'This has all of Fran's trademark quick wit and black humour.'

– Gráinne Murphy, author of *Greener* and *Winter People*

'I loved *Home Bird*. Fran drew me in to that world, I felt very present in it.'

– Jane Ions, author of *Domestic Bliss and Other Disasters*, shortlisted for the CWIP Prize in 2021

'Deliciously nostalgic, brilliantly funny.'

– Frances Quinn, author of *The Smallest Man*

'The story is ultimately upbeat, but there are no pat resolutions. The weighty themes are handled lightly, without worthiness or excessive sentimentality; the lightness of touch has real depth.'

– Anthony Ferner, author of *Small Wars in Madrid*

'A jewel of a book. Fran Hill can do what other authors spend a lifetime trying to achieve: disarm you in a sentence.'

– Deborah Jenkins, author of *Braver*, shortlisted for the Writers' Guild Best First Novel 2023

'Fran writes with such humour and humanity, it was an absolute tonic.'

– Victoria Mackenzie, author of *For Thy Great Pain Have Mercy On My Little Pain*, Winner of the Scottish National First Book Awards 2023

'Funny, warm and very moving. It'll make you laugh and ensure you have a gentle weep.'

– Lucinda Hawksley, author and biographer

'Like a perfectly risen souffle made with dangerously volatile ingredients, Jackie's story of dashed hopes, disappointment, optimism and resilience gripped me from the first line and wouldn't let me go.'

– Ruth Leigh, author of the Isabella Smugge series

FRAN HILL

Home Bird

Legend Press Ltd, 51 Gower Street, London, WC1E 6HJ
info@legendtimesgroup.co.uk | www.legendpress.co.uk

Print ISBN 9781915643063
Ebook ISBN 9781915643070
Set in Times.

Printed in India

Fran Hill is a full-time author and retired English teacher from Warwickshire who was in foster care as a child. Her first novel about Jackie Chadwick *Cuckoo in the Nest* was runner-up for the Paul Torday Memorial Prize in 2024. Her memoir *Miss, What Does Incomprehensible Mean?* was published in 2020. Fran lives with her gardener husband and has three grown-up children and two grandchildren.

To Hazel and Verity (who social-worked me in the 1970s) and to all the kind, long-suffering social workers past, present and future.

WEDNESDAY 23 MAY 1979

I had stood half an hour in stop-start drizzle when the huge wooden door, set implacably into the prison walls, was pushed open wide. I watched as Dad stepped out, dangling a brown paper bag from his fingers. He was accompanied by a guard.

I closed my umbrella and called, 'Over here!' but he'd already seen me.

His thick black hair – the hair I'd inherited - had taken on streaks of grey over the three years. I'd noted the gradual change during my visits. As he walked towards me, wearing the dark trousers he was no doubt arrested in, I realised that his hair and mine were now different.

He'd regained some of the weight he'd lost from his huge frame in the early days of imprisonment when he'd been deprived of a million calories a week in whisky, but nonetheless his shirt hung looser on him. Thinner in body and, I knew, in spirit. Perhaps something in the prison air smudged people's vitality as it smudged away time and left them behind everyone else, wondering how prices had risen so fast or what had happened to that newsagent on the corner.

But all was not lost.

'Behave yourself, Dave,' shouted the guard watching Dad go, 'or that Mrs Thatcher will slap you straight back in here.'

My father turned and stuck two fingers up.

'Dad!' I said.

The guard laughed and stepped back through the door.

It thudded shut and jangling keys on the other side locked it with a crunch.

'Hello, short-arse.' Dad patted me on the head. 'Thanks for coming.'

'It's study period on Wednesday afternoons. It was you or Jane Austen.'

'And you chose me, of course.'

'This time.' I shook the rain from my umbrella and fastened it up.

'I'm glad it's only you. I had visions of that bloody Bridget woman tagging along.'

'Come on.' I pointed down the road. 'Let's find a bus to the station before it rains again.'

Prison had been good for Dad in some ways. He'd admitted it during my final visit before his release. But he'd also said, 'I've ruined my chance to be a proper dad.'

'I don't need pushing on the swings,' I'd said, 'but there are things left on the dadding list.'

'Dadding isn't a word.'

'I'm a poet, remember,' I'd told him, 'or would be if homework let me.'

Now, Dad glanced back at the prison walls as though he thought they might follow him. 'The people who built that place knew how to do grim.'

'The people who built that used to include dead relatives in photos.'

'What?'

'I learned it in history.'

We reached the bus stop. As we waited, I said, 'I bought you a Mars bar.' I dipped into my anorak pocket. 'Happy release day.'

He tore its wrapper off.

'You don't have to eat it immediately.'

'I bloody do. You don't have any fags, do you?'

'Sorry.'

'I'm gasping,' he said. He stretched out the 'a' sound in

'fags' and 'gasping', partly because of his Devon upbringing and partly because of his addiction.

His instincts were right, though. Bridget had tried to come with me.

She and Nick had called round on Tuesday evening to the Victorian house in Leamington's Mason Street that I shared with three girls also fresh out of foster care. Social Services called it 'supported accommodation'. We could live there until we were eighteen or had finished full-time school or college if that came later. We had the number of a support worker should we open the front door to find a gang of murderers, so long as the murderers agreed to hang around while we dialled, of course.

I'd made my foster parents mugs of tea at what Bridget wanted to call a kitchenette but was really a work surface with a two-ring hob, an electric toaster and a cupboard above.

I had one wooden chair. Bridget sat on that in her smart blue jacket as though out to the theatre, her brown hair in its perfect bob. Nick perched on my single bed, polishing his glasses with a handkerchief.

'I've nothing to fear from my dad now,' I said.

Bridget said, 'We know.'

'So—'

'I'll have the car. I could pick you up from school at lunchtime and drive you there. The forecast says rain.'

'It's your birthday.'

'I'm not doing anything special. And I still have energy, despite everything.' She'd had trouble climbing the stairs to my first-floor room.

'And drive them both back?' Nick said to her.

She hadn't thought this through. I was imagining Dad's face when he found Bridget Wall at the wheel of his taxi back to Warwick, and I think she was doing the same.

'We'll be fine on the train,' I said. 'I'll take an anorak, a hat and two umbrellas if it will reassure you.'

'I suppose so,' she said, but as though someone had wrenched something precious from her. 'Do you want to come home afterwards for your dinner?'

She still called it home. And what I'd grown up in the Midlands calling tea she, from Oxfordshire, called dinner. I didn't hold it against her.

I said, 'I'd planned to fetch fish and chips to eat at the in-between hostel with Dad. I could drop in later. I have a present for you.'

Someone knocked at the door of my room as I spoke and Bridget jumped.

'It's probably Patsy,' I said. 'She moved in last month. Heather is her social worker, too.'

It was indeed Patsy. As I opened the door, we could hear Blondie's 'Heart of Glass' from the record player in the room next to mine.

'Spare sugar?' I said to her. She was wearing tight denims and a pink boob tube.

'How did you guess?' she cackled. Patsy's laugh didn't need a microphone.

'You're listening to Blondie for a change.'

'Ha ha.'

'Come in.' I waved vaguely towards my visitors. 'These are my foster parents, Nick and Bridget Wall.'

She shook their hands but no one seemed to know the next steps.

'And what do you do?' Bridget said, at last, as though at a cocktail party.

'As little as possible,' Patsy replied. 'I'd sit on my bum all day if I was allowed to.'

Bridget's neat eyebrows did their thing.

I said, 'Patsy's at college, learning hairdressing.'

Patsy pointed proudly to her head. Her red hair was in giant curlers. 'Move over, bloody Vidal Sassoon. Patsy's coming for ya.'

She laughed again and the room winced.

She pointed. 'Hey, you're not *Amanda* Wall's mum and dad?'

Nick said, 'For sins in a previous life,' and Bridget said, 'Nick!'

'She's in my class,' Patsy said. 'Fair hair, lanky kid. Legs to her armpits, lucky cow.'

Bridget seemed to recoil from this summary of her beloved and perhaps from the idea of close contact between Patsy and Amanda. She said to me, 'Did *you* know this?' as though I'd failed to pass on news of a kidnapping or imminent typhoon.

I said I hadn't made the connection, which I hadn't, and passed Patsy a bowl. 'I've put some sugar in this. Bring back what you don't need.'

'Cheers,' she said. 'He takes *four* in his tea, would you believe?'

I nudged her out. We weren't meant to have boyfriends in the house. I'd kept to the rule where my boyfriend Kevin was concerned, but Patsy wasn't a conformist.

'Who does she mean?' Bridget said, once the door was shut and we could no longer hear Blondie.

'Probably her grandad,' I said, 'or someone.' Which felt as true as I could make it.

'Are the other two girls at school? College?' Nick asked.

'No,' I said. 'One works at a shoe shop and the other in a factory. They're in the two attic rooms. They keep themselves to themselves.'

Bridget sipped her tea and said, 'Probably for the best,' but I think she meant Patsy.

I waited with Dad in a wide hallway that formed the hostel's reception area. Its mosaic-tiled floor was faded, the colours indistinct. A round clock on the wall said six o'clock. At the end of the hallway we could see a kitchen. Another door bore a metal plaque saying *Residents' Lounge*.

We'd been directed to a couple of plastic chairs by a

curly-haired woman at the desk who was saying into the telephone, 'Tonight could be tricky. We're stuffed to the gills.' On another chair sat a young man who didn't look much older than me – eighteen? nineteen? – with a battered sports bag on his knees.

He was smoking. I think he caught Dad looking at him. 'Do you want one?' he said and held out a packet of Woodbines and a box of matches.

Dad took them. 'You're a lifesaver, lad.'

'Except they cause cancer in mice,' I said.

I'd walked past this tall Georgian building at the edge of Warwick hundreds of times without knowing it was an in-between or halfway house for ex-prisoners while they waited for their accommodation. I said so to Dad.

'Me neither,' he said, 'and now look.' He sucked hard on the cigarette.

'It's only until Friday, then you'll have your own place.'

I glanced at the walls of the hallway, yellowed and dismal. Someone had tried out different shades of beige paint leaving several patches but even they didn't look too fresh, as though the council had thought about redecorating but the money had run out. Or perhaps the decorator, forced to work with so much beige, had gone off with depression.

The curly-haired woman put the phone down and called the young man forward, asking him to sign a form. She clipped it into a file. A second woman then appeared from the kitchen and led him up the wide stairway, saying, 'Yours is number eight, love.'

We approached the desk. 'Is this your daughter?' the woman said, kindly.

Dad put an arm across my shoulders. It felt heavy but good.

'I'm afraid no guests are permitted in the rooms, Mr Chadwick,' she said. 'I'm sure you understand.'

Dad shrugged and signed the form she slid over to him.

'And you've missed your tea. That's at five o'clock.'

'I thought I'd fetch my dad some fish and chips,' I said.

She chewed her lip. Eventually, she said, 'You can eat them in the kitchen, I suppose. There's a table in there.'

'Okay.'

'But no alcohol allowed.'

'You can say that again,' said Dad, miserably.

'No alcohol allowed,' she said.

I liked her.

I left Dad to the care of the second woman who said she'd give him a guided tour and I walked to the end of the road for cod and chips twice with some of the wages from my Saturday morning stint at the bakery. It made me feel grown-up, buying Dad a meal with my own money. As I took the change and the newspaper-wrapped parcels from the assistant, I wished he had been there to see me do it.

On my return, the woman on reception fetched Dad from the lounge. When she opened its door, I could see several other men in there, all smoking and watching TV.

I beckoned Dad into the kitchen, a huge square space with a table at the centre that could seat twelve. A tray sat in the middle of it, laid with salt and pepper shakers, HP sauce and tomato ketchup.

He stubbed out a cigarette in an ashtray on the kitchen counter.

'You've had two free fags today, then,' I said.

'Four.' He nodded in the direction of the lounge. 'Honour among thieves and all that.'

'Dig in.' I opened up my parcel. He did the same.

'What do I owe you, pet? The prison gave me a bit of cash.'

'It's on me. Use yours to buy your own fags.'

He laughed. 'It's on me,' he repeated.

'What?' I dolloped a heap of ketchup onto my chips.

'Nothing,' he said. 'It's just funny, you all independent and flashing the cash.'

'You're laughing at me, so that's the last time I do it.'

'I'll make it up to you, hoping I get this job at the pie factory in the morning.'

'You're telling *me* you'll make it up.'

I handed him a wooden fork. He stabbed at his chips with it. 'First proper fish and chips for three years.'

'They never made fish and chips?'

'Fish like leather. Chips sat for an hour in grease. And no vinegar.'

'No vinegar? That's medieval.'

He picked up the cod with his hands. 'This bloody fork is useless. We had cutlery, at least.'

'I'm sure there's cutlery in here somewhere.' We both looked round the expansive kitchen and its seven or eight potential cutlery drawers.

'I'll manage,' he said.

'You'll need cutlery for your new council flat.'

'I'll need everything.'

'Isn't there anything left from our old house?'

'It was all cleared out. I had no choice. That's what happens.'

'Even those boxes of Mum's things from the lean-to?'

'Even those.'

'Oh.'

He'd never told me this. I could see why he hadn't wanted to. I'd always intended to sort through those boxes of Mum's and he knew it.

Neither of us spoke for a minute, focusing on our food.

'I'm sorry,' he said, and I knew he wasn't merely apologising about the boxes.

I dipped a couple of chips in my ketchup. 'Only a couple of days and you'll be in.'

'It's got two bedrooms, you know.'

'Right.'

He winked at me.

'Dad, we've talked about this. It's best I stay where I am.'

'Best for who?'

'Best for *whom*,' I said. 'Eat your chips.'

Dad walked me to the bus stop, grumbling that they'd made him sign out formally. 'So much for freedom.'

He thought I was catching the bus back to Mason Street but I was going to see the Walls, as I'd promised, with the birthday present for Bridget which was in my satchel. I didn't want to say this to Dad.

'You don't have to wait with me,' I said as we stood in the bus shelter. 'I navigate my way around the transport network pretty well.'

He went quiet and I knew I'd hurt him.

'I don't mean it like that.'

'You do, but never mind.'

'I hope you sleep well at the hostel and that the bed's comfy.'

He said, 'It'll feel like a cloud.'

'Honestly. You go. I'm fine waiting.'

'If you say so.' He wandered off, pretending to look in shop windows.

'See you soon!' I called, but he didn't look back.

I arrived at the Walls' house at eight thirty. It was still light and they hadn't shut the curtains. I could see Bridget standing by the dining table, looking towards the windows as though waiting for me.

Scrub that. Waiting for me.

She flung open the front door while I was rummaging in my satchel. I didn't recognise the quilted yellow-orange flowered dressing gown she was wearing but I made no comment. She was usually in full battledress until bedtime: skirt, blouse, cardigan, earrings, perhaps a Tupperware container or two.

'Did you forget your key?' she said.

'You know I didn't.' I produced it. 'I never do. Happy birthday.'

She stepped back so that I could enter the house. I gave her a quick hug but she held on too long.

'Let go now,' I said. 'You're breaking my three-second rule.'

She did let go, but wasn't steady on her feet.

'Sorry, Bridget. I didn't mean to—'

She said, 'I'll put the kettle on and you can tell me everything.'

I walked into the living room and dropped my satchel on the coffee table. 'Not much to tell. He's out of prison. He's in the hostel. Done.'

'More than that,' she called from the kitchen. I heard her opening and shutting cupboards and the clink of teaspoons.

'She'll want a *lot* more than that,' Nick said. He was in one of the armchairs with a pile of history exercise books on his lap, writing a comment in the top one.

I sighed and dropped onto the sofa. 'I thought she might.'

'You know Bridget. She likes detail.'

I looked at his heap of books. 'What are you marking?'

'Terrible essays about Luddites.' He frowned. His sandy hair was disarranged, as though feeling it, too.

'That school keeps you busy.'

'Hm,' he said, quietly. 'Busier than I need to be right now.'

I knew he was talking about Bridget, but without talking about Bridget.

Amanda came downstairs, slender and pretty in a denim dress although she also wore a black leather studded bracelet and matching neck collar. She was exploring being a punk but having trouble committing.

She said, 'Hello. Is your dad still wearing his ball and chain?'

'Darling!' Bridget called through. 'You can't say that.'

But I'd preferred Amanda's response to Bridget's. 'That was funny. Well done.'

She plumped down beside me. 'Was it weird, seeing him?'

'I've visited plenty of times.'

'It's not the same, though.'

'Maybe.' I wanted to change the subject. 'How's college?'

'A pile of shit,' she said.

Bridget appeared at the kitchen door. 'Amanda!'

'Listen to your mother,' Nick said, or perhaps it was a tape recording he'd made once and flicked on for these occasions. His tone was affectionate, though.

'Hey, did your mum or dad mention they'd met Patsy?' I said to Amanda. 'She's on your hairdressing course.'

'And don't we all *know* it?' she said. I'd been about to offer a description but it seemed there was no need. 'I feel sorry for you having to live in the same house as *her*.'

'She's all right.'

'If you say so.'

Spotless wandered through and I stroked his soft Dalmatian ears. 'I miss having a dog. I hope he misses me.'

'I'm afraid that hound cares about nothing but sleep and food,' Nick said. 'I should have called him Sloth.'

I covered the dog's ears with my hands, just in case, and said to Amanda, 'No, you're right. It's not the same as visiting.'

Bridget came in with a teapot and cups on a tray. Her hands gripped the edge of the tray to keep it level. I wanted to leap up and take it from her.

She put it on the coffee table in front of me and Amanda. 'Do you girls want cake? I made a cherry and walnut.' She turned back to the kitchen to fetch it.

'Wait – open this first,' I said.

I'd bought her a cake knife with a china handle decorated with a bluebell pattern. She needed some help unwrapping it and I regretted my enthusiastic sellotaping.

'Oh!' She turned the cake knife over and over in her hands. 'I think I'm going to cry.'

'By the time she's thought it, it's too late,' Amanda said.

'But – it's so *pretty*.' Bridget dabbed at her eyes with a pure white handkerchief.

'Do you like the dressing gown I bought Bridget?' Nick said.

She flushed. 'That's why I've got it on,' she said, 'to show everyone how it fits. I wouldn't normally wear a dressing gown in the daytime. I'm not an invalid.'

'Of course not,' he said, after a pause.

She said, 'I'll go and fetch this cake, then. I need you to eat it so that I don't.'

I said, 'Can't ruin your reputation,' and didn't understand why she went straight to the kitchen without replying.

We could hear her opening a cake tin. Amanda said, quietly, 'Mum's had to give up leading her WeightWatchers group.'

'Oh. I didn't know.'

'Last night was her final meeting. She came home and went straight upstairs.'

'Right!' said Bridget, coming in with the cake on a flowered plate, but she said it tersely as though she knew we were talking about her and meant to put a stop to it.

Nick tried to help. 'Amanda's bought the new EP by The Clash, Jackie. She's been torturing us with it.'

Amanda ran her fingers over the studs on her bracelet. 'I'll play it to her after we've had cake.'

'Feel completely free not to,' I said.

Bridget passed the cake round. 'You're more disco, aren't you?' she said to me, asking a question to which she already knew the answer.

'I'd rather the Bee Gees.'

Amanda said, 'Ugh,' although I knew she had a clutch of their records. Her punk phase was recent news.

Uncle Nick said, 'So long as you don't start wearing chain mail or black lipstick, love, or come over all anti-establishment.'

'I might.' Amanda sounded defiant but also unsure. I don't think she knew what anti-establishment meant.

THURSDAY 24 MAY

I'd been home for an hour and should have been doing school-work but was deep into *The Grapes of Wrath* which Nick had lent to me. The telephone rang in the hall. I heard Patsy open her door and run downstairs. 'Bugger!' she said, and I knew she'd slipped on the stair where the carpet was worn to a shine. Then she called my name.

I came, more cautiously than Patsy had, down the wide staircase. She passed me the receiver.

'That should have been Pete,' she said, as though it were my fault, and ran back up.

It was my dad.

'Where are you ringing from?' I said.

'A residents' phone in the lounge.'

'Well? What's the news?'

'I got the job at the pie factory.' I could hear the relief in his voice, as though he'd been trying to keep it at bay in case it wasn't needed.

'That's great, Dad. Starting when?'

'Monday,' he said. 'I didn't think they'd take me but they'd had a letter of recommendation from my probation officer.'

'Has he actually met you?'

'Very funny.'

'What's the job?'

'I don't know exactly. On the shop floor, anyway. Three-month trial period, then the wage goes up. Once a week, I leave an hour early for my probation appointment.'

'Sounds good.'

'You won't be ashamed of your dad, will you? I don't think the fire service would take me back now.'

'I never asked you to try.'

'Do you fancy meeting up to celebrate, pet? A walk in the park and a cup of tea while it's light?'

'I've got homework and revision, Dad. I didn't get much done yesterday and I'm already behind.'

'That'll be my fault.'

'No, it's not—'

'Anyway, someone's waiting for the phone. I'd better go.'

I didn't believe him.

'Saturday afternoon, I promise.' I felt conflicted, and guilty that I'd been reading Steinbeck instead of working. Who else did Dad have to celebrate with apart from a few strangers in a hostel, even if they were generous with their nicotine?

'Right, then,' he said.

'Sorry I'm not there tomorrow to help you move in. I have mock exams.'

'My probation officer's coming. And it won't take long to unpack a toothbrush.'

'What about a kettle?' I said.

'He says there's a box with some basics like that. A charity, apparently.'

'Will you have a bed?'

'A bed, some chairs and a table, at least. Maybe a wardrobe.'

'A fridge?'

'Yep.'

'Good,' I said. 'Somewhere to put my cream cake for Saturday.'

Late Wednesday afternoon the previous week, my social worker, Heather, had collected me from Mason Street in her blue Volkswagen Beetle and taken me to the Walls' house for a meeting with Nick and Bridget to talk about my dad's release. He'd been sentenced to four years but had served three. 'Your expectations of the relationship and your dad's expectations might be different, Jackie,' she'd said when we'd all sat down. 'You need to be ready.'

I took a biscuit from a plate. 'I don't know *what* I'm expecting.'

'Obviously, he's your dad,' she said, 'but Nick and Bridget parented you for three years. He has to acknowledge that.'

'He does, in a begrudging, sullen, resentful, consult a thesaurus kind of way.'

Nick said to Heather, 'Do you think we should invite him here?' just as Bridget was picking up her cup of tea. She dropped it down again so that the cup clanked in the saucer.

'Here? What for?' she said as though he'd suggested having the Kray twins round.

'A cup of tea? A sandwich? I don't know.'

I said, 'I don't think Dad'll be looking for an invitation. He's not one for socialising.' I didn't add 'with people who have a double shed and a three-drawer freezer'.

'This kind of change can be tricky,' Heather said, 'while everyone readjusts. I know I'm relatively new but I've learned that already.'

I avoided catching Nick's eye. After we'd first met Heather, petite and with a complexion as pink and clean as a doll's, he'd said, 'How can she be a social worker? Surely she's only just weaned.'

'Dad's a totally different person,' I said now, 'from the one who went into prison.'

No one replied at first.

'We all hope so, of course,' Heather said.

'He needs people to believe in him.'

'He's lucky to have you to support him,' Nick said, which wasn't the same as 'We do believe in him'.

I couldn't blame them. But I'd seen Dad in his glory days – before the drinking and the anger and the assaulting of the

23

policeman that got him sentenced – and I wanted to see those days again. I needed to trust that he could get back there.

I asked Dad on the phone now, 'What did they give you for tea?'

'Some kind of stew with spuds. What exams have you got tomorrow, then?'

'I thought you said someone was waiting for the phone.'

When I'd said goodbye, I dialled the Walls' number. Bridget answered – the phone was on the kitchen wall – and I told her Dad's news.

'That's a good start.' She spoke slowly. Sometimes, at the end of the day, her speech was like this, each word deliberated over.

'He wanted someone to celebrate with.'

'Not with whisky.'

I said, 'Why does no one give him a chance?'

There was a long silence.

She said, 'You came to us at fourteen with a bandaged wrist. You jumped if anyone shouted.'

I sighed.

'We're worried for you,' she said.

'You should be worrying about yourself.'

She hesitated. 'The Parkinson's, you mean?'

'I suppose.'

'It's bad enough having it. If I add worry on top, I won't want to get out of bed.'

It was a rare admission.

FRIDAY 25 MAY

Kevin was waiting for me in the rain outside the school gate on Friday afternoon, still wearing his blue mechanic's overalls and heavy work boots. He often finished early on Fridays and would meet me for an hour or so, longer if I wasn't at the Walls' for tea.

'Happy half-term!' he said. 'I wish I got half-terms.'

'You don't have essays to write, though,' I said.

'And the education world can re*lax*.'

The rain had attempted to flatten his blond curls but without success. They'd bounced back waywardly. His hair was the same colour as his sister Kim's, my best friend at school. But where her hair was straight, his was a tangle of springs. He told people he was six feet tall but in truth he was five foot ten plus the hair.

Earlier that day, at break time, I'd sat with Kim and my other close friend Molly, eating iced buns.

Molly was a year older than me and Kim. We'd bonded over poetry although Molly had told me she'd given up writing poems now as who had time for things that never seemed finished? Her mother had multiple sclerosis and the previous year had seen Molly in school two-thirds of the time and at home preparing meals, vacuuming, shopping and helping her mother to the bathroom the rest. As a result, she was now retaking the Lower Sixth year.

All I knew about Molly's father was that he'd hightailed it the first day her mother's spoon had missed her mouth. Other than telling me this, she never talked about her dad. She'd said he was so dead to her that she called him 'the man who was married to my mother'.

She was in my English class but also studying music and biology. We were united in our worship of Mrs Collingworth, our English teacher. We didn't talk about it much but we'd both benefited from her kindness and, sometimes, her tenacity when we'd tried to avoid her in corridors.

Molly took a bite of her iced bun and said, 'Are you and Kim's brother in an "on" stage or an "off" stage?'

'I'm sorry,' I'd said. 'Sometimes I'm not even sure myself. But currently we're "on".'

'Oh, good.'

'I think.'

She put her head in her hands.

Kim said, 'Kevin never shuts up about you at home.'

Molly started humming the 'Wedding March' and, even more annoyingly, was in tune in a way I could never achieve. I snatched the bun from her plate. 'You get this back if you stop.'

She laughed, her grey eyes mischievous. 'I'm sorry. But you're like a yo-yo where he's concerned.' She took the bun off me. 'None of us can keep up.'

Kevin and I began to amble towards a bus stop. We'd planned for The Eatery in Warwick. It would only have taken fifteen minutes to walk but the rain looked stubborn.

'How's it going at the garage?' I said.

'Do you really want to hear about gaskets and exhausts?'

'Not really.'

We waited at the stop and other half-term-happy pupils from school joined us, huddling and giggling underneath the shelter so that Kevin and I were forced to stand close.

He put his arm around my waist, pulling me towards him. 'This is fun.'

'You stink of oil.'

'I've got Brut on.'

'You wasted your money. Come on, let's walk.' I nudged him out of the bus shelter.

As it was, five minutes later the rain sputtered to a stop and the sun, surprised to have another shot at the day, peeped out from behind juddery clouds.

'Will you come home with me after the café?' Kevin said, taking hold of my hand as we walked uphill into town. I'd had my hands in my pockets.

'Why?'

'Mum and Dad have gone away overnight to someone's wedding. Kim's out playing tennis.'

'The house is empty?'

He grinned. 'Yes.'

'In that case, no, I won't come home with you.'

We waited to cross the street. He said, 'It was worth a try.'

'It really wasn't.'

'I thought we were serious.'

'I'm serious about not having sexual intercourse with you,' I said, as we crossed.

He took his hand out of mine. 'You're jumping to conclusions again.'

'It's not far to jump.'

We talked very little until we reached the café which was busy with afternoon shoppers and a few school pupils. We found a corner table and ordered colas and packets of biscuits. Someone had left a newspaper behind. Kevin picked it up, scanning the headlines. 'Milk's gone up to 15p a pint.'

'Is that all you've got?' I said.

He put the newspaper down. 'What about the cinema, then?'

'You mean the back row and a good snog in the dark?'

An elderly lady on the next table tutted and said, 'Honestly!' to her companion.

Kevin sat back in his chair. 'For a girl, you don't mince words.'

I looked around the café. Photographs of old Warwick drunkenly dotted the walls. The castle. Tudor black-beamed houses. A horse and cart outside a grocer's.

'Anyway, Bridget's expecting me,' I said. 'She's trying a Delia recipe and wants me there for the great experiment.'

'We can ring her from the phone box and give your apologies.'

'You're not listening.'

'Fine.'

A waitress brought our order. Kevin stirred his drink with the straw.

'Only it's not fine. Your face says it's very unfine.' I snapped a chocolate biscuit in half.

'You know how I feel about you,' he said, 'since we first started going out.'

'That's only two years ago, officially.'

'Two and a half, including three long "breaks" you said you needed.'

'I know. I'm sorry.' I sighed. 'I was getting it in the neck from Kim and Molly today.'

'Well, what do you want? A marriage proposal? You're only a sixth-former.'

'Of course not.'

'You don't trust me. That's the issue. You think that if you let me go any further I'll drop you afterwards.'

'Of course I trust you.' But it wasn't true. I liked him. I may even have loved him. But that did not equal trust. He was right when he'd complain that I kept him at bay, only letting him kiss me and touch me over my clothing. I knew I was unusual from hearing the girls at school talk about their boyfriends. But I was content to stay unusual. Look what happens when you throw a lone seagull one of your chips, thinking you have a choice about what happens next.

'I don't trust you when you say you trust me,' he said.

I bit into the other half of my chocolate biscuit. 'Let's talk about something else.'

'Okay. Have you written any poems lately?'

'Not for ages.'

'What's stopping you?'

'I don't know.'

'You told me Keats had TB and *he* kept going.'

I looked at him. 'And you wonder why I won't let you go below the waist?'

The two elderly ladies were struggling into their spring jackets, ready to leave. One bent towards me as she went past and said, 'Don't give in, dear. You don't want syphilis – or worse.'

When they'd gone, I said to Kevin, 'What's worse than syphilis?'

'I don't know.'

'Still, we should listen to the old. Their age makes them wise.'

'Or jealous and twisted,' he said.

SATURDAY 26 MAY

The following afternoon, after work at the bakery in Warwick, I walked down the hill to see Dad in his new flat:
Number 12, Landor Court, part of a three-storey block in
Landor Close between the park and a parade of shops. I
climbed the two flights of concrete steps and he must have
heard me stomping up as he was waiting in the doorway.
'Blimey,' I said. 'You'll have to stop the fags, Dad, if you've
got to climb these every day.'

The door to the flat opposite Dad's opened. An unshaven
man in a vest peered out. 'Colin,' he announced.

'Dave,' my dad said.

'Jackie,' I said, making a mental note not to encourage
social interaction between the three of us if all we could
manage was a word each.

He looked us over. 'You haven't got a screaming baby,
either of you?'

'No,' Dad said.

Colin glanced at me.

I put my hands up. 'Not guilty.'

'Good. We can get some bloody sleep round here.' And
he went back in and shut his door.

Dad beckoned me into his hallway. 'I can cope with a few
steps. Remember, I used to shimmy up ladders into burning
buildings.'

'Long time ago, Dad,' I said, but I wished I hadn't because
it felt hypocritical, after all I'd preached to the Walls about

giving him second chances. 'Anyway, people your size don't shimmy anywhere.'

He showed me round the flat on what he called a 'tour' but which took under a minute. He seemed proud. Two bedrooms led left and right off the narrow hallway. In the larger bedroom was a single bed, a cheap wardrobe and chest of drawers. In the second bedroom, nothing. Then, the bathroom, which was tiny. At the end of the hall, a spacious square living room containing a small, past-its-best three-piece suite covered in brown Dralon, arranged around a small wooden coffee table. In one corner, a tiny dining table with four chairs squeezed round it, and in the other corner a cheap TV cabinet bearing a portable set. 'It's only black-and-white,' he said, 'but it's a bonus.'

At the window, which overlooked Warwick town, drooped a pair of insubstantial green curtains.

The living room led into a small kitchen with a fridge and cooker and what Dad said was space for a twin-tub.

'This is all from the charity?' I said.

'It's mostly second-hand, but it beats a cold cell and a cellmate who farts like a baboon.'

He'd been watching the horse racing. 'I'll switch this off,' he said.

'It's okay. I like it as background.'

'I'll make some tea, then. The kettle *is* new. And look in the fridge.'

I opened it. Two cream slices on a plate. I took them out. 'You remembered.'

'I'm your dad.' As we stood waiting for his kettle to bubble on the gas hob, he said, 'You'll stay and I'll cook you something later.' I noted the statement rather than the question.

'What are you cooking?'

'It's a surprise.'

'You mean, you haven't bought anything yet.'

'There's a shop across the street,' he said.

*

We walked to the small supermarket together after we'd drunk our tea and eaten the pastries. A tentative sun was doing its level best for us and I felt the warmth on my back.

Dad plucked a basket from a pile near the entrance and waved to the assistant at the till, a plumpish woman wearing a checked tabard. She'd over-lacquered her brown hair; it no longer had a life of its own.

'Doreen.' Dad nodded in her direction. 'How's tricks?'

'Not so bad, Dave,' she said. 'Long time no see.'

He turned to me as we entered the first aisle. 'What do you fancy, then?'

'A huge rump steak with a mushroom and cream sauce. Followed by lemon flan.'

'Is that the kind of food Mrs Posh Wall cooks you?'

'No. Don't be so touchy.'

'I'm not being touchy.'

'You're always touchy about the Walls. It's not the parenting Olympics.' I lowered my voice. 'Who's Doreen?'

'The shop assistant.'

'Yes, but how come you know her?'

'She used to be down the pub sometimes,' he said. 'What about a Fray Bentos pie, then?' He pointed at the pile of tins on display. 'Steak and kidney or mince and onion? Either'd be nice with a tin of peas.'

'Steak and kidney, then. Dad, she winked at you.'

'No, she didn't.'

But she had.

'I'll get this can of fruit cocktail,' he said, 'and some evaporated milk.'

'Remember I don't like the—'

'Cherries.' He gave my arm a little push as if to say, *See?*

'Bridget always forgot,' I said, but it wasn't true. It had happened once, and after that, she'd given my cherries to Amanda.

32

'You've gone pink in the face.'

'No, I haven't.'

But I was ashamed of my treachery. I felt it in my gut, like a squeezing hand. Why had I said that about Bridget?

We added more items to the basket: a pack of two toilet rolls, a sliced loaf, margarine, a bar of Cadbury Dairy Milk he tried to slip in while I wasn't looking. 'I deserve a treat,' he said, 'and these days it can't be whisky.'

'Did you get any chocolate in prison?' I said as we approached the counter to pay, joining a small queue.

'Ssh.' He bent right down to hiss it directly into my ear.

'What?'

'Tell the whole world, why don't you?'

'Ching,' went the drawer of the till.

We stood, waiting. 'Sorry,' I whispered. 'I didn't say it loudly.'

'You've got a voice like a foghorn sometimes.'

That's unfair, I said, but only to my own sense of injustice.

When it was our turn, Dad nudged our basket into the slot designed for it and Doreen began emptying it of our shopping, tapping prices into the till. 'Ooh, chocolate!' She smiled up at Dad. 'Someone's indulging themselves.'

'It's Saturday after all,' he said, dropping the chocolate into our shopping bag. 'Something to nibble on while watching the telly.'

She giggled. 'Indeed.'

As we began to walk back to his flat, I said, 'That woman was flirting.'

'Don't be daft.'

'Does she think she's in a *Carry On* film or something?'

He stopped without warning, so that I continued on a few steps before realising. I looked back.

He'd put down the shopping bag as though intending to go no further. 'I don't need a minder, by the way.'

'What?'

'I don't need a minder. I don't need you to keep an eye on me. Not any more.'

I shifted to one side to let a group of young boys pass by. 'I'm not minding you.'

'Could have fooled me.' He picked up the bag. As he bent to do so, the wind teased at his hair and for the first time I realised he had a tiny bald patch.

'Let's get back,' I said. 'The margarine needs to go in the fridge.'

'Let's.'

I put the shopping away and made us both another mug of tea. I took it into the living room where he was sitting in one of its two armchairs. He was turning the pages of the *Daily Mirror* but I sensed he wasn't reading. He had his pools coupon ready for the football results. I said, 'I couldn't find any sugar for you.'

'That's because there isn't any. Damn.'

'Shall I pop back to the shop?'

'So you can have another gander at Doreen?'

'No.'

We sat in silence for a few minutes, looking at the sports updates and cradling our mugs.

He took a gulp of his tea. 'I'm sorry, pet. I don't mean to be cranky.'

'Don't worry about it.'

He wiped his mouth with the back of his hand. 'I could kill for a beer. One single bloody beer, that's all.'

My tongue itched to tell him that one single bloody beer had always led to plural bloody beers in the past but, in case he thought I was minding him, I kept quiet.

MONDAY 10 SEPTEMBER

A week into the autumn term, I walked the half-hour route back from school to my bedsit in agreeable sunshine, jacket over my arm. I'd planned my evening. Tinned tomatoes on toast. Some butterscotch Angel Delight. A couple of hours for English and psychology homework, then an early night. I hadn't yet adjusted after the summer holiday.

But, as I neared Mason Street, with its terraces of tall houses, I saw twists of smoke stretching into the blue sky as though racing to be highest.

I turned the corner to see two red fire engines lopsidedly blocking our narrow street, flashing lights still revolving. Cars trying to turn into the street were wisely nudging their way back out before they got stuck.

As I approached the house, I saw Patsy standing on the pavement in her blue nightie and bare feet, her back to me. She'd told me that morning that she hadn't felt well and was staying home from college. I'd suspected a hangover.

I walked faster to reach her. A fist of orange flame was thumping out of an upstairs window – her room – and above it, both white smoke and darker grey smoke bucked and turned. Four or five firemen in yellow plastic trousers and round helmets were dragging a ladder on wheels towards the house and two more unwound hoses from the engine.

'Patsy!' I called and she turned. Her cheeks were marked with a mix of old mascara and tears and her hair was tangled and wild.

As I reached her, one of the firemen passed us, shouting, 'Move back, ladies!' and we shuffled together further along the pavement.

'What's happened?' I said.

She was still crying. 'I was downstairs trying to find aspirin and I smelled smoke. I went back upstairs and my bed was on fire.' She sniffed horribly and I gave her my clean handkerchief.

'Did you phone 999?' I nodded towards the fire engines.

'No, that lady did.' She pointed towards a neighbour in an apron and headscarf who stood outside her gate two doors away, looking at us with fret on her face. Patsy said, 'I ran outside and she heard me yelling.'

A fireman came out of the house, coughing and removing his helmet. 'Did you have candles burning, love?' he said to Patsy.

She shook her head.

'Leave a cigarette unattended?'

'No. I don't smoke.'

'Right.'

'Not today, anyway,' she added.

'It's okay,' I said to her when he'd jogged back towards the engine. 'It's the uniform, isn't it? You think you have to confess everything.'

One of his colleagues emerged from the house and stood next to us. 'I reckon we've calmed it,' he shouted to the other men. 'That room's gutted, though. I've been round the house. No one else.'

'The other two were definitely out at work,' I said to him. 'I heard them go this morning.'

'I'd told them that.' Patsy sounded offended.

'Good to have it confirmed,' the fireman said.

The neighbour in the headscarf beckoned me over. 'Do you need to phone anyone, pet?'

I went back and said to one of the firemen, 'Can we go back in?'

'Not unless you qualify as a fireman in the next ten minutes, my love,' he said.

Patsy and I followed the neighbour into her house and sat on the edge of her sofa. She lent Patsy a thin flowered housecoat to wear over her nightie. 'I'll go and put the kettle on and then we can phone people,' the neighbour said.

We heard water hitting the bottom of the kettle. Patsy wiped her nose with the housecoat sleeve despite having my handkerchief. She said, 'I've never worn a housecoat before. Do I look about fifty?'

'I admit, it's not Mary Quant.'

She wiped her nose with the sleeve again.

'You might get to keep it,' I said.

The neighbour brought in a tray of tea and a heap of French Fancies on a plate. Her telephone was on a table by the sofa.

I didn't know whether to ring Heather or the Walls first. I tried Bridget. The phone rang twelve times before she picked it up but I knew these days to give her time.

I explained what had happened and, once she'd established that I wasn't burned to a crisp or standing on a roof awaiting a helicopter, my hair aflame, she said she would telephone Nick's school and ask him to come and pick me up. 'He took the car today,' she said.

Patsy rang the Social Services on behalf of both of us and asked to speak to Heather Platt. She said to a receptionist, 'No, I can't call back later. I'm in a nightie and someone else's housecoat,' which wasn't the most precise explanation but had an emergency feel to it.

'How do you know the number off by heart?' I said, while she waited to be connected to Heather's office.

'I've had to recite it so many times in police stations. You don't want to know why.'

'I really do.'

We finished our tea, ate three of the neighbour's French

Fancies each, then decided we'd wait at the door for Nick and Heather to arrive. The neighbour was trying to distract us with news about her daughter's forthcoming wedding, the wedding dress design, and the relative merits of mushroom vol-au-vents versus quiche Lorraine, and Patsy was yawning ostentatiously in a deliberate attempt to stop her.

We watched the street as one fire engine left, leaving another behind manned by two firemen who said they'd stay to check the house again. They re-parked the engine so that traffic could pass.

'She was only being kind,' I whispered to Patsy.

'But who talks about pastry for that long?' she said.

It was half an hour later when Nick and Heather arrived together, both having run down the street from where I assumed they'd parked their cars. The neighbour came out to meet them.

Patsy said, 'They're in a race to comfort us.'

Heather called, 'Girls!' and they scurried up the garden path. She turned her attention to Patsy, leaving me to Nick, who clearly wanted to hug me but knew better.

We listened as Patsy, still dressed in the neighbour's housecoat, ran through the aspirin story once again for Heather and cried some more. We tried to reassure her. 'You're not responsible for the fire,' I said.

'Of course you're not,' Heather said.

'But I was in there when it started.' The sleeve came into use once more.

I thought back to what she'd just said about police stations. 'You didn't start it, though.' I hesitated. 'Did you?'

'No!'

Heather said to Nick, 'I'll sort Patsy out, and I need to get in touch with the other two girls. Can you take Jackie home with you?'

'What about this housecoat?' Patsy said.

'I've a spare jacket in the car,' Heather said, and she and Nick thanked the neighbour for all her help. Patsy gave the housecoat back to her. She took it between finger and thumb, holding it aloft as she carried it indoors.

Nick spoke to one of the firemen. 'We're thinking faulty electricals,' the fireman said. 'Nothing else seems obvious.'

Patsy looked pensive. 'Should I have told someone that sparks come out of the socket when I plug in my record player?'

At the Walls' house, Amanda was standing in the drive. 'I thought you'd be all sooty.'

'Are you disappointed?'

'A bit.'

'I've got nothing with me. I don't even have any clean knickers,' I said to Amanda upstairs on the landing once Bridget had checked me over for third-degree burns I might not have mentioned.

'I've got three brand-new pairs. You can have them. Mum bought them at the weekend.'

'They're not Minnie Mouse, are they? That's not very punk. Tell me you've moved on.'

'Do you want them or not?' she said.

'I'll accept your kind offer.'

There'd been a time when she would never have offered.

In the sunflower-yellow room that had been mine for three years, Bridget had put folded sheets, pillowcases and blankets on the bed ready for me to make it.

'She can't do the reaching over and tucking now,' Amanda said.

'Don't tell me *you* make your own bed now.'

'I won't, then.'

I sat on the mattress and she on the chair opposite, in our old positions.

'I think it's gammon and pineapple for tea,' she said.

'Sounds good.'

'Do you feel shaky? People feel shaky after a shock.'

'Nothing gammon and pineapple can't solve.'

'Have you told Kevin what's happened?'

'I'll phone him after we've eaten.'

She bit her lip. 'It's good, having you here again.'

'Don't go sentimental on me.'

'I miss you not being here.'

'Do I need to say it twice?'

'Maybe I'm trying to make up for the past and being such a pain,' she said.

'Please don't. Anyway, it's a temporary stay.'

'Where are you going, then?'

I had to confess that I didn't know.

TUESDAY 11 SEPTEMBER

'You can't go in today, surely,' Bridget said the next morning when I appeared in the kitchen, dressed for school.

'Why not?'

'You're wearing Amanda's blouse.'

'You'll need a better reason than that.' I poured cornflakes into a bowl.

She was leaning against the fridge for stability. 'You must have been upset by the fire,' she said, by which she meant she was upset.

'I'll be back by four.'

'I'll make you a cake, then.'

'So now we're *celebrating* the inferno?'

'You know what I mean. To cheer you up.'

'Honestly, don't go to the trouble.'

'It's no trouble.'

'You're so good to me,' I said, and her face lit up like a beacon.

I opened a drawer for a spoon.

'I don't know when I'll be able to fetch my clothes.'

'Heather will sort something out. There'll be news later, I'm sure.'

Later that morning, I was in a history lesson. Mr Wright was showing us a newspaper article about the funeral the previous week of Lord Mountbatten who had been assassinated in a

Provisional IRA bomb attack. The teacher was despairing at our ignorance of national affairs and the reasons for the Troubles. 'Do *any* of you watch the news?' he was saying as someone knocked at the classroom door. It was a first year message boy with a note to say that I had permission to leave school after dinner time so that Heather could take Patsy and me to Mason Street.

Heather's car was in the school car park, its engine running. Patsy was standing by it, waving as though I were miles away and might have missed her. It was unlikely. She was wearing a tartan Bay City Rollers cap as well as a yellow cheesecloth blouse and blue flared trousers too big for her.

'Who's letting us into the house?' I said, clambering into the back seat behind Patsy. Half of the seat was taken up by a large suitcase.

'The firemen,' Heather said. 'They're already there, investigating the cause. They're not keen, so we need to be quick.' She pulled down a sun visor against the afternoon brightness and backed out of the parking space.

'Whose is the suitcase?'

'I've been to Bridget's. She sent it. There's another in the boot.'

'I'm not hoping to bring back the actual furniture.'

Heather said, 'She insisted.'

I told Patsy that I liked the colour of her blouse and she said, 'Emergency clothes from the stinky children's home.'

Heather said, 'They're washed and ironed.'

'You don't usually wear a cap,' I said.

'*Vile*, isn't it? I didn't have any shampoo.'

'Your hair looked fine, I told you,' Heather said.

Patsy sighed. 'Fine for a *bag lady*.'

Heather waited at the school gate for traffic to pass. 'It's only for a couple of nights, Patsy, while we get you sorted. And the other girls are there, too.'

Clearly, I was the only Mason Street resident with a foster family ready to take me back in an emergency. I vowed to be more grateful.

'Anyway,' Heather said. 'I managed to persuade the firemen to let us in.'

I asked her how.

'I may have gone overboard with my deprived-teenagers description.'

'Do you need us to cry while we're there,' Patsy said, 'or scream for our mums?'

'Or wet ourselves?' I said.

'That won't be necessary, thank you,' Heather said, as we pulled out onto the road towards Leamington.

A fireman escorted us up the stairs. He carried up Bridget's two suitcases.

Heather had a large shopping bag for anything salvageable of Patsy's.

'Be careful where you tread, ladies,' the fireman said. 'It all seems intact but I can't admit to my boss that I let you fall through the floorboards.'

'Not a career highlight,' I said.

He looked older than my dad, and friendly. I wanted to ask if he'd ever worked with Dave Chadwick but stopped myself. I had little good news to pass on.

He led us round. Most of Patsy's room, as we expected, had been pillaged by the fire, the bed a heap of burned nylon bedspread, the curtains in black shreds. Her wardrobe, next to the window, was definitely an ex-wardrobe, a box of charred wood. Smoke hung in the air, hitting our palates.

Patsy had been cheerful in the car, despite her clothing cast-offs, telling us exaggerated stories about the horrors of the children's home, but she went pale now, looking around her room. Heather said, 'Don't worry. We'll go shopping when we've dropped Jackie off and buy you some basics.'

I looked forward to hearing how the shopping trip had gone, Patsy not being a basics sort of person.

The one intact piece of furniture, blackened but otherwise solid, was a chest of drawers tucked in a deep alcove near the door. Patsy pulled open the top drawer. 'My hairdresser things for college,' she said. 'All my rollers and scissors and my notes file.' She pulled open the second. 'And my underwear.'

'I'll wait on the landing,' the fireman said.

Heather passed the bag to Patsy, who scooped everything up and into it.

'What's in the bottom drawer?' Heather said.

Patsy opened it but seemed embarrassed. 'My Barbie collection.'

'Lovely.' Heather impressed me with her social-worker poker face. 'Put them in the bag.'

'They're all old,' Patsy said, transferring the dolls. 'I've had them for ages.'

I said, 'But that's a Beauty Secrets Barbie, isn't it? They only came out this year.'

Heather glanced at my lack of tact and it shrank back.

Patsy zipped up the bag. 'Most of them are old, I mean.'

The fireman pointed us into my room. The fire hadn't reached it but its door, as was the case with everything on the landing between my room and Patsy's, was smoke-stained and ugly.

Patsy and Heather helped me to pack up my clothes and possessions into the first case.

'Who is *this*?' Heather said, lifting up the giant toy gorilla the size of a toddler from my bed. 'This must be why Bridget sent the extra case.'

'Weston,' I said. 'Short for Weston-super-Mare, where he came from. The Walls took me and Amanda there for the day.'

'She's obsessed with it. She talks to it,' Patsy said. 'I've heard her through the wall.'

'You have not!'

Patsy looked at Weston. 'Actually, I'm not feeling so embarrassed about the Barbies now.'

'Weston will have to go through the wash with everything else,' Heather said, opening the second case and laying him in it. 'It all smells of smoke.'

'I'm pretty sure Bridget does a separate wash for gorillas,' I said.

WEDNESDAY 12 SEPTEMBER

After school, I telephoned Bridget from a phone box. 'I might be late for tea. Dad wants to hear the gory details about the fire. I may have to draw pictures. Or act it out.'

'Can't you just tell him in words?'

'Probably.'

'I suppose it's natural that he wants to know,' she said, 'as it's what he used to do.'

'And who he used to be.'

But first Dad wanted to boast about how tidy he was keeping the flat. I had to agree. He wouldn't win awards for dusting and he'd been sweeping the carpets with a dustpan and brush, but otherwise it was as neat as two plus two is four.

'Not up to your mum's old standards, obviously.' He looked around the living room where we sat drinking tea from two new Warwick Castle mugs he'd bought from Woolworths.

'I'm in admiration,' I said.

'I don't have any of those anti … anti-whatsits she used to put on the suite.'

'Antimacassars.'

'Anti-what?'

'Are you intending to buy some?'

'Not bloody likely.'

'I wouldn't worry, then.'

'I mean, can you see a ring around the bath?'

'Not from here,' I acknowledged.

'Then why not move in with me? It'll be like old times.'

'Dad, it was the old times that put me in a foster home.'

'I mean before that. Before the whisky.'

'Mum was here then. And that's going way back.'

'You're making this difficult.' He tipped his head back to drain his mug of tea. 'Of course, if you'd rather take the Walls' offer and stick with them in their fancy-pants three-bedroomed house with a lawn and a Kenwood Chef, it's your choice.' He stood, straightening his back to achieve the full six feet and three inches he owned. 'I'd quite understand.'

'Sounds like it.'

'You can walk to school from here. It's just across the park.'

'I can get the bus easily from the Walls'.'

He said, 'And I'm a new man.'

I couldn't argue. His eyes were clear these days and his face unflushed. He was keeping his job at the pie factory, had passed his trial period, was earning more money, and had even had a minor promotion. He'd assured me that he was avoiding friends he would normally meet in the pub.

'Where do you meet them instead?' I'd said on the phone.

'I don't. They're all in the pub. I'm Billy No-Mates, watching *Blankety Blank*.'

'Don't you get lonely?'

'Of course,' he'd said, 'and you can do something about that if you want.'

Another issue that strengthened his argument, although he didn't know it, was that I knew I was making more work for Bridget by staying there. Although I'd urged her to leave me to wash and iron my entire wardrobe of smoke-infused clothes, when I'd come home from school on Tuesday, there they were, ironed until they'd begged for mercy, neatly folded on my bed, and Weston was hanging disconsolately on the washing line by his ears.

She was incapable of listening to reason where laundry was concerned.

I wouldn't say this to Dad.

Now, he left the room and went into the kitchen. I heard

him refill the kettle, then the clank as he put it on the hob. He called through. 'It would be a chance for me to prove myself to you. To be a proper dad again.'

I followed him in. 'Your second bedroom is too small. I'd have to sleep standing up.'

'There's room for a bed, a narrow wardrobe and maybe a bedside table. I've measured up.'

'You've planned this all out.'

'I've cleared it with the council,' he said. 'I do things by the book these days.'

'Do you now?'

'You can get evicted if you move people in without telling the council. Or taken to court.'

'In which case, carry on doing things by the book. Please.'

'I even pay my gas bill on time.'

'Steady on, Dad.'

'So, when are you coming? This Friday? We could celebrate with a Chinese takeaway.'

'I don't think it's our decision.'

'Of course it is,' he said. 'I'm your dad.'

'It's not that straightforward.' I was trying to fend off his optimism, but he came and wrapped his body around me so that my nose was pressed into his chest. It was the closest contact we'd had since he came out of prison and although the logical part of me screamed, 'Don't do anything impulsive', all my traitorous innards were pulsing together, helpless against the love.

WEDNESDAY 19 SEPTEMBER

Dad had badgered his boss for permission to leave work early so he could attend the three o'clock meeting at the Social Services offices in Warwick. Heather had arranged it to discuss the choices for my near future.

Dad had clearly not come straight from the pie factory where he wore factory-blue overalls over jeans and an old shirt. He'd gone home to change into a smart brown jacket and trousers except that the trousers had a crease across the knees that showed they were fresh off a wire shop hanger.

He'd sprayed on enough Old Spice to fell a herd of rhinos.

He'd also arrived early. When I turned up, his large frame was precarious on a small wooden chair and he was telling Heather what he'd read in the paper about the Yorkshire Ripper's latest victim. This is how I knew Dad was nervous. (My mum used to tell him he was at his most inappropriate when he was scared.) Heather was sitting in an office chair near her desk, looking understandably wary. They both appeared relieved when I came in, Nick and Bridget not far behind me.

Bridget carried a stick. It was the first time I'd seen this. 'I thought we might be in an upstairs office,' she said.

'I made sure we weren't,' said Heather.

Heather had made a pot of tea and poured it now into regulation green cups while we all sat looking at each other as though we were strangers: a dish with a mix of odd ingredients that wouldn't work as a whole.

'I've bought a divan bed and new bedding,' Dad said into the silence. 'Sheets, blankets, an eiderdown.'

'We'll talk about practicalities in a moment,' Heather said. 'Let's not get ahead of ourselves.'

'Not the cheap muck, neither.'

'Would anyone like a biscuit?' Heather said, pointing to a plate of digestives she'd put on a low table that sat in the middle of the room.

'I'll have one,' said Dad, and took four. But at least that kept him from describing the pattern on the eiderdown.

Heather summarised the options. The renovation of the Mason Street house might take three to four months. During that time, I could either stay at the Walls' or with my dad. The room at the Walls' was more spacious and there would be someone there when I came home from school.

'Amanda would be thrilled to have you back in the fold,' Bridget said, substituting Amanda's name for her own.

'But is it too much for you?' Heather said to Bridget. 'Physically, I mean.'

'I told you not to do all that ironing,' I said.

I knew Bridget would have spotted Dad's trousers. She was probably starching his creases with her eyes right now.

'I can't see why I couldn't manage,' she said.

Nick put his hand on her arm. 'You would have to go easy, love, especially with what the doctor said.'

Heather's social worker antennae vibrated at the revelation. 'The doctor?'

'Darling!' said Bridget. 'You don't need to go into all that.'

But Heather pressed for information and Bridget admitted that the doctor had been worried about any further physical strain especially when he'd heard that I was staying with them again.

'I do the vacuum cleaning now,' Nick said. 'It took a while to persuade her.' I suspected this was understatement.

'I can always help with that, though,' I said.

'I understand you've had to give up your WeightWatchers role,' Heather said.

'Who told you that?' Bridget was like a cat threatened.

'Jackie mentioned it a while back.'

I felt guilty. At the time I'd told Heather, it was out of concern about Bridget's health. Now, in this context, it held more significance.

For a moment, no one spoke and the silence stretched.

Heather took it on. 'You could, of course, stay *temporarily* with your father, Mr Chadwick here. But, and I hope you don't mind me saying, Mr Chadwick, we do have some anxieties around that particular arrangement.'

When Heather talked like this, she sounded like someone who had to practise reading from the social worker's handbook in front of the mirror.

'You don't need to have "anxieties",' Dad said.

'Don't get huffy, Dad,' I said.

'I've got a regular job,' he said. 'I've already cleared her being at the flat with the council. I could even move into the smaller bedroom, if need be.'

'Need won't be,' I said, too fast for a grammar check.

'And I get home not long after half four, in time to put some tea on.' I knew he didn't finish work until five but I kept quiet. I was touched to see him fighting for me.

'As I said,' Heather told him, 'it would be temporary as far as Social Services is concerned. Jackie is eighteen in March next year and once she's finished full-time education in the summer, she'll be independent of us and free to make her own choices.'

I don't think Dad was listening properly by then. He'd sensed the shift in the room at the mention of Bridget's doctor and scooped up his chance. 'We found a bedside lamp to match the curtains,' he said.

Heather said she needed to speak to her manager but that she'd let us know the next day what decision was made.

'But whatever we decide,' she said, 'the most important thing is that Jackie feels – and everyone else feels – they can be honest about how things are going. Jackie?'

'Of course,' I said.

'And obviously I would check in with you occasionally, Mr Chadwick.'

'I've nothing to hide,' he said, sounding like someone with counterfeit fifty-pound notes under the bed and a body in the cellar.

It was only after I'd said goodbye to Dad and was in the back of Nick and Bridget's Morris Marina that I realised that, when he mentioned choosing my lamp, he had said 'we'.

SATURDAY 22 SEPTEMBER

I lay in bed on my first night at Dad's. The flat was quiet. Even though I could hear the murmur of the TV across the hallway, it was a soft, affable sound. I'd spent too many nights in our old house in our old life listening to him crash his way out of the back door to the outside toilet, kick furniture aside, or hurl empty bottles at the tiled fireplace. He was naturally a noisy clatter of a man: even a shift to another chair or the opening of a drawer in his bedroom made an impact on the flat. But the lack of suddenness was welcome.

I was pleased that I would still see the Walls regularly even though I was living at Dad's. After Heather had been round to inform us that Social Services had approved my stay with him, and after Bridget had cried while pretending to be running a head cold, they'd suggested I visit them each Friday after school for my tea, making routine what was currently occasional.

'That's a super idea,' Heather said, clearly relieved to have brokered the peace process.

Bridget said, 'I'll make Fridays the day I cook something special.'

'Please don't,' I said, 'otherwise I'll feel like a visitor who has to stand on ceremony.'

'All right, I'll do my cottage pie or chicken casserole.'

'That's more like it.'

'And perhaps a quick gateau.'

'You've used the word "quick" to make it sound easy. Don't go to extra bother.'

'I love making a gateau. I've got a new Mary Berry recipe.'

'You are unstoppable,' I said, and then regretted it. The Parkinson's was stopping her. Who was I to discourage her from keeping going?

'One thing, though,' I said. 'I often see Kevin on Fridays after school. I might not be here until six.'

'That's ideal,' Bridget said. 'Why not bring him along?'

'I'll see what he says.'

I knew what he'd say and it was exactly what he did say when I relayed the conversation to him later in the Bowling Green pub while he drank a pint of bitter and I sipped on a lemonade. He'd been to the Walls' house for a meal on several occasions since we'd started properly going out when I was fifteen and he'd endured Bridget's particular brand of hospitality to which she added a side dish of interrogation and a sprinkle of suspicion.

'I'm scared that I'll confess to something I never did,' he'd said to me then and after that had made me promise to discourage any future invitations.

From my bed, I could see a piece of woodchip wallpaper that had come unstuck near the ceiling. I stared at it as evening left us in half-light outside, and hoped the wallpaper wasn't an omen, like a magpie but in home décor. Tomorrow, I'd climb on a chair and stick it back. That's if there was any glue in the flat. Or perhaps Sellotape. That would do.

Make do and mend. My first night back with Dad and here I was, making do and mending again as though it had been waiting in my arteries in the years I'd lived elsewhere, ready to pump out ideas for how to keep a dodgy fridge going, fix a wobbly chair leg or cook a grown man a dinner using two slices of bread and a tomato.

I hadn't noticed, the years I'd stayed with Nick and Bridget, the absence of making do. Bridget had never given me a chance, leaping in with solutions like air into a vacuum. Had a corner of wallpaper begun to droop in my bedroom at Hollybush Close, she would have sensed it happen from the kitchen and been up there in seconds, slapping it into submission with wallpaper paste as though putting it on the naughty step. Bridget knew before I did if I needed a packed lunch, new socks, another toothbrush, a dictionary definition. I'd come to believe she kept all these things in her pockets.

I'd complained about it to my then social worker, Bobbie.

'But this is what parents do,' she'd said.

'I don't remember my own mum doing it. When she was still well, I mean.'

'It would have been your normal. You feel it now that you've been without it for a few years and, in fact, playing that role for your dad.'

It made me sad now to think how much Bridget's ability to leap in and rescue people had been lessened.

I closed my eyes and gave myself up to the night. If droopy wallpaper was the worst of my problems living with Dad, I could tolerate that. It was only day one.

FRIDAY 28 SEPTEMBER

It was Amanda's eighteenth birthday. She was older than me by six months.

'Well done,' I'd said to her on the phone on Monday, 'for organising your birthday on my usual visit day.'

'That's okay.' She'd sounded genuinely proud.

She'd phoned me with a request.

'Will you come out to celebrate after we've had whatever Mum cooks up?'

'Out where? I don't go out, except with Kevin occasionally, unless you mean to put something in the big dustbin.'

'Don't worry about where. I promise I'll sort something.'

'How come your promises sound like threats? Where are all your friends?'

'I'm seeing them on Saturday.'

'So, stay in on Friday with your parents.'

'What?' she said, as though I'd suggested popping out her eyeballs and swapping them round.

I surrendered. 'I'll come, if I must.'

'Wear something you wouldn't mind being photographed in.'

'I am *not* being photographed.'

'No, but imagine you were. It'll help with the look.'

'I don't need a *look*. Where are we going? Paris?'

*

There were two eighteenth-birthday balloons bobbing on the front door as I let myself in.

'Is that a new skirt?' Bridget said, meeting me in the tiny hall.

'From Dorothy Perkins.'

'We are honoured.'

'I didn't need this denim jacket, though.' I followed her into the living room and took it off. 'It's still warm out there.'

Amanda said, 'Jackie's coming out with me after we've had our tea,' and Nick and Bridget both said, 'Oh.' I realised she hadn't told them that the roast chicken Bridget had lovingly prepared, seasoned and basted wasn't the main event. I felt culpable by association, as though I'd plotted with Amanda.

'Coming out where?' Bridget asked.

'I'm glad you raised that,' I said.

'Into town,' Amanda said, obscurely.

Nick said, 'Who else is going?'

'No one in particular.'

'I'd prefer "no one at all",' I said.

'Why is everyone making a fuss about me organising a birthday outing?' she said.

We let her dwell on that. It wasn't as though there was a shortage of past history to go on.

Bridget served the meat onto plates in the kitchen and Nick carried them in, as well as accompaniments in dishes. 'I've made stuffing and pigs in blankets,' Bridget said but she sounded wearied, not energised as she used to be. 'Then we have birthday cake.'

As we ate, Bridget tried very hard not to ask me how my first week at Dad's had gone. She opted for indirect comments such as, 'We've had a busy week, haven't we, Nick? How was your week, girls?' and 'We have missed you and we've been wondering what you've been up to.'

'I've been up to nothing different than I would have been here,' I said, 'except that Dad sits there practising smoke rings rather than stroking a dog.' I put a piece of stuffing on my fork. 'And he prefers ITV. He's moaning that it's off-air because of the strike. He's having to watch BBC.'

Bridget also tried planting the questions on others, such as to Nick: 'You were wondering how long it takes Jackie to walk to school from her dad's, weren't you, dear?' He cooperated and said, 'Yes,' but she had less success with Amanda. 'Darling, you were asking whether Jackie had a desk to do her homework, weren't you?' and Amanda said, 'No, you started that conversation and I said she had mentioned a dining table.'

Other queries began with 'I assume'. 'I assume your dad is sober at the moment.' 'I assume your dad is keeping the fridge stocked' and 'I assume you have enough sheets and blankets'.

We ate Dundee cake, Amanda's favourite, after tea ('I know you prefer sponge,' Bridget said to me, 'so I've made some butterfly cakes too') and Amanda opened presents.

I'd bought Amanda 'When You're Young', the new single from The Jam.

'Yes!' She ripped off the wrapping paper. 'I don't have this one!'

'Don't sound so surprised,' Nick said. 'You told Jackie on the phone last week, and I quote, "I don't have their newest single".'

'You won't play it too loud, will you, darling?' Bridget said, in the least optimistic voice known to mankind.

'They're not as wild as some of the other punk bands,' I said.

'The lyrics are quite rebellious,' Amanda said, as though she felt I'd diluted her.

Nick said afterwards, 'I'll go and wash up.'

I followed him into the kitchen. 'I'll help.'

Amanda came in and looked at her watch. 'We need to go in fifteen minutes.'

'You come and help, too,' I said. 'We'll be done quicker.'

I tried to pass her a tea towel. She dodged it skilfully. Practice makes perfect.

'I have to go and change,' she said, and disappeared.

I called after her, 'Change into someone who likes drying up!'

On the bus into town, I asked her about Patsy. 'You're not best friends, then?'

'She says exactly what she thinks, that's her problem.'

'What's she said?'

'Oh, nothing in particular.' She looked out of the bus window. 'This is our stop.'

'Okay.' I still didn't know where we were going.

'What about her, anyway?'

'I just wondered.' I decided not to add, *I'm meeting her on Sunday.*

I'd had a telephone conversation with Heather and asked her where Patsy was staying. 'Not far from you,' she'd said. 'Nice experienced foster parents – living near the hospital.'

'Can I have the address?'

'We don't normally give them out.'

'The phone number?'

'I'll give her yours with your permission and she can ring you.'

'I'm planning to meet her for a social occasion, not to stalk and decapitate her.'

'It's protocol,' she said.

But, the next day, Patsy had phoned me.

Amanda and I climbed off the bus.

'A pub. I knew it,' I said, when she pointed us towards the Willoughby Arms. She was hurrying us along. She wore a black leather miniskirt I hadn't seen before and which Nick and Bridget had objected to, to no avail, when she'd come downstairs, tugging on the hem as though she knew what they'd say.

'This pub looks nice,' she said, as we approached.

'Stop pretending it's new to you. Isn't it all men in caps, reading *The Sun*? We'll be the only girls in here.'

'Not on Friday evenings. And I can buy a drink, legally, if you'll give me the money, seeing as it's my birthday.'

'I'm not staying long.'

'Don't decide yet. They have a live band on Fridays.'

I looked at her.

'Or so I've heard,' she said.

'Not a punk band, please.'

'I don't think so.' She pulled me through the door. 'And we might meet people I know.'

Sitting at a corner table were two young men. On their table were two half-empty glasses of beer and two packets of cheese and onion crisps. Brothers? They had the same squarish faces, dark hair and broad shoulders.

'Alec!' Amanda said, and the one who seemed older stood as we approached. She went to hug him and after some hesitation he returned the hug. She said to me, holding on to his arm, 'This is Alec, my boyfriend.'

We had all lost count of Amanda's boyfriends. She'd started collecting them when she was fifteen, like stamps or ornaments, these days scooping them up at college or at friends' parties, but she usually discarded them within weeks. The more Nick and Bridget tried to intervene, the more defiant she became. Once, she'd admitted to them, 'I'm only seeing him because you hate him.' When they backed off, she'd dropped the boyfriend as though relieved. 'He had bad breath, anyway,' she'd told me. 'And he listened to classical music.'

Amanda said, 'This is Ian, Alec's younger brother.'

Ian nodded towards me, said, 'All right,' and took a sip of his beer.

Amanda hassled me into a chair next to Ian and she sat next to Alec. For a few seconds, it was as though everyone was waiting for someone else to speak. I sensed Ian's eyes on me and I wondered what he'd been told. Amanda bent the truth like Uri Geller bent spoons and some disappointment was inevitable.

Near the bar, a three-piece band was setting up: two male guitarists in their forties or fifties and a female singer. If they were punks, they were well disguised.

'It's Amanda's eighteenth birthday,' I said to Alec and Ian to kick things off. I was surprised that Alec hadn't already mentioned it or offered to buy drinks.

'Alec knows,' Amanda said.

'Do I?' he said, and her face fell, but he put his hand in his pocket and brought out a flat blue box. 'Sorry,' he added, not sounding sorry. 'I don't do wrapping.'

'He doesn't do wrapping,' Ian echoed, confirming for me that whatever he was, it wasn't a raconteur.

'It doesn't matter,' Amanda said.

She opened the box. It was a gold chain bracelet, chunky, more like a man's watch strap than a woman's bracelet. She lifted it out. 'Oh, it's heavy!' She slipped it on to her wrist. It was clearly too big. 'I might have to get some links taken out.'

I waited for Alec to say he'd get that done for her. He didn't.

She kept the bracelet on, even though it kept slipping down over her hand and she had to shove it back. She wrapped herself around Alec for a thank you kiss but he seemed as though he'd rather have had it in words.

'Anyway,' she said, leaning back in her chair. 'What shall we get to drink? It's my eighteenth!'

I noticed Alec glance at Ian. 'I'm out of cash.'

Ian stood up. 'I'll get one.'

I took my purse out of my bag and pulled out a pound note. 'Here's something towards. Lemonade for me. Half a pint.'

He didn't thank me for the contribution.

'Babycham, please.' Amanda's voice was bright and artificial.

'As usual,' Alec said.

Amanda was coy. 'Ssh. Jackie thinks this is my first pub drink.'

I was irritated. Why was she playing silly games?

She turned to me. 'Have a Babycham with me. No one's watching.'

'You haven't read *1984*, then?'

'What?'

'It's okay. I like lemonade.'

We watched the guitarists as they connected leads to an amplifier and tuned up. The singer, a scrawny woman with short dark hair, a black dress and high heels, was drinking a Snowball while she waited. There were already two used glasses on the floor next to her microphone stand.

Ian returned with our drinks and a packet of peanuts which he opened and began to eat. He produced some cigarettes and lit one. Alec and Amanda had to ask to be offered one.

'Have you got a boyfriend?' Alec asked me, lighting his.

'Not a regular one,' Amanda said.

'Who's asking?' I said.

'Asking for Ian.' He nodded towards his brother. 'He's a bit shy.'

I picked up my lemonade. 'Suits me.'

The pub was filling up and the noise level rising around us only seemed to highlight the fact that everyone else was enjoying themselves.

'Come with me to the ladies',' I said to Amanda.

'I don't need to.'

'Come anyway.'

She rolled her eyes. 'Don't run off,' she said to Alec, and followed me.

'Are you trying to fix me up?' I said as she applied dark purple lipstick in the mirror.

'No.'

'I'm going out with Kevin.'

She scoffed. 'You hardly see him.'

'I'm busy with school. I see him once a week or so. Once a fortnight, maybe.'

'You're lucky he sticks around.'

'I don't have to be welded to him.'

'No danger there.' She clicked the lid back on her lipstick.

'How old is this Alec? I don't like him.'

'I'm not asking you to.'

'Do *you* even like him?'

'That's a stupid question.'

I said, 'You mean inconvenient.'

When we returned, Amanda moved her chair so that it was touching Alec's. I could see his hand on her exposed thigh. She giggled and kissed his neck. He kissed her too but there wasn't much tenderness about him. I thought of Kevin and the way he would stroke my palm with his fingers when we held hands.

The band began with a Gracie Fields song as she'd died the day before, but they did terrible things to it and when the singer said, at the end of the song, 'Rest in peace, Gracie,' I doubted it. Even I could tell the guitarists were out of tune and the singer's three Snowballs appeared to have substituted for some of the lyrics as she kept missing lines.

But it gave us all something to do to replace the conversation that wasn't happening at our table.

Ian bought another round of drinks, this time without my financial assistance. But as soon as he'd finished his, a half-pint, he stood and said, 'I'm off home.'

Amanda, almost sitting on Alec's lap by now, said to Ian, 'Aren't you going to see Jackie to her bus?'

'No, he's not,' I said.

He said, 'Suit yourself.'

When he'd gone, I waited five minutes then said, 'I'm going now. Are you coming, Amanda?'

She'd had two Babychams but was also drunk on her boyfriend. 'I'll stay here with Alec.'

I looked at my watch. 'It's ten thirty.' The guitarists were packing up and people were ordering their last drinks, perhaps stiffer ones after having listened to the band.

'He has a car, don't you, Alec?' She stroked the side of his face.

'I'll look after her,' he said. I didn't like his tone but she didn't seem to notice it.

I wasn't sure what to do. I put my jacket on. 'I'll phone you tomorrow.'

She waved, and drained her glass. As she put it down on the table, the bracelet slid off for the fourth or fifth time that evening and hit the tiled floor.

SATURDAY 29 SEPTEMBER

In some ways, living with Dad again was like living with a father I'd never known. Despite touches of the familiar, such as how his long legs struggled for room between his armchair and the coffee table, or his liking for cheese and crackers mid-evening, or his regular morning cough, so much was new territory. The last time I'd seen him so settled, Mum had been alive, I'd been at primary school, the three of us had been a family from the adverts on TV, and it was only other people who suffered car accidents that lost them their livelihoods, or alcoholism that lost them their dignity, or cancer that could creep through a woman's body as a burglar tiptoes through a house.

Now, here we were, choosing a vacuum cleaner on a Saturday afternoon.

He'd met me outside the bakery after work and we'd ordered a ham sandwich, a scone and a pot of tea in The Eatery.

'I'll pay for this,' he said.

'We can go Dutch. I've got my pay packet.'

'I'll pay,' he repeated, and I realised he wanted to be Dad. 'I still owe you for those fish and chips.'

'You owe me nothing,' I said, although I think we both knew that wasn't true.

In the electrical appliances shop later, I laughed when the salesman, who was so short and thin that Dad could have felled him with a breath, showed us an upright vacuum cleaner and said to Dad, 'Try out the action on this Electrolux, sir.'

Dad stepped back. 'I'm not that familiar.'

'It doesn't bite, Dad,' I said.

'I'll let the littlun do it,' he told the man, as though doing me a favour.

The salesman flicked the switch and I trundled the vacuum cleaner backwards and forwards on a piece of test carpet on which he'd scattered tiny scraps of paper. 'It's not too heavy,' I said, 'or too loud. It sucks everything up. I can't comment on technicalities.'

Neither could Dad when it came to vacuum cleaners so we had to trust the salesman's patter.

When it came to paying, Dad unfolded five pound notes from his wallet. He kept all his money in an old biscuit tin in a kitchen cupboard and I knew he'd been proud to see the tin fill up over the weeks, his cash managed wisely with some left for extras.

'It's another pound for delivery, sir,' the assistant said, 'or will you get the lassie to carry it?' He laughed at his own joke.

Dad didn't take it well. 'Why would I get her to carry it?'

'Of course, sir. Here's your receipt, sir.'

Dad picked up the box and hugged it to himself, at last able to prove some prowess. The salesman opened the door. Dad went through first, walking almost sightless into the high street from behind the box.

'You didn't have to get the hump with him, Dad,' I said when the shop door had shut.

'Bloody pipsqueak.'

Carrying the box back from town didn't prove easy despite his protestations. Several times other pedestrians had to take evasive action.

He'd also forgotten the two flights of concrete stairs up to the flat. I said as I walked up behind him, 'Should I take one end?'

'No need.'

Colin was waiting for us at the top, standing on his outside doormat and smoking. He'd watched Dad struggle up. He eyed the box. 'Someone's been shopping.'

Dad put it down to find his key.

'I've got mine, Dad,' I said. 'It's in my pocket.'

'You're all right, pet,' he said, but he was breathing hard.

'It's not a noisy one, is it, the Electrolux?' Colin said.

'No,' I said. 'We've just tested it in the shop.'

'Good. The bloody woman in that flat before you used to turn hers on to get the baby to sleep and leave it running in the hall.'

'It's a wonder she didn't set the flat on fire,' Dad said, opening the door, and on safer ground with fire safety than with household appliances.

'I wish she *had* gone up in flames,' Colin said, darkly, and disappeared into his hallway.

Over a cup of tea, Dad and I worked out between us, me reading the instructions and Dad inserting the bag, how to get the vacuum cleaner ready to go. 'Let's give it a whirl,' said Dad, flicking the on switch and running the machine backwards and forwards in the middle of the living room, as I had in the shop.

'That bit's clean now, Dad,' I said, over the noise. 'In fact, you might have accidentally mown the carpet.'

He switched it off.

I said, 'Shall we do the rest of the flat? This is fun, doing the cleaning together.'

'Leave the vacuuming to me. You do the bathroom. I had to clean toilets in prison.'

'Vacuuming can be your regular job, then. Saturday afternoons, when I get back from the bakery. I'll do the rest.'

'And then we'll see if I've made us a million on the pools.'

Later, cloths drying on the side of the bath, and the carpets happy for christening our new vacuum cleaner, we put two chicken pies in the oven and some potatoes on the hob to mash with real butter. I sat with Dad ready to watch the end of *Grandstand* on the BBC and tick the results off on his pools coupon.

I said, 'Cleaning makes me feel better as a person.'

'Your mother used to say that.'

'Did she?'

'Well, you didn't get it from me.'

He concentrated on the pools for a while. The voice of the announcer and the peace of the September afternoon and its friendly sunshine had me closing my eyes and giving myself up to something that felt like the colour green or a swim in a still lake.

He folded up his coupon and tore it in half. 'I've not made us millionaires. Sorry.'

'Next time,' I said, lazily.

'We can dream.' He lit a cigarette and sucked on it, blowing out the smoke.

'Maybe she could see us,' I said, looking at him, 'doing the vacuuming and cleaning together. Do you think she'd be proud?'

'Proud of you, maybe.'

'I remember her being proud when you were a fireman. She used to—'

'Those potatoes will be ready to mash, won't they?' he said.

He didn't like talking about Mum for long. Maybe guilt made his tongue unwilling to form the words.

But I'd felt her memory in the room. Had she come in with the sunshine? She'd been the sort who would.

After tea, I washed up. He came in, saying, 'Where's the Sellotape?'

'I'll get it. Sorry.' I'd left it on my bedside table after mending the droopy wallpaper. I didn't mention this in case he saw it as a criticism. I fetched it for him. 'What do you need it for?'

He tapped the side of his nose. 'That's for me to know and you to find out.'

He went into his bedroom. I heard paper rustling.

I was drying my hands when he came back. 'A present, lass. I found it this morning.' He handed me a small parcel wrapped in brown paper. 'Sorry it's so plain. But they only had pink, or flowers, otherwise.'

'I don't mind pink and flowers on wrapping paper.'

'I do.'

'Why have you got me a present?'

'Just open it.'

I hung the towel on its hook and tore open the paper. It was a book. *Poems for Every Day.*

He pointed. 'There's a date on each one. You can look up today's.' He sounded so pleased with himself, it hit the back of my throat.

I turned to 29 September. 'Blackberry Picking' by Seamus Heaney.

'We read this in school once,' I said.

'The whole book?' He seemed disappointed.

'No, no. This poem. Shall I read it to you?'

'Ah, no, pet.' He put a hand out as though stopping traffic. 'You know I'm not one for poems. But you are, so I thought you'd like it.'

'I love it, Dad. But you don't have to buy me presents.'

He ignored me. 'Look up your birthday date.'

'Okay.' I turned the pages to find 1 March. 'It's bound to be about spring.'

'I bet it's that "Daffodils" crap.'

It was. William Wordsworth. *I Wandered Lonely as a Cloud.*

'You'd already looked,' I said.

He seemed affronted. 'Any idiot could have guessed that for March the first.'

'I suppose.'

He said, 'I even know the first verse. We had it drilled into us at school. It's in me like Blackpool rock.'

'Go on, then.'

He looked coy but leaned against the counter and began, 'It's something like – I wandered lonely as a cloud, that floats on high o'er something and hills—'

'Vales.'

'Vales and hills, when all at once I saw a cloud—'

'Crowd.'

'I saw a crowd, a host of golden daffodils. Okay, maybe not Blackpool rock.'

I put the book down and clapped. 'That *would* have made Mum proud.'

His face changed. 'Don't be so soft,' he said, and walked into the living room. I followed him, carrying the book.

'Dad, I'm going into my bedroom to read some of them.'

'Okay, littlun.'

I sat on my bed and found my mum's birthday. 16 November. The poem was by Walter de la Mare and was called 'Autumn (November)' but it was all about phantoms and ghosts. I went back into the living room to sit with Dad.

While we watched *The Generation Game*, I noticed him playing with a thin silver chain round his neck. 'I haven't seen you wearing that before,' I said.

'I don't always.'

'Have you just bought it?'

'No.'

I stayed quiet. If he didn't want to tell me …

'It was your mum's.'

'Oh.'

He pulled it out from under his shirt.

I said, 'Oh, it's that locket and chain you bought her. I remember now.'

*

Mum had turned thirty not long before she died. I was twelve. She'd found it difficult to lean her head forward so that I could do up the clasp. It had hurt her, not that she'd said. I'd felt the hurt through my fingers as I touched the back of her spine. Perhaps there was cancer there, too. It seemed to be able to roam anywhere it liked.

'This must have cost real money,' Mum had said to Dad.

'No,' he'd said. 'I paid with Monopoly notes.'

'Dave.'

'Nothing's too expensive.'

Except that of course it was and in a way I was glad she hadn't been there to see the fallout while he repaid the debt – and probably others – for months. Toast for our breakfast, dinner and tea. Nothing in the fridge save milk and suspect bacon. Meanwhile, Dad found money for his liquid diet of whisky, and I never dared ask how.

'I kept the locket,' he said to me now. 'I wore it to court the day I was sentenced so it came to prison with me.'

'Oh.' I hadn't known this.

'I don't wear it all the time. On some days.'

'Her birthday?'

'No, more days than that.'

'Sad days?'

'I suppose.'

'That's like me and Mum's ring. I keep it under my pillow.'

I'd never told him this before. But the way he was talking about my mum made me bolder.

He tucked the necklace back under his shirt and took his fingers away from it. The conversation was done.

On the TV, Larry Grayson was congratulating the winners of the game and the closing music began. 'That bloody man grates on me,' Dad said, as though cheerfulness were a personal fault.

SUNDAY 30 SEPTEMBER

On Sunday morning, I telephoned the Walls' house. Amanda answered.

'What time did you get home on Friday night?' I said.

'What?'

'What time?'

'Friday? I think I was in bed by midnight.'

I heard Nick in the background, calling from the living room. 'More like two o'clock.'

She shouted, 'I'm closing this door!' and I heard it click shut.

'Where were you until that late?' I said.

'With Alec. Where do you think?'

'In the pub?'

'The pub closed at eleven.'

'In his car?'

She spoke more quietly. 'We went for a drive.'

'What sort of drive?'

She said, 'I'm going to hang up if you ask me any more questions.'

'I think he's a snake.'

'Right, I'm hanging up.'

'That was a statement, not a question.'

'He's my boyfriend, not yours.'

'You're worrying me,' I said.

She rang off.

*

Patsy and I met on Sunday afternoon by the river in the park. Temperatures were lower than usual for the end of September but there'd been no rain. 'The grass will be dry,' I'd said on the phone when we'd arranged it. 'We could bring picnics and flasks.'

'Picnics and *flasks*?' she'd said, and I'd held the receiver away. 'How *old* are you?' But a woman's voice in the background interrupted her. Patsy had sighed and said to me, 'Okay. Apparently, they're all the rage in this house.'

When I arrived, she was already sitting cross-legged on a tartan blanket and beside her a round basket had its contents covered with a polka-dot tea towel. I sat down. 'Embarrassing,' she said, 'carrying this through the streets like Little Miss Bloody Muffet.'

No one would have mistaken her for Miss Muffet in her bright green hot pants, matching jumper and sandals with four-inch platform soles.

'I like your clothes,' I said.

'Heather bought me a couple of things but …' She imitated vomiting. 'So, Marion took me shopping. She needed a *long* sleep when we got back.'

She peeled back the tea towel. Egg sandwiches. Homemade cheese flan. Pork pie. Bright red tomatoes in a plastic tub. Salt 'n' Shake crisps. Thick slices of buttered malt loaf wrapped in greaseproof paper. And a flask of tea.

'I've got two fish paste sandwiches and a bottle of lemonade,' I said.

'I'm banned from Marion's kitchen. She says I don't put lids on properly and I used a metal spoon on her new Teflon saucepan. And there was the freezer problem last Saturday.' She snapped open a bag of crisps as though they'd had something to do with it.

I waited.

She said, 'All I did was take a plug out for my hairdryer while I waited for a fried egg.'

'Drying your hair in the kitchen?'

'I was in a rush. Pete was taking me to the seaside in his new van.'

'Where were Marion and—'

'Harry. At their niece's wedding. They didn't get back until late evening. The freezer was half defrosted. Marion was up cooking joints of meat, in her wedding outfit, when Pete dropped me off at half three.'

I unwrapped my fish paste sandwich. Compared to Patsy's feast, it had lost its charm.

'They tried to be nice about it,' she said.

'Right.'

She handed me a wedge of pork pie and bit into hers. 'It didn't help that I'd left the back door open and a stray dog got in.' She laughed the Patsy laugh and a couple of birds took flight from the tree above us.

I said, 'I've missed you, Patsy.'

We ate the contents of Marion's picnic basket and I fed my fish paste sandwich to some ducks.

'Can you walk in those platforms?' I said.

'I walked here, didn't I?'

She made me carry the basket while we followed the river path and Patsy and her platforms fought for superiority. Walking shoulder to shoulder like this, though, brought a shift in conversation.

'If you've got a dad,' she asked, 'why haven't you been living with him?'

We hadn't talked about the reasons we'd been in care. 'He was in prison.'

'Thought so,' she said, matter-of-fact. 'Mine should have been but never got caught. The bastard.'

I wasn't sure what to say. We sat on a bench and Patsy wriggled her sandals off.

'No wonder my mum walked out on him. On us all.'

I remembered that she'd mentioned several siblings. I asked, 'How old were you?'

'Ten. Nine? Or maybe eleven.' She bent to massage her toes back into shape. 'We weren't doing birthdays. I know I was twelve when I was fostered because I had my first monthly that week and the woman had a mental breakdown at the state of the sheets.'

'That wasn't fair.'

'I wasn't there for long. Nor at the next one.' She sighed. 'I wish I'd gone to somewhere like Marion's straight off. Could have saved a lot of trouble.'

'Trouble that meant you needed the Social Services number at police stations?'

'How did you know that?'

'You told me the day of the fire.'

'Hm. *Never* pick a burglar as a boyfriend.' She said it soberly as though giving genuine advice.

Eventually, I said, 'That's a shame. It was on my to-do list.'

'Honestly, don't.'

'I promise.'

'You have *got* a boyfriend, haven't you?' she said, as though she'd think it careless of me if I hadn't.

'Kevin. I see him most weeks.'

'I've never seen him at Mason Street. Are you sure you're not making him up?'

'We're not meant to bring them to Mason Street.'

'Pff.'

I said, wondering whether I should, 'Is Pete the burglar?'

She punched me on the arm. 'Of *course* not! Give me some credit. Anyway, have you got enough money for two ice creams?'

We walked back, Patsy barefoot, towards the park's café. She'd put her sandals in the top of the basket.

'Marion and Harry have some bloody funny habits.'

'Habits they'd want you to tell me about?'

'For a start, Harry farts like a demon in the mornings, and Marion dyes her hair blonde and tells everyone it's natural.'

'Right.'

'I told Heather. Did you know that Heather broke up with her boyfriend?'

'How do you know?'

'I don't, really, but last week she looked as though she'd been crying, so I said had she broken up with her boyfriend, and she didn't say anything, so that proves it.'

'Definitely.'

'How old do you think she is?'

'I don't know, but I assume you're going to—'

'Twenty-four,' she said. 'I saw her date of birth written on a form on her desk but she covered it up before I could read any more and it's hard reading upside down anyway.'

I filed away the fact that I should tell Patsy nothing I didn't want passed on. Maybe she didn't mean to gossip but her tongue did it regardless. She'd previously told me some 'facts' about the other two girls at Mason Street and I was now revising those in my mind.

We – I – bought two 99s which we sat on the grass to eat while watching children play on the swings and slides.

I was biting into my Flake when I saw Nick, Bridget and Amanda coming along the path from the car park's direction, Amanda trailing behind like a wedding veil which thought it was at a funeral.

Bridget was using her walking stick.

I pointed. 'It's the Walls.'

'Bloody Nora,' Patsy said.

Bridget saw me first. She waved and turned to Nick, who then also waved. Bridget turned to Amanda and said something and Amanda looked as though she would wave but then presumably spotted Patsy.

Amanda was wearing a Sex Pistols tee shirt and jeans. Her blonde hair fell free over her shoulders.

'I can't stand that kid,' Patsy said.

'She's our age!'

'She hides it well.'

I went to meet them, leaving Patsy where she was.

'We decided on a change from Victoria Park,' Bridget said. She lowered her voice. 'Isn't that the girl from Mason Street who had her grandad round?'

Amanda caught up. 'What are you doing out with her?'

'Having an ice cream.'

She frowned. 'She's bad news.'

'What kind of bad news?' Bridget said.

'She's just a bit – frank,' I said.

'Frank?' Amanda scoffed.

Nick said, after a hiatus, 'Do you and Patsy want to walk with us?'

'Dad!' Amanda said.

'It's okay,' I said. 'We've been round the park already. Patsy can't walk in her sandals, anyway.'

'We'll leave you to it, then,' he said, and I went back to Patsy. We watched as the Walls passed us on the way to the river, Nick's supportive hand on Bridget's lower back. Amanda looked back at me and Patsy.

Patsy said, 'How long did you have to live with her?'

'Three and a half years. She's all right when you get to know her.'

'She's a shit punk, I know that.'

THURSDAY 4 OCTOBER

I gathered up my English folder and papers after Thursday's lesson and stashed them irritably into my satchel. Our class, mostly girls, had decided we didn't like Thomas Hardy and today's reading of his poem 'When I Set Out for Lyonesse' hadn't helped.

Mrs Collingworth had done her best. She looked serene enough, as always, in her usual light greens and soft cardigans, but it must have felt like lassoing runaway cattle.

Tracey had slapped down her poetry book when we'd read the Lyonesse poem. 'So, this is about the day Tom met his first wife, Miss?'

'Hardy to us, Tracey, especially in your exam.'

'Hardy, then.'

'That's right,' our teacher said. 'One of many elegiac poems he wrote to say how much he loved her.'

'Except that he wrote many of them *after* she'd died,' I said, 'so she didn't exactly get the benefit.'

'That's true. Good research.'

'And he'd already remarried so he was writing poems to his dead wife with his new wife in the house.'

'That's true as well.'

'Florence,' I said, checking my notes. 'And he took up with her while still married to Emma.' I made my voice as gruff as I could manage. 'I'll be down for tea soon, dear. I'm just writing about how Emma put magic in my eyes.'

She and the class laughed but she shook her head. 'Can

we discuss the language of the poem, rather than indulging in cynicism?'

'I think he wrote these poems out of guilt,' Tracey said.

I said, 'Guilt is why he kept his moustache that long and untidy, so that no one could see it in his lips.'

'Now that explains a *lot* about my Uncle Neil's facial hair,' another girl added.

'Class!' Mrs Collingworth said, and we quietened.

I wanted to point out that cynicism was a native language for some of us whose role models for romantic relationships had put us off hearts and red roses. I knew Tracey's parents had recently separated; I'd found her crying in the girls' toilets.

I hitched the satchel onto my shoulder and was heading to the door when the teacher said, as she cleaned the blackboard, 'How is your own poetry going, Jackie?'

I turned to face her. 'I think it's gone altogether.'

'The skill for poetry doesn't disappear. It'll be inside you, under your skin.'

'I wish there was a sixth-form poetry club.'

'I'm sorry. We have tried that but we get very few takers.'

'It was easier before A levels, especially now in Upper Sixth.'

'You're also doing psychology and ...'

'History.'

Everyone else had gone and I was left in the classroom with her. She started piling up exercise books on her desk, encouraging them into an orderly tower. Everything about her was orderly, from her calm brown hair to the way she'd nudge a desk into place if it dared shift out of line. 'You're living with your dad again at the moment, aren't you?' she said.

That was Mrs C – as we called her when she wasn't listening – for you. Sharp as a tack. But she let the query rest.

'Would it help if I set you a topic sometimes?' she said. 'A mini-prompt, to stretch your poetry muscles?'

'You don't have time to do that.'

'I'll be the judge of that, thank you. What about paper? There you are. Your prompt for the week. Write something on the theme of paper.'

'I'm not sure I'll—'

'Even a couple of lines,' she said. 'You're too good a poet. I'm not letting you go.'

'Like a dog with a bone.'

'Yes, but don't put clichés like that into the poems. They physically hurt me.'

A crush of pupils filled the corridor outside the classroom in pursuit of steak pie and mash. I went to join them.

'Thanks, Mrs Collingworth,' I said, as I left.

'Thank me with a poem,' she called after me.

After school, I had arranged to see Heather for our weekly Thursday meeting. She'd promised to bring Wagon Wheels. She collected me from school and drove us back to Landor Court.

She took off her jacket. 'I'd love to chat to your dad as well but I suppose he's at work.'

'So he tells me,' I said. 'I'll make us some tea.'

'You think he might *not* be?' She followed me into the kitchen. 'But—'

I laughed. 'You sounded just like Bridget then.'

'I never know whether you're being serious.'

'Me neither.' I poured the water into the teapot.

'I hear you're in touch with Patsy,' she said as we sat down in the living room, 'and she says she's on the same course as Amanda.'

'Is that all she said?'

'No, but that's all I'm telling you.'

'She doesn't hold back.'

'I'm glad you're friends with Patsy. You'll be good for her.'

'You make me sound like yogurt or muesli.'

'Sorry. It was meant to be a compliment.'

I poured the tea into our mugs.

'It all looks very tidy in here,' she said, looking round.

'Were you expecting rats?'

She blushed and I wished I could take it back, but she'd unsettled me and I wasn't sure where it had come from.

'We're on the second floor anyway,' I said to redeem the moment. 'They'd have to be adventurous rats.'

'They would.'

'Dad's making a big effort. We do the cleaning on Saturday afternoons when I get back from the bakery. He's bought a vacuum cleaner. I do the bathroom and kitchen. We've got routines.'

'And how does that compare to when you last lived with him?'

'There were other kinds of routines.'

'I was looking back at your notes,' she said, 'from when you first came to our attention.'

'Then you know.'

'It's not pleasant reading.'

'They're not pleasant memories.'

'Sorry, but I have to ask. Any sign that he's drinking?'

I hesitated. 'No. I mean, not that I've checked his wardrobe for empty bottles or asked if I can smell his breath.'

'He's lucky to have you. You're a loyal daughter.'

'Too loyal, probably.'

'You'd tell me, wouldn't you,' she said, 'if things started going wrong? The Walls would have you back in a flash.'

'If things started going wrong. A euphemism.'

'Don't go all wordy on me.'

'It means you're trying not to say something unacceptable, such as, saying that someone had soiled themselves rather than shat their pants.'

'Right, I think I get it.'

'S'cuse my French.'

She sipped her tea then put her hand in her bag. 'I nearly forgot. The Wagon Wheels.'

I said, 'I've thought of nothing else since you walked in.'

*

When Dad came home, he said, 'I think I saw that bloody Heather girl drive off. Does she have a Beetle?'

'Yes.'

'Well, I dodged behind a wall in case she spotted me.'

TUESDAY 16 OCTOBER

'Where are you going?' I asked my dad after tea a couple of weeks later. He'd appeared in the living room in jacket and trousers. I'd heard him raiding the biscuit tin for cash.

Again, he smelled of Old Spice. The trousers I recognised from the Social Services meeting. He still hadn't ironed out the creases. The jacket was grey, though: a new one. I reached over to turn the volume down on *It's a Knockout*, leaving people in foam rubber suits to roll over logs and leap obstacles silently.

I stared at my father. 'You don't have a grey jacket.'

'What's this, then?' He flapped it at me.

'Have you bought it specially?'

'I'm allowed to buy myself a jacket. I've got a job in case you'd forgotten.'

'You've spent too much recently, especially on me. You know there might be a recession, don't you? They said so on the news.'

'They say a lot on the news.'

'Where are you going?' I said again, conscious of repeating myself but unable to stop, like when you start a machine accidentally and can't find the button again.

'Out.'

I followed him into the hall and watched him trying to smooth his hair down in front of the mirror.

'It's Tuesday,' I said.

'Thank you for the information.'

'Are you meeting someone?' I tried to sound teasing.

'I might be.'

I hesitated. Should I say it? But I still couldn't find that button. I think it had got lost in my fears. 'Is it Doreen from the shop?'

I had visited the shop on my way home from school the day before to pick up a can of baked beans.

She'd nodded as I walked in but her hair had stayed still. 'Hello, Jacqueline. Buying chocolate for your dad?'

'No,' I'd said, and went to the aisle for beans.

As I'd paid for them, she said, 'Beanz meanz farts!' and laughed, as though we'd known each other for years.

'Not in our house,' I'd said.

'What if it is Doreen-from-the-shop?' Dad asked now.

'Are you going to the Roebuck?'

'What if I am?'

'Are you going to answer every question with a question?'

'I'll have *one* shandy if that's what you're fretting about. And we're going to the Berni Inn. It's her birthday.'

'It must be a big one for a new jacket.'

'What do you want me to do? Fetch up in my pyjamas or a string vest?'

I tried another tack. 'How come Doreen knows my name?'

'What do you mean?'

'I bought the beans from that shop yesterday and she called me Jacqueline.'

'It's not a crime,' he said.

'That means you've been talking to her about me.'

'Would you rather I denied your existence?'

I bit back the words, *It wouldn't be the first time.*

He tilted towards the mirror again, licked a finger and ran it firmly over his eyebrows. They had a few hairs that stuck out, perpendicular to the rest, as though planning escape. He didn't usually care about them.

This was more worrying than the new jacket.

When he'd gone, I turned off *It's a Knockout*. It seemed frivolous now. I called Kevin's house but his mum told me he was out with a couple of his mechanic friends.

Instead, I worked on a poem about letters in response to Mrs C's 'paper' prompt.

I still wrote occasional letters to my mum's parents, Nanna and Grandad. They lived in Glasgow and although I had visited them once the previous year, Bridget and Nick putting me on a train despite Bridget's premonitions of a crash, an ambush or, at the very least, food poisoning from a British Rail sandwich, letters were our main communication. I updated them on school and included anecdotes about my friends. I didn't mention Dad. Theirs were usually filled with news about Grandad's job with the council and his plans for retirement or about what was growing in their garden, but in between the lines I read my mother.

I also wrote to my Auntie Pat in New Zealand, although less often. She would include memories of my mother, her sister, in her letters, but the undercurrent of hurt made them painful to read, the sentences themselves feeling the injury. She never mentioned my dad, even in response to my news about the flat and our new vacuum cleaner. This absence of mention I took as unforgiveness.

I read the final draft of my poem to the same mirror Dad had used for his eyebrows, pretending as I always did now to read to Mum. She'd read poetry to me since I was a baby, perhaps even as I exited the birth canal.

I'd called the poem 'Opening the Post'.

Their lines are anything but straight.
They weave and curl, avoid and duck

the truth. The truth in black and white
can be too much, lack tenderness.
Sometimes the words hold bruises
that nothing can soothe, not even time
which everyone says is a healer
because it's a comfort to imagine so.
The planting of dahlias, visits to neighbours,
a shop closed as owners move abroad:
the lines slip crooked down the unruled page
as though weary of choosing safe words.

SATURDAY 20 OCTOBER

We were in the kitchen after tea, waiting for the kettle to boil and for Mike Yarwood's show to begin our evening's TV. Dad was opening a brown envelope that had arrived that morning as I'd left for the bakery. 'It looks official,' I'd said to him then but he'd put it on the kitchen counter.

After my morning at the bakery, I'd met Kevin in Warwick for a bacon sandwich and a walk in the park, but when I'd returned home, and Dad and I had cleaned the flat together, the envelope had remained on the kitchen counter, unopened.

I'd been living with Dad for a month.

'Who's it from?' I said, as he unfolded the sheet of paper and scanned it.

'No one much.'

'Must be someone.'

'Nosey parker. It's my probation officer. I forgot an appointment, that's all.'

'Dad,' I said.

'Don't nag.' He put the letter in his trouser pocket. 'I hope you don't nag that lad of yours.'

'No.' He rarely mentioned Kevin. I think he was in denial. On the other hand, I wasn't encouraging them to spend time in each other's presence.

'Should I come up and meet your dad some time?' Kevin had said that day when he'd walked me back to the flats, although he'd sounded tentative. Kevin's knowledge of my dad – although he knew he'd been in prison – was sketchy, just as all my friends' knowledge was sketchy. I preferred sketches to full-colour illustrations.

'He's not one for guests,' I'd said.

'Oh, okay.'

'And if he sees you, he'll have to acknowledge that you're real and that I'm not twelve any more.'

'You're not *twelve*?' he'd said, earning himself a punch in the arm.

There wasn't much room in the boxy kitchen for both Dad and me but, still, more room than in our old kitchen, and sober Dad took up less space anyway.

I say sober Dad. He would tell me he was having shandies when he went out. I tried to trust him in the way people had to trust rollercoasters and aeroplanes when they were first invented.

'What was it like, in prison, having doors shut on you?' I said.

He looked at me. 'What's brought this on?'

'Just thinking about this small kitchen and what it would be like to be locked in with someone else for hours. I would get panicky.'

'You get used to the locked doors.' He reached easily into a top cupboard for a new packet of tea. 'You can get used to anything.'

'I've never got used to the yolk of eggs,' I said.

'True.'

'At the start, then. The first night.'

He put two spoons of tea in a pot and added boiling water. 'They put you in a cell on your own.'

'I thought that was for punishment.'

'Not on the first night. It's to settle you in.' He stirred the tea round and round in the pot, more times than he needed to. 'The doors in prison,' he said, and I felt responsible then for making him think back, 'aren't like the doors in this flat.

They shut with a clang and a crash and then, of course, there's always a key turned.' He stopped stirring for a moment. 'Nothing says guilty like those keys.'

I took two mugs off the draining board. 'You were guilty, though, Dad, weren't you?'

'You mean the policeman?'

'Yes.'

We'd never talked about this.

He sighed. 'I didn't think so, at first. I tussled with him. I didn't know he'd fall and crack his head open.'

'Unintended consequences,' I said.

'Consequences all the same. I deserved them. I had plenty to feel guilty about.'

'You mean what happened with Mum?'

He stood at the sink, looking out of the window at the rooftops of Warwick houses. 'And much more.'

'You don't need to feel guilty about *me*, Dad,' I said to his back.

'Don't I?'

And, because I wasn't sure, I didn't reply to that.

'I hated thinking of you behind that door,' I said. It was easier to say these things when he wasn't facing me. 'Uncle Nick found me a library book about modern prisons to prove you weren't slumped against a damp brick wall with a rat eating your foot.'

'Did he now? Well done, Uncle Nick.'

Stupid, stupid of me to mention Nick. It was a sure-fire way to set Dad bristling.

'What was in your cell?' I said.

'You've watched *Porridge*.' He still didn't turn round. His voice had an edge.

'A toilet? A little table?'

'In prison you're more focused on what *isn't* in the cell, not what is.'

I tried to lighten things up and compensate for mentioning Nick. 'What did you miss most? Me?'

He didn't skip a beat. 'No, I missed bloody whisky.'

'Oh.'

'I still do,' he said. 'At least the locked door meant I had no choice about it.' He turned to face me at last and in the small space I stepped back. 'Did you know that some men deliberately put themselves in there to have that door locked on them and keep them away from temptation? Steal a pack of ciggies, threaten a policeman, throw a brick through a shop window. Anything to keep them from doing what they know they shouldn't. I didn't understand it before but I do now.'

He seemed to have forgotten about the tea. I poured it into our mugs, stirred sugar into his and passed it to him. It had been a long speech for Dad and throughout it his face had been pulled out of shape as though he'd lost control of it.

I bit my lip. 'You're doing really well, though, Dad. Aren't you?'

'Am I?' He walked into the living room and turned up the volume on the telly. The theme tune to Yarwood's show arrived in the quiet room like a raid.

'That's loud,' I said. 'We'll have Colin knocking. Or the lady downstairs.'

'Let them bloody try.' He gripped his mug as though it would be the first thing he'd throw.

Later, as I left him watching the telly to go to bed, I said, 'Try not to miss any more probation appointments.'

'No need to go on,' he said, although there clearly was every need.

THURSDAY 25 OCTOBER

When Heather took me to The Eatery after school, she said she knew about Dad's missed probation appointment. 'Sometimes,' she told me when we'd ordered tea, 'the right hand does know what the left hand is doing.'

'It's like MI5,' I said.

'Not exactly. It's for your protection and welfare that we try to maintain contact with the other agencies involved with your family. Do you see it that negatively?'

I wasn't sure how to see it. She worried me when she took refuge in jargon.

'It was a one-off,' I said. 'I asked him. He says he'd offered to do overtime and forgot the appointment. He needed extra cash.'

This was the story Dad had given me when I'd asked him again about the letter. I wasn't sure whether he had told me the truth or a story made up for convenience. I slept better when I believed the former.

She'd bought us slices of Victoria sponge. 'He wants to buy me a record player,' I said, picking up my cake. I wasn't being totally honest. He had mentioned a record player but for the living room. He was building up his record collection again. Pink Floyd. Thin Lizzy. Elvis Costello.

'Lovely!' she said.

'And he knows I need new clothes for school. I wore my denim skirt the other day and got told it was too casual. We're supposed to wear office dress.'

'He's looking after you.' She was clearly reassured. It saved me from adding more detail. I'd warmed to my theme and had been about to mention new toiletries and a rug.

'He is. I think the experiment is proving a success.'

She checked her watch. 'It's four thirty. What time does he get home from work?'

I remembered that Dad had fibbed about this at the meeting in September to give the impression of round-the-clock care. I didn't want to get him into trouble. 'About now,' I said, trying not to sound definitive. 'Sometimes a bit later.'

'I'll run you home and drop in. He shouldn't be surprised. He knows I'm keeping an eye.'

'Don't you finish by five?'

'It won't take long. You're on my way home.'

She parked the car by the shops and we crossed the road to Landor Close. I looked up at our windows. Dusk was beginning to fall but no lights were on in the living room or in his bedroom, the rooms on that side of the flats.

Oh, Dad, I thought. Where are you?

She walked up the two flights of steps behind me and was standing on the top step, waiting as I put my key in the door and opened it. As I did, I heard the toilet flush. The hall was in darkness.

Dad emerged from the bathroom. 'Hello, littlun,' he said. He couldn't see Heather. 'Must be a bug. I've got diarrhoea like the bloody Victoria Falls. Knocked off early, fell through the front door and got to the lav just in time.' He walked into his bedroom, switching on lights as he went and calling back, 'Don't go in there until I've lit a match.'

I whispered to Heather, 'You're welcome to come in, but—'

She put a hand up as if to stop me. 'It can wait, given the circumstances.'

FRIDAY 26 OCTOBER

I came home from school early. We'd broken up for the autumn half-term but I wasn't going to the Walls' for tea. Nick had telephoned the day before to say that Bridget's parents were visiting. 'You're still welcome,' he said, brightly. 'You're always welcome.'

'I'll give it a miss, thanks,' I said. I'd met Bridget's parents several times and they didn't improve on repeat.

'Lucky you,' he said, all brightness gone.

I'd phoned Kevin to see if he was finishing work early but he wasn't.

I let myself into the flat, expecting no one home. Dad's tummy trouble ('I knew I shouldn't have eaten that sausage roll from the back of the fridge') had cleared up overnight and he'd gone to work as normal.

I shut the front door. There was a pink suitcase in the hall.

In the living room, I found Doreen, the shop assistant with the rigor-mortis hair. She was standing on a chair at the window, wielding a tape measure. As she reached up in her short dress, I could see the top of her stockings, held up with suspenders.

'Oh, hello, chuck,' she said, as though we'd seen each other only that morning and she'd made me buttered toast and jam.

'What's happening?'

'I'm sorting out some new curtains for your dad.'

'How did you get in?'

'Your dad gave me a key, chuck.'

'Why?'

'So I could open the door.' She laughed at her own joke.

'Where are the usual curtains?'

'In the twin-tub, getting a good clean before they go in a drawer.'

I went into the kitchen to stare at the twin-tub and listen for a moment to its joshing and sloshing as though that would help me know what to say next.

Going back in, I said, 'Dad can't afford new curtains. Those came with the flat.'

'We can always find money for new curtains,' she said, which didn't address my concerns.

I tried another tack. She seemed unassailable. 'Why is there a suitcase in the hallway?'

'Oh, don't you worry about that.' She hopped expertly down from the chair as though she measured curtains for men she wasn't married to three times a week, then reached for a pad of paper on the coffee table. 'Let me just write these numbers down, chuck, before I forget them, then we can put the kettle on. Your dad will be home before long.'

Home?

'I don't like being called chuck,' I said. This wasn't wholly true. The bus driver said it and I liked it. A couple of teachers said it. The lollipop man at the zebra crossing said it.

That just left Doreen, then, and anyone else in my Dad's living room wearing baby-blue frilled suspenders.

'Jackie, then. Your dad says you don't like Jacqueline, either.'

So, they had discussed me. This would have been in the Roebuck, Dad with his shandy, or so he kept telling me, and Doreen with a Babycham or a Martini, her soft thigh pressed up next to his on the bench seat.

'You're the opposite of my son, Stuart. He hates being shortened to Stu. His dad – my ex – does it all the time and it drives him mad.'

She had a son? An ex-husband? Doreen obviously came with accompaniments. Would I come home tomorrow to find the son and husband, too, in the front room? Measuring skirting boards, perhaps, or adding a picture rail?

I watched as she wrote a series of numbers with a short pencil she'd had behind one ear. 'I saw some nice floral curtains in Debenhams.' She looked around at the beige walls. 'They'll pep this room up something lovely.'

I'd told Dad myself that I thought the walls were boring, but I said to Doreen now, 'I think they look fine as they are,' and disappeared into my bedroom to stare at my homework.

Later, I heard Dad's footsteps up the concrete steps and then his key in the front door.

'That'll be Dave,' Doreen called from the living room.

I opened my door. 'I know. I live here and this happens at the same time every day.'

'You *are* funny,' she said, then called, 'Hello, love!'

I looked out into the flat's tiny hall. Dad filled it, his shoulders nearly touching the walls either side and his head having to dodge the light fitting.

He hung his coat on the hook. 'Doreen?'

'Surprise!' she said.

'I thought it was tomorrow, we agreed. Saturday.'

'Agreed what?' I said.

'I needed to talk to the littlun first,' Dad said, lowering his voice to a whisper and nodding towards me.

I waved at them both. 'Whispering won't make me invisible.'

'A day early makes no difference,' Doreen said, 'and the shop was closed today for redecorating,' as though that were sufficient reason for relocating where you weren't welcome.

'Is she moving in?' I said to Dad.

'Not in those words.'

'What words, then? Choose some others.'

'You know I'm no good with words.'

'You are,' Doreen said, giving him a playful punch. 'You're the one who finished the crossword in the pub the other night.'

'He doesn't do crosswords,' I said.

'Let's not call it moving in,' Doreen said. 'Let's call it staying for a while. Is that better?'

I asked Dad if he'd told the council. 'What happened to doing things by the board?'

He didn't want to meet my eyes. 'Don't split hairs.'

'I won't take up much room,' she said.

'Haven't you got your own place?' I asked her.

'I shared a flat with a friend. She's advertising for someone else.'

'You could always reapply.'

'Jackie,' Dad said.

She'd said 'staying for a while', though. I'd have to hope.

But – Doreen's suitcase. It was as pink as possible. It yelled pink, pink, look at me, I'm pink. Even its handle was pink.

If suitcases could look permanent, this one did.

I could be grateful for one thing only. Heather had visited yesterday and not today.

SATURDAY 27 OCTOBER

Doreen had an edge. She'd been in the flat barely twenty-four hours before I realised she did not think of herself as a lodger. Physically, she was cushiony, with curves and softness, but any opposition did not receive a gentle landing. She offered the same inflexibility to what she seemed to see as potentially mutinous household objects and spent Friday evening and Saturday morning organising them and rearranging the flat.

'Don't you work at the shop today?' I asked on Saturday morning as I ate cereal before going to the bakery.

She looked delighted that I'd asked a question. 'No, chuck. Monday, Tuesday, Wednesday, Friday. Day off Thursday. Start at nine, finish at five. Sometimes I do an extra—'

'Thanks,' I said. If I didn't stop her, I might get her bowel routines, too.

On Friday evening, she'd introduced a magazine rack for Dad's newspapers and her collection of *Woman's Realm*, designated a drawer in the kitchen as 'medical' and catalogued cleaning materials into one place, shipshaping them into the cupboard under the sink. 'I need to know where everything is,' she'd said, shutting its door and wringing the dishcloth she'd used to clean the cupboard as though strangling a puppy.

Dad and I had watched her from the hall. He seemed awestruck.

I felt the same but without the awe. 'Why do you need to know where everything is? Nothing's going to jump out and attack you.'

'Cheeky sod,' she said, light-heartedly but as though that had been an effort.

'I used to keep some medicines in the bathroom cabinet,' Dad said, but his voice had already waved the white flag.

'Best to store them together,' she said, 'then we all know where we are.'

I knew where I was and I didn't want Doreen there with me.

On Saturday afternoon, the three of us were watching the racing on telly. Dad had shifted from his usual position in the armchair and gravitated to the sofa with Doreen, sitting thigh to thigh. I tried not to look. Then Doreen yawned and said, 'All that organising takes it out of you, Dave,' but whatever it had taken out of her, it wasn't her sex drive. They disappeared into the bedroom 'for a nap'. I turned the telly up to maximum so I could hear horses galloping instead of my father and a woman I barely knew. When they re-emerged, she was childish, sliding innuendoes into the conversation ('Shall I put the kettle on, Dave, or would you rather I took it off?'), but I was glad to see Dad reticent to play the game in front of me.

The pink suitcase, once she'd unpacked it on Friday, had found a new home on the top of Dad's wardrobe. I'd heard them wrangling about it in the bedroom. I'd been in mine, making notes on ideas for a poem.

'It's a bit bright, Dor,' he'd said.

'That room needs a splash of colour. It's all browns.'

'Different browns,' he said, flatly.

'Where else is it going to go?'

I wrote *Back to her old flat, along with her?* in my note-book. I didn't feel I could say it aloud but at least it was there in black and white.

They were getting ready for the pub by six thirty on Saturday evening to meet, according to Doreen, 'Joan and Michael for drinks and chicken in a basket'. The names were new to me and, I suspected, to Dad.

Kevin had rung during the afternoon. Dad had answered. 'It's that lad.' He'd handed the phone over quickly as though it were hot.

'Do you fancy the disco later?' Kevin asked me, his voice expectant.

But I wasn't in the mood for what Donna Summer and Rod Stewart had to say. Not only that but until I'd acclimatised to Doreen's presence I was afraid that I would cry it out, the news being so unfamiliar and raw in my mouth. 'Maybe next week,' I'd told him.

'Don't hold back on the enthusiasm,' he'd said.

Doreen wore a sparkly green dress and matching clip-on earrings. She'd set up the board in the living room to iron the dress, along with other clothes from her case that she said had come out creased as though we were at fault. While doing so, she'd complained about Dad's iron. 'Where's the steam button?' she'd said, turning the iron this way and that.

'The what?' Dad said.

'Does that answer your question?' I said.

'We can get a new iron in Woolies.' She nosed its point along a sleeve. 'I can't have an iron without steam.'

Dad said, 'I thought they ran on electricity,' and nudged me to make sure I'd heard the joke.

'Boom boom,' Doreen said.

They were almost ready to go, Doreen applying last-minute lipstick using the mirror in the hall. She turned to me. 'You can sort your own tea, chuck, can't you?'

'There's a cooked sausage in the fridge that needs using up,' Dad said.

'Party time!' I said.

The telephone rang. Doreen reached for it, but Dad stretched across and picked it up. 'Hello,' he said. 'Who? Oh. Michael. Sorry. Yes, we're just setting off.' He put the receiver down and said to Doreen, 'It was Michael. He couldn't remember what time we'd arranged.'

'Mind like a sieve,' she said.

Dad said, 'You gave this Michael and Joan my number?'

'What do you mean, *this* Michael and Joan? Anyway, it's my number now as well, isn't it?' She put a hand on his arm.

I wondered whether Dad could sense these tiny freedoms being plucked from him, one by one.

'I don't want you answering the phone, Dor. You're not supposed to be here. What if it was the council? Or Social Services?'

'At six o'clock on a Saturday?'

'You know what I mean.'

'If you say so.'

'I'm not saying don't use it. I mean, don't answer it.'

'I suppose it's for the best.' She blotted her lips with a tissue. 'I don't want to get you into any trouble.'

When they'd gone, I heated up the sausage in a pan and fried an egg. I ate it with three slices of bread and margarine in front of Larry Grayson, washed up, then made a sign for my bedroom door that said *Private*, securing it with Sellotape.

Dad and Doreen arrived back after eleven, waking me up. I'd climbed into bed at nine, wearied by change.

I heard Dad in the kitchen, saying, 'She ate the sausage, then,' and I was touched that he was checking I'd had some tea but then he said, 'Where have the crackers disappeared to? Did you move them, Dor?'

I was listening carefully. Was he slurring his words? I didn't think so. All the 's' sounds in sausage, crackers and disappeared had come out spot on.

'You're not having a snack now, surely,' Doreen called from the bedroom.

'Oh, here they are. I always have a snack before bed. There's a lot of me to keep going.'

'Ooh, you can say that again,' she said, with a titter, and I put the pillow over my head in case there was more, but not before I heard her come out of the bedroom and Dad say, 'Leave off a minute, love. I'm just cutting a piece of cheese.'

SUNDAY 28 OCTOBER

The next morning, I pulled on my Sunday jeans and went to the kitchen for some breakfast.

Doreen was in there, wrapped in a lilac dressing gown, making tea for herself and Dad. She was unlacquered, with bed hair set free from its usual tethers.

'Morning!' she said. 'I trust you slept well.' She put her hand to her head in case any of her hair escaped and ran off.

'Your trust is misplaced.' I squeezed past her to reach inside the bread bin.

'Oh. Apologies for breathing.' She tried another tack. 'The sign on your bedroom.'

I waited.

'I'm not invading.'

I opened the fridge, peering inside. 'Where's the margarine? The Blue Band? It's usually in the door.'

'We're getting Stork now and it's on the top shelf.'

'Are we? Dad only likes Blue Band.'

'He likes Stork now as well,' she said, pouring milk into mugs.

I found the Stork, dug a knife into the pack and spread it thickly on two slices. I sensed her watching.

'Do you want a spade, chuck, the way you're lathering that on?'

I said nothing, opening a jar of jam.

'Don't use the same knife as you did for the margarine,' she said.

I pretended not to hear.

She picked up the two mugs. 'Did you pretend not to hear that?'

'I'm sorry to be rude, but you're not my parent.'

'No, chuck, and I'm not trying to be.'

'You're not *not* trying very well,' I said, and she walked back to Dad's room, shutting the door behind her firmly, as though the door had the last word.

FRIDAY 9 NOVEMBER

I took the bus after school to the college where Amanda was reluctantly being formed into a hairdresser and waited for her outside the gates. We were going to the Happy Plate café in Leamington before heading back to the Walls' for tea. In the chill of the early dusk, soft lights were appearing in the windows of tall houses opposite the college.

Other students, stumbling joyously with Friday relief, emerged from the gates with satchels and rucksacks, lighting cigarettes as they walked.

Amanda had told me on the telephone that she had to stay after her final class to speak to a tutor.

'What about?' I'd said.

'I'm getting a prize for most reliable student.'

'Wow! That's incredible.' Which it was, in the truest sense of the word.

'As if,' she'd said.

'What have you done wrong?'

'What have I done right?'

You couldn't say she had a skip in her step as she approached. She wore a black leather jacket with an abundance of zips, but she looked cold. 'There goes my weekend,' she said, solemnly, dipping into her bag for a packet of Benson & Hedges and her matches.

'Extra homework?' I said.

'Pages and pages of notes on customer service principles.' She almost spat the consonants as though holding them partly responsible. 'I'll die of writing, alone in my bedroom.'

Amanda was, like her mother, prone to exaggeration and it was best not to respond otherwise it could progress to ridiculous levels of hyperbole and perhaps the apocalypse.

'Before you die,' I said, 'either of making notes or smoking, let's go into town for Horlicks.'

We sat at our favourite table, furthest from the draught of the door. Amanda was on her third cigarette by now. Only one other table was occupied.

While we waited for Horlicks and biscuits, afternoon Radio 2 playing in the background, I said, 'I prefer The Eatery in Warwick. I was there yesterday with Heather and Dad.'

She rolled her eyes. 'Dream date.'

'Dad only came for twenty minutes and then the café closed. But enough time for her to assess whether he's – I don't know – developed an opium habit.'

'Right.'

'Or let me develop one.'

He's done neither, I thought. But he'd definitely picked up a Doreen habit, yes, and one Heather would have learned about had we met at the flat as she'd originally suggested. 'We're having a big change-round,' I'd said, truthfully, on the phone. 'The café would be better. Dad can pop in on his way back from work.'

I said to Amanda now, 'He behaved himself. Quite the gentleman.'

'I wish Alec was.' She'd lost interest in my anecdote. 'I know he's ignoring my phone calls. He gets his flatmate to answer and say he's out.'

'Oh.'

'And he invited me back to the flat last Saturday evening when the flatmate was at the pub then spent the *whole* time watching a film.'

'And what did you do?'

'Tried to look tempting.'

'But if he was looking at the screen—'

'Exactly!'

I was lost for words but fortunately she had plenty for the gaps.

'My parents have decided to hate him anyway.'

'I didn't like him either.'

'I'm well aware.'

'Do they know he's twenty-two? He's a plumber, isn't he?'

'No, they don't, because I told them he was eighteen and doing mechanics at college.'

'Amanda!'

'I know. But I can't not have a boyfriend, can I?'

'They're not essential,' I said. 'Not in the same league as – say – teeth, or kneecaps.'

We broke off while the counter assistant brought our drinks and two packets of Custard Creams and I gave her some coins. Amanda stubbed out her cigarette in the ashtray, screwing it down hard as though it were Alec's commitment.

It was unfortunate that, as Amanda usually dumped the boyfriends, the one she actually liked was losing interest.

'Have you slept with him?' I said.

'A few times.'

'What's a few?'

She stirred her Horlicks. 'Whenever he wants, I guess.'

'So, maybe he's only—'

'Don't say it,' she said. 'I know.'

I opened a packet of Custard Creams and bit into one. 'How is your mum?'

Amanda's eyes filled with tears. 'It's not fair that she's got Parkinson's.'

'No,' I said.

'I feel bad that I'm such a rubbish daughter.'

'You did not make your mother ill.'

'I suppose. But she can't even take Spotless out for long walks any more, not that the lazy oik has complained.'

'I do miss him.'

'Their lives have totally changed. But I can't live a boring life as well, staying in every night, watching telly, making my bed, doing my homework on the right day.'

I smiled at her description of boring. 'At least you don't have a Doreen,' I said, although I hadn't meant to. The words had appeared on my lips in a surprise move, as though they knew that the knowledge would turn to poison inside me.

'A Doreen? The malt loaf?' she said, and I loved her so much right then even though she was feckless.

'I wish.'

I told her about my dad's lady friend moving in and all the changes she'd made already and, once I'd begun, I hardly drew breath. 'I can't find anything. The tomato soup is where the cereals were and the cereals have replaced the orange squash. There was always a spare key on the telephone table in the hall and Doreen thinks it should be hidden somewhere but we can't remember where. We usually keep the toothpaste and shampoo on the side of the bath but she rearranges them artistically on the windowsill with a candle.'

This last fact drew an 'ugh' from Amanda.

'I'm hoping she's temporary,' I said. 'She has a son, apparently. I think he's older than us.'

'Living with you?'

'Don't even utter those words.'

'What's his name?'

'Stuart. He's in Birmingham, though. I hope never to meet him.'

'Is she *meant* to be living with your dad?'

This made me sure I'd said too much. 'Please don't say anything to Nick and Bridget. Promise me. It might get my dad into trouble with the authorities. I'm not sure of the rules.'

'You're not supposed to have other people living there without the council knowing. Someone in my class says her mum—'

'Don't tell me.'

'Okay. I guess you didn't share this with Heather yesterday, then?'

'What do you think?'

'Ditto regarding Alec,' she said. 'Don't say anything to Mum and Dad. I told them he was The One and these climbdowns are the pits.'

I had a horrible thought. 'And Patsy.'

'What about her?'

'You wouldn't say anything about Doreen to her at college, would you?'

'I don't go anywhere *near* her.' She shuddered.

'She's not a virus,' I said.

FRIDAY 16 NOVEMBER

I fell asleep again after my alarm had rung and woke fifteen minutes later in the middle of a dream in which I was late for registration but my teacher was Heather in Doreen's lilac dressing gown, writing on the blackboard.

My pillow was spotted with blood. I flipped it over, but the clean side laughed as if to say, 'Who are you fooling?'.

Tiny spots of blood, but old companions. My head-picking habit was back. I'd found myself doing it recently when sitting in bed, reading before I turned out my light. So far, I'd kept it to evenings except for yesterday when Heather caught me at it in the café and I'd told her it 'might' have been an allergic reaction to shampoo, modal verbs being so helpful for being evasive.

I needed to stop the habit myself before they sent me back to the educational psychologist I'd seen in 1976 who was an educated man in everything except personal hygiene and who had dragged so much information out of me, I'd felt lighter on my feet.

I tugged a brush through the knot and snarl that was my morning hair, even though it caught on the sore spots. I didn't feel like being kind to my head.

Dad was in the kitchen, dressed for work, leafing through the newspaper. 'Looks like the miners are going to strike,' he said. 'Could be power cuts. Thatcher's got a problem on her hands.'

I found it difficult to engage. There was enough going on in our own house without other people's bad news.

He called to Doreen who was in the bedroom, getting dressed. 'We'll need to be stocked up on candles in case, love. And I don't mean the poncey lavender ones you've got in the bathroom.'

'You could have asked me, Dad,' I said. 'I could easily pop to the shop later.'

'No need. Doreen can bring some back.'

'Oh.'

After school and before I went to the Walls' for Friday tea, I took the bus to Warwick and visited a florist on my way to the church graveyard where Mum was buried. This would be the first time on my own. The Walls had taken me on special days and, before that, I'd always gone with Dad.

It would have been Mum's birthday.

The shop door sang a carefree 'ting-a-ting' as I opened it: fine for buying wedding flowers or a congratulations bouquet but surely less suited for honouring the dead.

The middle-aged woman in the shop wore a badge saying, *Nora Brown, Manager*. She had kind eyes, the type that invite immediate trust. You'd want them in a counsellor or perhaps a surgeon about to amputate a limb, but they're welcome in florists, too.

'What can I do for you?' she said.

'It's my mum's birthday.'

'What does she like? We've got lovely chrysanths in.' She pointed to a display. 'Lucky mum, to have a daughter buying her flowers. I wish I did!'

'She likes chrysanths,' I said, and now I'd collaborated with her on using the present tense, there was no going back.

'Something like this?' She picked up a tall container filled with yellow and orange flowers with large, happy heads. 'I could make you a bunch. She'll be delighted.'

'How much would that be?'

'Let's call it ninety pence and a free birthday card. Then you're sorted.'

I was very much not sorted. I was out of sorts, my heart thumping with memories, and hoping she wouldn't ask about cakes or what we were doing to celebrate.

'Write the card while you're here?' She took a pen out of her apron pocket.

'It's okay.'

She put the pen back. 'No problem.' She smiled and said, 'You'll be wanting to think about what to put in the card,' and she wasn't wrong.

She wrapped the flowers expertly in pink paper then put my coins in the till.

'Happy birthday to Mum. Tell her best wishes from the florist.'

Mum's gravestone had been white originally but was more of a faded grey now.

'Hi, Mum,' I said. I unwrapped the flowers and laid them in front of the stone. They screamed colour, stark against the weathered gravestone. 'The florist says happy birthday. She's nice. You'd have been good friends.'

Near the grave was an old wooden bench, mossy and worn. I sat on it and retrieved a Penguin biscuit from inside my satchel. I always ate a Penguin biscuit when visiting Mum's grave. They'd been her favourite snack and Dad and I had established it as a ritual.

The first time he'd suggested it, I'd questioned him. I would have been twelve. 'It doesn't seem fair that she doesn't have one.'

'Rubbish,' he'd said. 'If there aren't Penguin biscuits where she is, I'll choose to go down and not up.'

It had satisfied me.

'Cheers,' I said to Mum's grave now, holding up the

biscuit like a glass of champagne. 'Maybe Dad will be along after work.'

Was she there? Did she know how much I wanted to tell her about Doreen and ask what to do?

Amanda was staying overnight with a friend so it was Bridget, Nick and me sitting around their dining table later, eating Bridget's beef stew.

I wondered which 'friend'. I assumed Alec. Patsy had told me on the phone that Amanda had missed several days of college. 'Then she turns up and whines, "I don't know what to *do*." The tutor's getting proper naffed off.'

Patsy's own college attendance hadn't always been regular but I didn't point this out. I said, 'Don't forget the bakery tomorrow if you want that job.' There was a vacancy for a Saturday afternoon assistant. I'd told the shop manager, Sheila, that I knew someone who'd be suitable. I hoped Patsy would prove me right. I could imagine her yelling, 'That's eighty-nine pence, Mrs Jones, and how are your varicose *veins*?'

'Is Amanda okay?' I asked Nick when Bridget was in the kitchen. I wondered whether her absences from college had been due to illness.

'Fine in herself. Why?'

'No reason.'

As Nick served out the beef stew so that Bridget could sit down after cooking, we joked about how Bridget was and always would be queen of her kitchen, and woe betide anyone who intruded or changed things around.

I oh-so nearly said something about Doreen.

For someone so soft and feminine, dressed most of the week in a shop assistant's checked tabard, Doreen was an elemental force. I could fend her off easily enough when she criticised the way I spread margarine, but I was more worried about

Dad. He was conflicted between the two of us. She'd want to watch some documentary about an actress or Mexican temples on BBC2 while I wanted *Top of the Pops*, and even though Dad liked *Top of the Pops*, he'd say, 'Doreen's right. You can hear all that on Radio 1.' And he'd sit through the documentary, pretending interest.

Before Doreen arrived, Dad and I had added to our Saturday routine an hour in the local café with a newspaper before coming back to watch the football results. But when we suggested that the three of us go, Doreen said, 'Ooh, their tea is like cat piss,' and Dad agreed, 'It's not the best.'

End of discussion.

Doreen's Saturday afternoons were for relaxing, anyway. She preferred Sunday mornings for housework and Dad and I were redundant as she whisked through the flat with vacuum cleaner, cloths, steaming soapy water and disinfectant, like Superwoman but with dusters.

'What's that furniture polish?' I'd said, when she first buffed up the furniture. 'Is it Pledge?' It was the same one Mum had used and the smell drove me into my room to write poems or pick at my head.

'It's the best.'

'I think I'm allergic to it,' I told her. 'It makes my eyes burn.' I rubbed them for effect.

Dad was listening. 'Oh, pet.'

'I could see what else there is, I suppose,' Doreen said, and the following week she used something different.

I'd held fast on cleaning my own room but she feared my standards weren't high enough. Fully aproned up, she'd peered around my door the previous Sunday without knocking. 'Shall I give this a once-over?'

'No,' I replied. 'I've already cleaned it and that would be a twice-over.'

'So sarky,' she said, and shut the door.

I called, 'Can you knock next time, please?'

But, more than any of that, she'd brought alcohol into the

flat from the off. A bottle of Gordon's gin had nestled in the pink suitcase among the frilly underwear and the bright-coloured shift dresses she favoured. She'd put the gin under the sink with the Domestos as though it were another house-hold essential and would pour herself a gin and tonic at five thirty before tea, asking Dad if he wanted one. 'Not for me, love. You know I'm trying to steer clear,' he'd said at first, and he'd made himself a mug of tea or poured a cream soda from the Corona man who came by in his truck on Saturdays. Or he'd light one cigarette after the other and suck on them as though trying to inhale self-control.

But 'Not for me, love' had changed over the first few days to 'I'd love to – you know I would'.

One day, he'd said, 'Gin's not my favourite but I'm itching for bloody something,' and I'd said, 'Dad, you promised,' at which he blustered out of the kitchen and into his bedroom, slamming the door.

I'd tried to reason with her. 'Dad's been trying so hard,' I said when he was having a bath one evening, I think to avoid giving in.

'One won't do him any harm.'

'He never stops at one.'

'I can't not have my daily gin,' she said, as though gin were a vitamin or an angina tablet.

'I'm not saying you shouldn't. Just don't offer him any.'

And for a few days after that she didn't. But the founda-tions had been laid.

Now, having my tea with Bridget and Nick, with Spotless in his usual place under the table in case of scraps, the words *Dad's lady friend has taken over our flat* were queuing up in my mouth and ready to roll. Perhaps the sentences themselves knew to do the right thing even while I stacked up reasons not to.

But, as I was about to speak, Bridget yawned, loud and

wide, in a very un-Bridget-like fashion, and I said, instead, 'You're tired.'

She said, 'I had another bad night last night.'

'I didn't know you were having trouble sleeping.'

'I can't remember what I've said and not said to which person and about what sometimes.' Even her words seemed weary.

Nick pointed upstairs. 'I've taken up residence in your old bedroom some nights, Jackie.'

'Why?'

'He thrashes around, twists and turns in his sleep,' Bridget said. 'Always has. But these days, it wakes me, and I can't do without the sleep. My limbs don't work otherwise.'

'That room is strikingly yellow, Jackie,' Nick said. 'I can't believe we put you through that when you lived here.'

'Why do you think I wore my sunglasses?' I said.

They both laughed.

I couldn't mention Doreen now.

Nick had referred to my stay in the past tense, anyway.

Present tense with the florist. Past tense with the Walls. I would have told Mrs Collingworth about the way grammar had influenced my day if it hadn't come with so much baggage.

'Anyway,' Nick said, putting his knife and fork together, 'this time next year we should have more room.'

'How come?' I said.

'Thanks to my dad. He's selling his house to buy a bunga-low. He wants to give us enough to extend ours.'

Nick's dad, a widower, had moved from the Midlands to South Wales on retiring.

'I've tried to dissuade him but he thinks we need a couple more rooms to give us flexibility. Convert the garage, perhaps. Add a bedroom upstairs.'

'That's kind of him.'

'It is,' said Bridget. 'Too kind.'

'He managed care homes for years,' Nick said. 'He knows

the value of space when – well – when people aren't moving around so easily.'

I'd met Nick's father a few times. A wise, kind man who wore thick paisley sweaters and corduroy trousers and added his rumble of a voice to a male choir.

'I'm not care-home material yet,' Bridget said, her voice as tart as lemons, and she started scraping and stacking our plates as though to prove it. 'There's no need to turn this house into one. You'll be wanting a lift put in next. Or my bed brought downstairs, with Spotless.'

'He's right, though, darling,' Nick said. 'He's got the money. He wants us to have it now, and to do some good. Carpe diem and all that.'

'What does that mean?' Bridget said.

'Seize the day,' I told her. Mrs Collingworth, who was my form tutor as well as my English teacher, was always saying it in registration to motivate us. It had minimal effect which is why she was always saying it.

Bridget put a lid back on the casserole dish that had held the stew. 'I'm not sure I'm up to seizing anything,' she said, all the lemon sourness gone from her voice and replaced by sorrow.

When I let myself into the flat, Dad was in the kitchen with a plate loaded with cream crackers and half a pound of cheese and Doreen was watching TV. Although she'd taken charge of all our main meals, she didn't approve of Dad's evening snacks and left him to prepare them. Perhaps she thought he would sense her disapproval and stop.

'Do you want a couple of these, pet?' he said.

'Okay.' I didn't need them, but I loved any chance to be just me and Dad.

He reached for a small plate in the cupboard and passed me two crackers topped with cheese. I crunched savagely into the first one – snap! – hoping Doreen would hear.

'Branston?' he said.

'No, thanks.' I kept my voice down. 'I went to Mum's grave today. I took flowers.'

He put down a knife and looked at me. 'Did you remember the Penguin?'

'Of course.'

He bent towards me for a brief squeeze. 'You are a better person than I am.'

'I agree.'

'I remembered,' he said, 'but I was on the phone to my probation officer. Then I forgot.'

'Don't worry.'

He ruffled my hair. 'Would you like some money for the flowers?'

'No. That's not why I told you.'

'I know, pet.'

'You could go tomorrow. She won't mind if you're a day late.'

'I might. It's been a while.'

Doreen came into the kitchen. 'Am I missing something?'

'Yes,' I said, and went into my bedroom.

Half an hour later, after I'd read for a while, I went to fetch a glass of water. Doreen was in the kitchen, pouring gin into two glasses from a new bottle of Gordon's.

I nodded towards the glasses. 'Is one of those for Dad?'

'I can't drink them both,' she said, although I'd seen evidence to the contrary.

'Did he ask you for one? He doesn't like gin.'

She turned to face me. 'Your dad's not a child. He can make his own choices.'

Dad wandered in, holding an empty beer glass. 'Stop worrying. It's a one-off.'

'A two-off,' I said, 'by the looks of it.'

'I've had a bad day,' he said.

I walked to my room so that I wasn't facing him. 'Start on the gin, Dad, and there'll be more bad days to come.'

I shut my door, but I heard Doreen say loudly, as though she meant me to hear, 'You shouldn't let her cheek you like that.'

'She's got a point,' he said.

'She's got a tongue on her, that's what she's got.'

WEDNESDAY 5 DECEMBER

It was after ten and I'd been watching *M*A*S*H* with Doreen and Dad and then some politics programme that I'd watched alone as they'd both dozed, their heads too heavy for them. Doreen had been drinking gin and Dad whisky. A bottle of Bell's had found its way to the Domestos cupboard but, when I'd commented on it, he'd told me not to interfere and to get on with my own life, as though he saw his life and my life as parallel lines and not a Venn diagram.

It had cheered me up to chat to Patsy on the phone earlier that evening about her first couple of weeks at the bakery although it had been hard to keep her on topic. I wanted to know how she'd found the work, not a speculative account of Sheila's love life or the news that the assistant who worked part-time Monday to Fridays had got growths in her womb bigger than a beach ball.

'I think the customers like me,' she'd said at last. 'If they look poor, I throw an extra bun into the bag.'

'You can't do that!'

'Sheila hasn't noticed.'

'You might get into trouble.'

'I'm not scared of trouble. That's *peanuts*, that is.'

'You're like Robin Hood,' I said, and even though we were on the phone, I could sense her blushing.

Her ego was big enough already so I didn't tell her that

Sheila had commented, 'She could charm the sun out of the sky,' and had thanked me for recommending her although she'd added, 'Shame she doesn't come with a volume control.'

'We're heading for bed, pet,' Dad said now, stretching and rubbing his eyes. 'Turn the telly off when you're done.'

'Don't forget to pull the plug out,' Doreen added, unjustifiably abrupt, as though I'd been in the habit of forgetting.

I'd learned to stay up half an hour later than they did with the telly still on. I preferred *Sportsnight* or a play in which nothing happened than to lie in my bed on the other side of a thin wall, listening to the sounds Doreen made and to Dad shushing her. I'd heard – and Kevin certainly seemed to think so – that sexual intercourse was meant to be pleasurable but Doreen sounded as though she was undergoing surgery without anaesthetic.

I heard them moving between bathroom and bedroom and waited until it had gone mercifully quiet before switching off the TV and yanking out the plug with force, just for Doreen.

I was in my bedroom about to undress when someone knocked at the front door. Not keen to answer this late, I ventured back into the hall and called Dad.

He appeared from the bedroom in striped pyjamas. 'Was that a knock?'

As if in reply, another knock came. He frowned.

He padded along the hall in his bare feet and opened the door. I stood behind him and peeked round.

Standing on our new outside *WELCOME!* doormat – a Doreen purchase which grossly misjudged Dad's attitude to visitors – was a young man, older than me but not by much. He carried a shabby sports holdall and a large carrier bag. In the stark yellow gleam from the automatic light at the top of the stairs, I saw dark, uncombed hair. He wore a duffle coat and scruffy shoes.

'Can I help you?' said Dad, sounding doubtful about whether he'd like to.

'Is my mum here?' he said.

'Your mum?'

'Doreen. Is she here?'

Doreen's voice floated from the bedroom. 'Stuart?' She arrived, tying the belt of her silky dressing gown, and squeezed past Dad to face her son. 'Is that you?' she said, late in the process.

'I've got nowhere else,' he said. 'Dad's thrown me out. I've already spent two nights on the streets.'

Whenever Doreen had spoken of Stuart, the main impression she'd given was that he was – to quote her – 'a waste of space of a boy' and that she hardly saw him.

She was seeing him now and, to do that, she must have given him Dad's address. Our address. I waited for Dad to say, 'How did you know where we lived?' but he didn't.

'Can I sleep here for the night?' Stuart said.

I cut in. 'Sorry, no room at the inn.'

'Jacqueline,' Doreen said.

'I've had nothing to eat, Mum,' he said.

'Oh, son. You poor love.'

There was a pause.

'You'd better come in, lad,' Dad said, at last. 'But we've only got the sofa.'

'You're in for an uncomfortable night,' I said, looking at his height. He wasn't as tall as Dad, but not far off.

'Better than a doorway,' he said, and stepped inside suddenly, like a Jehovah's Witness. That meant all four of us were in the hall together as though in a lift but, regretfully, without the emergency button.

'Thanks, Dave, love,' Doreen said.

'One night,' Dad said, but you couldn't have called him assertive.

'One night,' Stuart echoed. 'Cheers, mate.' The term of address seemed overly familiar, but weeks later, when he was still with us, I realised *he'd* meant 'One night *at a time.*'

Stuart smelled stale, like a basket of dirty washing. He followed my dad into the living room and curiosity made me bring up the rear. Doreen filled the kettle in the kitchen. Dad said, 'You might have to hang your legs over the end. It's only a two-seater.'

'I haven't slept for two nights,' he said. 'I could sleep in a ditch.'

'In which case—' I began, but Dad said, 'Jackie!'

Doreen came in. 'You can tell me all about it in the morning, love. You'll be wanting to kip down,' but Stuart said, 'I could murder a cheese sandwich,' at which point Doreen instantly upgraded him to egg and chips.

I lay in bed, hearing the sizzle and spit of Doreen's cooking, and worried that in the middle of the night I would meet Stuart in the hall on his way to the toilet. I wondered if he had pyjamas in either of the bags.

THURSDAY 6 DECEMBER

In the morning, when I'd dressed, I went to fetch breakfast. The door to the living room was still shut. I hoped it would stay that way until I left for school and that when I came home all sign of Stuart would have disappeared and any skin cells that had flaked off him been hoovered up.

I was rinsing my cereal bowl, looking out of the kitchen window at other people's rooftops, when the living room door opened. Neither Dad nor Doreen had emerged yet.

'Any chance of a cuppa?' Doreen's son said from behind me, his voice with a morning rasp to it that said twenty fags a day.

I kept my gaze on the rooftops in case I turned round to see a naked man. I'd never seen a naked man and wasn't in the mood for my debut.

'Where's the tea?' he said.

'In the cupboard.'

'Which one?' He came to stand beside me. Phew. Clothes. 'What are you staring at over there? Have you seen a UFO?'

His rumpled shirt hung over a pair of flared jeans. His bare feet were dirty. But his eyes reminded me of Spotless's eyes: chocolatey-brown and hungry. There was intelligence in them. I recognised it in the way you know when someone else has suffered like you, or when they too love animals.

Still, he was in my dad's flat and, for me, as welcome as an itchy rash.

'The tea's in there,' I said, pointing, and went to clean my teeth.

I heard him fill the kettle and then he called, 'Is there any sugar?' but I left him to find out for himself. It wasn't as though the choice of cupboards was extensive and he had plenty of time, because if I was sure of one thing, he didn't have a job at the bank to hurry to.

As I picked up my satchel from the hall, Dad appeared. 'Did I hear the lad?'

'You're late for work, Dad.' I checked my watch.

He looked shifty. 'I'm not feeling my best today. I might ring in.'

'What's the matter?'

'I think I'm trying to fight something off.'

Whatever it is, it's not Doreen, I thought.

I said, 'Isn't Thursday Doreen's day off?'

'Oh, is it?' He put a finger to his head as if to say, *Silly me. I forgot.*

I didn't have energy to play his games. 'At least you'll both be here to say goodbye to Stuart when he leaves,' I said, and let myself out of the flat, but not before I heard Stuart shout, 'I love you too, baby!' from the living room.

Outside our block of flats was a brick shelter underneath which our metal dustbins sat, all labelled with the flats' numbers in thick white paint. Idly, I lifted the lid from ours. I don't know what made me do it. Fast-disappearing hope, perhaps.

Someone had thrust them down under newspapers, presumably hoping to conceal them, but there they were: three empty bottles of Bell's.

MONDAY 10 DECEMBER

At the end of my English lesson, the last lesson of the day, Mrs Collingworth deftly shut the classroom door when everyone else had left. 'How's the poetry going?' she said, turning to me. 'How did you get on with the poem about signs?'

Since she'd set me the 'paper' prompt back in October (and presented me with a clean exercise book in which to write), I'd shown her three or four attempts, including my 'Opening the post' poem about letters. She'd begun to ask me for copies to keep in a folder. 'I always keep examples of pupils' best work,' she'd said.

'Signs' had been her most recent prompt.

'I tried a sonnet,' I said.

'You have a great ear for rhythm. You need it for sonnets. I'd love to hear it if you're not rushing for a bus.'

'I walk back these days. Dad's flat is the other side of the park.'

'Excellent.'

'I'm not sure the poem's finished.'

'Poems rarely are. They're best left fuzzy, in my view.'

'I called it "Signs". I couldn't think of anything more original.' I retrieved the exercise book from my satchel and opened it.

'Go on, then.' She sat in her teacher's chair and folded her arms.

'Don't you have marking to do?'

'Just read the damn poem.'
'Okay. Here it is.'

You look for good signs. Stop here! for cream teas.
The sun will shine tomorrow. Money off!
A mile until you're home. Pink-blossomed trees.
Two for the price of one. An easing cough.

You hope for true signs. Promises: they're kept.
Letters come from those who said they'd write.
Kisses are sincere. The facts correct.
Doors are locked and rooms are safe at night.

Lament the sad, the bad signs. Artful words.
The dropping of the gaze. The alibis.
The hidden, veiled. The sudden caw of birds.
The rosebush in the flower bed that dies.

Stop here! for cawing, blossom dead and gone,
for veiled sunshine, two dropped flowers for one.

I closed the exercise book.

Mrs Collingworth said, 'Jackie, are you sure you're *okay*?'

'Tickety-boo.'

'But that's so mournful. Beautifully done, but mournful. What's been happening?'

'You always say that when you read a poem you shouldn't make assumptions about the poet.'

'You mean what your class didn't manage with Thomas Hardy?'

'And I've been reading Sylvia Plath's poems. She makes it impossible.'

'She does. But I wouldn't be doing my job if I didn't ask you.'

'I know.'

'So – what's brought on the ominous bird imagery and the dead flowers?'

I sighed. 'Disappointment, I suppose.'

'In yourself?'

I realised she was right. I thought she'd say 'disappointment in your dad' but she'd judged better than that. I was disappointed in myself for making what seemed like the wrong decision and in not having the guts to reverse it and find myself back in a safe place. It could have been so easy. One word ('help') to Heather in the café the previous Thursday would have made all the difference. But instead I'd used all the other words I knew, skirting around that one as I would huge spiders or thin ice.

'And,' I said to Mrs C, 'disappointed in the way things – people – don't always turn out …'

'The way you hope?'

'Yes.'

She opened a drawer in her desk and took out a leaflet. 'I think you should try this,' she said. 'It's a poetry competition for fourteens to eighteens run by a London publishing house. The deadline is mid-January. You should enter.'

I said, 'Even though things don't always turn out the way you hope?' But I took the leaflet.

THURSDAY 13 DECEMBER

Mrs Collingworth stopped me on the way to morning assembly. 'Your psychology teacher—'

'I know. I'm retaking the test.'

'Ten per cent, though?'

'It's better than five.'

'Did someone else get five?'

'No,' I admitted.

'This doesn't happen to you, Jackie. What's going on?'

'I'm adjusting to Upper Sixth, that's all. Why does everyone assume my life is imploding?'

I knew I was being rude. And this was Mrs Collingworth, who'd been my ally all along and deserved none of it.

But before I could apologise, she'd spotted another pupil she needed to talk to and was pursuing them down the corridor.

Heather cancelled our café meeting: she had staff training and would see me next week instead.

I phoned Kevin. I'd only spoken to him a couple of times on the phone since refusing his disco invitation a few weeks earlier.

I told him I could do some schoolwork in the library then meet him.

'Okay, I'll see you in the Bowling Green at five,' he said. 'I think I can stretch to a lemonade for you.'

'I'll be legal soon.'

'I'll dump you then,' he said. 'I'm not made of money.'

The school library. The Bowling Green. I'd have sat on a bench in the park if it hadn't meant frostbite.

Places to go rather than head straight home.

Mrs C had asked me earlier what was going on and I'd hurled the concern back at her. But I wouldn't have known where to start.

Those routines I'd complacently told Heather about: now only a memory as the flat creaked and juddered under the weight of four of us.

On my return from school since Stuart had arrived, he'd be in situ in the living room, idling his afternoons away with *Jackanory* and *Grange Hill* while slugging beers. The days of using the dining table for my homework seemed over.

He kept the TV volume unreasonably loud, too. Trying to write about a First World War poem or the rise of fascism wasn't easy against a background of children's television.

'Are you hard of hearing?' I'd asked him.

'No,' he'd said.

'Are you trying to muffle the sound of your own laziness?'

'Bog off,' he'd said.

To give him credit, Stuart was also a reader. He'd arrived with dog-eared copies of Frederick Forsyth and Graham Greene and had joined the library. ('How did you get a ticket?' I'd asked. 'Gave them this address,' he'd said. 'It's not yours to give,' I'd said.) On opening a fourth beer, though, he'd fold over a corner of the page and abandon reading for semi-consciousness.

He was also cleaner than when he'd first arrived. 'Put your clothes in the family washing basket,' Doreen had told him, to my disgust.

A tray from the kitchen became my desk. I'd sit on the bed, my back to the wall, and lean the exercise book on it.

But my handwriting, a neat script with small loops and hooks inherited from my mother, would suffer, and my neck ached. Also, I wasn't doing Thomas Hardy or Wilfred Owen justice. They'd made all that effort, staying up late, agonising over this or that adjective and the best metaphor for despair. Yet, here I was, assembling half-hearted essays on which Mrs C would write *Expand this idea* and *Explore the irony further* and, when she wearied of this, *Ditto above.*

I did no better with my psychology studies, as my test result had showed. It felt pointless, studying dry theory from textbooks when case studies cavorted under my own roof. A classmate had asked the teacher, 'How do I find evidence for reasons for addictive behaviours in humans?' and I wanted to answer, 'Come and watch my household. Tickets on the door.'

I found history easier. Kings and queens. Wars and conflicts. Political changes. Dates and places. Names and titles, gained and lost. I took refuge in certainties.

Since Doreen and then Stuart had moved in, I had developed new antennae, like an insect evolving. I'd forgotten what it was like: this continual state of high alert. Someone moving to the kitchen, jangling keys, unscrewing a bottle, set the antennae buzzing, as did the sound of Dad's money tin.

When Doreen first came, I'd heard Dad say, if we'd run out of bread or bacon, 'Help yourself from the tin, love.' More recently, he'd said it less. She'd helped herself too freely: a new dress here, a bottle of perfume there. A Mediterranean cruise couldn't be far behind.

'How come Doreen always borrows from you?' I'd asked Dad. 'What does she do with her own wages? She's saving all that money on rent, for a start.'

But I knew. Doreen loved her Kays catalogue, leafing through it in the evenings while drinking gin, and finding the bargains more astonishing with every sip. Like Bridget, she had a love of kitchenware ('You could do with a decent set of pans, Dave.'), but where Bridget had the money in the bank, Doreen only had it in her imagination.

When Doreen arrived home from work, she'd say to Stuart, 'Have you been sitting there all day, son?' but Exhibit A was in the kitchen, waiting. Dirty plates and teacups, knives and forks, open packets of cheese on the counter, a knife sticking out of the jam like Excalibur. 'You should think about moving on,' she'd say, but without conviction, unless she meant to the next beer or from one chair to another.

'The phone hasn't rung while you've been here, has it?' she'd asked him.

'No, and if it did, I wouldn't answer. I'm not taking bloody messages.'

'Good. Keep it that way. You're not meant to be here. Dave would be knee-deep in it.'

'I'm not thick,' he said.

Dad would be home before Doreen, assuming he hadn't stayed off with a mystery ailment. A few days before, I'd found him watching *Blue Peter* with Stuart, home suspiciously early. Doreen had said, 'Isn't your boss getting ants in his pants about you?' and he'd said, 'He knows I'm a good worker. He won't let me go that easily.'

'As long as you stay good,' she'd said.

'What's that supposed to mean?' he'd said, the first time I'd heard open defensiveness used against her. It had been over three years since he'd used the tone with me, but my antennae recognised it and warned me, setting them complaining at too much to do.

Kevin and I spent only an hour in the pub, its bay windows happy with Christmas lights and the bar busy with custom and chat. Meanwhile, our conversation was stilted, as though we'd only just met. I felt depressed about my psychology test but didn't want to tell him. He clearly knew something was wrong. So I toyed with a beer mat whose message was, *Courage! Take some cans home now!*

'I'd best get back, Kevin. I haven't finished my homework.'

He didn't object.

'Shall I walk you home?' he said, outside the pub.

'It's two minutes. You're in the opposite direction.'

'Shall I kiss you goodbye here, then?' He leaned in. His mouth on mine, as always, gentle, unassuming.

I pulled away. 'You smell of Guinness.'

'Might be because I've just had a Guinness,' he said, but I knew I'd pained him.

I arrived home at six thirty. Usually, Doreen would have been clearing up after tea. I'd told her I'd be late so not to cook me anything and I'd make a sandwich.

Stuart was in his usual position. There were beer bottles on the coffee table and a mess of stubs in the ashtray. He'd had what looked like cheese on toast. Like a toddler, he never ate the crusts. They were heaped up on the plate.

A library book was on the floor, face down.

'Where is everyone?' I said.

'That's a bit rude,' he said. 'I'm here.'

'You know what I mean.'

'Gone to the Roebuck, I think.'

'This early?'

'This early.'

'Oh.'

'Come and watch *Nationwide*. This stunt performer has jumped eighty feet high on a motorbike.'

'Have people got nothing better to do than kill themselves?'

'Well, aren't you the life and soul?'

'Isn't it time you were finding somewhere else to live?' I said.

'Says who?'

'Says the council. You're not supposed to be lodging here. Neither is your mum.'

'I'm not lodging. I'm borrowing your dad's sofa. And she's borrowing your dad.'

'Shut up.'

'You're going to ring the council, are you, and split on him?'

'I could tell my foster parents or my social worker. They'd tell the council.'

'And then what would happen?'

I fetched a glass of squash and some crisps and took them to my room. I couldn't look at his face any longer, especially as I didn't want to think about the answer.

SATURDAY 15 DECEMBER

I dressed ready for work and came into the kitchen to find Stuart there, wearing a light brown suit and matching tie, taking a bowl from the cupboard.

'Why are you in a suit?' I said, staring. He looked smart and neat and – I hated myself for thinking it – appealing in a David-Essex-who-never-made-it kind of way.

'The suit? I can take it off for you if you like.'

'You're all right. I'm not desperate.' I put two slices of bread under the grill, edging around him so as not to make contact. 'Where did you get it?'

'Borrowed it from a friend of Mum's. I'm going to an interview.'

'On a Saturday?'

'It's at a garage. Sales. It's what I did in Birmingham until – until it ended.'

'You got the sack, you mean.'

'I never said that.'

'But did you?'

'Why should I tell you?'

'How did you get into doing that?'

'I did a year's business course at college.'

'Instead of A levels? How old are you?'

'Twenty,' he said. 'What makes you think I was A-level material?'

'Your books,' I said, pointing in the direction of the living room. 'And your eyes look clever.'

'You've been looking, have you?'

'Not really.'

'Yeah, well. Things don't always go to plan.'

'What happened?'

'It didn't go to plan. I've just said.'

'What do you mean?'

'What's with all the questions?'

He poured cereal into the bowl and splashed milk onto it. Some spilled over the edge and onto the suit. 'Bloody hell,' he said.

I passed him the washing-up cloth. 'Dab it.' He did, and handed the cloth back.

He opened the fridge. 'Do you want the marg?'

I took it.

He opened a drawer. 'And a knife?'

'I didn't ask you to play butler.'

'How did you get to be so cheerful?' He took his bowl and spoon and walked away.

'Good luck getting the job,' I called. 'Then we can have our room back.'

He didn't answer.

After work, I collected my wages, left the warm bakery, saying hello to Patsy who was arriving, and pulled on my thick coat. I'd arranged to meet Amanda in the park café.

She was there already at a window table except that the windows were misted with condensation. The café's noisy heaters threw out damp, bathroom-type air with abandon.

She wore her black leather jacket over a black polo neck and sported a nose stud.

'How did you persuade your parents to let you do that?' I said.

'I didn't ask them. It was my money.'

'You mean, their money that they give you?'

'Same difference.'

'How did they react?'

'How do you think?'

I hung my coat on the back of a chair. 'I thought you might have ordered already.'

She grinned. 'I thought I'd wait for your wage packet.'

I said, 'Now that you've spent your own cash on perforating yourself.'

I queued at the counter and brought back hot chocolates and toasted teacakes. Amanda had rubbed a circle in the condensation so we could see outside to the park where children in coloured bobble hats and mittens climbed ladders and seesawed.

I said, 'All their little noses are as red as cherries, and they don't care so long as they can play.'

As though she hadn't heard me, she said, 'Did you remember the shirt?'

'Bugger. Sorry.'

I'd bought a shirt from Dorothy Perkins which was too tight. It was the kind of cornflower blue that suited Amanda. 'You can have it, so long as you don't slash holes in it,' I'd said.

'I'm at a party tonight,' she said. 'It would go with my black trousers and this leather jacket.'

'More bugger.'

'I could come back to yours and get it.'

'Haven't you got anything else to wear? Dad isn't expecting visitors.'

'I'll wait outside. It's fine.'

But as we neared Landor Close, she said, 'I wish I'd gone to the toilet at the park. I'm getting desperate.'

'It's up two flights of stairs,' I said, as though this might convince her bladder to behave differently.

'I'm bursting.'

'Okay.'

I opened the front door and Amanda, hesitant, followed me in.

Dad and Doreen were in the kitchen, constructing a meal of

ham sandwiches and alcohol. They both stared as we arrived in the hall as though they'd turned on the telly and found the wrong channel.

'My friend needs to use the lav,' I said, and nudged her towards it.

I intended to grab the shirt from my room and be ready to leave. I couldn't think of one conversation topic that I wanted Dad, Doreen and Amanda to embark on.

I couldn't locate the shirt at first. Then I found it in a bag at the bottom of my wardrobe, ready to take to Amanda.

I heard the toilet flush and Amanda emerged into the hall.

'Who's this, then?' Dad said. It had been years since he'd seen her.

'It's Amanda Wall.'

'Oh. That Amanda.'

Doreen didn't understand his reticence. 'Let's give Jackie's friend a proper welcome, Dave.' She came towards us, all mother figure and flowery apron. 'Pleased to meet you, love. A school friend?'

'Amanda is – was – my foster sister,' I said, 'when Dad was away.'

'Oh, I see.'

'She's off now, anyway,' I said, which is when the front door opened and in came suited-up Stuart, except that the suit was now creased, he was tie-less and his face said beer, beer, beer.

He stood in the hall, a hand against one wall to steady himself. 'I didn't get the job, before anyone asks.'

'Oh, I'm sorry, love,' said Doreen. 'They don't know what they're missing.'

His eyes were on Amanda. 'But the day's looking up. Who's this?'

'No one you need to know about,' I said, and shouldered Amanda into my room rather than pass Stuart in the hall. I shut the door.

She looked round at my room with its small wardrobe and box of a bedside table.

I said, 'Here's the shirt. Try it on.'

She took her jacket and jumper off and put the shirt on, doing up the buttons. 'Have you a mirror?'

'Not in here. It looks great. Better than it did on me.'

When she had her clothes back on, she sat on my bed. 'Who is that?' She spoke quietly, as did I.

'Oh, Doreen's son. He visits sometimes.'

'He had a key.'

'I know. She gave it to him so he can let himself in.'

'Was he a bit pissed?'

'Probably.'

'Not bad-looking, though.'

I sat on the bed and spoke right into her ear. 'He's a scrounger. Don't even think about it.'

'Brown eyes. Like Spotless.'

'I've noticed.'

'Oh, you like him, then. I'll leave him for you.'

'I do not. And I don't want you anywhere near him.'

'Tall.'

'He doesn't eat his crusts,' I said, foraging for arguments. 'He doesn't wash his hands after peeing.'

'Horrors!'

'How's it going with Alec?' I said. A low blow, but I thought it might help.

'It's not.'

'Oh. What happened?'

'Let's not go there.'

'Did you bunk off college for him? Patsy said something.'

'Patsy's a loudmouth.'

'I was worried.'

She waved me away. 'He had a few days off. Anyway, he's history.'

'Okay.'

'Thanks for the shirt.' She put it in its bag. 'Do you want money for it?'

'Do you have any?'

'No. Only bus fare. What times do they run from here?'

'Wait there. Don't move.'

Dad and Doreen were in the living room. Stuart was in the bathroom, I assumed to change out of his suit.

'Dad,' I said. 'Have you got that timetable for the Leamington buses?'

The cheap TV cabinet contained a drawer where Dad kept a jumble of timetables and leaflets. He pointed to it.

'There's one in ten minutes,' I said when I returned to Amanda and sat next to her to read the timetable. 'You'll get that easily.'

I was sure Stuart had waited to hear my bedroom door open as we emerged into the hall. He'd changed into jeans and a brown jumper the colour of his eyes. He glanced at the timetable I held. 'I could hear you two whispering,' he said. 'Was it about me?'

'Don't flatter yourself,' Amanda said. But as I let her out of the front door, she looked back at him, and I remembered my mother reading to me from a children's Bible the story of Job's wife who, despite warnings, looked back at Sodom and found herself turned into a pillar of salt.

Five minutes after Amanda had left, I was in my bedroom when the front door slammed.

I opened my door. 'Who went out?' I called, and Doreen shouted, 'Stuart's gone to fetch some bread rolls.'

He came back after twenty minutes. I ambushed him in the hall. 'Where are the bread rolls?'

'They'd run out,' he said.

'Of the shop?'

'You're not funny,' he said.

THURSDAY 20 DECEMBER

On the last day of school before the Christmas holidays, I poured milk on my cornflakes. No one else had stirred. Their drinking had stretched into the early hours. Thursday was Doreen's day off so she had time to nurse a hangover but it seemed to me like a day wasted. Surely the point of a day off was walks in the park or a bus ride to the next town to browse the shops.

Stuart was free to lie in and often did. Somehow, he'd found a way to sleep on a sofa three sizes too small for him, curled up like a newborn. I admired the feat although I hadn't admitted this to him, saying instead, 'I suppose all wildlife adapts to new habitats.'

Dad, however, should have been getting up for work.

I was rinsing my cereal bowl when I heard Dad's raised voice to Doreen. 'You did *what*?'

He burst from their room in his pyjamas and stood in the kitchen doorway. His face was grey and his hair a tangle.

'You'll never guess what she's done,' he said.

I emptied the washing-up bowl and said, 'If it's changing where the towels are kept, I'd already spotted that.'

He ignored me. 'Go on, guess.'

Why was he telling me? Surely it was between the two of them.

Doreen came out of the bedroom in her dressing gown and stood beside him. 'It's a fuss about nothing,' she said, although her voice didn't sound sure.

'Nothing?' He was breathy, as though he'd been running.

'What is it, Dad?'

Stuart came out of the living room. 'Don't let me intrude. People need to piss.' He went into the bathroom.

'Your dad has to move on,' Doreen said to me. 'She's been gone – what is it? – six or seven years.'

'Who's been gone?' I said, but only because I needed time to process. I wasn't sure if I'd heard right.

'Maggie,' she said, at the same time as Dad said, 'Your mum.'

I'd heard right. 'What's happened, Dad?'

Doreen tutted and went back into the bedroom. Perhaps she didn't want to hear what she'd done all over again.

'That solid silver locket.' He touched his neck as though it, and perhaps comfort, were there. 'Doreen found it in my drawer while doing what she calls a sort-out.'

'She hasn't thrown it away?'

'No, she's bloody sold it. For a few measly *quid*.' He shouted the last word to make sure she heard but I suspected she was listening anyway. He slammed the palm of his hand on the kitchen surface and the bread bin jumped. 'I need a drink.'

'It's eight o'clock in the morning.'

I shouldn't have said it.

'I know what the bloody time is. I don't need you to tell me.' But his voice broke on 'tell'.

'Dad, I'm on your side, remember.'

He shook his head. 'A few quid, pet.'

Doreen came back. 'I'm sorry, Dave,' she said, in a not-sorry voice. 'Someone around here has to find ways and means. There was nothing in the tin.'

I thought, *start your own tin*?

'And how do you think I feel,' she added, 'knowing you're hanging on to the past like that?'

'You didn't have the right,' I said to her.

'Don't you have a heart, Dor?' Dad said. 'That meant a lot to me.'

She said, 'It's not as if you've worn it lately.'

'That doesn't mean I didn't want to keep it.'

'It wasn't the only thing I sold. There were rings and bracelets of mine, too.'

'What the hell difference does that make?'

She put a hand on his arm. 'It does you no good, being sentimental.'

He shook her off. 'How would *you* know?'

'Puh,' she said. 'I'm going back to bed.' She shut the bedroom door with a loud click.

I checked my watch. 'I have to get to school, Dad.'

'You'd better, then.'

'Don't have a drink. You need to go to work.'

He patted my hair. 'I'll do my best, pet.'

The toilet flushed and Stuart came out of the bathroom. He clearly thought twice about venturing into the kitchen – he would have had to squeeze past Dad – so he headed back towards the sofa.

I left for school but soon realised I'd forgotten to pack my textbooks. The incident that morning had made me miss out stages in my routine. All day long and in every lesson, as teachers showed their displeasure at my lack of organisation, I was reminded about the silver locket.

Heather dropped me home after our Thursday café meeting, during which I told her the entire plot of *Tess of the d'Urbervilles*, which I was reading, to stave off inconvenient questioning. I wondered what awaited me at the flat. Doreen had wounded Dad and when Dad was hurt, he could lash out like an animal cornered.

But when I peered round the door of the living room, I found Dad, Doreen and Stuart, with Doreen reading out crossword clues to the others as though they were all marvellously old friends and in the pub of an afternoon.

'Boredom!' she said. 'Begins with T. Six letters.'

'Er – tedious?' said Stuart. 'No, that's seven.'

'Tedi*um*,' said my dad, awarding himself a swig from his glass.

Stuart had a swig too as runner-up.

No one noticed that I'd arrived. I fetched some orange squash from the kitchen and took it to my room.

This was Dad papering over the cracks in his relationship with Doreen, I decided. He wasn't strong enough to tell her to leave and to reclaim the money tin and bathroom windowsill and kitchen cupboard for himself and for me. He needed a woman and Doreen would do for now, Kays catalogue addiction, locket-selling and all.

That morning, I'd told him we were on the same side. It had felt true, in which case, why was I in my bedroom, alone?

Later that afternoon, Doreen switched the radio on and sang along with Abba in the kitchen as she fried chips. She knocked on my bedroom door. 'Do you want two fish fingers or three with your chips?'

'Not for me. I'm writing to my Nanna and Grandad.' I said 'my' deliberately. I felt she'd taken enough of what belonged to me.

She tried to open my door but I pushed it back forcefully with my foot to stop her entering, the way people do in public toilets. I heard her tut. She said, 'Well, writing letters isn't going to stop you being hungry.'

I didn't agree.

SATURDAY 22 DECEMBER

I worked overtime the Saturday before Christmas, alongside Patsy. Sheila had praised us for selling so many mince pies. 'How do you do it?'

We didn't admit that Patsy was telling customers that the bakery up the road was using last year's mincemeat.

I arrived home at two. 'Hello,' I called from the hall but there was no answer. I could hear racing commentary from the TV.

I peered round the door. Stuart in his armchair, his head nodding over the book on his lap; Dad and Doreen on the sofa, draped over and around each other like a heap of curtains. They were all in their nightwear and I wondered whether they had intended daily life to begin, or just to wait until bedtime came round again.

Dad's resentment about the silver locket had either drained away or he'd tucked it somewhere it didn't show.

'I brought us back some currant buns. A present from Sheila.'

'Thanks, pet,' said my dad, without looking round.

'I'll put them in the kitchen, shall I, for later?'

'What?'

'I'll put them in the toilet, shall I?'

'Thanks,' he said.

The coffee table bore a plate with the remains of bacon sandwiches, including Stuart's crusts.

'Is there any bacon left?' I said.

'Sorry, chuck,' Doreen said. 'I would have saved you a rasher or two if you'd asked.' She still hadn't looked round.

'I shouted from the bakery but you didn't hear.'

'Ouch,' said Stuart.

The racing commentator's voice filled the room, as a race reached its climax, his pitch higher and higher. Dad and Stuart shifted closer to the TV as though that could make horses run faster or better.

I went into the kitchen and put my wages envelope on the counter while I poured some squash. What should I do for the rest of the day? Spending quality time with the other residents of the flat wasn't hooking me.

I sat on my bed for a while. I heard Dad in the kitchen opening and shutting cupboard doors, then the rustle of a crisp packet. He went back into the living room. Then I heard Stuart say, 'I fancy some crisps too,' and the same routine was repeated by him.

Doreen called, 'Bring me some, son.'

The sound of three people crunching crisps – I could hear them even though my door was shut – was suddenly too much. Stuart had a habit of crunching down on the crisps, so that everyone else could experience them with him, rather than putting them whole in his mouth.

I went into the hallway and telephoned the Walls' house to speak to Amanda. 'Do you fancy coming into Warwick?'

There was a hesitation. 'I suppose I could.'

I was hurt. 'I said come to Warwick, not stab yourself with needles.'

'I don't have any money.'

'I do. I've just got my wages. I can treat you to a hot chocolate.'

'Okay.'

We arranged to meet at The Eatery.

I put my head around the door of the living room. 'I'm going up into town.'

'Who with?' Stuart said.

'What's it to you?'

'Keep your hair on, chuck,' Doreen said.

In the kitchen, I picked up my wage packet and slipped it into my jeans pocket.

'Bye!' I shouted from the hallway, but no one responded. I shut the front door, then noticed plotting clouds, so I let myself back in to fetch my umbrella. As I stepped into the hall, I heard Dad say, 'Go and fetch the new bottle, Dor.'

The Eatery was busy with Christmas shoppers, gossip and newspapers. I found a table and waited for Amanda. She arrived half an hour late.

'You've got new boots,' I said. They were black, adorned with mini chains. She wore them with a short skirt and thick tights.

'A present from a friend.'

'Which friend?'

'Oh, no one you know.'

She sat down, shrugging off her leather jacket. A waitress came to take our order.

'So, what mischief have you been up to this week?' I said, while we waited.

'What do you mean, mischief?'

'Don't take offence. I'm only joking.'

'I've been busy with college.'

'Now you *are* making me suspicious.'

'And a few other things.'

'Such as?'

We sat quietly for a moment. I wasn't sure why. She usually had a complaint or other and I was missing it.

A waitress brought our steaming mugs and, while Amanda sipped at hers, I slid my pay packet out of my pocket, intending to transfer the money into my purse.

Amanda's eyes widened, looking at the figure written on the packet. 'Three pounds fifty!'

'I did overtime.'

'Still.'

'You could get a job if you wanted one. I could ask at the bakery. You get free cakes sometimes.'

'What time do you have to get up?'

'Seven.'

'*Seven?* On a Saturday?'

'Your face.'

'Anyway, I get free cakes at home,' she said, and then looked sad. 'Most weeks, anyway.'

I knew Bridget wasn't baking as much as she used to.

'Second thoughts,' I said. 'Patsy works there, too.'

'Ugh!' she said.

I emptied the cash from my wage packet onto the table. 'That's funny.'

'What?'

'Oh, nothing. Just—'

I could only see one pound note and two fifty-pence pieces.

'Just what?' But she was watching a table of three boys. 'They're from college,' she said. 'Idiots.'

'Stop staring at them, then.'

Where had my money gone? I checked the envelope again.

I thought back. Stuart. The sod. He must have taken it while he was in the kitchen, looking for crisps.

I would need to tell Dad. Perhaps this would finally convince him to kick Stuart out. A thread of hope began to sew itself into me.

But I couldn't tell Amanda. She might mention it to her parents and that could set off a chain of events I wasn't prepared for.

We finished our drinks. She was clearly not in the mood for talking and I wasn't sure what I'd done.

I put my coat on. 'See you Christmas Eve.'

'I guess.'

'You don't need to guess. I'm coming on Christmas Eve. Your mum and dad invited me.'

'Oh.'

'It'll be lovely to see you, Jackie. Your company is always so stimulating.'

She was looking at her watch. 'I need to go,' she said, and headed for the door.

Outside, the bad-tempered clouds were making good on their threats. I put my umbrella up and set off for home, rehearsing in my mind how to start the conversation.

At the flat, I found Dad and Doreen preparing to go to a birthday party. Doreen was wrapping a present on the dining table and Dad was trying and failing to be helpful with Sellotape.

'Whose birthday party?' I asked. They'd said nothing about it earlier.

'Someone from the pub,' Dad said.

'Where's the party?'

'At the pub,' Dad said.

'Don't they have a house?'

'Don't you have something else to do?' he said.

Dad had his usual jacket and trousers on and I think he'd Brylcreemed his hair. Doreen liked it slicked down but it made him look as though he'd been rained on. I didn't like the way she was trying to discipline Dad's hair in the way she did hers.

She was wearing a tight pink shift dress, low cut at the front and, from what I could see as she bent to wrap the present, a bra that lifted and separated, and then lifted some more.

'Where's Stuart?' I asked.

'Having a bath,' Doreen said. 'He's going out, too.'

'You'll be all right on your own, pet, won't you?' Dad said.

'I thought he had hardly any money,' I said. 'How can he be going out?'

I saw Doreen look at Dad. 'She's quite the Gestapo, isn't she?' and this riled me and gave me my starter.

'He's taken money from my wage packet. It was in the kitchen and one pound fifty of it has disappeared.'

'Don't be ridiculous,' Doreen said. 'Why would he do that?' She put a final piece of Sellotape on the parcel and tapped it with satisfaction.

'Your manager's made a mistake,' Dad said. 'Did you check the money was right when you left work?'

'Why would I? Sheila's never messed it up before.'

Doreen walked past me, teetering on stiletto heels as though she'd already had two gins, which she may have done, and knocked on the bathroom door. 'Stuart!'

'What?' There was a pause. The bathroom door opened and Stuart stood there, a towel wrapped around his waist. I wanted to look away but also needed to see his reaction. I kept my gaze carefully on his face.

'Jacqueline's lost some money from her wage packet,' she said.

He shrugged. 'So?'

'I haven't *lost* it,' I said. 'Someone's *stolen* it. S. T. O. L. E. N.'

'I don't know what she's talking about,' he said.

'I'm right here. Did you see my wage packet in the kitchen earlier today?'

'Maybe. I can't remember.'

He adjusted the towel as though he thought it was coming loose. I hoped not.

'Who else would it have been?'

'I think you've made a mistake, love,' Doreen said. 'Or your manager has, as your dad said. We can lend you a pound if you're short.'

Dad came into the hall. He didn't repeat the offer.

'Have we finished here?' Stuart said. 'I need a slash.' He shut the bathroom door.

'It isn't a mistake,' I said, but if Stuart wasn't going to own up, what could I do?

'We're going to be late if we don't get a move on.' Doreen adjusted a bra strap which was protesting at being overworked.

They left, leaving a heady mixture in the hall of Dad's Old Spice and the musky scent that Doreen bought from the Avon lady. Stuart was still in the bathroom. I sat on my bed, not wanting to risk meeting him if he legged it to the living room starkers. He kept all his clothes – the few he had – in the holdall in the corner and I didn't know if he had taken any into the bathroom.

Doreen had been to charity shops for trousers, shirts and jumpers for Stuart and taken money from Dad's tin to buy new pants and socks. 'I'm not buying my son second-hand Y-fronts,' she'd said when Dad protested.

'If you want him in brand-new pants you can use your own wages.'

'Then how would I pay for the curtains in our bedroom?'

'I never asked for new curtains. What was wrong with the old ones?'

'They didn't block out all the light.'

'That's why God gave us bloody eyelids,' Dad said, and I loved him for the joke. I'd punched him on the arm to acknowledge it and he'd grinned. These moments were scarce. I had to grab them as the starving grab at bags of rice.

From my room, I heard Stuart come out of the bathroom. Twenty minutes later, he shouted, 'I'm off, honeybun,' and the front door slammed.

'Peace, Weston!' I said to my gorilla.

I pulled some English homework, a comparative essay about two Wilfred Owen poems, out of my school satchel and went to use the dining table. But the room was dispiriting. Stuart's bag gaped open, clothes spilling out, and the coffee table was littered with the day's detritus. The dining table itself was covered in what was left of Doreen's birthday wrapping project as well as red and green Christmas paper chains that she had been making. They should have looked cheerful.

I returned to my room and sat on the bed, writing half-heartedly. I didn't feel like comparing poems. I was too busy comparing life now with life in the distant past.

After ten minutes, I gave up, relocated to the living room, cleaned up the coffee table and turned the TV on but most of the programming was red and green too, accompanied by tinsel, smiles and the baby Jesus. None of it fostered any Christmas cheer in me whatsoever and I climbed into bed at nine thirty.

I'd been asleep for a couple of hours when I heard the first key in the lock. Someone yawned in the hallway – Stuart. The living room door clicked shut.

An hour later, in came Doreen and Dad, giggling together in the hall. I heard her say, 'Watch out. The Gestapo might still be up,' and she laughed again.

'Oops,' Dad said. 'I tripped over the welcome mat. Not very welcoming!'

'That's what you get for having *only a couple*,' Doreen said, loudly as though I were meant to hear it.

I heard Dad peeing in the bathroom and he was treating the whole flat to it because he hadn't shut the door.

It was the first time he'd done that since I moved in.

SUNDAY 23 DECEMBER

The issue of my disappearing wages niggled as we ate Doreen's huge roast dinner on Sunday afternoon. I'd raised the issue several times that morning only for the three of them to unite enthusiastically over the manager's mistake theory, Doreen yelling, 'Are you still banging on about that?' over the sound of the vacuum cleaner.

'Drop by the bakery tomorrow and find out what's what,' Dad said when we were in the kitchen together. I had no other option. He clearly wasn't willing to pursue the issue with Stuart.

Now, Doreen kept asking me, 'Do you want more gravy, pet?' as though you could drown suspicion in gravy as well as your Yorkshire puddings.

Stuart had been with us for nearly three weeks. Dad said, 'Well, lad. What are your plans for Christmas?'

Stuart looked up from his dinner. He tended not to talk while eating, scraping up his food as though worried someone was timing him. He rarely thanked his mother for cooking. I was thanking Doreen a lot more often to show him up. He said, 'I can't afford to buy presents if that's what you mean.'

I faked shock. 'What about my new Swiss watch?'

'I didn't mean presents,' Dad said, but he didn't clarify.

'Dad meant, have you decided where you'll be for Christmas?' I said.

Doreen looked at Dad. 'I'm not sure that's what he was saying.'

'I haven't found anywhere else to live,' Stuart said. 'I have been looking, honest.'

I wondered where he'd found time to do this in between sitting on his arse watching TV and sitting on his arse watching TV.

'It's Christmas already,' Doreen said. 'He may as well stop here, Dave. We're putting the tree up.'

'We have a tree?' I said to Dad.

'I had an artificial one at my old flat,' she said. 'My friend's dropping it by later. It's got silvery branches.'

I had a brainwave. 'Does your friend still need a permanent flatmate? Couldn't Stuart go there?'

Dad shook his head at me.

'And stay with my friend Rita?' Doreen said. 'That would be odd.'

'No more odd than stubbing out his fags on our sofa cushions and making Eiffel Towers out of beer bottles.'

'Silly girl.'

'Idiot,' Stuart said, through a mouthful of sprouts.

'You're being rude, Jackie,' Dad said.

'What about your own dad?' I asked Stuart.

'He can't go to his dad's,' Doreen said.

'He'd murder me,' Stuart said.

'Solution!'

Dad said, 'Jacqueline, you're not too old to be sent to your room.'

Doreen said, 'I think she is, love,' and I was grateful for her common sense and angry with her at the same time.

I toyed with my dinner. The gravy was congealing anyway. Doreen always put too much thickening in gravy and if you left it long enough it resembled jelly round a pork pie, which I hated. Bridget's gravies were usually shiny like newly polished shoes and just thick enough to offer a crisp roast potato a velvety winter coat, or perhaps I am quoting an advert.

'So that's Christmas sorted, then,' Doreen said, spearing a cube of swede.

'I'll start looking for a place in the new year,' Stuart said, leaving us to wonder to which new year he referred.

MONDAY 24 DECEMBER

Dad and Doreen slept in on Christmas Eve morning and were both snoring like boars on the other side of my bedroom wall.

I ventured into the hall. I'd left the book of Wilfred Owen's letters I was studying for school on the living room floor. I put my ear to the door and heard the rustling of pages, so I knew Stuart was awake. And there was a light on.

'Can I come in?' I said, knocking.

'Be my guest,' he said.

'Are you decent?'

'I'm under two layers of blanket.'

'I left my book,' I said, walking in. I reached down beside the armchair in which I'd sat, picked up the book and glanced back at Stuart, lying on his side on the sofa, a magazine in front of him.

He had it open at a double-page spread. A woman lay on her back, her legs wide apart. I had never seen such a photograph before.

A hot feeling started at my feet and worked its way up my body. I didn't know what it was called but I felt as though I'd done something very wrong while people were watching.

I looked away from the magazine and at Stuart's face. 'That's disgusting.'

'What's wrong with it? It's only a woman with her clothes off.'

'It's much more than that.'

'If you say so.'

'You're not even trying to hide what you're looking at.'

He said, 'Why would I?' but flipped it shut. The front cover said *Playboy*. 'It's not my magazine, anyway.'

I said, 'I'm sure.'

'It's not. I found it under the sofa.'

'You're lying.'

He laughed, as though he didn't care whether I believed him or not, and I realised he was telling the truth. 'Your dad probably looks at it with my mum. Ask him yourself.' He slid the magazine back under the sofa. 'You really have no idea.'

'I don't want those kinds of ideas.'

'Turn the light off as you go. I'm going back to sleep.'

I flicked the switch, shut the door and went back to my room.

Every time I thought about the photograph, I felt ashamed for remembering, and then more ashamed that Stuart might have been right and that my dad looked at the same photos with Doreen. I didn't want to think about it.

Would Stuart say something? I decided not. He wouldn't want Dad or Doreen to know he'd found the magazine.

I wished I could unsee it, not carry it around with me, like someone else's rubbish.

Later that morning, an extra visitor arrived for Christmas: the garish silver tree that Doreen installed by the window, bedecked with mini angels and an aisle's worth of Woolworths baubles and tinsel, like a glam rock star in tree form. Underneath it we laid presents, including one from me to Dad: a woolly scarf. I'd also wrapped chocolates for Doreen. I'd initially bought nothing for Stuart but gave in, finding a copy of *On the Road* by Jack Kerouac from a second-hand bookshop. I hoped he'd get my drift.

All three were drinking, going hard at the spirit aspect of Christmas, and had started at nine. Dad and Stuart were on whisky. Doreen was drinking something clear, either gin or vodka. The number and range of bottles in the cupboard under the sink was increasing.

In the middle of the coffee table was a box of Black Magic, its lid open and the top tray nearly empty.

'Isn't it too early for all this eating and drinking?' I'd said, when I'd first come into the room.

'It's Christmas Eve,' Doreen said.

'Scrooge,' Stuart said.

Dad stared into his drink as though needing somewhere to look rather than at me.

I'd made myself a mug of tea. I'd offered to make a pot but it wasn't as popular a menu choice as poisonous liquids. 'Don't forget I'm at Amanda's this afternoon, Dad,' I said, sitting in the spare armchair. I'd learned to say 'Amanda's' not 'Nick and Bridget's'.

'Oh, the lovely Amanda,' Stuart said. 'Amanda with the blonde hair. Amanda who gets the Leamington bus.'

'Shut up.' The way he said Amanda's name now seemed coated with a layer of *Playboy* and it made me feel sick.

'You'll miss a lovely tea I've got planned,' Doreen said.

'Doreen's made a Christmas pudding for tomorrow,' Dad said, then added, when I didn't respond, 'It's home-made.'

'I got you the first time,' I said.

I knew she'd made a pudding. She'd talked so much about it, I was surprised not to have seen it in the papers. I think she felt that making it, along with putting up the tree and suffocating it with sparkle, would cement her maternal role in the household. Two Sundays back, she'd commandeered the kitchen all afternoon, stirring pudding mixture in a new china mixing bowl and spooning it into a new pudding bowl, both ordered from the Kays catalogue.

She'd bought brandy and what didn't go into the pudding was going into Doreen while she listened to Radio 2 and sang along. She asked if I'd like to stir in the lucky penny but I remembered doing it for Mum and said, 'Stuart can do it.' Stuart said, 'I'm not a child.' So, it was down to Dad and a slosh of the brandy into a glass persuaded him. 'Make a wish,' Doreen said, and he'd breathed something dirty in her ear, the brandy fumes no doubt sorting out any excess wax.

Now, Dad said, 'What time are you going to the Walls?' as though he couldn't wait to be rid of me.

'Nick said he'd pick me up at two. I'm not sure whether the buses are running.'

It was the wrong thing to say. 'Ooh, a chauffeur,' he said. 'Picking up Lady Muck. What is it? A Bentley?'

It was the nastiest thing he'd said since he came out of prison even though I knew it was the whisky and brandy, the guilt and the self-loathing talking. They made an influential foursome.

Doreen had felt it. 'Dave,' she said. 'It's not the littlun's fault.'

She'd adopted Dad's term of address for me and usually it annoyed me but here it seemed well meant.

'It's a Morris Marina,' I said. 'And, no, it's not my fault. I'll go and get ready.'

Doreen looked at her watch. 'It's only twelve. Have a bit of dinner with us before you go? I've boiled a nice piece of gammon.'

'I don't have an appetite,' I said. 'The smell of whisky takes it away.' And I went to my room to wait there until two o'clock. But as I crossed the hall, I heard Doreen say, 'I know, but she's worried about you,' and my dad reply, 'I can take care of myself.' This claim had already been disproved many times but he was clearly sticking to it.

My room was cold. I sat underneath the blankets, trying not to pick at my head and working on the poem I was writing for the London competition. It wasn't shaping up as happy. The theme was nature and, although I'd intended to write something hopeful about trees or the sea, a few nights previously, at two in the morning, I had heard a man shouting in one of the neighbouring flats and a woman screaming back. Unable to shut out the noise, I'd turned on my light and started writing.

Now, I changed some verbs and cut out extra words until I was pleased with it, if you can be pleased with a poem so depressing that it could have stripped the joy from every one of Doreen's Christmas angels.

I read it aloud in a whisper to see how it sounded.

And so that my mum might hear, if she was able to listen.

Not for you
The sky is black and so are people's hopes this night:
black like holes, silhouetted shadows, rotted teeth,
scored-out words that should never have been written
and soot from burned-out houses where tragedies played out.

There are stars but they are not for you and you and you
so don't go reaching up to pluck them in your naivety
for they are designed only for certain fortunate hands
which they will turn to silver at the first contact.

There is a sun that others can expect of a morning
to bless their windows, paint stripes of happy on their walls
but it is not your sun unless you mean heat that curls you dry,
pursues you down alleys, into corners and nooks.

There is a cloud. Here, a gift, at last, wrapped in grey.
Let it sit on you and make itself comfortably at home.
You said you wanted a companion, something nearby
to talk to when the black falls without fair warning.

I waited outside the flats for Nick's car, shivering even beneath my thick coat and scarf in the afternoon cold that wheedled past normal protections. I'd dressed in smart jeans and a Christmas-red jumper. My bag contained presents for Nick, Bridget and Amanda, although I hadn't had as much to spend as I'd have liked because of my missing wages. The streets were quietening and shops shutting as people drifted home to their Christmases, ready to hunker down, peel sprouts, write cards for neighbours, rescue the glass baubles from the baby's grasp.

I was experiencing Christmas in two homes this year and I wasn't sure that I belonged in either of them. Perhaps I would have felt more at home in Mason Street, eating a mince pie with Patsy and watching a Christmas film on my tiny TV set.

But Spotless, appointing himself chief welcomer, licked my hand as Nick ushered me into the Walls' living room. Nick said, 'Here she is,' as though I were the hired entertainment.

I would try to forget what might be happening back at Landor Court and what state Dad might be in by the evening.

Amanda was on the sofa, flicking through a *Jackie* magazine Christmas edition. She wore black trousers and a grey tee shirt with a slash in each sleeve.

'All dressed up for the celebrations, then,' I said but she ignored me. I tried again. 'Merry Christmas.'

'Hello,' she said, not looking up.

'Don't worry. I always linger on the Marc Bolan pictures as well.'

She pinked up, and I was sorry I said it, especially given my conversation with Stuart about the *Playboy* magazine. Was I a hypocrite? I wasn't sure. I felt as though I was wandering around in new territory.

'I'm sorry. I didn't mean anything bad.'

But she shrugged as though she didn't care. It was as if she'd regressed three years and gone back to the Amanda she'd been when I'd first joined the household. Someone distant and sullen.

Bridget looked tired, having poured all of herself into the roast beef dinner and a jam roly-poly which she proudly told me were both making great progress in the kitchen.

I'd noticed tiny changes these days in the way the house was furnished. An occasional chair placed just outside the kitchen door so Bridget could stand and talk to those in the living room with her hand on its back. A side table by the armchair for her drinks. A couple of small rugs removed, I think so that her shuffling feet didn't trip.

At one point during the afternoon, she wanted an extra cardigan from upstairs and Nick offered to fetch it for her. She said no but didn't object when he walked up the stairs behind her, a subtle hand on the small of her back.

Bridget forced us all to pull crackers and wear hats as we ate our roast dinners, as though it were Christmas Day. 'You won't be here for the day itself, Jackie. Make the most of it while there are four of us. It'll no doubt be quiet with your dad tomorrow.'

If only. I imagined Dad, Doreen and Stuart, hats lopsided, reading out silly jokes about elves or reindeers and laughing over minuscule tape measures and fortune-telling fish that curled in their hands. It felt like a TV sitcom I would watch, but not want to appear in.

We opened presents after our meal. Nick and Bridget had bought me a set of three notebooks, all with pretty covers, and a new fountain pen. 'For your poems,' Nick said.

I'd bought Bridget a recipe book and Nick a new novel by John le Carré.

I opened Amanda's gift to me – a stationery set – and Amanda opened a blue pendant I'd bought her. 'It's the same colour as the shirt I gave you,' I said. 'I'm sorry – it's not very punk, now I think about it.'

'That's so pretty, darling,' Bridget said, un-punking it even further. 'Go upstairs and try it on with the shirt. Show us.'

She said, 'I'm not a performing seal.'

'You don't have to,' I said.

'I'm sure Jackie would like to see how it looks,' Bridget said.

'Shall I come up with you?' I said to Amanda.

'No, thanks.' She heaved herself from the sofa.

I sniffed my armpit. 'Do I smell or something?' But I didn't think she'd heard me as she was already going upstairs.

'Don't worry,' Nick said, when we heard her door shut. 'It's just Amanda.'

'No, that's *old* Amanda.'

'You don't live here,' he said, laughing, and I know he didn't mean it to hurt, but it was like a pinch, as was the fact that Amanda clearly didn't want to be alone with me.

We waited for her to re-emerge but five minutes later she called down to say she was feeling tired and needed to sleep. She slept – if that's what she was doing – until six o'clock when Nick drove me home.

Doreen, Dad and Stuart had entertained themselves for the afternoon with a 'Who can get the drunkest?' competition. I looked at them, their bodies heavy in the chairs as though the drink itself lay on their chests like a wrestler, and in my mind awarded them all equal first place in their contest before going to my room and writing poetry with my new fountain pen. I tried not to pick at my head but found this impossible and at one point blood smeared the page of my notebook. I drew a line around the stain, like the outlines drawn around bodies at crime scenes to mark the site of the tragedy.

TUESDAY 25 DECEMBER

In the end, though, Christmas Day with Dad, Doreen and Stuart held more natural cheer about it than Christmas Eve had at the Walls'. Dad put Doreen's new album of traditional carols on the record player he'd bought us back in September and perhaps the household felt it crass to bicker while Good King Wenceslas was making so much effort with the poor man gathering winter fuel. I helped Doreen in the kitchen, doing my best to meet her exacting standards for sprout preparation. Dad attempted the seasonal crossword in the paper while Stuart read a new library book.

We kept the TV on while we ate our Christmas dinner, squeezed around Dad's dining table, elbows almost touching. It was *Top of the Pops* of 1979 (we'd had a vote on which programme and Doreen lost) and even she nodded along to Boney M. and Roxy Music. I imagined the Walls eating without any background TV or radio, trying to keep the conversation light despite Amanda's nose stud and mood swings, and finishing their Christmas dinner precisely at 2.45, to make a cup of tea in time for the Queen.

Doreen had roasted a turkey whose sides were burned because she had overestimated the size of Dad's oven but her roast potatoes were crispy and her bread sauce thick and tasty. There were four different vegetables, pigs in blankets, and cranberry sauce in a china dish. She'd boiled a small ham, too. Her gravy was characteristically glutinous but goodwill to all men and all that.

The sauces and the ham were left on the kitchen surface for us to help ourselves. They didn't fit on the table.

'Did we need that ham as well, Dor?' Dad had said, gazing at the spread.

All the plates and dishes tussled for space with glasses for red wine, something they rarely drank but which Doreen said was compulsory at Christmas. I said I must have missed that bit of the Nativity story.

She'd bought Christmas crackers and I won against Stuart, which pleased me. The gift was a tiny pack of cards. Stuart's suggestion that we played strip poker didn't go down well with my dad and shut Stuart up for a while. Doreen set fire to the Christmas pudding which flamed too eagerly and she said, 'Ooh, Dave, get your hose out and put out the flames.' Dad blushed, which I found a comfort. He still had a conscience, and I wished he didn't let alcohol rob him of it so easily.

We watched the Queen's speech while eating Christmas pudding and brandy butter, and when she spoke about remembering those who had gone before us, I looked at Dad hoping he would see Mum in my eyes, but he'd just found the penny in his pudding.

Afterwards, I helped Doreen wash up, which took an hour, especially as she kept taking breaks for wine. 'I thought we'd drink more of it with the meal,' she said, clearly happy that we hadn't.

She sat us all down with obvious anticipation to open presents. Dad unwrapped his woolly scarf and wound it round his neck even though the room was warm with three bars of our electric fire glowing. Doreen opened her chocolates and offered them round. Stuart said, 'Great choice, kid,' when he unwrapped the Jack Kerouac, and I said, 'Feel free not to patronise me any time.'

Dad had bought me Christmas socks but then Doreen passed over a second, larger parcel. 'Your dad doesn't know about this one,' she said, as though that had been a good idea. I unwrapped it. A new satchel, its leather stiff and unmarked.

It felt like a box in my hands. I wasn't sure what to say as I didn't need a new satchel. I liked my old one and would be finishing school in June.

Dad said, 'That's quite a surprise!' speaking for both of us. He tried to sound jovial, but it fell short.

'That's very thoughtful, Doreen,' I said. 'It must have been expensive,' I added, for Dad.

'I knew you'd love it.' She clapped her hands together.

She'd bought both Stuart and Dad a bottle of expensive whisky. Dad gave her a bracelet in a velvet blue box.

'Ooh, are they proper diamonds?' she said.

'Leave off, Doreen,' he said. 'It cost enough as it was.'

'It's lovely, anyway,' she said, and I thought the 'anyway' unnecessary.

'Thanks, Mum,' Stuart said. 'Sorry I'm too skint for presents.'

'That's all right, son,' she said, but he was getting regular dole money now so a lavender soap on a rope surely wasn't beyond him.

I phoned Patsy at six o'clock to see how Christmas Day with Marion and Harry was progressing. 'Do they have the family round?' I asked her.

'Thankfully not,' she said. 'They're meeting tomorrow at the daughter's house.'

'Are you going?'

'And be a spare *part*? Not likely. What did your dad buy you?'

'Some Christmas socks.' I didn't mention the satchel.

'That's such a dad present.'

'What about you?'

'It's embarrassing.'

'A Barbie, then.'

'Maybe.'

'Kissing Barbie?' She'd mentioned this new version.

'You press a button on her back and she puckers up,' she said.

'Hours of entertainment.'

'You're taking the mickey.'

'No, I'm pleased if you're pleased. It's just not my bag.'

'Marion almost took it back to the shop, though, after the plumber had been.'

I waited.

'They had to call a plumber Christmas Eve.'

'What for?'

'The bath wasn't draining. Marion keeps asking me to use the hair catcher thing in the plughole and I always forget.'

'Ouch.'

'Harry said plumbers were expensive and even more so at Christmas.'

'I bet Harry did.'

'Enough hair to set up a wig shop, the plumber said. Anyway, your mate, Amanda.'

'What about her?' Did I want to know?

'Drinking *vodka* in a classroom,' she said.

'When was this?'

'After we'd done curly perms. Or maybe it was soft perms.'

'I mean, how long ago?'

'Just before the end of term. She's hardly been in. And when she did come in, she brought vodka.'

'Bloody hell.'

'In a Coke bottle. Is she stupid?'

I didn't trust myself to speak.

'Her mum and dad would have got a letter,' Patsy said.

'How do you know that?'

'I heard the tutor tell another tutor she was writing it. She'll be lucky to stay on the course. I won't be sorry. She's a waste of time.'

'That's a harsh judgement,' I said.

'Someone has to say it. She's got a screw loose.'

TUESDAY 1 JANUARY 1980

On New Year's Day, I woke at nine to hear Dad and Doreen having a row in their bedroom. I was surprised they were awake as they'd stretched the New Year's Eve celebrations well beyond the eve and into the new year itself and may only have stopped at February if supplies had allowed.

Stuart hadn't been with them, going out and not saying where.

I'd experienced the turn of the year lying in bed, listening to the church clock's optimistic strikes, and trying not to listen to Doreen simpering in the way she did when Dad was kissing her neck. My clock had said three when I'd heard them go to bed, and three thirty when Stuart's tread on the concrete steps woke me again and I'd listened as he jabbed his key at the keyhole in the way I'd seen, in a sex education film, newborns bob for the nipple.

Now, Dad was trying to keep his voice low but Doreen had cast off restraint. 'What did you expect?' she was shouting. 'Marmite sandwiches?'

There'd been conflict about this all week. Doreen had been, again, raiding the money tin more often without telling or asking Dad, hence our lavish Christmas including my new satchel and the superfluous ham.

I couldn't hear his reply exactly. His voice rumbled on and then she said, 'Pardon me for trying to make Christmas special.' She came out of their room and started running a bath: unusual as she usually bathed at night.

Dad hammered on the locked bathroom door. 'None of us have had our morning pees yet. My bladder's fit to bust.'

'I hope it does!' she shouted back.

'It's not fair on the littlun,' he said. And although my bladder was coping well, I felt I should offer support so I climbed out of bed and peered around my door.

'Yes, I'm busting, too.'

The living room door opened. 'What's going on?' Stuart said, his voice rough with lack of sleep, his hair sticking up.

'Your bloody mother's having a bath,' Dad said, as if that would explain everything.

'And?'

'We all need a pee,' Dad said.

'So do I,' he said, 'but I'm not yelling about it, waking everyone up.' He closed the door.

'I'll have to pee in the kitchen sink,' Dad said to the bathroom door.

'Don't you bloody dare,' Doreen called back.

'Out of the bedroom window?' he said. He went back into his room.

Five minutes later, I heard Doreen open the bathroom door. I think she had hurried up, worried he would urinate on passers-by.

The sound of Dad's urgent peeing soon echoed down the hall and the toilet flushed.

He knocked on my door. 'Your turn! Then Stuart.'

I opened it. 'I hope this coordinated peeing is a one-off. I'd rather plan my own schedule.'

Later, at ten thirty, Stuart stood at the kitchen door wearing a coat, one of Doreen's charity shop finds. I was fetching a late breakfast of toast. Doreen was peeling potatoes. 'I'm off out,' Stuart said.

'Where to?' Doreen said.

'Just out.'

'Will you be back for New Year's dinner?'

'What is it?'

'What do you mean, what is it? Either you want your dinner or you don't.' She sounded more hurt than irritated.

'Only asking.'

'It's roast chicken.'

'What time?' he said.

Dad must have been listening and arrived in the hall. 'It's not a bloody hotel, lad. If you don't like the arrangements, you can sling your hook.'

'Keep your hair on,' Stuart said, but we all knew he wished he hadn't. A long silence followed until Dad returned to the living room.

'Living on the edge,' I said to Stuart.

'Sod off,' he said, and left the flat.

Dad said to Doreen later, 'I've had enough. He has to go. *He's* a parasite—'

Had he been about to say 'as well'?

She said, 'You can't say that about my Stuart.'

'Your Stuart, according to you not so long ago, is a waste of space.'

'It's not totally his fault.' Her voice was maudlin. 'You haven't met his dad.'

I bit into my toast and said, 'Maybe you should invite *him* for New Year's dinner as we now have an open-door policy.'

Dad laughed, which pleased me, though I preferred his laughs without the bitter edge.

I took the toast into my bedroom, ate it while looking out of my window, then pulled on a thick jumper. In the kitchen, Dad and Doreen's argument rose in pitch, returning to the theme of money. I said to Weston, 'Sorry to leave you listening to this,' grabbed my coat from the hook on the back of the door, and went into the hall.

'I won't be long,' I said, and was out of the front door

169

before they could question me. But I heard Dad say, 'See? Even the littlun can't take it any more.'

I walked into the park. A milky sun travelled with me, sparkling the frost on the grass and offering a touch of warmth. I planned to comfort myself with a mug of Horlicks in the café, but it was closed, and I remembered it was a bank holiday. Families had braved the outdoors, though, and children squealed on the swingboats and shouted down the long slide while their parents congratulated their successes. Older couples – perhaps grandparents – watched, cosy inside their tweed coats. A group of teenage roller skaters slalomed up and down the paths, arms akimbo for balance.

I followed the river path, watching the swans and imagining their webbed feet under the surface of the water, paddling like madness, belying the serenity of their progress along the water and the purity of their white feathers. I thought of Mrs Collingworth and how her lessons were smooth and peaceful as though they took no effort. Yet I knew from hints she'd dropped how she stayed up until the small hours some nights and, judging by the coffee cups on her desk and the piles of marked books when we shambled into her room in the mornings, clearly arrived at school long before we did.

I was leaving the river behind me, turning back towards the main park, when I saw Amanda. She was with Stuart.

They were on a bench and either it wasn't the first time they'd spent time together or things were progressing at indecent pace. Stuart had his back to me. Their heads were touching, and his arm was around her shoulders. She was looking up into his face and stretching for a kiss in a way that made me feel as though my toast and marmalade might make a return journey.

I stepped towards them and she must have sensed the

movement. Her body stilled and her eyes widened as she stared at me over his shoulder. They begged me, 'Please. Say nothing.'

I had a few seconds to decide what to do and where my loyalties lay, but no one could say I hadn't practised.

I turned back and walked – almost ran – the way I had come, not noticing swans, white feathers, the water, the children on the slide, tweedy grandmas, the roller skaters, the dark windows of the holidaying café. At the edge of the park, I hesitated, realising I didn't want to go home yet. Instead, I wandered up the hill into town, passing both Tudor and Georgian facades. Peering into the windows of closed shops and more empty cafés, I wished they'd been open so I could throw away time browsing shelves or ordering a second pot of tea. What I was reluctant to do was to return home only to have to sit with Stuart, should he turn up, while Doreen asked us whether we wanted leg or breast.

I arrived home at one. Doreen was whisking unease into the gravy in the form of cornflour, and Dad was in the living room.

'Your son isn't back,' I said to Doreen.

'He's called Stuart, pet.'

But I didn't feel like giving him a name.

'He'll be home for his dinner, I'm sure,' she said.

He did return and she added a fourth plate to warm, so she hadn't been sure at all.

'Where did you go?' she asked him.

'For a walk.'

'On your own?'

'That's for me to know.'

I didn't know how to handle this. I needed to talk to Amanda first. But it took everything I had not to punch him.

'Dave's got some whisky open,' Doreen said. She tried to give him a couple of glasses. 'Fetch me a drop, son.'

'You ask him, Mum,' Stuart said, and I realised he was wary, having cheeked Dad that morning. 'I'll have a beer.'

In the living room, he slumped into his usual armchair, poured his beer, picked up his library book and found the page.

Dad said, 'Hm.'

The mood around the table, compared to Christmas Day, was muted. Dad was sleepy, and his eyes were closing even as Doreen was soliciting his admiration for her roasted parsnips. When she served out the meat, she said to Dad, nudging him, 'Here's a nice plump and tasty bit,' but Dad said, 'Not too much for me, Dor,' which put a pin in her New Year balloon.

Doreen had tried a new trifle recipe called 'Sherry with added sponge, jelly, custard and cream', and we were busy inhaling it when she announced, 'I've Christmas crackers left over!' as though crackers could substitute for happiness. The announcement fell like a dropped stone but I offered to pull one with Stuart and, as it went 'crack', imagined I'd shot him right between the eyes. It gave me pleasure with which to start an uncertain new year and, as a bonus, woke Dad up.

'What New Year resolutions do we have, then?' Doreen said. She turned to Stuart. 'What about you, son?'

'Find himself a new place to live?' I said. 'The Canary Islands?'

'You think you're so smart,' Stuart said.

'Quite the comedian,' Doreen said.

But Dad said, 'The Gobi Desert? Australia?' and Doreen and Stuart exchanged glances.

I felt a stab in my gut at Dad's support, even though he'd pronounced it 'Aushtralia'.

At five o'clock, I was in my room and could hear Doreen gossiping on the phone to her sister who lived in Coventry. I checked my purse for coins and seized my chance.

'I need to phone someone,' I said to Dad, 'but Doreen will be ages. I'll run to the phone box.'

'Okay, pet.'

'Okay,' Stuart said.

'I wasn't talking to you,' I said to him.

I dialled the Walls' number. Amanda picked up the receiver on the first ring as though she'd been waiting. I pushed in coins.

'Is Bridget in the kitchen with you?' I said.

'No, she's resting upstairs. Dad's in the shed.' She was whispering, though.

'What the hell are you doing? I told you Stuart was bad news.'

'Your opinion,' she said.

'It's not my *opinion*. I live with him.'

'Something I only learned from him, not from you.'

'I couldn't tell you in case you told your mum and dad. He shouldn't be here. Anyway, that's not the point.'

'I like him,' she said. 'He followed me to the bus stop that Saturday.' She knew what I wanted to know.

'Why didn't you tell me this when we met before Christmas?'

'Why do you think?'

A woman knocked on the window of the phone booth. 'Will you be long?' she called.

I shook my head and turned my back to her.

'Apparently you were caught with vodka at college,' I said.

'How did you know that?'

I didn't answer.

'Patsy,' she said.

'What did your mum and dad say when they got the letter?' She paused. 'They didn't get the letter. I'm not daft.'

'Amanda! They're bound to find out somehow.'

She said, 'Don't deny you think Stu is good to look at.'

Stu? His mum had said he hated the abbreviation.

'So are *tigers and snakes*,' I said. 'You're being an idiot.'

'Don't exaggerate. He's not dangerous.'

My heart was thumping with frustration. How could

I convince her? I said, 'I found him leering at *Playboy* magazine.'

She actually laughed. 'You are so innocent.'

'I'd rather stay that way.'

'Please yourself. But you can't tell others what to do.'

'I think your mum and dad should know. Is this why you ignored me Christmas Eve? You were already seeing him? If you were hiding it, how come it's a good thing now?'

She went silent and then said, 'If you split on me, I'll tell Mum and Dad that two people have moved in and your dad will be in a heap of trouble. It's illegal in a council flat, isn't it, at least without permission?'

She didn't sound sure but neither was I. Would he lose the flat? Could he go back to prison? Who could I ask without them wondering why I wanted to know?

I said, 'Have you and he – I mean – have you let Stuart …?'

'That's none of your business,' she said, and hung up.

I replaced the receiver and coins pumped out to remind me that Amanda hadn't stayed around to listen to sense.

Back home, Dad and Stuart were both asleep in the living room, overflowing ashtrays and the empty bottles belying the hours they had sat smoking and drinking together, as though tobacco and alcohol were a kind of glue, bonding people with nothing else in common.

Doreen was in the kitchen with her friend and confidante, gin, putting the remains of the chicken in a margarine tub. 'I'll make sandwiches with this,' she said, 'for our packed lunches. When are you back to school?'

'Tomorrow.'

'Oh,' she said. 'I was going to say you'd have the flat to yourself.'

'Why?'

'Stuart's spending the day with his friend, someone who's moved into a flat at the bottom of Leamington.'

'Has the friend got a spare room?'

'Give over, chuck.'

But as soon as I'd had the thought, I regretted it. If Stuart had his own room, he could take Amanda there. Otherwise, his options were limited. He couldn't bring her here. These days, predicting who would be home and when had become less easy.

'Ah well,' I said. 'I've got used to him now.'

She glanced at me. 'That's a rapid U-turn,' she said. Doreen may have lacquered her hair each morning until it stood motionless in terror, but she had her wits about her.

WEDNESDAY 2 JANUARY

In English, Mrs Collingworth collected the essays on Wilfred Owen's poetry that she'd set us over the Christmas holidays. 'Not *one* excuse,' she said, moving expertly around the classroom to gather exercise books, but, as Canute found, you don't always have control, whatever your status.

She said to Raymond, the boy with no essay, 'What do you mean, you didn't hear me give the homework? Everyone else heard.'

'I didn't hear, Miss. I don't know why. Perhaps I was absent.'

'I don't remember you being absent.' She picked up her meticulous attendance record from her desk to check it and he began to sink in his chair. 'Not that kind of absent, anyway.'

Molly nudged me, amused.

Mrs C said to him, 'Can you hear me now?'

'Yes, Miss.'

'I think we're talking loss of interest, not loss of hearing. See me after school.'

Mrs C's interrogations were kind but in the way Dettol is kind to wounds, which is why I'd let her take my exercise book even though I knew it contained a half-finished essay. The previous evening's attempt to fix it had proved futile.

She hunted me down later that day while I was in the lunch hall with Molly and asked me to see her in her classroom when I'd eaten. Molly said, 'What does she want to see you about?' I hadn't confided in her.

'Whatever it is, I don't feel so hungry for these meatballs and gravy now,' I said.

'Shut the door, please,' Mrs C said as I entered her room.

'So no one can hear me scream, Miss?' I said, but her face didn't join in with the joke.

I stood by her desk.

'You're not in trouble. But tell me.' She pointed towards my essay and her mark: *5/20.*

'I'm sorry.'

'The question should have been easy for you.'

'I know.'

'So tell me.'

'I started it too late.'

'Yesterday, you mean.'

'More or less,' I said. 'A lot happened over the holiday.'

'You were busy?'

'In a way.'

She bent to write *Finish by next Monday* on my essay and said, 'That's not the main reason I want to see you, anyway.'

'Oh.'

'There's blood on your collar today, and I noticed the same before Christmas.'

My hand went to my neck. 'It's probably just a spot.'

'Give me credit. You had some help with this head picking before, didn't you?'

'I'm in control of it.'

She paused and rearranged stationery on her desk. 'You have an appointment with the school nurse. Tomorrow break time.'

'I do?'

'You do now.'

'Please don't contact my dad. He has enough problems.'

'Problems that make life difficult for you?'

'I didn't say that. Honest, I'll get myself together.'

'I have reason to believe you'll get on well with Nurse Broughton,' she said, enigmatically.

'Does she head pick too?' I said.

This time, she smiled.

FRIDAY 4 JANUARY

I'd turned up to the nurse's office next to the sick room on Thursday but a note on the door had said she'd been called to an emergency and would be in touch about rearranged appointments. When Mrs Collingworth asked me quietly in Friday's registration period whether I'd remembered my nurse appointment, I said I had remembered it, yes.

Nick wasn't yet home when I arrived at the Walls' for tea. His birthday would be the following Monday. I'd brought a present.

I'd almost cancelled, trying to talk myself into a headache during afternoon school. After my last conversation with Amanda, I couldn't see us engaging in friendly chit-chat over one of Bridget's starched tablecloths. But that was cowardly. Perhaps she'd had a change of heart and, as the vegetables were served, would confess all in tears and ask her parents for relationship advice.

Perhaps the vegetables would turn into unicorns and fly off.

Bridget was in the kitchen, putting candles in a cake, monitored by Spotless who hoped for dropped icing or crumbs.

They'd bought a high stool for the kitchen so that Bridget could perch.

'It's not Nick's birthday until Monday,' I said.

'I know, but it's a school night and he'll have marking. We knew you were coming so we brought it forward.'

'Don't rearrange the calendar around my visits. What if I disappoint?'

'We couldn't celebrate anything without you.'

'You managed before 1976.'

She looked at me, eyes wide in what seemed genuine perplexity. 'I have no idea how.'

We were scarily near sentiment. I tapped my satchel. 'Good thing I brought his present, then. It's in here.'

'New satchel?' she said.

'Christmas.'

I'd said to Dad, 'I don't want to use the one Doreen gave me. It's all rigid and lacking in personality.' But he'd said, 'Don't upset her, pet. Do it for me.'

'Amanda should be home soon,' Bridget said, and I was pleased to see I'd dragged her back to practicalities. She checked the kitchen clock. 'I don't know why she's not already here. We told her this morning it would be her dad's birthday dinner.'

'What are we having? I smell rosemary.'

'Leg of lamb,' she said.

A leg of lamb? A special effort.

'Did Amanda know *I* was coming?' I said.

'Exactly. That's why I'm puzzled.'

'Did she say she'd be here? In actual words?'

She picked up the oven glove. 'I'm not sure. We assumed.'

The front door slammed. 'There she is,' Bridget said, letting out a long breath as though relief had softened her body.

But it was Nick. He called, 'Happy Friday!'

'Oh,' she said.

'It's Nick,' I said, unhelpfully.

'Don't come in the kitchen, Nick,' she called. I noticed she found it hard to project her voice. I wondered if he'd heard.

I went to greet him. 'Don't go in the kitchen. Secrets.'

'You mean a cake.'

'Ssh.'

'Happy un-birthday,' I said.

'It got rearranged.' He smiled and put his school briefcase on the floor.

'Shall I make a pot of tea?' I said.

'What would we do without you?'

'What you did before 1976,' I said.

'Hm. We weren't managing very well, if you remember.' He took off his work jacket. 'Then you came, and everything changed. You brought us to our senses.'

Bridget said from the kitchen, 'Exactly what I said.'

I already felt like a traitor and this 'Isn't Jackie great?' refrain compounded it. I was reminded of King Duncan in *Macbeth*, bestowing honours on the person he thinks his most loyal soldier when that soldier's just told the audience that all he can think about is killing the king and grabbing the title.

At six fifteen, we sat watching the early evening news, but it's hard to take in steelworkers' strikes and housing bills when what you want is a key in the door.

Bridget said, 'I can't leave the potatoes in any longer, and the cabbage has been sitting a while.'

'I feel its pain,' Nick said. 'I'm famished.'

'It's not my fault,' she said. Bridget sounded so disappointed and there were shadows under her eyes as though Amanda had smudged them in with a soft black pencil.

'Let's get on with it, Bridge,' Nick said.

'You make it sound like a trial we have to get through rather than a birthday meal.'

'I didn't mean it like that, darling.'

I was angry with Amanda, making her parents tetchy with each other even without being present. They'd worked so hard to strengthen their marriage and needed that strength even more so now.

'I'll come and help,' I said. 'We can make up a plate for her and keep it warm.'

We ate, the three of us, pretending that there wasn't another place laid and a seat empty.

Nick and Bridget distracted themselves by asking questions about my life with Dad, another thing that made me angry with Amanda. Without her to focus on, I was a sitting target.

'He really enjoyed Christmas and New Year,' I said, failing to expand on the aspect he'd enjoyed most.

'He didn't mind you coming here on Christmas Eve?' Bridget said. 'And leaving him on his own?'

'He didn't mind me coming.'

'At least you were there Christmas Day.'

'Yes.'

'Did you buy each other presents?'

'He bought me some Christmas socks,' I said.

'Lovely!' Bridget said, as though Christmas socks prophesied a bright and happy future.

'And I had the new satchel,' I said.

'This all sounds very positive,' said Nick, which I think meant, 'Your dad still has his job, then.'

As insurance, I said, 'I bought Dad a scarf in case he's cold on the walk to work.'

I'd prepared all these answers already in case Heather and I had met the day before but a secretary had phoned a message through to school to say she had a hospital appointment. I was relieved. Things rehearsed and said twice can begin to sound manufactured if you don't get the intonation right.

After Nick and I had washed up, we sat down with tea and the birthday cake. Bridget and I offered our inadequate rendition of 'Happy Birthday' so that he could blow out his candles and I gave him his present.

'*Kane and Abel*,' he said, unwrapping it. 'Jeffrey Archer's new one. How did you know I wanted this?'

'A little bird.'

'Me!' Bridget said.

'Thanks for the great tip-off,' I said, reaching out and squeezing her arm. She seemed to shiver with pleasure.

This positive moment in the evening was over very quickly. It was seven thirty. We sat watching a quiz show for an hour but the room answered every question with Amanda, Amanda, Amanda.

At eight thirty, I said, 'I'd better go. I have work tomorrow.'

'I'll drop you back,' Nick said.

'No, I'll get the bus.'

'It's freezing out there.'

'I've got my big coat.'

'If you're sure.'

I wasn't. The local buses weren't known for their heating systems. But I didn't want Bridget left alone with her disillusionment.

Stuart wasn't in at home. I watched a thriller that wasn't thrilling with Dad and Doreen then went to bed, waking at three in the morning to hear a key in the door then the light switch click on in the bathroom.

SATURDAY 12 JANUARY

For the first part of January, after the holiday's excesses, Dad's conscience, or perhaps his probation officer, seemed to have given him a talking-to. He made it to work each day and when he came home put the kettle on or poured fizzy pop. Even when Doreen said, 'Wouldn't you like one of Stuart's beers?' Dad said no and Stuart tried not to look relieved.

I began to time it so that when I heard his heavy tread up the outside steps, I'd be in the kitchen ready to say 'Tea, Dad? There's a fresh pot,' before Doreen supplied him with other ideas.

He looked happier in himself and was arguing less with Doreen.

I head-picked less when he was peaceful, although some mornings my pillowcase was stained, because some things, even if you master them in the daytime, carry on without you at night.

Schoolwork was easier, not having Dad at the front of my mind like the constant thrum of a headache without the physical pain.

All this had made my weekly café meeting with Heather on Thursday so much more natural. 'You're chatting away today,' she'd said, because when it's safe to let words go without examining them on the tongue first, conversation feels good. She'd added, 'You seem so content to be with your dad,' and, right then, there was truth in it.

Also, I hoped it meant I could forget the school nurse. She hadn't chased me or, if she had, the note was lost in transit. It happened all the time. The school had recently reduced the size of appointment slips to a sliver in a paper-saving exercise but so often they became snarled up with other papers and notes, only to be found weeks after the said appointment, if ever.

I was grateful.

My (completed) Wilfred Owen essay had earned *18/20* and a *You've made my day* comment from Mrs C which I carried around like residual warmth for hours. In psychology, I put my hand up to answer questions and the teacher said, 'Thank goodness. I thought we'd lost you.' My history class travelled on a coach to a Roman fort and I earned a merit on the way back for aiming a sick bag under a boy's chin in time for him to vomit up his packed lunch. Also, my write-up of the fort visit (minus the vomit incident) was sent to the school magazine.

But I still needed to confront Stuart about Amanda.

Stuart was spending much less time in the flat and more with his friend in Leamington and, I suspected, with Amanda. But was it my business? I was tired of other people's business being my business but seemed to carry it around with me all the same like a shadow.

Doreen had gone out with a friend to the Saturday sales. Stuart was home for a change, parked for the afternoon in front of the telly. Dad said to me in the kitchen, 'Fancy our usual café?'

Usual? I didn't say it in case I spoiled the mood.

I poked my head around the door to say to Stuart, 'We're going to the café.'

'Not for me, thanks.'

'You're right,' I said. 'It wasn't.'

We found a table and the waitress brought us tea and

toasted teacakes. A radio was playing pop songs and the chink of cutlery and babble of customers made it homely. I wished we could stay for hours, perhaps days.

'You can be mother.' Dad nodded towards the teapot.

'In the absence of alternatives,' I said, without thinking.

'Indeed.'

'Sorry. That came out wrong.'

'It's okay, pet. It's no surprise you're bitter.'

'I'm not,' I said, stirring the tea in the pot.

'Even after what I told you while I was in prison?'

Ah, so this was why we'd come. That was the last time we had spoken of it.

'Look, we can't be certain Mum's death was your fault,' I said. 'The doubt is a comfort.'

'You mean, that she missed that first appointment?'

'Yes.'

'But I hit her,' he said. 'And she didn't want to go to the appointment – looking like that.'

'I understood all this in 1976, Dad. There's no need—'

'You were younger.'

'But not stupid.'

'No. You've never been stupid, pet.'

'Maybe the disease was advanced by then anyway. It could have made no difference.'

He picked up his teacake but perhaps just for something to do as he didn't bite into it. 'I suppose.'

'That's how I prefer to think of it.'

'Do you mean you've forgiven me?'

'Is it called forgiveness? Maybe it's giving you the benefit.'

'You're a kind girl,' he said.

I poured his tea and then mine and added milk from the jug. I could sense him watching me. He ran a hand through his hair and I knew it had taken courage to bring me here for this conversation.

'It must be hard for you, having Doreen around instead,' he said.

'I don't think of Doreen as an instead.'

'No, me neither.' He put half the teacake into his mouth.

'Can we talk about Stuart,' I said, 'while we're on the big issues?'

'Okay.' I couldn't judge his expression. It seemed he'd anticipated this topic, too.

'He stole my money. Nothing's ever been done about that.'

He picked up his teacup and cradled it in both hands. 'Ah.'

The door to the café opened, letting in a foursome of chattering elderly ladies in coats and soft hats. They shut the door and fussed their way to an empty table, ushered by a waitress. I was sure Dad had welcomed the pause.

'What do you mean, ah?' I said.

'About that.'

'Go on.'

He put his cup down, reached into his pocket for his wallet and pulled out two pound notes. 'It wasn't Stuart who stole it.'

'What do you mean?'

'It wasn't Stuart.'

'Who was it, then?'

He looked down at the pound notes. 'It was me. I took your money, pet.'

I searched his face for a reason that he would lie to cover Stuart – or perhaps Doreen. That would have made more sense.

'I was desperate,' he said. 'Doreen had emptied my tin of cash and I'd run out of whisky.'

I looked at the man sitting opposite me and wondered who he was. 'You heard me blaming Stuart, and you didn't say anything?'

'I know. I'm ashamed.'

'You weren't ashamed *then*?'

'I was,' he said, 'but whisky trumps shame.'

'Right.'

'And then shame leads you straight back to the whisky,' he said, his voice sunken and hopeless.

I took the notes and folded them into my purse. 'I even feel guilty taking these from you, Dad, and I shouldn't. You're not getting your change.'

'I wouldn't ask.'

'And now you've given me something else to try to forgive. You're building up a list. I might have to buy a notebook.'

'I'm trying to do better. You must have noticed.'

I ate my teacake. I felt like making him wait. 'You'll have to say something to Stuart about this.'

He looked down at the table. 'Don't make me do that, pet.'

'You're joking.'

'Please. You won't tell him it was me, will you? Or mention it to Doreen?'

I stood and started pulling on my coat. 'Do you remember when I was about seven, I visited you at the fire station and you'd rescued an old lady that morning from a kitchen fire?'

'I do remember,' he said, looking up at me. 'I suppose you thought me the bravest man in the world.'

That evening, when Doreen came back and we'd eaten our tea, she persuaded Dad to go to bingo with her.

'Bingo?' he said. 'We never go to bingo.'

'My friend won fifty quid last week. We could have a holiday.'

'We could pay some bloody debts before any holiday.'

I hadn't been aware there were debts or maybe I'd been pretending.

'Come on,' she said. 'Someone has to win.'

He grumbled, 'And plenty more lose,' but he went into the bedroom. His wardrobe door creaked open, then shut. I wondered whether, after our talk that afternoon, he would be glad to be out of the flat and not watching TV with me.

But bingo probably meant drinking.

*

I said to Stuart in the kitchen, when they'd gone, 'I owe you an apology.' He was layering sandwich spread on slices of bread.

He looked up. 'Oh, can't wait to hear this.'

'I accused you of stealing my wages, and now I find you didn't.'

He waved the sandwich spread jar at me. 'Tell me something I *don't* know.'

'I made a mistake.'

'You certainly did,' he said. 'You need a new manager.'

I didn't comment on this and he went back to his sandwich-making.

'There's plenty else you owe *me* apologies for.' I'd found my way in.

'Sounds like you have a selection.' He put his sandwiches on a plate.

'Let's start with Amanda.'

Something sly crossed his face. 'What's that got to do with you?'

'Everything. She's my friend. And foster sister.'

'You're not her bodyguard.'

'We're very close.'

'Which must be why you're not speaking at the moment. *That* close.'

'She knows she's doing the wrong thing, that's why.'

'You don't know anything about us,' he said.

'I know I don't trust you any more than – than I'd trust a ship with a gaping hole in it.'

'Very poetic. Unfortunately, you've got me wrong.' He walked into the living room with his plate and I had no option but to follow.

'How come?'

He slumped into the armchair. 'I really like her. It's not something casual.'

'I don't even want to know what that means.'

'Suit yourself,' he said. 'I wasn't going to tell you.'

'Does Doreen know about her?'

'She knows there's a girl. She's not like you, all third degree.'

I went back to my bedroom and made notes from my psychology textbook, trying to replace in my mind my fears for Amanda with information about the construction of the human brain.

I heard Stuart put his plate on the draining board in the kitchen. When I looked out, he was in the hall, his coat on and a scarf round his neck that Doreen had bought. 'Where are you going?' I said.

'To join Mum and your dad at the bingo. Where do you think?'

As soon as he'd left the house, I dialled the Walls' number. Nick answered. When I said I'd like to speak to Amanda, he said, 'You're not the only one. She's always with friends in the evenings these days and out late.' His voice sounded heavy with worry.

'Which friends?'

'Oh, various. I can't keep up with all the names. But we can't shackle her in her room these days. Could you talk to her for us?'

'She's too busy to speak to me, too,' I said.

'Have you spoken to her since my birthday tea?'

'No.'

'We had a very worrying night. Did she tell you where she was?'

'Honestly, we haven't talked.'

'That's very strange. I'm sorry.' He sounded puzzled, as well he might.

I tried to divert him. 'How has Bridget been today?'

'She's not too good. A bit shaky.'

Bridget, in the background, was calling, 'Never mind about me. Does Jackie know who these friends are?' and Nick repeated her question.

But if Bridget was feeling shaky, I wasn't going to shake

her further, in case, like a tree in autumn, she lost all her leaves and was left bare and at the mercy of the elements.

After the phone call, I sat on my bed, reading and rereading my nature poem for the competition. I'd written it out four times because I kept making mistakes and didn't want to send an entry with crossings-out, although Mrs C had said, 'It's about the poetry, and every poet makes last-minute corrections.' But it didn't feel right, especially as many other aspects of life felt untidy and it would feel good to make something perfect.

I copied onto the envelope the name and London address Mrs C had given me, folded my poem and slid it inside before I could scan it again for weaknesses.

I licked the envelope and sealed it, then the stamp. These felt like sure and definite actions. I enjoyed them.

It was nearly eleven when Dad and Doreen arrived home. I'd been trying to sleep so that I didn't hear what I feared. I failed, and so, as Dad tripped up the steps on the way to the flat, and Doreen said, 'Mind out, Dave!' and when they came into the hall and Dad said, 'Ssssh!' even though his uncoordinated body was stumbling its way noisily through the hall into the kitchen, and when Doreen said, 'You should have stopped at four, like I said,' I heard every single detail.

TUESDAY 15 JANUARY

I queued with Kim and Molly at dinner time. 'I need proper food,' I said. 'I'm in the library after school.'

'You're such a swot,' Kim said.

'I wish that was why. I'm way behind on English again.'

At 4.30 p.m., the librarian said, 'Time to go home, Jackie.' Darkness had fallen along with a clinging mist and, as I walked towards the gates, a couple of teachers had climbed into their cars and turned their headlights on so that yellow beams, spectral in the dim light, stretched across the car park.

Kevin was at the school gate and started walking along beside me. He was wearing his work overalls and carried a rucksack over one shoulder. 'Slow down. You're almost running.'

'Trying to keep fit,' I said, but I steadied my pace. I wasn't being fair. 'How did you know I'd be late out of school?'

'I rang home and Kim said.'

'You're like a stalker.'

He said, 'I've phoned you at home three times now since the new year. Your dad keeps telling me you're not in.'

This wasn't strictly true. I'd heard Dad answer the phone and had asked him to say, should Kevin call, 'She's not available', which he had.

'If you want me to have words,' Dad had said when we'd first talked about it at Christmas, 'just let me know. I'll give him what for.'

'Kevin's decent, Dad. I've got too much else to do, that's all.'

'You can rely on me,' he said, which would have been convincing had he not been holding on to a chair back to stay vertical.

Still, they were opportunities for him to look after me and he seized them. We were both aware of their rarity.

Kevin said now, 'How can you not be in three times on freezing January evenings?'

'I have things to do. You don't know everything about me. Maybe I'm training for an Arctic expedition.'

'It's not a joke, Jackie. What's going on?'

'Nothing.'

'Actually, you're right. *Nothing's* going on.'

'Not that again. You're sex-obsessed.'

Two boys who had been behind us snickered. They laughed as they ran off.

'Stop deliberately misunderstanding,' he said. 'How about the cinema at the weekend?'

'I'm not sure.'

'There you go. Another evasion.'

'Okay, then, let's say no.'

'Right.'

We waited at a zebra crossing, having to double-check for bicycles or quiet cars swallowed up by the mist.

I said, 'Let's give it a break for a while. I'm trying to concentrate on my A levels. I've got exams, remember.'

'Another break?' he said. 'How many before we say we're not going out any more?'

I said, 'That's up to you.'

As I spoke, I felt myself distanced, listening from afar to my insincere sentences. I didn't want to call them lies.

I wanted to be with him. I knew this was mutual. But for those kinds of intimacies, you need space in your brain uncluttered by other people and what they drag along with them. I didn't have that space.

'Oh, it's like that?' He pulled his rucksack further over his shoulder. 'Let's call it a day, then.'

'Let's.'

I watched as he walked down the road, trying hard not to look at his broad shoulders and the way he bounced a little from side to side.

The mist helped me, absorbing him into itself, and it's always nice, especially when everything else is going wrong, to have the weather batting for you and not against you, even if it is icy droplets.

WEDNESDAY 16 JANUARY

At dinner time, with our plates of beef stew, Kim, Molly and I negotiated our way around the long tables for three spare seats. The stew hadn't looked promising in its giant silver vats, guarded by a grim dinner lady, and it looked no more promising now that we were fated to have it inside us.

'Are these meant to be dumplings?' Molly said, pushing one with her fork.

I said, 'In the same way I'm Olivia Newton John,' and moved three dumplings to the side of my plate.

Molly laughed, but Kim didn't.

I put a cube of beef on my fork. 'What's up?' I said to Kim. 'Have you got pains?' Kim's periods often kept her at home for several days each month. Sometimes, she'd go white in registration and hold her belly. I knew Mrs C kept watch and would tell Kim's teachers to go gently.

Kim laid her knife and fork on her plate. 'It's not that. Kevin says you've chucked him. Again.'

'Oh.'

Boys at the other end of our table were joshing and nudging each other, water spilling from their glasses. I concentrated on them for a while.

Kim said, 'You're messing him around. Even my mum said so last night.'

I envied her the family. They had no doubt listened to Kevin, taken his side, rallied round, defended him. And I felt sad about her mum. Christine Price had welcomed me to their cramped home many times, first as Kim's friend and then Kevin's girlfriend, too, baking Swiss rolls and chocolate sponges to honour my visits.

Molly said, 'She's not messing him around. Maybe she doesn't have time for a relationship. She has to be honest.'

Although I didn't talk about Dad much to Molly, just as she didn't talk to me about her mother's disability, I knew she understood what it was like to have the margins of your life filled in so that the page was crammed.

Kim said to her, 'You wouldn't say that if you'd seen your older brother in tears.' And she got up, picking up her plate with its unfinished meal.

'Aren't you going to have sponge and custard?' I said. We usually fell on sponge and custard like wolves, mainly because it wasn't tapioca pudding.

'Is that all you're worried about?' she said, and went to stack her plate on the trolley. Molly and I watched her go.

Molly said, 'Don't worry. She won't let this break you up. She can't.'

'You haven't been to their house. They're so loyal to each other. As tight as – as tight as – something tight. As thick as thieves.'

She raised her eyebrows.

'I know,' I said. 'Resorting to clichés. Ominous.'

THURSDAY 17 JANUARY

Heather and I had arranged to meet in The Eatery after school. Had it only been the previous Thursday that I'd been frothy with chat and good news from home?

In the time since, I seemed to have accumulated even more that I couldn't tell her, so today I leapt on her general questions such as 'How are things going?', offering anecdotes from the classroom, telling her stories about Patsy in the bakery, and sharing the fact that I'd tidied my room and found a book under the bed I thought I'd lost.

What also helped was that Heather's style of speech rarely involved direct questions such as 'Is your father drinking?' but, like Bridget, she was covert. 'I trust your father is behaving himself,' she asked.

I said, 'Compared to how things were when I was younger, he is an absolute paragon of virtue,' and she laughed. Laughing distracts people from their train of thought, so that when the waitress came with hot water for Heather's teapot and another lemonade for me, it was like an iron, smoothing over the creases as though they'd never been there.

'I expect your teachers are pleased with you,' Heather said, and because I could truthfully answer, 'I hope so,' she assumed I was being self-effacing and everyone likes self-effacing. It's an attractive quality that keeps people off your back.

I justified the half-truths by telling myself that it wasn't me I was trying to protect, but my dad. If it had been me, I would have said, 'My dad moved his girlfriend in, and she's taken charge of the *Radio Times* and keeps gin under the sink, and then her son arrived and lives on our sofa, and now he's taken up with Amanda and my teachers think I'm a slacker when I'm not and Dad stole from me and can't keep off the booze and Kevin thinks I don't love him so I'm scalping myself and writing like Plath.'

But I didn't, even while the most vulnerable and soft parts of me screamed, *Tell the truth, tell the truth.*

Heather said, as we were leaving, 'I have so many cases on my list with complex problems. It's lovely to hear all your positive news.'

I said, 'We could meet every other week rather than every week if you're stretched.'

I was half joking but she was already malleable, like soft clay or bread dough. 'If you're sure,' she said. 'In fact, I was going to discuss that possibility with my manager.'

I put my coat on. 'We could telephone in the intervening weeks, if there was need. You could chat to Dad that way, too.'

'That's so thoughtful of you,' she said.

FRIDAY 1 FEBRUARY

It was Dad's thirty-eighth birthday. I'd cancelled going to the Walls' for tea. Dad had mentioned a new Pink Floyd album recently. I'd bought the LP from Woolworths the day before when I'd been in Warwick to meet Heather.

I hurried across the park from school as I needed to wrap the present before he came home from work but, when I arrived, he and Doreen were next to each other on the sofa holding glass tumblers containing a clear liquid. It could have been water, but only in the same way cows could be fish. My stomach twisted with disappointment that he wasn't even trying.

On the coffee table was the Pink Floyd LP.

I was confused. 'Did you find that in my room, Dad?'

He frowned. 'Don't be daft. I don't go in your room.'

I bit back the words, *You went in my pay packet.*

He said, 'It's my present from Doreen.' He pulled her close to kiss her and I shut my eyes until it was over.

'I'm sorry, chuck,' Doreen said to me, detaching herself from Dad's face. 'You should have mentioned that you'd bought it.'

'You're drinking,' I said to Dad. The words were out before I'd thought them, skipping past the censor.

He said, 'Cut me some slack on my special day.'

I felt reckless. 'Let's hope it stays special.'

He said nothing.

'How come you're both home?'

'I took the afternoon off,' Doreen said.

Dad said, 'I wasn't feeling too good this morning.'

I said, 'Are you feeling better, now you've got your medicine?'

Doreen said, 'You've a sharp tongue, missy.'

'Leave the lass alone,' Dad said.

'Is Stuart here?' I asked. 'I like to know who's in the flat, in case someone's built bunks in my room and moved in an aunt.'

'You're being ridiculous,' Doreen said. 'Stuart's at his friend's. He stayed overnight again.'

'He might as well move in,' said my dad. 'Something there appeals to him. Do they have a colour telly?'

In my room, I slid the LP and redundant silver wrapping paper from under my bed. 'Now what?' I said to Weston. I hadn't kept the Woolworths receipt.

The only other person I knew who liked Pink Floyd was Nick.

In the living room, Doreen was topping up Dad's glass with the gin bottle, so he must have drunk nearly a whole glass in the thirty seconds I'd been out of the room.

'I thought you didn't like gin,' I said.

He didn't reply.

'Here's the one I bought,' I said, waving it at him, 'but I'll give it to Uncle Nick.'

I thought I saw Dad flinch when I said 'Uncle', such a soft and friendly word, usually.

'So I've nothing to give you,' I said, although on my bed-side table was a card with a funny picture of a man saying, *Older and wiser. That's your story, anyway.*

When I returned to my room, I tore it in half so that I couldn't relent.

Ten minutes later, Dad knocked on my bedroom door. 'We're getting birthday fish and chips. Do you want fish or a chicken pie?'

'I'm not hungry.'

'It's my birthday.'

'There'll be others,' I said, 'hopefully.'

He opened my door and poked his head round. 'You're taking this too far.' I saw his gaze switch to the torn card, but he didn't comment.

'I'm not the one taking things too far.'

Soon, Dad's steps echoed down the stairwell and fifteen minutes later they came back up. The aroma of vinegar sneaked under my door as did the rustle of paper. I dived beneath my blankets until they'd finished the meal but the tang of it had diffused throughout the flat. If vinegar could speak, it would have said, *Cut off your nose to spite your face.*

Doreen and Dad's voices became louder and louder as the evening progressed and they laughed at sitcoms. At one point, a glass was dropped in the kitchen and Doreen giggled as she cleared up the shards with a brush and dustpan as though starring in a sitcom herself.

I found a pimple at the back of my head and gouged at it with a fingernail until the nail filled with blood. I felt disgusted with myself and wondered whether Dad felt the same after gouging at his self-respect with alcohol he didn't even like.

FRIDAY 8 FEBRUARY

It had been three weeks since I'd been to the Walls' for tea. Last week, Dad's birthday. The Friday before, Nick and Bridget had been invited to eat with friends.

Although I'd missed the Walls, I hadn't missed my own ducking and diving while they questioned me about school, Dad, life at the flat and, to borrow from *The Sound of Music*, what do you do with someone like Amanda.

Amanda herself I hadn't seen since the new year when I'd spotted her with Stuart.

Bridget and I had a cup of tea together while she asked for the highlights of my life. As she'd chosen the word 'highlights', I could safely not include finding out that my dad would steal his daughter's wages but told her instead that the school had decided to stop serving the tapioca after a pupil survey.

When Nick arrived, I gave him the Pink Floyd album, summarising the drama of last Friday's events to 'Dad had one already'. Mrs C's teaching on precis skills had not gone to waste.

Where was Amanda?

Nick said, 'She's staying overnight again at her friend's house in Warwick.'

'Which friend?' I said.

'I think she's called Catherine, isn't she, love?' he said to Bridget.

'Catherine or Kathleen,' Bridget said. 'She's mentioned

both, unless she's mixing them up. She has so many new friends these days, which is a good thing, I suppose.'

It seemed the norm now, the three of us at the table (still set for four because if the Prodigal Son could spend all his dad's money on prostitutes and still get a fatted calf, Amanda could come home for cottage pie).

We started on stewed fruit and custard. 'We're worried that she's not working hard enough at her hairdressing course,' Nick said.

'She'll pull all the stops out when it matters,' I said.

'We wish she had your dedication,' Bridget said. She gazed at me indulgently. 'You're doing so well.'

Bridget had no up-to-date facts with which to support this optimistic thesis but she wasn't to know that, since January, when I'd reassured my teachers with a brief upsurge in achievement and participation, my schoolwork had taken a back seat, been relegated to the back burner, was playing second fiddle, and all the other metaphors that meant poor grades and disappointing exam predictions.

'You're letting things slip again,' my psychology teacher had said. It was an unfair assessment because, if I'd felt I had any control over the slippage, I'd have done something about it.

We'd been given a letter that week to take home: an invitation to a parents' evening the following Monday. I'd passed it to Dad who'd given it a cursory glance, although he'd had trouble focusing, then used it as a coaster for a glass.

While Bridget was in the downstairs toilet, I went upstairs to use the bathroom then peeked into the sunflower-yellow bedroom.

On the chest of drawers by the bed, Nick's alarm clock. His pyjamas were folded on top of the pillow and the windowsill was stacked with books. I looked into the double room they'd shared, feeling like a trespasser, but I needed the information.

One pillow in the centre of the double bed.

The trespasser feeling was odd because for three years I'd been a central part of their household and now I felt on the periphery.

It was my own doing. I only had to speak.

Only. A word that carries so much weight, I thought, as I sat on my bed at home. I picked up my poetry notebook and began to write.

Only
Four letters but each one a stone.
Take them one by one in your hands
and tell me you're not aching.
That's words for you, my friend.
Innocuous like the backs of babies' knees
until they stray into sentences
where they sit, implacable:
toads by the side of the road,
mothers with their arms folded,
tanks in a row, guns drooling.

WEDNESDAY 13 FEBRUARY

I walked out of the gate after school with Molly and we saw Amanda standing on the opposite side of the road, dressed in punk black, including a black woolly scarf and black mittens which seemed both a match and a mismatch. I waved and she gave a vague wave back but didn't come across.

'I'd stay and say hello,' Molly said, 'but I have to rush back to Mum.'

I hadn't told Molly about the rift between me and Amanda in case telling her something led to telling her everything. Considering our tongues are held captive inside our mouths, they have such a tendency to blab independently. Best not to start.

I crossed over to meet Amanda and said, 'Why are you skulking as though you're in a spy film?'

She had a nose ring now as well as the stud.

'Thanks for the welcome,' she said.

'Sorry, but you've been avoiding me for, what, six weeks now, and don't deny it.'

She swapped a black canvas bag from one shoulder to another. It wasn't her college bag. 'I don't deny it.'

'Have you split with Stuart?' I tried not to sound hopeful.

'Can we talk in the Happy Plate?'

'So now you want me for an agony aunt?'

She looked embarrassed.

'Haven't you been to college?' I said.

'Day off.'

'Who said it was a day off? You or them?'

But she didn't answer. We started walking towards Leamington. On the way, I asked her about Bridget. She told me that Bridget's consultant wanted to increase her medication.

'Is it not working?'

'Her knife and fork keep slipping from her hands.' I heard a catch in her voice.

'That's upsetting,' I said. 'Yes, I've seen that.'

'She can't prise the lids off Tupperware containers. Sometimes, she can't get them on.'

We walked in silence for the last five minutes.

The café was busy. We had to wait by the door until a table became free. When we sat down, I said, 'I'll treat you to this. As we haven't met for a while, I have money in my purse.'

'Okay.'

A waitress appeared.

'Do you want tea, or a cold drink?' I said to Amanda.

'Lemonade. And biscuits. Rich Teas or something,' she told the waitress. 'Not Custard Creams.'

I ordered tea. 'You're getting very picky,' I said, when the waitress had gone.

I asked her how college was going and she said 'What?' as if she didn't know what I was talking about.

'You're doing a hairdressing course. You know. At that big building that has tutors and classrooms.'

'You're so amusing,' she said, darkly, and described a lesson in which another student's perm had gone wrong and someone had ended up with green hair. But there was something desperate about her, as though beneath her words were other words, like hot springs, aching to burst through earth.

The waitress came with our drinks and biscuits. Amanda opened a packet of Nice biscuits, and nibbled around the edge of one.

'It's not going to matter now, college,' she said.

'What? Have you resigned?'

'Resigned? You don't resign from college.'

'You're worrying me. I'm forgetting the words.'

She sipped lemonade through a striped straw then said, 'I'm worrying myself.'

'Why?'

She grabbed my hand. I looked down at it, and she gripped it harder. She said, 'You can't tell my mum and dad. Or anyone.'

'How can I promise that? What if you're in danger?'

She lowered her voice, although the café was noisy with talk. In fact, she almost mimed it. 'I'm having a baby.'

'Say that again.' There was a slim chance she'd said, 'I'm happy with Maybelline.'

'A baby,' she said. She looked frightened.

'What? I can't believe it.'

She let go of my hand. 'Try being me.'

'No, thank you.'

'Trust me. You don't want to. No change there. You never have wanted to be me. It's the other way round.' She ate the rest of the biscuit and picked up the crumbs with a finger.

'I meant, I wouldn't want to be having a baby.'

'Nor do I.'

'I don't know what to say.'

'Good,' she said, 'because I don't want advice. I just wanted you to know.'

I looked around the café, wondering what conversations others were having over their scones and pots of tea. Most faces were animated, glad to be socialising, or so it seemed. Perhaps Amanda and I looked like that to others, too, or maybe they were sharing news of a death or asking what to do when a child has night terrors. People's faces aren't reliable.

I said to Amanda, 'Is it Stuart's?'

'Of course. Who else's?'

I tried to look reassured. 'Shouldn't you—'

'I said, I didn't need advice.'

'But how do you know it's true?'

'The usual ways,' she said, 'if those sex education videos were right.'

'You haven't seen a doctor.'

'Of course not.'

'Periods?'

'Gone.'

'Sick?'

'I feel as sick as a pig, but I haven't actually been sick.'

'Sick as a dog, you mean.'

'Don't correct me. I hate that.'

'Irritable?' I said, before I could stop myself.

She stood up as if to go.

'Sit down, idiot,' I said. 'You need me.'

'I don't.'

'So why are you telling me?'

I saw her gulp twice. 'I don't know. It's made it all true.'

'Have you told Stuart?'

'No. That's the other reason I came to see you. I want you to tell him.'

I ate a whole Rich Tea while taking this in.

'He'll be angry with me,' she said.

'Angry with *you*? It's not all your fault. It takes two, unless this was an immaculate conception.'

'What even is that?'

'Tell me you're joking.'

'I don't know what went wrong. Sometimes he's a bit … eager.'

I wasn't quite sure what this meant. I didn't admit it. 'He'll have to step up then, now he's a daddy.'

'I thought if you introduced the idea, he'd have time to get used to it.'

'He's not responsible father material. Unless you want him to pay for an abortion.'

'I don't want that.'

'Or you could give the baby away.'

'I couldn't. Why go through the effort of a whole pregnancy only to hand it over to someone else?'

'There's only one other option, then,' I said, 'and I'm no expert but I think it involves nappies and feeding and cots. Add to that, crying through the night, and that's not just the baby.'

'You're not much comfort.'

'What do you want me to say?'

'Tell me I'm not pregnant and I imagined the whole thing.'

'Okay. You're not pregnant and have imagined the whole thing.'

She picked up another biscuit and bit into it.

MONDAY 18 FEBRUARY

I was trying and failing to do homework in my room after school.

Stuart was in the flat. Dad and Doreen weren't home. I should have plucked up courage to speak to him about Amanda while I could. Arthur Miller wasn't getting a look in.

Then I heard Dad arriving. It was only four o'clock.

I went into the hall. His face was ruddy and he steadied himself against the wall as he took off his wet shoes. He wasn't wearing work clothes.

'Whatever you're about to say,' he said, 'keep it to yourself.' His words were the kind with no boundaries, running into each other with abandon, like puppies out of control.

'Have you been in the pub?' I said.

He sighed, a long breath. 'Brick wall.'

'The pub closes at three.'

'Not if he's still got customers,' he said. 'Or perhaps one keen one.'

'What about work?'

He wriggled out of his coat and hung it on its hook on the wall, missing the first time.

'What *about* work?' He pushed past me and went into his bedroom. I heard the bed springs creak under his weight.

Five minutes later, I knocked on his door. 'Dad, remember there's a parents' evening at the school from five o'clock.'

Mrs C had said to me, 'Remind your dad about it, won't you?' so I would have felt guilty not doing so, but I didn't want him to attend. Should she ask whether I'd reminded him, I could safely say that I had. I didn't need to tell her that I'd done so over the sound of thunderous snoring.

Heather had asked when we'd met the previous week if there was a parents' evening coming up. She'd seemed particularly harried that day and checked her diary twice while we were there, as though anxious that she was forgetting things. I think she felt that if my teachers got a look at Dad and he passed muster, this might substitute for a check from her that she didn't have time for.

At five o'clock, Doreen arrived home and put the kettle on. She was taking off the yellow checked tabard she wore for work, folding it up. I watched her from the kitchen door.

'Why isn't Dad at work?' I said.

'Hello to you, too.'

'He's been in the pub.'

She lit the hob. 'He's got no work.'

'What?'

'Sacked. Too many absences. I thought they were meant to make the heart grow fonder,' she added, with a sour laugh.

'It's not really a joking matter.'

'Hark at you! Comedian when it suits you.'

'It's not funny.'

'You'll soon change your tune,' she said, 'when we're eating egg and chips five times a week and the gas gets cut off.'

'He hasn't had that many absences.'

'That's the problem with you youngsters.' She reached into a cupboard for a cup. 'So certain of your facts.'

'Surely they gave him a second chance.'

'He'd already had his second chance. And his third. And fourth.'

'Oh.'

'I don't know how he thinks we're going to manage on my wages. He's not spending them on whisky, I know that.'

'He'll get another job,' I said.

'And pigs might bloody fly.' Her eyes flicked to the cupboard where Dad kept his money tin and not for the first time I wondered whether her attraction to Dad was in direct correlation with the weight of the tin. 'He had an appointment with his probation officer today,' she said. 'Looks as though that may have bitten the dust.'

'He can't miss those.'

'It seems he can.'

But at least I now had a further line of defence should Mrs C's questioning be too searching. He'd double-booked.

While I dressed for school the following day, Doreen had the radio on in the kitchen but there was no sign of Dad's heavy step into the bathroom or the clunk of a wooden drawer. I listened harder, in case I'd missed something.

But Doreen was only making one packed lunch.

THURSDAY 21 FEBRUARY

After that morning's English lesson, Mrs Collingworth asked me to stay behind. It was dinner time and I hadn't eaten yet that day, as Doreen and Dad had been in the kitchen rowing. It being her day off, she was making bacon and egg sandwiches for herself and Stuart. Dad had assumed the bacon and eggs were reserved for teatime. What else did she think she'd cook, he wanted to know, seeing as the fridge was otherwise empty, as was the money tin?

So, I'd been packing my satchel quickly after the lesson, hoping for an early spot in the queue with Molly.

'I won't keep you long,' the teacher said. 'I know you'll want your dinner.' Sometimes I wondered whether Mrs Collingworth knew me better than I knew myself.

'Save me a place,' I called to Molly as she left.

Mrs C was stacking textbooks. 'Your dad didn't manage it on Monday. It was a shame not to see him.'

'He double-booked. Sorry.' I'd told Heather the same on the phone and she'd said, 'I must fix to see him soon.'

'I'm sure you keep him updated,' Mrs C said, 'and there'll be a report at Easter.'

'Is that a threat?'

'You know me better than that.'

'Sorry.'

'I hear a rumour,' she said, 'that when it comes to you and the school nurse, never the twain shall meet.'

'Oh.'

'I think you said you'd been to the appointment.'

'I did go. She wasn't there. She'd left a note on the door. And she didn't rearrange. Or, at least, no message came.'

'She did send one, she says. It will turn up one day far into the future.'

'I suppose.'

'I wish you'd told me the whole truth,' she said.

'Sorry.'

'Accepted.'

'Anyway. Things got better.'

'Hm. I'd rather hear, "Things *have* got better." Are you still seeing your social worker?'

'Thursdays.'

'You're trying harder with your essays. This week's Arthur Miller was a good B.'

I'd stayed up most of the night to finish it and had fallen asleep in psychology. The teacher had thrown a board rubber to wake me.

'And the head picking?' she said.

'I'll go and see the nurse if you want me to.'

'I've already asked her to send you another appointment.'

She opened her handbag and took out a lipstick and a mirror, applying a shade of pink to her lips. It felt intimate, like a compliment to me. I decided it was for persuasive effect. Mrs Collingworth knew exactly what she was doing.

FRIDAY 22 FEBRUARY

During registration, Mrs C passed me the thin slip of paper. *Nurse. Friday 1p.m.*

At dinner time, after burning my mouth on liver with mashed potatoes and shovelling down rice pudding that had a skin so thick and hard you had to invade, I went back to the nurse's office and knocked. The door opened.

Nurse Broughton (or Nursey B as everyone called her) was an unusually tall woman with a body like a tube, dressed in full nurse's uniform, fob watch and all. Her face, serious and sober, as though she were about to hand out a life sentence, contrasted with her reputation. Everyone liked her.

'Sit down, Jackie,' she said, pointing me, with an impossibly long, bony finger, to a plastic chair. She sat opposite me, her skirt rising to expose thin knees. 'Comfortable?' she said, looking straight at me, her eyes a deep green like pondweed, only kind.

I said, 'Are you going to tell me a story?'

'No. That's your job.' She sat back and crossed one leg over the other. Her feet must have been size nine, at least. 'Tell me everything.' Her voice was as soft as furs.

'Can't I just choose some relevant details?'

She laughed and I wasn't expecting it.

'Okay, I'm here because I pick at my head and make it bleed,' I said, cruelly.

'So I gather. Is this when things worry you?'

'No, when I'm gloriously happy.'

She leaned far forward and poked my arm. 'Mrs Colling-worth told me about you. You won't scare *me* off with your jokes like a porcupine's bristles.'

No one had ever said this before. I felt known, as though I might want to be her friend for ever and ever. I wondered how it would feel to be hugged by her. Perhaps like being hugged by a knobbly tree, but you'd endure it for the affection.

'What kind of moments make it hardest to stop?' she said.

I began to relax. 'When I don't like what's happening.'

'An example?'

'I suppose – being made to eat egg yolks.'

'Stop it.'

I looked down at my lap. Her eyes sucked you in. 'Okay. People arguing.'

'You mean you and your father?' she said, and I realised I'd said too much. I couldn't mention Doreen or Stuart, or Dad's drinking, in case she passed news on. Here I was again, choosing my words, tiptoeing through sentences as though they were mini landmines.

'Yes.'

'Okay.'

'And when I worry about him,' I said.

'And there's been plenty of reason in the past.'

I looked around the room. 'Have you got a whole file on me?'

'We're like the Secret Service in here.' She waved in the direction of a filing cabinet.

She didn't probe further. We sat in silence and I heard a clock ticking on the wall behind me.

'Don't you need dinner?' I said.

'Are you saying I'm skinny?'

I felt my face heat up. 'I didn't mean – I didn't want to take up too much time.' If I didn't get out of there, all my defences would melt like ice cream in August. I'd have to plan better for next time.

'Let me decide that,' she said, smiling. One of her front

teeth overlapped its neighbour. 'We'll do this every two weeks on a Friday. I'll send a reminder.'

'If I must.'

'It's always your choice.'

But in fact I craved more of her bony tenderness even though I'd need to hold back on detail. And it was only once a fortnight.

She stood and so did I. 'I hear from Mrs Collingworth that you're a poet,' she said.

'Trying to be.'

'Wait there.' She opened the top drawer of the filing cabinet and lifted out a magazine which she passed to me.

I looked at the cover. '*Agenda*.'

'It's a literary magazine. You can have it. I've got other copies.'

'What's a literary magazine?'

'Literary magazines publish poems, short stories, reviews, articles about literature, that kind of thing.'

I looked at the contents page. She pointed. There was her name. Constance Broughton. Constance.

'They took six poems of mine. I've had a few printed elsewhere but this is my best achievement so far.'

I had never met a published poet. 'That's what Mrs Collingworth meant, then.'

'She mentioned that we might have something in common?'

'Obliquely.'

'Goodness,' she said. 'You *are* a wordsmith.'

'If you're a poet,' I asked her, 'why are you here, being a nurse?'

'Only the very lucky get to be full-time poets,' she said. 'Not many poets live in mansions.'

'Damn,' I said.

She opened the door and nodded towards the magazine. 'There's a good piece in there about different poetry forms, too. And you can tell me next time what you think of my poems.'

That evening, when I'd returned from the Walls' house, I stayed in my room and pulled *Agenda* magazine from my satchel. I turned to the nurse's poems. At first, I told myself aloud, 'Nursey B wrote these,' and then, 'Nurse Broughton wrote these,' but it was only when I said, 'Constance Broughton wrote these,' that it sounded right.

Her theme was loss. Each poem explored a different aspect. The loss of a parent. The loss of colour from trees in winter. The loss of youth. Beauty. A child. Memory. They were short poems, some only one verse. Two were sonnets. One was a villanelle, a form I remembered studying for O level when we read 'Do Not Go Gentle' by Dylan Thomas. Her style was sparse, frugal with description, but in the lack of description, there was power.

I didn't understand everything they meant, but I had learned by then not to be worried about this, thanks to Mrs Collingworth.

One of the sonnets contained these lines.

They ask me to wear black and bend my head.
I strut your memory high in yellow and red.

I thought back to my mum's funeral. She had begged Dad and me not to wear black. Dad, who had wept continually every time we visited her in the hospice as though he carried tears for many more than one person, had refused to promise. She'd said she understood but I think it had made her sad.

When she died, I'd tried to persuade him to follow her wishes but whisky and the guilty variety of grief combined had made him fearsome and I retreated. He hired a formal black suit for himself and a plain black dress for me, with what money I didn't know. I felt he was punishing himself – and me, although I didn't deserve it – by cloaking us in thick darkness like condemned criminals.

The night before the funeral, when he had been rendered useless by drink despite having vowed to stay sober, I looked in Mum's chest of drawers in their bedroom and found a pink lacy petticoat. It was too big for me but I wore it to the church underneath the dress. I tucked it in as best I could, and willed the elasticated waist to prevent the petticoat from slithering down my legs when I walked to the lectern to read the poem I had written for the occasion.

I hoped Mum, in some way, knew about the petticoat. What I didn't want was everyone else finding out.

Now, I stroked my hand across the pages of the poetry magazine.

'Constance Broughton,' I said aloud again. 'Constance Broughton.' It made it real, and not only had she shown me her poems, but she had allowed me to know her Christian name, usually a taboo at school.

There was a rap at my door. 'Talking to ourselves, are we?' Stuart said.

'You can bugger off,' I said.

SATURDAY 23 FEBRUARY

Dad and Doreen had gone to the pub on Saturday evening, leaving me alone in the flat with Stuart. Dad, to his credit, had asked me recently, 'Do you mind being left with him?'

'I'd rather you stayed home and weren't in the pub at all,' I said.

'I wanted to make sure you felt safe.'

'Right, Dad.'

I went into the living room and sat on the sofa. Stuart was watching a Tarzan film and eating crisps.

'Oh, a rare honour,' he said.

'I'll stay so long as you put the crisps in whole instead of biting them. I swear Colin could hear it from next door.'

'Pardon me, I'm sure.'

'Granted.'

'Help yourself to a beer.' He pointed to his supply on the coffee table.

'I thought you'd be with Amanda,' I began.

'I haven't seen Amanda all week.' He put a crisp in his mouth in the way I'd asked and crunched it. 'She's gone weird on me anyway.'

'Meaning?'

'Wants to catch up on *college work*.' He made quotation marks in the air.

I couldn't conjure up a first sentence for my announcement.

'She can suit herself,' he continued. 'She was getting clingy.'

On the screen were elephants. Tarzan was meant to save them from the effects of a man-made dam that would drown them.

I said, 'I saw Amanda on Wednesday.'

'Lucky you,' he said. He opened the third bottle, judging by the empties, and poured it into his glass. I would need to get to the point.

'How can you afford all this beer?'

I'd heard him begging Doreen for money. She couldn't resist him, especially as he'd claim he needed a new shirt or train ticket for a job interview. But no shirt or train ticket or job interview appeared, so he was either lying or he was lying.

'Amanda told me some important news,' I said.

He didn't answer.

'It's news you need to know.'

'Why?'

'Because you're involved.'

He put down his glass and sat up straight. 'If she's up the duff, I don't want to hear it.'

I was shocked. 'Up the *duff*?'

'Up the duff. Bun in the oven. Knocked up. In the family way.'

'You can stop with the synonyms. I knew what you meant. I didn't think you'd be such a bastard about it.'

'Ooh, out come the claws,' he said. But he looked uncertain. 'Are you telling the truth?'

'Amanda. Is. Pregnant.'

'How does she know?'

'You want a run-through of the signs?'

He lit a cigarette, the last one in the packet. 'Might not be mine.'

'I wish it weren't. But it is.'

He sucked on the cigarette, his lips tight, then breathed out smoke. 'Why are *you* telling me?'

'She's fragile,' I said.

'She has a habit of slapping. She's not that fragile.'

I didn't comment. I'd been slapped by her myself.

'Has she told her mum and dad?' he asked.

I wanted to leave him stranded. 'I don't know.'

'I'll borrow money off Mum. Tell her to stave off blabbing. It can be fixed.'

On the TV, a beautiful Indian princess implored Tarzan to help the elephants.

'You're a lump of shit,' I said to Stuart and left the room, but not before he'd thrown an empty cigarette packet at me.

It missed.

I called from the hall, 'No wonder you got her pregnant with an aim like that.'

I'd labelled him a lump of shit but in truth I didn't fully believe that. Despite everything, there was something about Stuart that I liked. Once or twice, we'd discussed the books we were reading and he'd seemed a different person. It reminded me of a Thomas Hardy poem we'd studied at school called 'The Man He Killed'. In it, a man acknowledges that the soldier he shot in the Boer War could, in other circumstances, have been a friend, but that they'd been pitted against each other to serve someone else's conflict. If I hadn't shot him first, the man says, he would have shot me, but in another context, I'd have stood him a drink.

That night, Dad and Doreen fought about money again on their return from the pub after eleven. I lay in bed, listening. They seemed to use their pub trips these days, which had strayed into weeknights as well as weekends, as a temporary break in proceedings before – ding ding! – returning to the ring.

Either they didn't see the irony in spending money at the pub only to argue when they got back about how much they didn't have, or they saw it and pretended they hadn't. Maybe deliberate ignorance was something that developed in people in response to the shock of finding yourself an adult.

That night, it seemed, Doreen's friends had turned up at the pub and Doreen had appointed herself their benefactor but with Dad's wallet, thin as it was.

'I'm not a bottomless pit,' Dad said. They were in the kitchen.

'No, you're a tight git,' she said.

Stuart must have come out of the living room. Dad said, 'And you can bugger off back in there. This is a private conversation.'

The living room door closed.

I continued to listen to their private conversation as, I'm sure, did Stuart, seeing as they were conducting it at top volume.

'You can use your own wages,' Dad said to Doreen, 'for your pals.'

'Oh, and how do we stock the fridge and cupboards?'

I heard a cupboard door open and the drag of the money tin. 'Empty,' he said.

I knew bills awaited payment. I'd seen the envelopes.

She said, 'Heave your arse out of bed on Monday, then, sign on the dole, and get yourself a job. Have you told your probation officer you got the sack?'

'The factory got to him first.'

'Well, God only helps those who help themselves,' she said.

'*You're* the bloody one who's been helping herself.'

There was a silence. I thought they had moved out of the kitchen. But then Doreen said, more quietly, '*Don't* you dare raise your fist to me, Dave Chadwick.'

'I didn't mean to.'

'Oh, I think you did.'

He said, after another long silence, 'Maybe you should move back to your old flat for a while. Until I'm settled.'

'Are you throwing me out,' she said, 'because I bought my mates some drinks?'

But she didn't sound that upset. They were less and less

affectionate these days. Perhaps this was evidence that I could hope.

'I can't move back,' she said. 'She's found a permanent flatmate now.'

'Oh, then you'll have to sort something else.'

'What would you know about sorting things?' she said, and I heard the bathroom door shut. There was no more movement for a while. Was he standing in the kitchen, alone?

The fridge door opened, then shut. He said, 'Bugger it!' He was looking for cheese. I knew there was none.

If Doreen moved somewhere else with her pink suitcase, I thought, presumably Stuart would too with his shabby holdall. It would be Dad and me. We could rewind the tape.

That's if we hadn't lost the cassette.

SUNDAY 24 FEBRUARY

In the morning, there seemed no fallout from the previous evening's fight between Doreen and Dad. Perhaps they didn't even remember it. This felt anticlimactic, a volcanic eruption without a hint of lava. Doreen was hoovering the flat as usual, Dad and Stuart obediently lifting their feet out of the way like lambs. Dad was reading the Sunday newspaper. Stuart had started a new novel and was deep into it.

I put on my coat and left the flat without announcement – I'd have had to shout over the vacuum cleaner and I didn't feel like telling them anything, let alone making an effort.

I rang the Walls' house from the phone box. Amanda answered. 'Mum and Dad have gone to a christening,' she said.

'Whose christening?'

'Some baby.'

'Well, yes.'

She yawned.

'You sound tired.' I said.

'And I feel so sick.'

'I told Stuart you're pregnant.' She went quiet, and I wondered whether she wanted the truth. I decided she could have it. 'He suggested money for an abortion.'

'I don't want to do that.'

'I know. I don't think he's going to win any Father of the Year awards, Amanda. You need to tell your mum and dad.'

'I wouldn't know where to start,' she said.

I walked into the park. I didn't want to go home yet. I tried to imagine Amanda, like these other young mothers, gathered in conversational huddles while their toddlers ran around, parcelled up in thick coats and oversized hats, or asked to be lifted onto the climbing frame. The women looked in their twenties and thirties. Husbands stood, hands in pockets or tight under their armpits, chatting with other husbands.

So many reasons why Amanda wouldn't know where to start.

FRIDAY 29 FEBRUARY

It was the last day of the half-term holiday in a leap year. 'You can ask your lad to marry you today,' Doreen told me that morning. She was buttering toast.

'He's not my lad.' I hadn't spoken to Kevin since the middle of January.

'Your dad said there'd been a cooling-off,' she said, as though her own relationship was a bed of fragrant, cheerful roses. She and Dad seemed to have stepped back from the idea of breaking up but the peace felt a tenuous one, like a rope that's fraying or a wire coming loose.

'Then you know, if Dad told you.' I poured milk over my cornflakes.

'You'd like to get married, though, chuck? Have a family?'

'It's not top of the list.'

She put a hand on my arm. 'You can talk to me any time, you know, if you and your lad are having problems.'

'He's not my lad. Could you pass me the sugar bowl, please?'

She did so and put her head to one side in a sympathetic gesture that reminded me of Bridget when she was trying to help and failing, except that Bridget's hair moved and Doreen's stayed put.

'Well, you know where to find me,' she said.

Unfortunately, this was true.

'Don't forget that your dad and I are taking you out tomorrow for your birthday,' she said. She bit her toast and added, 'As promised,' as though I'd begged them to plan something, which I hadn't. And they wouldn't tell me where we were going.

'I told you, I hate surprises,' I said.

'Well, you're getting one. Don't be a grump.'

They'd raised the idea the previous Wednesday evening of taking me out for a birthday meal after work on Saturday. We'd been eating fish fingers and chips on our laps and watching *Nationwide*.

'But I've been invited to the Walls' at teatime,' I'd said. I shouldn't have.

'Oh, they'll have bought you a fur coat and a diamond necklace,' Dad said.

'Don't be ridiculous, Dad.'

'I meant at dinner time anyway,' Doreen said. 'You can go to the Walls' afterwards.'

'I suppose.'

She said, 'Okay, maybe *we* can all go out – me, your dad, and Stuart – and leave you here to stew in your own juices.'

'I'm game for that,' Stuart said.

'Steady on, Dor,' Dad said.

'Of course, I'm grateful,' I said, 'and dinner time would be fine, but I'd rather know where we're going. I don't like surprises.'

'So you said,' Doreen said.

'She gets that from me about not liking surprises,' Dad said, 'like that bloody Heather woman dropping in this morning.'

'What?' I said.

'What?' Doreen said.

Stuart said, 'Ouch.'

Dad told us that Heather had phoned him at ten that morning to say she would be passing his flat in fifteen minutes and could she drop in for a catch-up? The probation officer had been in touch with Social Services about Dad being sacked from his job so she hoped he'd be at home.

'I nearly had a seizure there and then,' he said.

'Where was Stuart?' I said.

'At the library,' Stuart said. 'I wish I'd been here to watch.'

'A bloody disaster, that'd have been,' Dad said.

He explained that he'd spent the fifteen minutes clearing away evidence of live-in girlfriends and their offspring ('including the extra toothbrushes in case she needed the lav') as well as of alcohol consumption. He left the local newspaper on the table, open at the jobs pages. When Heather arrived, he'd endured twenty minutes of what he termed 'interfering la-di-da chit-chat' before ushering her out of the door.

'Then I took the bottle of whisky back out of the airing cupboard,' he said.

His account had been funny and I loved to see him in storytelling mode, but it also made me uneasy. 'What if she comes without notice another time?' I said.

'I've thought of that. I booked her into the diary for a month's time.'

'Since when did you own a diary?' Doreen said, mockingly.

'Since last week.' He produced it from his back pocket. 'WHSmith, half price, seeing as it's February. I bought it to write job interviews in. She was impressed.'

'You're a lucky beggar,' Doreen said. 'Anyway, about this birthday dinner. I'm not letting her wriggle out of it.'

I said to her, 'But I know you can't afford a meal out.'

'She's right, Doreen,' Dad said.

She stabbed at a couple of chips. 'We'll leave it to the Walls, then, shall we?'

There was a pause.

'No, we bloody won't,' Dad said.

'Then I'll book us somewhere for one thirty.'

SATURDAY 1 MARCH

Patsy arrived for her afternoon shift at the bakery, the door pinging, as Sheila was giving me my wage packet. 'Happy *eighteenth*!' Patsy shouted past the noise of customers and tills.

A chorus of 'It's your birthday?' from Sheila, three colleagues and a regular customer had me scuttering out of the floury warmth of the bakery into the wind-whipped outdoors before I got cuddled.

'You'll get your present tomorra!' Patsy called.

My instructions from Doreen had been to catch the bus into Leamington after work and she and Dad would meet me on the main street. The day was bitter and I pulled on the knitted birthday gloves that she had presented me with that morning.

The gloves had been one of two presents I'd opened in the living room, at Doreen's insistence, before heading off to the bakery. The three of them had watched me, yawning and still in their nightclothes, as though only taking a temporary break from sleep.

'They're Marks and Sparks,' Doreen said.

'Thank you. I needed some warm gloves.'

'Told you, Dave,' she said. Doreen loved knowing things about me.

Dad had bought me a box of Milk Tray. 'All because the lady loves,' he said in a deep voice as I unwrapped them, but added, 'Doreen fetched them. I was having a kip.'

'That's not how it works in the advert.'

'I haven't bought you anything,' Stuart said. 'When can I go back to sleep?'

I said, 'I'm feeling more and more special.'

'You're *wearing* the gloves!' Doreen said, when I climbed off the bus.

I said, 'I took a wild guess at their function.'

She jabbed my shoulder with a finger and said, 'You're such a card.' I could smell alcohol on her breath. She was wearing high heels as though out for an evening. A brisk wind did its best to ruffle her hair but the hair was winning.

Dad, dressed in trousers and jacket, looked flushed.

They'd been celebrating my birthday without me in one of Leamington's pubs.

'My hands are very cosy in these,' I said, grabbing the chance to be grateful in case it didn't happen again that day.

Doreen took hold of my left arm and Dad took the other.

'This way,' she said, as though she were a tour guide. *Look to your right, and there's your dad, choosing his steps carefully. Look to your left, and you'll see a woman who's half gin.*

They'd booked a table at the Berni Inn.

'Plush, isn't it?' Doreen stroked the velvet flock wallpaper as she and I took off our coats and laid them on the empty fourth chair next to me. They sat on the bench seat opposite. 'We came here for my birthday in October.'

A waitress hovered.

'Poncey bloody wallpaper,' Dad said. 'What's wrong with a bit of Anaglypta?'

'Don't spoil the day,' Doreen said.

'How is that spoiling the day? Bloody hell, woman.' He shifted around, trying to get comfortable and find room for his legs.

'It's lovely in here.' I looked around. I'd been several times but with the Walls. I would have to select my words.

I picked up a menu. The waitress took out a notepad. 'Can I get you—'

'Gin and tonic for me, chuck,' Doreen said. 'Make it a double.'

Dad made as if to protest but then said, 'A pint of bitter for me.'

'I thought you'd have a Guinness,' Doreen said.

He shook his head.

'You'll have something, won't you, littlun?' she said to me.

'A Coke, please,' I said to the waitress.

'I didn't mean a *Coke*.' Doreen spoke as though I'd ordered deadly nightshade cordial. 'You're eighteen today.'

'Happy birthday,' intoned the waitress, as if a button had been pressed. She looked my age.

'Try a Babycham,' Doreen said, 'or a Martini and lemonade.'

The waitress's pencil was poised.

'No, thanks. I'm happy with Coke.' I nodded to the waitress who still hadn't written anything and said, 'Coke, please,' because no one else seemed to be listening.

'What kind of birthday is that?' Doreen said, when the waitress had gone. 'It's hardly worth bringing you out if you won't let your hair down.'

'Leave the lass alone,' Dad said, into the menu. 'She's got her head screwed on, that's all.'

'What's that supposed to mean?' Doreen unfolded her napkin huffily and put it on her lap.

'I'm having the gammon and pineapple,' he said, 'with chips.'

Doreen seemed surprised. 'You're not having the mixed grill?'

'Look!' He slapped the menu down. 'Why don't you order for us all? I fancy *gammon*.'

She tutted. 'Pardon me.' She played coquettishly with her pearl drop earrings.

I picked up the menu. I didn't want to look too familiar with the choices. I ran my finger down the steak options and ummed and aahed. 'I'll have a rump steak. With a mushroom and onion rings. And a jacket potato.'

Doreen's face had *Wouldn't you prefer chips?* written all over it.

The waitress brought the drinks and took our food order. Doreen ordered the mixed grill for herself. Then she poured tonic into her gin, although not much, and took a long gulp. Dad made quick progress with his beer. Both visibly relaxed, sitting back. Dad grinned at me and said, 'Happy birthday, pet.'

I envied them. All my Coke would do was make me gassy and that was no help with enduring tense family occasions.

'Have you been here before, chuck?' Doreen said, so I had to confess that I had and with whom.

Dad said, 'Might have bloody known,' and we sat in silence for a few minutes listening to the music playing through the speakers: Art Garfunkel's 'Bright Eyes'.

'Isn't this about rabbits dying?' he said.

'Dave, don't,' Doreen said. 'I'm having a mixed grill.'

I was stirring the Coke round with my straw when I turned, thinking I'd heard a familiar voice. The bad news was, I had. It was Stuart, asking the waitress where we were sitting. 'I think my mum booked,' he was saying. 'Doreen Baker.'

'This way, sir,' she said.

Dad turned to Doreen as if incredulous. 'Surely you didn't tell him where we were going.'

'I might have mentioned it,' she protested, 'but I never said he could come. Maybe he's forgotten his key.'

I thought it more likely that he'd forgotten not to turn up to other people's birthday meals.

He arrived at the table, the waitress behind him, her note-pad and pencil ready.

'What the bloody hell?' Dad said.

Doreen was indicating that I should move our coats off the vacant chair next to me.

Stuart said, 'I was passing by. I've been to get some shoelaces.' He waved a paper bag at us for proof then took off his denim jacket, hung it on the back of the vacant chair, and sat down.

'Passing by?' I said. 'Not passing away?' I moved my chair further from his.

'That's not funny, chuck,' Doreen said, but Dad and Stuart had both laughed.

'I'll pay my share,' Stuart said.

'Pay your share, my arse,' Dad said.

'He might as well stay now he's here,' Doreen said.

The waitress asked him, 'What would you like to order, sir?'

He asked me what I was having.

I said, 'Less fun than I was before you came.'

Unmoved, he turned to Dad. 'What are you having?'

'He's not having the mixed grill,' Doreen said.

'Gammon and bloody pineapple,' Dad said.

'I'll have gammon and bloody pineapple,' Stuart told the waitress, 'and a pint of bitter.'

The waitress eyed us warily as though at the aquarium, watching piranha nibble at each other. 'Chips or jacket potato?' she said to Stuart.

'Chips, of course. Who comes out and has a jacket potato?'

'Jacqueline does,' Doreen said.

'*Jackie* happens to like jacket potatoes,' I said.

He said to me, 'I hope there's Bacardi in that Coke.'

'Don't *you* start,' I said.

Still, contrary to all my expectations, when our plates arrived, the mood at the table shifted to something more pleasant and it was Stuart's arrival that had shifted it. Everyone was happy with their meals when they came, even if Doreen wasn't happy with other people's. We passed the salt and pepper like civilised folks. I donated two onion rings to Stuart. And when Dad wanted sauce for his chips, Doreen waved down the waitress who tiptoed over in case she got drawn into battle then seemed relieved at the request for ketchup.

Stuart began to offer more intelligent conversation than Dad or Doreen had brought with them. As the minutes ticked by and the chips went down, both were disappearing from us into lovey-doveyness, kissing and holding hands, their brains left empty of oxygen as their bodies' resources fled to their vital organs. 'A bottle of Mateus Rosé, please,' Doreen said, putting her hand over Dad's mouth.

This left Stuart my only choice of companion and he seemed at least to have arrived sober. I remembered Mrs Collingworth's carpe diem advice and vowed to squeeze the best out of his presence, even if he had taken up room in Dad's flat with that presence and in Amanda's womb with his offspring.

I was surprised when he asked about my psychology lessons and what I studied in them. 'I've heard of Freud,' he said. 'Isn't he the Oedipus complex man?' And shock made me chatty as I explained what I'd learned. He listened, his brown eyes on me.

Doreen interrupted, her words slurred. 'What the bloody hell is she on about?' And he said, 'Give it a rest, Mum.' She shrugged and turned back to Dad. The table was very much them and us.

'Repression means trying to exclude unpleasant or unacceptable thoughts from your consciousness,' I said to Stuart.

'I know what repression is. I'm not a complete dumbo. I told you already I was doing A levels.'

'You didn't tell me you'd started them. You said you were *going* to. Why did you stop?'

He slurped from his drink. 'I wasn't putting the time in.' He dropped his voice. 'My dad pulled me out of school to do something "useful" instead.' He sounded sour. 'That's when I started at the garage.'

'Why weren't you putting the time in?'

'Because I'm lazy?'

'You said it, not me.'

'And because – well – warring parents, and all that goes with that. School took a back seat.'

He glanced at Doreen but she was talking to Dad, in between letting him kiss her neck, about whether they could afford desserts.

'We can't come to the Berni and not have a pudding,' Dad was saying, so he was drunk enough not to remember that he was skint.

'Black Forest gateau all round, then!' Doreen said, triumphantly, when the waitress came, before any of us could ask for apple pie. We let her. I knew how Dad felt sometimes in the face of her bloody-mindedness.

Stuart said to me, as we were eating our gateau, 'My dad thinks A levels are for posh kids. You're lucky with yours.'

We both looked at Dad.

'In that sense, anyway,' Stuart said. He grinned and I couldn't help smiling back.

After the meal, the waitress arrived with the bill and it turned out that Stuart's offer to pay his share would need to be delayed due to lack of funds, and perhaps lack of integrity. I was disappointed in him.

I took out my wage packet and Dad was about to accept my offer but was shouted down by Doreen. Dad and Doreen began sniping at each other, tempers frayed, voices raised – forgive me if I don't lay out all the detail – so the waitress called the manager who extracted payment from Dad with a threat to call the police then escorted us out.

We travelled home on the bus together in near-silence. Stuart and I sat behind Dad and Doreen. Their lolling heads told a tale. Also, the talk Stuart and I had been having had seemed possible at the Berni but not now. He smoked three cigarettes, hard and desperate, as though each one didn't offer what he'd expected.

*

Later, I left everyone sleeping and caught the bus to the Walls'
for five thirty. They'd hung eighteenth-birthday balloons on
the front door.

'Here's the birthday girl!' Bridget said, as I entered the
house. She was in a matching yellow skirt and jumper and
wore clip-on flower earrings but her feet were in slippers,
not the usual soft shoes she wore for at-home occasions.
It was as though she'd made so much effort with the skirt
and jumper that she'd run out of energy to sort anything
below the knee. Next time, perhaps, she'd go without tights.
Parkinson's was cruel.

Nick, wearing a frilly apron, and not looking like Nick,
came from the kitchen to greet me. He bent to peck me on the
cheek before I could protest. 'Happy birthday, pet.'

'You're taking liberties.' I took off my coat. 'Is she here?'

'Upstairs,' he said. 'Sleeping, I think. She's always nap-
ping these days. She climbs into bed after college and sleeps
much of the weekend. Goodness knows what's tiring her out.'

'Perhaps all the socialising.'

'That's slackened off lately,' Bridget said. 'You don't
know why, do you?'

'I can't help you, I'm afraid,' I said, sincerely.

I'd sat for an hour in the school library the previous week
after school and made notes on a book about pregnancy I'd
dared not take out in case the librarian sent a note of concern
to Mrs Collingworth in the form register. Warwick Grammar's library walls had ears. One girl in the fifth year had
borrowed a book on venereal diseases and had consequently
earned six sessions with Nursey B and a few lessons off to
visit the clinic. People found out and no one would sit next
to her, not having listened in sex education, presumably, to
how VD got spread.

Amanda was still in what was called the first trimester, I'd
worked out. Tiredness. Nausea. Breast enlargement (which

would have pleased her were it not for the associated surprise child). I couldn't remember the others.

'Maybe she's working hard at college,' I ventured.

'Maybe I'm a lizard,' Nick said.

Bridget said, 'Darling!'

I sat on the sofa and she sat next to me, lowering herself down as though a sudden jolt would snap her. Nick poured four glasses of pineapple juice and brought them in. 'The birthday meal will be served at six,' he announced, and went back into the kitchen.

Amanda came downstairs, her hair in a tangle and a red pillow mark on one cheek. She was in green striped punk-free pyjamas. She curled up in an armchair and rubbed at her eyes.

'Morning,' I said.

I hadn't seen her since mid-February when she'd told me about the pregnancy. I couldn't see any evidence of it on her abdomen but the book had said that might not happen until much later, perhaps six months along.

I could have been imagining it, but despite having crawled out of bed, her skin seemed different. Brighter and glowing, as though she'd had a facial.

I didn't know what to say to her that was safe in front of Bridget and Nick. Any question could have led to mishap.

'How's college?' I began.

'As shit as usual,' she said, so that was the end of that. She could at least have played ball.

Okay, so, how's the pregnancy, then? was on the tip of my annoyed tongue.

Nick came in, drying his hands on a towel. 'What's the birthday girl been up to so far?'

'I went with Dad to the Berni Inn,' I said.

'Oh. You didn't have steak, did you?'

I should have thought. Steak was Nick's fail-safe recipe. But I hadn't known he was doing the cooking.

I didn't feel I could lie. The room was fraught with lies. 'I never mind having steak twice.'

'I could find a chicken Kiev in the freezer,' he said.

'We should have asked,' Bridget said. She hated culinary crises like this.

'I didn't know I was going until we were there. It was a secret.'

'How lovely,' Bridget said. Translation: *How surprising that your dad is behaving like a proper parent.*

'If you really don't mind another steak,' Nick said, 'I'm about to grill them.'

'Are we having jacket potatoes?'

'Chips.'

'There you go, then. I had jacket potato at the Berni.'

See? I said to Doreen in my head.

Amanda yawned, wide and loud, and I caught the yawn from her. I did feel weary. It took it out of me, being with the three of them, treading softly, watching for trip hazards.

Still, at least the causes for my tiredness wouldn't last nine months, or perhaps nine years. Nineteen years? When did parents stop worrying? It wasn't happening for the Walls.

'I've made a Black Forest gateau for pudding,' Bridget said, 'in case you think I've made Nick do everything.'

'I wouldn't think that,' I said.

'And I sliced the beef tomatoes.'

'I love beef tomatoes.'

'And I refilled the pepper pot.'

If she kept going, I thought, she'd soon get down to the lighting of the oven or the turning on of a tap. But I knew why it was happening and it was tragic, watching her cling on to basic tasks like someone hanging on to a cliff edge, letting go, inch by inch, and unable to save themselves.

Amanda seemed more her normal self during the meal and ate her steak and half of mine. Spotless was under the table, keen to help, but ignored.

Bridget said to Amanda, 'You have such an appetite these days!'

I offered to slice the gateau so that I could give myself a

tiny piece. I noticed Bridget glance my way and was sure she was about to say, *Did you have Black Forest gateau at the Berni Inn, too?* so I said, 'I sold more doughnuts than anyone else this morning,' and she took the bait.

'They'll make a baker of you yet,' she said.

'Except that I want to be a poet.'

She looked worried. 'Can poets earn livings? So many have died young.'

I added, 'Or perhaps a psychologist – and a poet in my spare time.'

She seemed reassured.

After the meal, Bridget seemed determined to clear up our gateau plates but it meant her walking to the kitchen, using both hands to hold them, with no free hand with which to steady herself. She stumbled as she reached the kitchen and two plates fell. One landed on the kitchen lino and broke in half.

Spotless whined from under the table.

Bridget cried, suddenly and loud, like a child would.

Nick rushed to pick up the broken plate before she stepped on it in her slippers. Amanda took the rest of the plates from her – although there was a tussle, Bridget unwilling to let go of anything at all.

I said, 'Let's sit down, Bridget.'

She followed me to the sofa. 'Stupid, stupid,' she said, pulling a handkerchief from her sleeve and dabbing her eyes. 'I thought I could hold on.'

Spotless loped over to Bridget and put his chin on her knee.

'I need a newspaper to wrap the bits in,' Nick said, coming in to fetch one from the magazine rack. 'At least we decided against the best china, darling.'

'It doesn't matter what china it was,' Bridget sniffled. 'It's not that the *china* is broken. It's that—'

We waited for her to say it. But she didn't need to, and I'm glad the words didn't make it into the room because the curtains and carpets and polished surfaces and the dust-free books and everything which had been cared for by Bridget might have wept until the morning.

I helped Nick wash up while Amanda stayed with her mother, leafing through magazines, then we sat around the coffee table on which was a small pile of presents.

Nick said, 'Your lad phoned us.'

'Who? Kevin?'

'Is there another one?'

'No. But we're not really going out at the moment.'

'He didn't give that impression. He rang and said he didn't have your new address. I didn't think it was right to tell him so he came round here.' He pointed to a paper bag on the pile.

I picked it up.

'Open it then,' Bridget said. 'We all need a cheer-up.'

Inside the bag was a card and a wrapped present which felt like a book. I opened the card. I didn't read it out. It said, against a picture of a bouquet of flowers, *To someone special*, and inside he'd written, *To Jackie. I miss you. Love, Kevin.*

'What does it say?' Amanda said.

'Nothing unusual,' I said.

'Open the present.'

It was *The Bell Jar* by Sylvia Plath.

'Didn't she gas herself?' Amanda said.

'Well, that is cheering,' said Bridget. 'What a strange birthday present.'

'It's an autobiographical novel,' I said. 'Kevin knows I love her poetry.'

'Is her poetry any happier?' she said.

'I could quote you some lines.'

'Don't worry, dear,' she said. 'I think I'd rather have a sherry.'

'On a Saturday?' Sherry was a Sunday drink in this house.

'Would you like a drop?' Nick said to Amanda.

'If you are,' she said.

'What about you?' Nick said to me. 'Now you're legal.'

'No, thanks. Anyway, I wasn't born until eleven p.m. so technically I'm not.' I wished I'd remembered this earlier for Doreen.

Nick poured the sherries and I opened three presents from Nick and Bridget: some coconut-scented bath bubbles, hand cream and shampoo.

'I bought them in town,' Bridget said, 'and wrapped them.'

'They're perfect. I love coconut products.'

Amanda gave me coconut-scented soap.

'What a coincidence,' Bridget said. 'You went to Boots as well.'

'Mum,' Amanda said. 'She's not daft.'

By eight o'clock, Amanda was yawning again. 'The sherry's made me sleepy,' she said, patting her lower abdomen absent-mindedly.

Her mother laughed. 'It won't be down there already, darling.'

A near miss.

Nick offered to drive me home. I gathered my presents and cards together.

'I won't come to the door,' Bridget said. She was folding a blanket across her lap.

Outside, a mean and stinging sleet was falling. 'Another birthday done and dusted,' Nick said as he started the car. 'Did you enjoy yourself?'

I said, 'I had a lovely time.'

At home, I peered around the living room door. Dad and Doreen were asleep on the sofa, snoring in front of the TV, and Stuart was massacring prawn cocktail crisps. The coffee table looked forlorn under its weight of bottles and glasses. I thought back to the inch of sherry that the Walls had drunk, thinking themselves rebellious.

'I'm off to bed,' I said, quietly.

'Happy dreams, sweet pea,' Stuart said.

I put my nightie on and sat in bed to read and reread Kevin's card, tracing his words with my fingers, and then I started *The Bell Jar*. I hadn't read it out to the Walls but he'd written inside the book, *Because you're going to be a famous poet, too.*

SUNDAY 2 MARCH

Marion and Harry's house, where Patsy was staying, was ten minutes' walk from Dad's. 'Come round on Sunday afternoon,' she'd said on the phone during the week. 'I'll make you a *cake*.'

'Remember I don't like fruit cakes.'

'I know.'

I said, 'You need to check with Marion and Harry that it's okay.'

'They won't mind,' she said. 'I've told them how sensible you are.'

'I meant, check they'll let you in the kitchen to make a cake.'

She screeched a laugh and I heard Marion call, 'Patsy, dear. Please.'

I rang the bell of a semi-detached house with a brick archway over a small outdoor porch. A woman answered, dressed in a winter coat and scarf. She was round and friendly. I tried hard not to look too closely at her dyed hair.

She stepped out of the house. 'Jackie, presumably,' she said. 'We're just off to see family.' She pointed to a car in which a man in a jacket sat at the wheel, waving. I waved back, self-conscious.

'Thanks for letting me come,' I said to Marion.

'Patsy said you were sensible.'

Strange, how easy it is to project an impression, meanwhile being everything but. Had I been sensible, I wouldn't have been carrying around untruths in every pocket and seam and hem and trim of myself.

She smiled. 'Happy eighteenth.'

I heard the thump of footsteps on stairs as I stepped into the house and Patsy appeared in the spacious hall, wearing jeans and a tight orange top and with her hair in rollers. I shut the front door. 'Happy *birthday*!' she said.

She pulled me into a large, rectangular living room with a bay window. In the bay was a table on which sat a huge chocolate cake, dotted with candles and girded by a pink ribbon, next to two small plates and flowered napkins. 'I'll confess now,' she said. 'Marion made it. I did cream the butter and the sugar with the electric whisk but she wasn't happy when it wouldn't stay in the bowl so she told me to go away.'

'It's a giant cake.'

'She doesn't do small cooking. I'm bulging out of my clothes like a burst sausage.'

'A startling image.'

'I'll get a knife,' she said, and I held my breath as she ran out of the room, tugged a drawer out of its moorings, slammed it, and came back in with a long carving knife. I stood back.

'Shall I be mother?' she said, but before I could reply she'd dug the knife in and was cutting slices that would each feed four and a surprise guest. She slid them inexpertly onto the plates. 'Cake is *served*!'

She hadn't lit the candles but I didn't like to interrupt. They were falling out of the slices she'd cut, though. 'Bugger it!' she said.

'It doesn't matter.'

'We can light the rest.' She ran back into the kitchen. Another drawer received ill treatment.

'Make a wish,' she said, once she'd lit those that had remained upright.

I wished silently that Dad would stop drinking and that life would return to normal.

'Do it out loud,' she mumbled through a mouthful of cake.

'That's not how this works.'

'Please.'

'Okay. I wish we could settle back into Mason Street soon.'

I sat in an armchair and started my fat wedge of cake, wondering how I'd finish it.

She sat on the sofa, attacking hers. Crumbs escaped from her plate like kamikaze pilots and who could blame them?

'How old were you when your mum died?' she said.

A Patsy U-turn.

'I was twelve. She had cancer.'

'Is that when you got a social worker?'

'No, later. Dad wasn't very good at coping after she'd died.'

'He was a pisshead, wasn't he?'

I flinched. 'That's one word for it. But he'd got depressed after a car accident lost him his job. So there was that as well.'

'Do you have any aunties or uncles?' She put her empty plate on the floor.

'One aunt in New Zealand.'

'That's no help.'

'Not for everyday needs, no. But we write to each other. What about you? Aunties, I mean.'

'There's one in Ireland.'

Somehow I felt she'd wanted to get this auntie into the conversation.

'Is she a help?'

She stood. 'Let's get some tea on.'

In the kitchen, I picked at my cake and watched her fill the kettle to its limits, struggling to lift it onto the hob. I estimated boiling point would arrive around midnight.

'Is she?' I said. 'Helpful?'

She sloshed milk into two mugs and put the bottle back in the fridge without its cap. 'I stayed with her a couple of years ago. She was a help then.'

'She fostered you?'

'Sort of.'

Now, I couldn't work out whether she wanted to talk about this aunt or not. The signals weren't clear.

'She lives by the sea,' she said.

'Free holidays!'

'It wasn't so much a holiday.' She sounded sad.

She picked up a tea towel and began drying what was on the drainer. Then she dabbed at her eyes with the cloth and I realised she was crying.

'What's up, Patsy?' I put down my plate and went over to her, wondering what to do. She bent her head into my shoulder. I was worried that the rollers would attach themselves to my jumper, like burrs, and that I would be attached to Patsy for ever.

But she stepped back after a few seconds.

'I miss her,' she said, taking in a huge, juddering breath as though trying to control the tears. It didn't work. 'I miss her every day.'

It seemed she must have been closer to the aunt than she'd suggested.

I took the tea towel off her and gave her my handkerchief. 'Let's go and sit down while we wait for the kettle.'

She blew her nose and shook her head. 'No, it's fine. I've got a card and present for ya.'

She ran into the hall and upstairs. I picked up the kettle and emptied half the water out, putting it back on the hob.

A couple of minutes later, she came back and thrust an envelope in my hands. 'There's your card.' The ink on the envelope was wet and came off on my fingers. 'Sorry it looks like a card for an old lady. It was the only one Marion had.'

I opened it. 'Thank you.'

'And here's your present.' She gave me a brown paper bag.

I looked inside the bag and pulled out a toy baby gorilla, like Weston, only twenty times smaller.

'I thought Weston might like a child,' she said. 'Happy birthday.'

I stroked it. 'I love this. Thank you!'

She blew her nose again.

'Are you okay now?' I said.

'You're a bit shit with people crying, aren't you?'

'I'm sorry.'

'I'll have more cake instead, when the kettle's boiled.'

As if it had heard, the kettle began to hum and then whistle.

'That was quick,' she said. 'It usually takes ages when I make tea.'

At home, I introduced Weston to his offspring. 'What shall we call her?' I asked him, and he suggested that I should name her, as I'd named him, after the place he and I had first met – Weston-super-Mare.

Super-Mary now sat beside him on my chest of drawers.

MONDAY 3 MARCH

Every time I'd opened *The Bell Jar* over the weekend, the turns of the pages themselves had words to say and they said, *Why have you let go of someone so precious?*

And it wasn't just Kevin. I had seldom spoken to Kim lately.

The passive construction is more accurate: I had seldom been spoken to by Kim.

We shared no academic classes in sixth form and, although I still sat to her left in Mrs Collingworth's form room, Kim was friends with the girl on her right. Most registration periods, when we were allowed to talk, my view was of the back of her head, her shiny blonde hair bobbing as she chatted. Once, overhearing her conversation, I'd said, 'You never told me about that,' and her head whipped round as though I'd touched her with a hot poker.

Molly said to me on Monday as we waited for Mrs Collingworth to arrive to English, 'Should I talk to Kim for you?'

'It won't do any good.'

'You don't know until you try,' she said.

She reported back the following day at break time.

'Kim says Kevin has started writing terrible poetry.'

'Poetry? That's not Kevin.'

'Apparently it's Spurned Kevin.'

'You're making this worse. What else did she say?'

'She was about to make it up with you but when he started writing the poetry she changed her mind as they're all about heartbreak.'

'Is she serious?'

'Completely serious. She says you've destroyed him.'

'Why won't she say these things to me in person?'

'I think she's torn. She'd feel treasonous, talking to you.'

'Treason's a bit strong. I'm not Guy Fawkes.'

'She actually mentioned Guy Fawkes.'

'She did not.'

Molly grinned. 'Honest, I think she'll come round.'

THURSDAY 6 MARCH

The next day, I met Heather in The Eatery after school. We took the one free table. A coachload of pensioners had taken over the rest, spooning jam onto huge scones and comparing various Warwick Castle mementoes they'd collected. Their many woollen coats draped over their chairs, making the café seem soft-furnished for the day.

We'd ordered tea and toasted teacakes and Heather asked me how Dad's job-hunting was going since he'd signed on at the dole office.

'I think he said something about an interview,' I said.

It was true. He'd said, 'I hope I get an interview for that one.'

'Is he managing, money-wise?' she said.

'We've cut down the caviar and oysters.'

She smiled. 'And how are things with you?'

I hesitated. The list of things I couldn't say was now so complex, like knitting out of control.

'So-so. Plodding on.'

'That's an old person's phrase,' she said, dropping her voice.

'What's the young person's equivalent? I can't think.'

The waitress brought our tea. We waited while she arranged it on the table.

Heather said, 'Maybe "nothing unusual has happened".'

This tested my integrity. What defined unusual these days?

'I'll stick with plodding on,' I said. 'I've never been trendy anyway.'

'Okay.'

'I've been writing a poem,' I said, 'if you'd like to hear it.'

'Oh.'

'You're not a poetry fan.'

'It's not that. It's not the kind of news I expected.'

Me neither, Heather. I'd seized on it to fill a gap.

'It's either that, or I read you my class notes on schizophrenia.'

'I'll take the poetry. Actually, I don't mind some Patience Strong.'

The teacakes arrived. 'I really do mind Patience Strong,' I said. 'Too cheesy. Please don't quote any or I won't be able to eat this.'

She laughed. 'Let's hear yours, then. What's it about?'

I reached into my satchel for my poetry exercise book. I'd worked on the poem in the school library at dinner time. 'It's about the park.'

'What's it called?'

'I don't know yet. I haven't decided.'

'Right.'

'It needs improvement, but here goes.'

It felt alien, reading poetry to Heather.

The river is a soft arm
lying quiet along the length
of the park's body.

People walk, following its stretch,
as swans pride their way
past nervy coots.

I was pausing, as Mrs Collingworth said we should, between verses.

'I like the swan description,' Heather said.

'There are two more verses.'

'Sorry.'

I continued.

A willow dips into the water
while sparrows wait for news
within its greenness.

A child falls. Its cries
split the calm of the day
into shards.

I closed the exercise book and slid it into my satchel.

She said, 'I was enjoying that until the last verse. But then—'

'Sorry. You're supposed to be lulled into a false sense of security and then plunged into despair.'

'In that case, it worked beautifully. I hope that doesn't reflect your current mood.'

'It's not necessarily autobiographical.'

'I see. Not necessarily. I recognise the park, though.'

'Try not to.'

'I'm sorry I interrupted. It's the same at classical concerts when you're not supposed to clap between movements.'

'I've never been to a classical concert,' I said.

'No.'

'I didn't mind being interrupted. At least it's a response.'

She looked at her watch. She'd only eaten half of her teacake. 'I'm afraid I have to go promptly today to visit a family on my case list.'

I tried to look disappointed. 'Never mind. What time did you say you'd be there?'

'I didn't. I'm dropping in unexpectedly. There are things they're not telling me.'

I stood and pulled on my coat. 'I can walk back from here.'

'If you're sure.'

'You have a difficult job, don't you?'

'It relies on people being more honest,' she said. 'I'm not a mind reader.'

FRIDAY 7 MARCH

'You're quiet,' I said to Molly as we packed our bags after English, Friday's last lesson. Mrs Collingworth had split the class into pairs for discussion about a scene in *All My Sons* and I'd been paired with Molly.

I'd asked Molly at one point, 'The characters say one thing and mean another, don't you think?'

'Maybe,' she'd said, playing with a pen.

In the girls' cloakroom, Molly and I unhooked our coats. 'You don't have to talk about it,' I said.

'You mean, tell you everything.'

'Has something happened?'

She took such a deep breath. 'I'm moving up to Northumberland.'

'What?'

'My aunt lives there. She's been staying with us for a fortnight and now all hell's broken loose. We're going to live with her so she can look after Mum.'

'Oh.' I'd expected her to say, 'I have a headache'. or 'I didn't sleep well last night'.

She fastened the toggles on her duffle coat. 'We were managing. Mostly.'

'Has your mum got worse?'

She said, 'I've been trying not to notice.'

I understood. 'Sometimes it's easier.'

'Easier but not best for anyone,' she said, sighing, 'or so my auntie says.' She checked her watch. 'I have to get my bus.'

We walked out of the school building together towards the row of buses, some of their engines rumbling, headlights on as the day began to fade.

'Mine's not here yet,' she said.

'I'll wait with you.' We sat on the low wall that bordered the car park and pulled our coats tighter against the cold. 'What about your A levels?'

'I'm going to a school near my aunt's. Somewhere called Alnwick.'

'Oh. After Easter?'

'No,' she said. 'My last lesson is next Friday.'

'But – that's in one week!'

'My auntie doesn't hang about.'

We watched in silence for a minute or so as a teacher tried to corral the restless pupils queuing for Molly's bus. Other buses trundled off with their cargo.

'What will I do?' It sounded whining and selfish but I felt whining and selfish.

'You've got Kim, and Kevin,' she said, and paused, 'if you can hold on to them.'

'Whoa!'

'I don't mean to be harsh, but—'

'Have you been wanting to say that all this time?'

'No,' she said. 'I really do sympathise. But – it can be maddening, the way you hold him off. And you lost Kim as a result.'

I was stung.

She said, 'Do you remember when I was the smelly girl in the third year poetry club?'

'You weren't smelly.'

'Don't lie.'

'Not that smelly. And it wasn't your fault.'

'You agreed to be my friend,' she said.

'I liked you.'

'What if I'd said I didn't need friends?'

'That's silly.'

'So you can see it when it's other people.'

'It's not the same.'

A bus turned into the school gates, its headlights making us blink.

She said, 'If I had someone like Kevin wanting me as a girlfriend, I wouldn't think twice.'

'He wants me to let him – do more things.'

'Of course he does. But if you say no, he'll wait.'

'He says so.'

'Kim thinks the same.'

'You talk to Kim about this? I didn't know there was a committee.'

She said, 'Did you know Kim has to have an operation?'

'Why?'

'Her heavy periods. I think it's called endo-something.'

'She never said.'

'She won't, will she? You're not exactly on menstruation terms.'

'Ouch.'

'That's my bus,' she said, standing up, 'but think about it. I need to know you and Kim are friends before I go.'

I watched her climb on. She waved when she'd found a seat and stuck out her tongue.

Amanda had told me that she had to stay after college for a hairdressing demonstration and would go to a classmate's house after that. So, I set off to arrive at the Walls' for five thirty, determined to spill the pregnancy beans. What Molly had said about doing what's best for everyone surely applied to foster sisters and, if Molly could be brave and move away to Northumberland, I could be brave, too.

I would start, I decided on the bus, by asking about progress on the house's extension. Bridget had come round to the idea, Nick had said on the phone. 'I sold it to her because it means you can stay whenever you like.'

I would then say that there was a further reason for extra rooms that they might want to consider and, when they asked me the reason, I'd say because Amanda is having a baby and you'll need a nursery. If Amanda later asked – *when* Amanda later asked – why I'd told Nick and Bridget her secret, I could honestly say they'd asked me a question and I couldn't lie outright.

Who's the father? they might ask, but this was Amanda's story to tell, and I intended to be far away when she did.

Despite my forward planning, each time the bus stopped, I considered jumping off and catching one the opposite way, so, when I arrived at the house, I surprised even myself.

I took out my key. 'Hello,' I called from the hallway.

'Up here,' I heard Nick shout, and the panic in his voice propelled me up the stairs.

Bridget was lying on their bedroom carpet, her body bent in a strange position beside the bed. She seemed asleep. Nick was kneeling next to her, his hand on her shoulder.

'What happened?' I threw my satchel down and crouched beside them.

Nick's eyes were wide, like a child's. 'I'm waiting for an ambulance. She came upstairs to fetch something. I heard a crash and she yelled out.'

'Is she unconscious?'

'I think she's banged her head on the bedside table.'

I needed to be able to help. 'Shall I put some things in a bag for her?'

'I don't think she'll be hungry.'

'No, I mean knickers, toothpaste—'

He looked distracted. 'There's a bag in the wardrobe.' He waved his hand, not in the direction of the wardrobe.

It felt intrusive, looking through their chest of drawers to find underwear, a nightie and socks. I unhooked Bridget's new dressing gown from the back of the door and added it to the bag then fetched her pink toothbrush and toothpaste from the bathroom.

She had one slipper on. I slid the other back onto her foot.

We sat in silence, watching Bridget's breathing together, until we heard a siren's wail.

'I'll run and flag them down,' I said.

Outside, the ambulance was parking up, its siren tamed although its lights still on. I waved my arms anyway to confirm they were at the right house, and so that I could tell Nick I had.

Neighbours came to their doors or peeked from behind curtains. Ken from next door shuffled down his path and called, 'What's happened, love?'

'Bridget,' I said. It would have to do.

Two ambulancemen hurried towards me, one young, one much older and burlier. Each carried a bag. 'Are you the patient?' said the younger man, his face earnest.

'She's been waving like a flag in a gale, mate,' his companion said, moving towards the front door. 'Sorry, love. He's new.'

'She's upstairs,' I said, and followed them in.

I watched from the landing as they knelt by Bridget, listening to her heart, checking her pulse. Nick told them what he'd told me.

'She's got Parkinson's,' I heard him add.

'I see,' said the older ambulanceman. 'Bless her.'

'I should have come upstairs with her,' Nick said.

'You can't be everywhere, son,' said the man, which made me gulp something down that there was no time for.

Bridget was brought downstairs on a stretcher. She was beginning to wake up but was mumbling and restless.

'Don't worry about the potatoes, love,' I heard Nick say.

I stood and watched with him as they settled her in the ambulance. They'd asked him to wait. He held the bag I'd packed for Bridget, to which I'd added items from her handbag: a comb, lipstick, a tiny mirror.

Nick's face was pale under the street light outside their house. The glare picked out its contours, making him seem unearthly.

'Do you know which classmate's house Amanda has gone to?' I said.

'She didn't tell us. We've stopped asking. I didn't even know it was a classmate.' I thought he might cry.

'Should I stay here and wait for her?'

'You're a love,' he said.

'Have you got your wallet and keys?'

He looked at me as though he didn't understand the question. 'What?'

'I'll fetch them.' In the house, his jacket, the keys and wallet in the pockets, was on the back of a chair.

Five minutes later, the ambulance drew away, its light still flashing, and the neighbours dropped their net curtains or shut their front doors to resume watching *Nationwide* and get the tea on.

Ken, though, had waited on his front step. 'Did she have a fall?'

'She'll be all right,' I said, to reassure us both.

In the kitchen, I found Spotless, oblivious in his bed in the corner, very much not a rescue dog.

Two pans were simmering on the hob, one with potatoes and one carrots. The vegetables were soft and ready. For something to do, I added butter and milk to the potatoes and mashed them in the way I thought Bridget would have. I put the mash in a large Tupperware container, using a smaller one for the carrots. In the fridge were three pork chops on a plate under a piece of kitchen foil, and a bowl of defrosted apple sauce.

It felt unnatural to do all this, as it had foraging through Bridget's chest of drawers. She hated presenting aspects of herself unfinished or unpolished. Rarely would she leave anything for others to complete, if she could help it. Sometimes, these days, she couldn't help it.

I sat on the sofa, eating Jelly Babies I had in my satchel. I hadn't sat in this house alone since I'd left to move into Mason Street. My status had been visitor since then, however welcome.

At nine o'clock, I heard Amanda's key in the door. I went to greet her. She smelled of smoke and cider and not at all of concerned expectant mother. 'Oh,' she said. 'You're still here.'

'Come and sit down.'

'I need my bed. I'm tired.'

'Come and sit down,' I said, in my best Mrs Collingworth.

She cried as I told her what had happened, and I had a lump in my throat that seemed too big for it. She said, 'Should I go to the hospital?'

'No. Your dad said wait. He'd phone.'

'I hate waiting.'

'Let's put the telly on. It'll fill the gaps. Do you need something to eat? You're eating for two, remember.'

'I don't want to remember,' she said.

In some ways, it was like old times. Amanda and I, as we had when I'd lived there, watching *Hawaii Five-O* together with our minds instead on whatever crisis her parents were having. Amanda flicked through *Just Seventeen* magazine but I knew she wasn't reading.

In other ways, they were new times. Amanda was pregnant, only three people knew, I was one of them, and now the idea of revealing this to Nick and Bridget seemed as farcical as it had earlier, on the bus, seemed logical.

I dialled my dad's number. 'I'm going to be late home,' I said, 'in case you were worried.'

'Okay, pet.' He put the receiver down before I could explain why.

At ten thirty, the phone rang. Amanda ran to the kitchen to answer it then came back to say, 'Dad's home in twenty minutes. They're keeping Mum in for tests. What's concussion?'

'When you bang your head and go unconscious, I think. Shall I look it up?'

'No, you're bound to be right.'

'Is she awake?'

'Yes, but talking strange.'

'That's probably temporary.'

She took a deep breath in and let it out again. 'I wasn't here.'

'How were you to know?' I said, but perhaps she was talking more generally. 'She's in the best place.'

'People always say that,' she said, 'almost as though someone's already floated to paradise.'

'Wow.'

She grinned. 'That was a bit poetic, wasn't it?'

'I'm proud.'

'Of that, anyway,' she said, chewing the inside of her mouth.

I pulled on my coat. 'Better go for the bus.'

'Dad said he'd take you.'

'It's okay. He'll be knackered.'

'I'm glad you were here,' she said.

Don't be, I thought. I came round to grass you up.

FRIDAY 14 MARCH

I'd phoned Nick on Saturday, Sunday and Monday to ask how Bridget was and he'd said they were running tests. On Tuesday afternoon, he'd phoned me to say that she had been sent home. 'She'll be fine,' he said, 'but it's set her back.'

'Shall I still come round on Friday? I'll bring her some flowers.'

'It's the Chelsea Flower Show here already. Amanda cleaned the florist out.'

'Okay, shall I come early and help cook?'

'We'll have fish and chips,' he said.

I hurried to say, 'I'll fetch them on my way there. I know what we all like.'

'You're an angel.'

I wanted to feel helpful. In other ways, I felt anything but. Nick and Bridget needed to know about Amanda's pregnancy, but if I didn't feel I could tell them, how would Amanda? I'd read a magazine article once at the dentist about women whose families only knew of their pregnancies when they were on their backs on the bathroom floor in a puddle of fluid and the baby's head appearing if not already off to primary school. Bridget and Nick didn't deserve this.

I'd add some mushy peas and pickled eggs to the order, I decided.

*

That morning, I was about to leave for school, hauling an overstuffed satchel onto my shoulder. I was sure the old satchel had held more, having stretched and loosened since the third year when the Walls had bought it for me.

'That looks heavy, chuck,' Doreen said from the kitchen. She was dressed for work in her checked tabard and flat shoes, eating toast while standing in the doorway.

'It's a body,' I said. 'It wouldn't fit in my drawer.'

She ignored me. I think she had her own joke ready and wanted to deliver it. 'I thought maybe you had the kitchen sink in there.' She looked back towards our sink melodramatically.

You couldn't fault her effort sometimes. But I wasn't in the mood. I decided on frankness. 'Two exams at school today, so I had to bring my books home to revise last night.'

I could sense her thinking back to the previous day. I'd taken refuge in my room as soon as I'd come home from school, told Doreen I didn't need any tea, and hadn't emerged except for the bathroom. I'd bought Tuc biscuits, a bottle of cola and a Crunchie from the shop. Friday would bring a two-hour history exam in the morning and a two-hour English exam in the afternoon. There'd been a psychology exam the previous week. About all of them, I felt the way condemned prisoners feel. They know they're going down. The question is whether it's thirty years or forty.

As ideal settings for revision go, however, Number 12 Landor Court wasn't up there with libraries or quiet corners in bookshops.

There'd been an ongoing all-evening row between Dad, Doreen and Stuart. It was like listening to a radio play that you hated from the opening lines but you couldn't reach the dial to turn it off.

Before tea, Stuart had dropped a beer glass in the kitchen and had proved yet again that he wasn't made for a career in hospitality by sweeping it up without sweeping it up. Dad had gone in with bare feet and yelled when he'd trodden on the shards. Doreen tried to pick bits out of Dad's feet with her eyebrow tweezers, saying, 'Keep bloody still,' while he, it sounded like, thrashed about, accusing her of pushing glass into his feet rather than pulling it out.

'Why would I do that?' she'd shouted.

'Why do you bloody do anything?' he'd replied.

All of their interactions were conducted at the kind of high volume that alcohol fuels, as though as it sloshes past the vocal cords it turns them up a notch.

The furore died down but started up again when Dad realised that Doreen had bought four steaks to cook for tea with money from his tin where he was now keeping his dole money once he'd cashed his giro at the post office. She'd promised not to take money from the tin which is why there'd been a temporary truce of sorts.

In my absence, Dad ate my steak too at the same time as railing against the price of it. Doreen said, still loud, 'No problem guzzling it down, then?'

'I would have had half of that if I'd been asked,' I heard Stuart complain.

'You weren't,' Dad told him.

'Who wants Bakewell tart?' Doreen said, but in the tone you'd use to say, *Who wants a slap?*

She knocked on my door, saying, 'There's Bakewell tart going spare,' but I said, 'It's not the only one,' and she left me alone.

For the rest of the evening, they'd sniped over what to watch on telly and who should get up to replenish the drinks, then indulged in some drunken, futile political opinions while watching the news. Eventually, they'd all crashed into bed around eleven o'clock, and I'd utilised the small hours to finish my revision, turning my light out when my clock said two thirty.

If it had been a one-off, that would have been something. But there'd been several similar evenings. The telly stayed on regardless, the sniping continuing over Dave Allen's jokes. Sometimes Doreen would throw an insult or Dad an accusation and then there'd be audience applause except that Allen was timing that deliberately and Dad and Doreen by accident.

Now, Doreen rinsed her toast plate and said, 'I hope we didn't disturb you too much.'

I left her to think it through and let myself out of the front door.

I heard her call, 'Good luck!' as I shut it, and Dad's voice from the bedroom saying, 'Good luck with what?' I had mentioned my mock exams to him but perhaps the memory had been sluiced away by the drink along with the volume control.

I came across Molly in the corridor after registration. It was her last day. She had insisted on sitting all her tests despite this. 'The new school said some marks would be useful,' she'd said.

'You can have my marks,' I'd said. 'I don't want them.'

'I bet you'll do better than you think.'

'I bet you'll lose all your money.'

'Shall we meet up at break time?' I suggested now, leaning against the wall to let pupils past on their way to lessons. 'I'm seeing a teacher at dinner time.'

This wasn't strictly true. I had another appointment with Nurse Broughton.

'We can't. Didn't your form tutor read out the notice? They're messing around with break time because of the exams. We'll miss each other.'

'Oh.'

'Can you postpone the teacher? It's our last supper.'

'Please don't call it that.'

'Sorry,' she said. 'Can you?'

'I'll sort it out. Anyway, it can't be a last supper. There are only two of us. And hopefully no Judas.'

'Three,' she said. 'Kim'll be with us.'

'Oh.'

'Is that all right?'

'What did Kim say?'

'I told her what I told you. I need to know you're friends. It will be easier for me to leave. So I think she's happy to give you another go.'

I said, 'You make me sound like a tombola.'

I knocked at Nursey B's office on my way to the history exam. 'It's my best friend's last day,' I said.

'I heard about that,' she said, like some kind of mystic. 'Are you free straight after school?'

The history exam was the torture I'd anticipated. Led into the hall in silence, we were pointed towards single desks in alphabetical order, carrying our pens and anxiety. My desk, by the double doors leading to the school field, let in a draught which played around my shins for two hours. I hedged for too long over my choice of questions but settled on the rise of the British Empire and how the British economy recovered from the depression in the 1930s.

I'd been in those lessons. I'd made notes. I'd even reread some of those notes the night before.

I'd managed to scoop nine O levels, hadn't I, only two years before?

I'd ranked in the top three in all my classes in the Lower Sixth.

I had a brain. It must still be there. I could feel it whirring and clonking, although unfortunately not about the British Empire.

I finished the exam early. One invigilator saw that I'd stopped writing and scurried down the aisle to see if I needed more paper.

I almost laughed aloud.

For the remaining twenty minutes, I watched other pupils write. I looked out of the hall windows towards the school field. Trees only just in bud were teased in the March breeze. Younger pupils, perhaps second years, were playing with hoops and balls and skipping ropes, as free as ribbons, while a teacher sat on a wooden chair, reading a newspaper and waving occasional instructions.

When the invigilator said, 'Pens down,' some sighed with frustration. How I envied them.

Molly and Kim were standing together outside the doors of the school dining room. Molly waved. 'We thought we'd wait. That physics teacher's on duty who doesn't let you save places.'

'Hello,' I said to Kim. It felt awkward because sincere greetings had been rare for months. We'd probably touched elbows or bumped legs under the desks in registration, that's all.

'Hi.' She looked pale, like someone who normally wore thick make-up and then one day decided to go without it.

'Did you have an exam this morning?' I asked her.

'Biology.'

'Ugh.'

'It was.'

'You had history, didn't you?' Molly said.

'More like history had me,' I said, and Kim laughed.

Perhaps things would be all right. Or had Kim only agreed to have our dinner together for the sake of Molly? On Monday, would we be back to edging around one another?

We collected our cutlery, plates of chicken casserole and bowls of chocolate sponge with pink custard, loading them onto our trays. Molly led the way towards three empty seats.

'I bought a present,' Kim said, when we'd sat down. She

handed Molly a paper bag. Inside was a bar of Cadbury Fruit and Nut chocolate, Molly's favourite.

'So did I.' I reached into my satchel. I'd bought the same thing.

'Great minds,' Kim said.

'Suits me,' said Molly. 'I'll need supplies for the journey.'

We began to eat, but Kim was only toying with her meal.

'Not hungry?' Molly said.

'Usual problem,' Kim said, and I stayed quiet, because I wasn't supposed to know.

Molly said, stabbing at a piece of chicken, 'Look, you two. I need a promise.'

Kim and I looked at each other. I saw a wariness in her eyes that I also felt.

'I know you've missed each other,' Molly said.

'Have you missed me?' I said to Kim.

'My mum says I'm an idiot. Have you missed me?'

'Like a severed leg. You know. It feels as though it's still there, but it isn't.'

Kim looked doubtful.

'It's a compliment, honest,' I said.

Molly said, 'I feel like I'm on my deathbed here, dealing with stubborn long-lost relatives.'

'What happens now, then?' Kim said.

Molly said, 'You two fell out over Kevin. Why don't you just not mention Kevin, like people agree not to talk religion or politics?'

Kim looked at me. 'Okay. Agreed.'

I said, 'Yep. Agreed.'

'Well, that wasn't too hard, was it?' Molly said.

Kim abandoned her chicken casserole and started on her chocolate sponge. She said to me, 'A fortnight ago, I spent two nights in hospital.'

I glanced at Molly. She had clearly known.

Kim said, 'Molly came to see me. But the other person I wanted there was you, and Mum offered to phone you.'

'Why didn't she? Kim, I would have come.'

'As Mum said, I'm an idiot.'

She turned to Molly, 'I wish you weren't leaving.' Her voice crumbled.

'Me too,' I said.

'It's not ideal,' Molly said.

She was only a year older than me and Kim but right then she seemed adult and responsible, already growing away from us.

I blinked in case any tears thought they'd try their luck. Kim was already crying.

'Anyway,' said Molly, picking up her spoon. She'd always been awkward with emotion, like me. 'I know what I'll miss most.'

'What?' I said.

'I don't know if they'll have pink custard in Northumberland.'

Nursey B was dabbing at her uniform with a wet cloth when I arrived. She asked me to sit down. 'Someone was sick on me.'

'Ugh.' I put my satchel on the floor.

'Occupational hazard.'

'I hate clearing up sick.'

She came towards me, a large wet patch on her skirt. 'When have you had to clear up sick?'

I realised that the unguarded confession was a gift to her. I should have learned my lesson after all the practice with Heather.

'Go on,' she said, sitting opposite me. 'Tell me.'

I shrugged. 'It was a long time ago.'

'You were a child.' It was a statement, not a question.

'Before I was fostered.'

'Ah. Drinkers don't always get to the toilet bowl in time.'

She stayed silent in a way that makes you feel that you must fill in the spaces.

'He'd be sick in whatever was nearest sometimes. A wastepaper bin. A basket of washing.'

'Dirty washing?'

'Not until he'd been sick.'

'Right.'

'Or onto the rug by the bed,' I said.

She crossed her skeletal legs, one over the other, and leaned towards me. 'You shouldn't have had to do that.'

'I suppose.'

'At least that's not happening now.'

I could truthfully confirm that it wasn't. But I had heard him being sick in the bathroom some nights. There were few secrets in a flat that small.

'And how is the head picking?' she asked.

'Not brilliant.'

'No?'

'Dad's searching for a new job. I'm probably worrying about that.'

'Can I look?' she said.

'At my dad?'

'At your head.'

'That's usually for head lice, isn't it?'

'Kill two birds with one stone.'

'I do *not* have head lice.'

She stood and I let her examine my head. Her long, cool fingers were gentle, feeling her way around my scalp, lifting my hair to see where my scalp met my neck. This was where many of the sorest spots were, some scabbed over already, some new and raw.

I said, 'Are you going to ask me about holidays, like at the hairdressers?'

'I'm going to ask you whether you'd like ointment for these.' She smoothed my hair down and went to open a drawer, taking out a tube. 'This is antiseptic and soothing at the same time.'

'Thanks.' I put it in my satchel.

She washed her hands at a basin in the corner and sat down again.

'What do you think is making you do this?' she said.

'Can't we talk about your poems now?'

'No.'

'Half the time I don't even know I'm doing it.'

'I suppose that's something, that you're not doing it deliberately.'

I'd lied. Sometimes I did. You shouldn't lie to people who share their poetry with you.

'I could refer you back to the educational psychologist,' she said.

'Is it still an old man called Mr Bayfield with body odour?'

I could see she tried not to smile. 'It is Mr Bayfield, yes.'

'No, thanks. Can we talk about your poems now?'

She checked her watch. 'I've got five minutes.'

I didn't know what to say even though she'd given me the chance. I said, after a while, 'If I was the sort of person who cried, I would have cried.'

'Is that all your feedback?'

'I think so.'

'Well, that's a huge compliment,' she said. 'I mean it.'

I stood up.

'You're going now? I'd quite like to talk about why you're not the crying type.'

'I'm due at my foster parents' for tea.'

'Convenient!'

Bridget's fall had formed her into a different kind of woman. When I arrived with the fish and chips, she was lying on the sofa, sleeping, a quilt untidy on her body. Bruising had been merciless to the left-hand side of her face. Underneath the quilt, she wore her dressing gown.

I tiptoed into the kitchen to find Nick buttering slices of white bread. I put the packet of fish and chips on the counter. 'They'll need warming up,' I said. 'It's cold outside.'

Spotless stepped out of his bed and leaned against the

kitchen cupboard as though to stay as close to the fish and chips as possible.

I heard the inexpert clatter of trays and cutlery behind me as I came back into the living room. Still, Bridget didn't wake and I found this sad. Until recently, the crash of kitchen equipment would have been like a clarion call, pulling her upright like a puppet straightened.

I watched her sleeping but it felt voy … voy … I went over to the bookcase and pulled out a dictionary. Mrs Collingworth's words were in my ear: *If you don't look it up now, you'll never look it up.*

Voyeuristic. That was it.

I glanced up to see Bridget looking at me, beginning to pull herself to a sitting position. 'What are you trying to find?' she said. The words came slow.

'Voyeuristic.'

'Why? Isn't that a peeping Tom?'

'I heard it somewhere.'

'Goodness. What have you been listening to?'

'I don't remember.'

'Bless you. Always ready to learn something new.'

'Should you be sitting up?' I said.

'Why not? Were you planning to drop chips into my mouth while I was lying down?' She hoisted herself around and sat back against the cushions with a sigh as though the very act of getting vertical had stolen something from her.

Nick came in with a large teapot and mugs on a tray. 'Bridget's hospital stay has made her cynical,' he said, 'unless they sent the wrong woman home in the ambulance.'

'It's called frustration,' she said.

'Do you think it's permanent?' I said.

'The frustration? Probably.'

'I meant the cynicism.'

'Also probably.'

I poured four mugs of tea. Nick hadn't brought milk out. Perhaps he didn't even know where Bridget kept her milk jugs.

She called to Nick. 'Darling, when did we stop having milk in our tea?' but her voice was weak, as though someone was sitting on it.

I went into the kitchen, bringing back a whole bottle. I made as if to put it on the coffee table.

'Take that back,' she said, 'and find a jug. We're not philistines.'

'Only kidding,' I said, but I'd made her laugh, and my heart jumped.

When I came back in, Amanda had appeared and was rearranging the quilt over her mother's knees. 'Who are you?' Bridget said to her. 'I don't recognise you.'

Nick said, 'See what I mean?'

Amanda straightened up. I tried hard not to look at her abdominal area. 'Hi,' she said.

'I've brought fish and chips.'

'Did you remember the mushy peas?'

'You can fetch them yourself next time. I've got pickled eggs as well.'

'Lovely,' Bridget said.

While we waited for the fish and chips to reheat, I gave Bridget a Mother's Day card. I'd stood for ten minutes in Woolworths, choosing. Three years, and it never got easier, with none saying *To My Foster Mum*. One had said *On Mother's Day* on the front, illustrated with a vase of daffodils, and I thought *Yes!* but opened it to find a rhyme.

You've been a perfect mother
since my birth and from that day.
You've loved me every minute
in every kind of way.

Whichever way you looked at it, this stretched the truth.

Another had said *For Mothering Sunday* illustrated with a Victoria sponge which looked far less plump and inviting than one of Bridget's. Inside, the card was blank. I'd written

Thank you for everything. Your cakes are better than this. and signed my name.

'Should I open it now,' she said, 'or leave it for Sunday?' But she was already opening it.

She cried as I'd known she would, with or without the treacly poem.

Then she looked again at the front of the card. 'That cake needed more eggs.'

We ate our fish and chips around the coffee table with trays on our knees. Amanda made a chip butty for her mother.

'Look at my hands shaking,' Bridget said, at one point. I'd already noticed, while she'd opened my card. 'I can't make this pickled egg stay still to cut it,' she said, 'especially with no grip either.'

'Darling,' Nick said. 'Shall I help?'

'Don't you dare,' she said. 'I'll pick it up in my hands, like a savage.'

'Has that only just started?' I asked her.

'I've been trying to ignore it,' she said. 'But however hard I concentrate now, my brain won't stop them from shaking.'

'I thought everyone with Parkinson's had shaky hands,' Amanda said.

'Everyone thinks so,' Bridget said. 'There was I, confident I'd bucked the trend.' She speared a piece of fish as though she were the one killing it.

'The shakiness might not last, Bridge,' Nick said. 'It could be a temporary blip. You did hit your head.'

'Nothing about this bloody condition is a blip,' Bridget said, and because she never swore, we all laughed, including her.

After we'd washed up, Nick said that he'd talked that day to a builder. 'The garage will be a downstairs bedroom,' he said, 'with a toilet and sink, then another bedroom upstairs on top of the garage.'

'Will we be here when they do the work?' Amanda said.

'We'll try to coordinate it with a holiday in early August. Somewhere with a beach.'

By then, Amanda would have had to tell them about the baby, surely. Otherwise, I could foresee awkward conversations around swimming costumes.

SUNDAY 16 MARCH

On Mothering Sunday morning, I told everyone I was going for a walk and visited Mum's grave. I'd bought daffodils on Saturday after work and kept them in water in my bedroom overnight.

I laid them on the grave and sat on the bench to eat my Penguin biscuit. The day hadn't decided yet whether to offer sun or cloud but there was a touch of mildness in the air.

'I'm sorry Bridget got a card and not you,' I said, 'but you have flowers and she had a picture of a mediocre cake.'

I sat for fifteen minutes or so watching many others arrive at the cemetery, filling vases, placing flowers, tugging at weeds. Mothering Sunday had put her arms around them and gathered them to this place: those who'd loved their mothers, and perhaps those who wished they'd loved them more.

Later, Doreen was clearly relying on Stuart to have remembered Mothering Sunday but he said nothing even while he munched her roast pork with home-made apple sauce and a lime cheesecake with cream. After the meal, she produced a box of Black Magic she'd bought herself. He started on them, taking the orange creams from both top and bottom layers.

'What brought all this on?' Dad said, also oblivious (and skint).

It wasn't my place to say. And the longer the day went on, the more embarrassing it would have been for Doreen to announce, 'It's Mothering Sunday.'

We watched the early evening news, though, and, during

the local bulletin, the newsreader reported on a woman in Coventry who'd had triplets that morning. 'And Mother's Day will always be special for her,' the newsreader said, 'with three cards and three presents!'

'Bugger it,' Stuart said.

'Ah,' Dad said.

'Sorry, Mum,' Stuart said. 'Other things on my mind.'

But Doreen said, 'I didn't even realise myself. I don't care about that sort of thing.'

Dad didn't help. 'Did you go up to the grave, pet?' he said to me.

'I did.'

'Did you take flowers?'

Doreen and Stuart were concentrating hard on news about a Warwickshire butcher who had gone out of business because he gave people salmonella as well as chicken.

'I took some daffodils.' I wished Dad would stop.

'Good. They were her favourites.'

'I remembered.'

'God bless her soul,' Dad said.

'Bloody hell*fire*,' Doreen said at his unexpected turn to religion. 'I'm going to have a bath.'

'A bath? It's quarter past six,' Dad said. 'What about tea?'

'Can I go for a slash first if you're going to wallow?' Stuart said.

Doreen spent the rest of the evening in pyjamas and dressing gown, smelling so strongly of rose-scented soap that Dad complained, and drinking gin like water. I made Dairylea sandwiches for us all at half past seven but she'd fallen asleep, so Stuart ate hers, too.

WEDNESDAY 19 MARCH

I walked up the stairs to our flat after school. I was thinking about Bridget. Nick had telephoned the previous evening to say that she had jettisoned the quilt on the sofa and returned to a mostly upright position. She had re-established control of the kitchen and was rearranging cupboards and drawers to cement this. 'She loves it when I can't find the tin opener,' he'd said.

'Isn't that going to get annoying?' I'd said.

He said it was worth it to see her smiling more, particularly as Amanda was worrying them stupid, spending hours in her bedroom. 'We're almost nostalgic for all the parties and nights out.'

Before I reached the first floor, I could hear Dad and Doreen yelling as though communicating across a canyon. Should I turn on my heel, walk the other way, wander into town to scan the windows of gift shops and sweet shops and the antiquarian bookshop with its leather-covered volumes?

As I reached the flat, Colin appeared, a Woodbine balanced on his lip as usual in the tiny ridge that had formed over the years. His jumper was stained with egg or cream or perhaps loneliness.

'They've been like that for an hour now,' he said.

'I'm sorry.'

'Wouldn't worry.' He puffed on his fag. 'There's nothing good on the telly.'

I smiled but I knew the smile had no heart.

'Let me know if you want someone to punch their lights out for you,' he said, and went back inside.

I admired his optimism as I thought he'd used up all his strength on being unemployed for as long as possible.

Our conversation had happened against the backdrop of continual shouting so I didn't need to twist my key so quietly. I nudged the door open. They were in the living room, or they would have heard me.

I stood in the hall. They were right near the door so must have been standing, not sitting. 'Nothing left for the rest of the *month*,' Dad was saying. I could imagine him looming over Doreen, trying to wield physical dominance where he didn't have emotional dominance. His big hands flailing.

'He needed a train ticket,' Doreen said.

'He can buy his own bloody train ticket.'

'I thought you'd be glad to see him go.'

'I am. But not on my dole money.'

There was a silence.

'He's got some bloody girl pregnant,' she said.

'What? Who?'

'He won't tell me.'

'And he's buggering off?'

'He's buggered off,' she said.

'A charmer,' Dad said. 'I won't miss him.'

'Just as you won't miss me?'

He said nothing to that.

'You won't, will you?' she said.

'You can think what you like,' my dad said. 'I won't miss you raiding my money.'

I heard footsteps. 'I'm taking these curtains.'

His footsteps. 'You're taking nothing. You paid for those with my money, just as you've paid for everything since, save your poncey soaps.'

Bottles clinked.

'And you can leave those there,' Dad shouted.

'What happened to all my worldly goods I thee endow?'

'Don't be ridiculous. We're not even bloody married.'

'And whose fault is that?'

They'd considered marriage? Something in the pit of my stomach shrivelled.

Doreen's voice was quieter now. 'You haven't told her about us, have you?'

'Why would I? It was years ago.'

'So easily *brushed* under the carpet!'

'Don't be stupid.'

'Worried about losing your hero status?' Doreen said.

'She doesn't need to know.'

'Did Maggie know?'

'Don't call her that. Margaret to you.'

'Well, did she?'

'Of course not. It would have killed her.' I heard the catch in his voice.

'Listen to yourself,' she said.

'Doreen, don't go. You don't have to.' But I knew Dad and that voice wasn't Dad with conviction.

She said, 'I should have done it weeks ago.'

I pushed the living room door wide open and walked in. Doreen was standing by the dining table, her best jacket on.

'Jackie,' Dad said. He sat down heavily in the armchair recently vacated by Stuart. Its structural features had long since given themselves up. It creaked and strained.

'Eavesdroppers never hear anything good,' Doreen said.

Dad shook his head as though he could shake off Doreen, me, and the mess he'd got himself into, like a dog who's been in water.

Doreen said to him, 'Are you going to tell her?'

'Shut up,' he said, but he was disadvantaged, sunk down in the chair.

She turned to face me. 'Before your mum died, your dad and I—'

'You can save your breath,' I said. I headed for my bedroom

but stopped when I noticed Doreen's pink suitcase against the hall wall by the telephone table, her handbag balanced on top.

'Give me a goodbye hug, then, chuck,' Doreen said, coming out into the hall.

'Don't call me chuck.' I went into my bedroom, where I stayed, lying on my bed, until I heard the front door click shut and her suitcase being dragged down the steps. Bump. Bump. Bump.

I wanted to go to Dad but I could hear him crying in the living room, each sob a regret, perhaps. I didn't want to embarrass him.

An hour later, I ventured in. 'Dad?' He'd moved to the sofa. Angela Rippon was reading the news on the telly.

Stuart's holdall, which had sat like a fat canvas toad in the corner, had gone. The absence of the bag, and of him and Doreen, made the room seem generous, as though there was now room to stretch and lean. I took in a deep breath and let it out again, allowing my lungs the freedom of the space. Ornaments had disappeared from the windowsill and the magazine rack had lost its women's journals. The blankets Stuart had been using were in a heap on the dining table.

Dad couldn't have been feeling the sense of space. He was bent over his drink as though protecting it or making it part of him. His eyes were puffy, his nose red. 'Both gone, love,' he said into the glass.

'Where's Doreen going to stay?'

'I don't know. I didn't ask. She said something about a job in Birmingham.'

'Maybe back to her ex, then. Isn't that where he is?'

'Can we not talk about her?' Dad said.

I sat beside him. On the news, a doctor was explaining why oily fish was good for the brain. 'Do you want a cup of tea, Dad?'

'No. I want peace and quiet.'

'Shall I go to my room?'

He shook his head. 'I don't mean that, pet. I want you to sit there and watch telly with me, and then we'll get a Chinese takeaway. That kind of peace and quiet.'

'I can buy the takeaway.'

He looked shamefaced but didn't protest.

'Are you sad she's gone?' I said.

He lit a cigarette and drew on it, puffing smoke out towards the fireplace. 'I'll give it more thought tomorrow.'

The doctor was showing the camera tins of pilchards and sardines and saying, 'These could change your life!'

'What did Doreen mean,' I said, 'about you and her, before Mum died? Is it what I think?'

He said, 'I don't know what you're thinking.'

Neither of us spoke for five minutes or so. The sports news came on. The weather. Light winds. Perhaps a spot of rain in the Midlands. I picked at my head. I didn't care if Dad saw. In fact, I hoped he would. There was blood under my fingernails he ought to see.

I said, 'I didn't think you would have any more shocks for me. But they keep coming. Like grenades.'

He looked as though he would speak, but he had nothing to give. He reached over for the bottle and went to unscrew the cap.

'The cap's here, Dad. You left it off.'

'So it is,' he said.

On the way to fetch the Chinese takeaway, I phoned the Walls' house from a phone box. Amanda answered and I pushed in several coins. I heard her call, 'It's for me!'

'Is it safe?' I said.

'I'm shutting the kitchen door. They're upstairs, sorting laundry.'

'Your mum's letting Nick help her?'

'I know.'

'I've got some news,' I said.

'Good or bad?' she said.

I hesitated. 'I suppose it depends.'

'What is it?'

'It's Stuart,' I said. 'He's gone.'

'What do you mean? Gone where?' She was keeping her voice to a whisper.

'I don't know. Maybe back to Birmingham?'

'Why? Did your dad kick him out?'

'Didn't need to. He's taken himself off. I don't think he—'

'—wanted to be a daddy,' she said. She sighed. 'I guess we knew that. I knew that.'

'I'm sorry.'

'It's not your fault.'

'No, I mean, I'm sorry he's been such a bastard to you.'

'Not all the time. We had some good times.'

'I won't ask for more detail,' I said.

'I wasn't going to give you any. Look where good times have put me, anyway.'

'Are you upset about him?'

There was a pause. 'I don't know yet,' she said. 'You're presumably not.'

'Well—'

'At least you'll get your living room back.'

I said, 'And the kitchen. Doreen's disappeared off as well.'

'Where?'

'Not sure. Perhaps Birmingham too. But I can't say I'm sobbing.'

'I bet.'

'It's a shame about Stuart,' I said. 'I did have a decent conversation with him about Freud. I was very near liking him.'

'Is Freud a band?'

'No.'

She said, 'Actually, Stuart was waiting for me yesterday when I came out of college.'

'You've seen him?'

'He wanted to know if it was true. He seemed surprised I didn't have a big bump.'

'Ignoramus.'

'I showed him a book about pregnancy that I'd borrowed from the library. I think that was proof enough that I had it in my bag.'

'So how did you leave things?'

'He said he'd be in contact,' she said. 'He didn't say anything about leaving.'

'How touching,' I said. 'When are you going to tell your parents?'

'I can't. How can I tell Mum? It will set her back.'

'You can't leave it for ever.'

'I can leave it a few months,' she said. 'I'm not showing yet. Not on my tummy.'

'What do you mean?'

'My chest,' she said. 'It's like balloons blowing up.'

'Do they do maternity clothes in black with slashes in and studs? Otherwise, I think you might have to have a break from being a punk.'

She said, 'I was getting bored, anyway. Everyone was so *angry* all the time.'

'Your mum and dad will be relieved. Maybe it will help them cope with the baby news. "Mum, you're going to be a granny but it's fine because I love Barry Manilow now."'

'Oh, shut up,' she said. 'It's all right for you.'

'It's very much not all right for me either. It's just a different kind of not all right.'

'But at least you don't have a baby growing inside you,' she said, 'whose daddy has legged it and whose mummy wanted to be a hairdresser.'

It was the first time she had professed enthusiasm for life in a salon. That's perspective for you.

'This is true,' I said. 'I'm sorry.'

THURSDAY 27 MARCH

'I don't like to nag,' I said to Dad.

It was four o'clock and I'd arrived home to find him asleep in front of children's TV. He'd woken up and grumpily accepted the offer of tea.

I was holding the local newspaper open at the jobs pages. I said, 'I don't *like* to nag, but I have to.'

He took the paper off me and scanned the advertisements. 'Ha. Pie factory, machine operator,' he said. 'They won't take me back. Even my bloody mother won't take me back.'

'What?' My nan lived in Devon and we hadn't heard from her for years. She'd written to Dad when he was first imprisoned to say he was banished from the family.

'I rang her this morning,' he said.

I wanted not to be cynical but I wondered if this was about money. I decided to believe it was about love and family.

'What did she say?'

'I won't repeat it. Suffice it to say, I'm not invited for a holiday.'

'I'm sorry, Dad.'

He shrugged. 'That's how it is. Burned my bridges there.' He turned his attention back to the newspaper.

'Are there other possible jobs?'

'Warehouse manager.'

'Ooh, manager,' I said.

I tried not to follow his eyes around the living room, strewn with the detritus of his day.

'Machine operative,' he said.

'Right.'

'Off-licence shop assistant.'

'Maybe not that one.'

'Office assistant. School leavers welcome. Look, why don't *you* go for a job?'

'Be serious. Anyway, I'm at school *and* I've got a job.'

I hadn't meant it as a barb but he took it that way, dropping the paper on the floor.

I drank my tea. 'Isn't your probation officer worried about you?'

'He's a nag, too.'

'When is Heather coming to see you again?'

'Oh, bloody hell,' he said. He hauled himself up, fetched the diary from the drawer in the TV cabinet and flicked through the pages. 'Monday.'

'At least you won't have to clear away evidence of Doreen and Stuart this time.'

'A right little Job's comforter, you are.'

We sat watching Tina on *Blue Peter* telling the nation how easy it was to keep things secure with sticky-backed plastic.

'Are you missing Doreen?' I said.

'I'm not missing that Stuart, that's for sure.'

'That's a yes, then. Has she sent you her address?'

'No. Why would she?'

'I thought she might, hoping you'd convince her to come back.'

'Are you missing them?' he said.

I stayed silent.

He yawned. 'I'm missing her cooking. And the bed isn't so warm.'

'I'm not missing her cooking,' I said. Since she'd left, we'd reverted to toast and beans some nights, especially if I had homework or revision. But I preferred toast and beans with Dad than a roast with Doreen and Stuart. Before I'd been fostered, mealtime routines had been chaotic because of Dad's drinking. This time round, I insisted we eat at the same time. But I wasn't sure how long I could keep this going.

'Hasn't she even tried to phone?' I asked.

'Nope,' he said. 'Now can you shut up about her?'

I wanted us to travel back in time, like on a magic carpet, back to cleaning the house together on Saturdays, sipping tea in the café, watching *Top of the Pops*, meeting one another in the kitchen, me in my school clothes and him in work trousers. But whisky had kept that carpet on the ground and although I did meet him in the kitchen in the mornings, he had reverted to his old daytime uniform of vest and underpants that made him seem less of a man and twenty years older.

Later that evening, he fell asleep in front of the TV, still holding a half-full glass. It was balanced precariously in his lap so I bent to rescue it. He sensed the movement and woke up. The glass tumbled to the carpet and he grabbed at it like a man crazed, but too late.

I expected him to be cross but not that he would get up, tower over me and roar at my head that it was my fault Doreen had left as I'd never accepted her.

'That's unfair, Dad,' I said. 'I did my best.'

'To persuade her to go.'

I was braver than I had been at fourteen. I looked up at him. 'Dad, she went because you lost your job and then you lost her respect.'

He raised his hand then as though the word 'respect' had jerked on it.

I shrank back and I think he felt the movement all the way through his body. He dropped back onto his chair, his head in his hands. 'I'm sorry, pet.'

I headed for my bedroom, calling behind me, 'I don't have to stay here either, you know. I have choices.'

This was true, but I didn't want to make those choices. I

wanted him to shop for pork pie and pickled onions and red tomatoes and have them ready when I came home from the bakery on Saturdays.

I stayed in my room, working on a poem. When the phone rang in the hall, I let it ring, but Dad shouted, 'Answer it, pet.'

It was Patsy.

'Marion's driving me *insane*,' she began at volume 11 out of 10, and I hoped Marion wasn't in the house.

'Why?' I slid a fingernail under a scab at the back of my head.

'She wants to know where I am *all* the time. If I'm too long in the *bath*room, I get an interrogation.'

'She's your foster parent,' I said. 'And she's probably more worried about nights out and you coming back at breakfast.'

'But I'm seventeen! At least you've already had your birthday.'

Patsy wouldn't be eighteen until the end of August.

I repeated what my social workers had said many times about Bridget. 'It's called caring.'

'I wish she wouldn't.'

'You don't mean that.'

'I can look after myself.'

'Says the girl who saw sparks coming from a plug socket and didn't mention it.' It was out before I could stop it.

'That fire was an *acc*ident.'

'I'm sorry. I'm really sorry.'

'Everyone around me thinks I'm still a child,' she said, 'as though I hadn't ...'

She left a pause as though she expected me to probe. But I was too tired to take it on.

'Do you want to meet up over the holidays?' she said, after a while.

'I don't know, Patsy. I've got revision.'

'You poor thing,' she said, sincerely, as though I'd

announced a terminal disease. 'Well, I'm working a few weekday shifts at the bakery anyway. Maybe I wouldn't have had time either.'

I knew I'd hurt her.

'Shouldn't be long before Mason Street,' I said to try and repair the breach.

'Yeah. Then I can go out with Pete and stay out for *weeks*.'

I heard a woman's voice in the background and realised that Marion must have been there all the time.

FRIDAY 28 MARCH

I knocked at Nursey B's door on the last day of the spring term. She was at her desk, writing notes. She put her pen down and we sat in opposite chairs as usual. She stretched her legs out before her and crossed them at the ankles, her man-sized feet in sensible shoes with laces.

She tried small talk. 'What was for school dinner today?'

'Roast pork and gravy,' I said. 'Peas like bullets.'

She laughed and tried bigger talk. 'Any plans for the Easter hols?'

'Some.'

'Anything more specific?'

'Revising,' I said, morosely. 'Revising some more. And some more.'

'Did you get your report this morning?'

'Unfortunately.'

'You've read it? You're meant to take it home first. It's sealed.'

'I haven't read it. I'm assuming.'

'Don't assume. Your teachers understand more than you think.' She paused, then went in for the kill. 'Did the ointment help?'

I hadn't been using it. I had tried, but it made the spots soft and slippy, and soft and slippy was frustrating. I didn't know how to explain this. *I prefer crusty scabs* seemed ungrateful.

'I'm sure it will help,' I said, carefully.

She uncrossed her legs and sat up. 'You haven't been using it.'

'I kept forgetting where I'd put it.'

'Nice try.'

'The dog ate it?'

She didn't smile. 'Is it because it softened up the scabs?' I chewed my lip.

She said, 'You know how when your Dad used to drink?'

'Yes,' I said, alert to keeping her in the past tense.

'And he knew it was the worst thing for him?'

'Yes.'

'But he carried on doing it anyway?'

'Yes.'

'We call that self-destructive behaviour.'

'I suppose.' I took in a deep breath. Something was building in my chest.

'That kind of behaviour is a sign of distress,' she said. 'It blocks things out. Things you'd rather not look at.' She covered her eyes with her hands to demonstrate.

'Right.'

'What are you not telling us, Jackie? What is it you don't want to look at?'

I had an urge to leave the room but also I loved Nursey B. I wanted her to massage my head again.

'You're like a poem,' she said. 'I need to peel back the layers to find out what's really going on.'

Her sparse upper body leaned towards me and those green eyes were like a sea in which to swim but her face was so thin, her cheeks almost hollow. I thought of nurses often portrayed on TV fully fleshed, smiling, bustling.

The thing in my chest pushed up towards my throat and I tried to swallow it down.

'It is too much for you to carry,' she said slowly, in her deep voice. It sounded as though she was singing to me.

My eyes stung but I couldn't stop the tears. They were

going to arrive whatever I did in the way sunrise, death and wasps do.

I bent forwards, put my face in my hands and cried. My hands were soon wet.

She waited, passing me a clean white handkerchief from her skirt pocket. I put my face in that instead. Every time I thought I would stop crying, I began again. Instead of watching me, she moved around the room, shifting papers, opening a drawer. Someone knocked at the door and she yelled, 'Not now!' I heard footsteps shuffling off.

Gradually, the tears began to dry up.

'Tell me,' she said, sitting down again.

I blew my nose. 'I don't want to get anyone into trouble.'

'I understand.'

'There's too much to tell.'

'I can take it.'

I looked at my watch. 'I've got English.'

'No. You've got Nursey B, and you're staying here.'

'You'll tell everyone else,' I said and, as I spoke, I wasn't sure how that would feel.

'Not everyone,' she said, pretending to think about it. 'I'll probably miss out – er – China. Perhaps New Zealand.'

And because this was so inappropriate of her, I opened my mouth to let out all the waiting words. 'It all started with Doreen.' I balled the handkerchief in my hand, squeezing it.

She said, 'Tell me about Doreen.'

I began with the baby-blue suspenders and the measuring up for curtains. These details were fixed in my mind like photographs. And once the first fact was out, others followed, as though attached.

Doreen's arrival.

Stuart's arrival.

Whisky's (re)arrival.

Doreen's departure.

Stuart's departure.

Whisky's (non) departure.

I omitted the arrival of babies.

'Thank you for sharing this with me,' she said, when I'd finished. She hadn't interrupted at all.

'I'm worried about betraying my dad.'

'It's not betrayal.'

'It feels like it. What if he gets prosecuted?'

'I thought you said they'd both left.'

'They have.'

'Then I doubt that very much.'

'Oh.' I realised then that I'd got so used to crafting my words and choosing silence over truth that even when that danger had passed, my guardedness hadn't.

She said, 'I'll ring your social worker later. She'll decide how to handle it.'

'I don't suppose you want this handkerchief back. There's a lot of me in it.'

'I've got a laundry basket.' She pointed. 'Pop it in there.'

I said, dropping in the handkerchief, 'Should I go to English?'

'No. Sit down. Do you have a book in your bag?'

'Yes. I'm reading *Oliver Twist*.'

'I'm reading Daphne du Maurier,' she said. 'So I'm going to fetch us some tea. Then we'll sit and read and eat biscuits without a care in the world. How does that sound?'

'Deluded,' I said.

She laughed.

When I left school later that afternoon, I found Kevin by the gates, hands in his duffle coat pockets, eyes screwed up against the low sun.

'Oh,' I said, although I'd rather have said, 'Wrap your arms around me and snuggle into my hair.' After my time with Nursey B, my limbs felt weak, as though I'd done manual work.

I hadn't seen him since January although I'd sent a short note to thank him for the birthday card and present he'd delivered to the Walls. Kim and I had kept our recent agreement not to speak about him. It had felt unnatural at first but had worked for us, plus we'd had threatening letters from Molly demanding to know whether we were keeping to the contract and getting along.

'Are you going to the Walls' house for tea today?' Kevin said.

'No. They're at a hospital appointment.'

'Have you been crying?'

'I might be running a cold.'

'I miss you.'

'How come you're here?'

'You're not listening. I miss you.'

'I meant work.'

'Afternoon off,' he said. 'The boss's birthday.'

I put my satchel on the pavement and shifted to let other pupils pass. 'Kevin – I'm not ready to—'

'Do you miss *me*?' he said. 'Be honest.' He pointed to himself. 'The face of a god, no?'

I tried to keep the smile inside but it begged for liberty. 'If you say so.'

'Just friends? We've done it before. Can I walk with you? We could stay in the park for a while.'

'It's cold.'

'Not if we're on the move.'

'You're not going to try anything on?'

'Oh, give me strength,' he said, raising his arms to the heavens. 'I could walk on the other side of the road if it helps. Or you could catch a bus and I'll run along behind.'

'I'm only saying.'

'Let's just wander. Please.'

'I've got a school report to show my dad.'

'Will a couple of hours make any difference?'

I said, glumly, 'Probably not.'

We walked towards the park in silence for a few minutes. I felt that he was letting me adjust to his presence.

'You had me writing dreadful poetry,' he said, as we neared the bridge over the river. 'By rights, I should never speak to you again.'

'Why did you?'

'I don't know. Maybe it made me feel nearer.'

'Are you still doing it?'

'My family begged me to stop.'

'I did hear something about that,' I admitted.

We sat on a bench, staying close together for warmth, or so he claimed, and watched the swans parading.

'Is that why we call it swanning around?' Kevin said.

'Epiphany!' I said.

'You're a sarky sod. We're not all English swots. Do you want a Polo?' He pulled a tube of them out of his coat pocket but, as he did, a piece of folded paper fell on the ground. He bent to pick it up.

'What is it?' I said.

'Nothing.'

'One of the poems?' I was teasing and didn't expect him to say yes.

'I'm not showing you.'

'Why have you brought it, then?'

'I forgot it was in this coat.'

'You're lying.'

'Okay, I'm lying.'

'Show me.'

'You'll laugh. It's only one verse anyway.'

'I won't.' I put my hand on his arm. 'I promise. I think it's lovely that you tried.'

'Do you want a Polo or not?'

'I want a poem first.'

He unfolded the paper. 'Read it for yourself. I'm not reciting it like an idiot.'

I took the paper.

He'd written:

Her hair is black but her heart is pure.
She is the girl for me, I'm sure.
Her smile is sunshine, she lights my way.
I miss that smile every single moment of the day.

'It's rubbish, isn't it?' he said.

'Well ...'

'What?'

'You've used a comma after sunshine instead of a full stop.'

'Oh.'

'But that doesn't matter.'

'It's not a good poem.'

'Not yet. But that doesn't matter either.'

I put my hand around the back of his head and drew his face towards mine. We didn't kiss, but I put my cheek next to his and we sat like that for a while.

I gently pushed him back. 'Have you really missed me every moment?'

'Except when I'm asleep,' he said.

'Of course.'

'Or watching football.'

'Right.'

'Or eating sausage and mash. I don't think of anything else when I'm eating sausage and mash.'

I punched him on the arm then took a Polo.

We walked along the river, running a competition to see who could make the Polo last longer. At one point, he reached for my hand and I curled my little finger around his.

'Actually, Kevin,' I said. 'Your last line didn't scan. I won't sleep if I don't say.'

'I knew it.'

'But at least you can sing and play guitar. I sound like a wounded toad.'

'I didn't like to mention it.' He searched his pocket. 'Have you still got the poem?'

I tapped my own pocket.

'To put under your pillow?' he said.

'To throw darts at.'

'Can I kiss you?' He leaned towards me.

'No.'

'Okay. Shall we do one more circuit of the park?'

'It's beginning to go dark.'

'Just one.'

I knew what he meant. We were trying to grasp time and stop it from moving.

'It's half past five,' I said. 'I ought to ring Dad first and let him know I'll be out longer.'

'There's a phone box by the park gate.'

'He'll be wondering,' I added, because you can always hope.

In the phone box, I dialled Dad's number, my coins ready. But no one answered.

I tried again with no result.

'Where else would he be?' Kevin said when I emerged from the phone box and told him.

'I don't know,' I said, although I did.

We walked around the park again, stopping to sit on a fallen tree trunk. The temperature was dropping and the light weakening so we snuggled up close. He put his arm around my shoulders. 'How is it, living with your dad again?'

'Let's not talk about it. I like *this* moment.'

At the edge of the park, he said, 'I'll walk you to your street.'

'No.'

'Let me,' he said. 'I don't want to say goodbye yet.'

*

We wandered through the churchyard at the edge of the park and turned towards the Landor Court flats. Lights were being turned on in homes and off in workplaces and shops. Kevin said, 'Kim's operation is soon.'

'She told me,' I said. 'We're telling each other things these days.'

'My two favourite girls. I'm glad you're back together.'

I turned to face him. 'Hey, did she put you up to this?'

'What?'

'Turning up today. She did, didn't she?'

'She may have had a hand in it.'

'Hm,' I said.

'Anything to stop me from writing poetry.'

'You might carry on.'

'I won't need to if I can talk to you. I say things better in conversation.'

'You're not wrong there,' I said.

As we approached Landor Court, we saw a man ahead of us, his tall, uncoordinated figure weaving a slalom on the pavement, and, in the dusk, the height and the turn of his head told me it was Dad. I deliberately slowed.

'Just checking I've got my key.' I dipped into my satchel, faking a search.

'Okay.'

'Here it is,' I said, pulling it out.

Dad was losing pace and we were catching up. He stopped and reached out to a lamp post, letting it bear his weight. He had his hand on his upper chest as though trying not to retch.

'Had a few too many,' Kevin said.

'So it looks.'

'One of my uncles is like that. I think he had a baby who died.'

'That's sad.'

'I think I'd turn to drink if I had a baby who died,' he said, which hit something just underneath my earlobes.

Dad started off again, blundering along the pavement, and turned into Landor Close.

Then he tripped. We watched him fall, his long arms windmilling as he realised what was happening but couldn't stop the momentum, like someone careering downhill on a steep slope except that here the steep slope was beer or whisky or maybe both.

We heard the thud of his head on the pavement.

We ran towards where he lay, face down, his legs in the road, his arms out like Jesus on the cross, his head still. The alcohol came off him in waves as though he'd washed in it. What I could see of his face was grey, and in those few moments seemed to become greyer.

Kevin knelt beside him and said, 'He's knocked out.'

A woman ran over from her shop. 'I was locking up when I saw him fall,' she said. 'Do we need an ambulance?' But she didn't wait for an answer. 'I'll call one.' She hurried back.

A young couple approached with a pram. The girl bent down to peer at Dad. 'Don't move him until the ambulance gets here,' she said, 'in case he's broken his neck. I've seen it on the telly.' This wasn't a great endorsement but it was all we had. She put her face close to his. It was strange to see her fresh, young face next to Dad's. 'He's breathing okay. But he's clean out.'

'His legs are in the road,' I said. Somehow this seemed the saddest thing, Dad's long legs, clad in a pair of old trousers, stuck out into the road like something discarded.

'You can't change his position,' she said again.

Astute!

But Kevin was now standing at the junction to the close, waving traffic away.

A small group of pedestrians gathered, staring down at my father's disarranged frame as though hoping for more drama, and I was glad when we heard the siren, shrieking out into the falling dark of the evening. Traffic edged away to let it through and the ambulance came to a halt, the doors flinging wide.

'Do we know who he is?' said a female ambulance worker, kneeling down with her fingers on Dad's neck.

'No,' said Kevin.

'Yes, I do,' I said. 'He's my dad.'

When Dad was being transferred to the ambulance, Kevin said to me, 'What can I do to help?' I could see he had other questions – who wouldn't have? – but there was no time for them.

'You go home. I'll phone you.'

'Do you want me to come with you?'

'No.'

But the afternoon seemed to have tethered me to him and him to me. It took an effort for us to separate.

The hospital was a two-minute ambulance journey from Dad's flat. I sat on a fold-down chair and watched him. On the way, he began to wake up, but held his head like Munch's *The Scream* painting and groaned. The ambulance worker tried to keep him calm. 'Not long, Mr Chadwick.'

'It hurts,' Dad kept saying, although his words were blurred and I didn't know whether that was the drink or the injury. Neither did the ambulance worker. Inside the vehicle, the smell of alcohol had replaced much of the oxygen.

His trousers were wet at the front. It made me love him more but I couldn't have explained why.

'Let me see your head,' the ambulance worker said at one point, leaning over Dad. 'Oh, that's quite a bump.'

Dad threw up what looked like a pint of beer onto her chest.

'I'm sorry,' I said to her.

'Don't be,' she said. She tapped Dad's cheek. 'Mr Chadwick. Don't go to sleep on us.'

*

When we reached the hospital, Dad was pushed on a stretcher on wheels into the casualty department and behind a cubicle curtain. I tried to follow but a nurse wearing a badge saying *Staff Nurse* asked me to wait in the main department while he was assessed. 'The receptionist will want some details from you,' she said.

'How long will it take to assess him?'

'We'll look after him,' she said.

The casualty waiting area hadn't changed since the last time I'd been there with Dad in 1976, the day he had hurt my wrist and had reluctantly come with me to have it X-rayed. The department's bright lights meant that, if you hadn't looked ill on arrival, you did now. Rows of wooden chairs acted as a deterrent, I imagined, to anyone thinking they might spend the night here with a minor complaint, but it hadn't deterred everyone and there were patients holding clumsily bandaged arms or with hands on their stomachs.

After a receptionist who looked like a grandma had taken Dad's details, writing them on a form in black capitals as though he'd already died, I skim-read two old copies of *Woman's Weekly* and pushed coins into the drinks machine for a hot chocolate drink that, if it had seen chocolate, hadn't seen it for long.

A tall male doctor in glasses and green surgeon's clothes approached after an hour. 'Do you belong to Mr Chadwick?' He sat beside me and looked relieved to be sitting down.

'What's happening?' I said.

'He's got a small subdural haematoma. It's a bleed on the brain from the fall and he needs surgery. How much alcohol do you think he's had?'

'Over a lifetime?'

He smiled. 'Just today.'

'I don't know. He looked pretty far gone. He must have

been drinking all day.' I thought back to what Kevin had said about the uncle. 'He's not a very happy person.'

'We'll test his blood, and monitor him carefully tonight, then operate first thing.'

'He's not going to die.' I tried to frame it as a statement even though it wanted to be a question.

He didn't respond to this.

'*Do* people die from this?'

He didn't want to say it. I could tell.

'Can I see him?'

'We're taking him to critical care. Do you live nearby?'

'Ten minutes' walk.'

'Pyjamas? His toothbrush and comb?'

'I'll fetch them.'

As he walked away, and I began to put my coat on, the double doors behind me opened and shut. I could feel the draught.

It was Kevin. Seeing him twice in one day felt good, as though it were as natural as the tide or the strike of a clock. 'I didn't want you to be alone,' he said.

'Thank you.'

'Well, Mum told me you shouldn't be. What's the situation?'

'I need to fetch Dad's things.'

'I'll help you carry them.'

'It's only pyjamas and toiletries.'

'I'll walk beside you while you carry them.'

The flat seemed to know what had happened, judging by the reverent quiet as I let Kevin and myself in. It was missing the hubbub and clamour of Dad's huge presence. I switched on the hall light but it exacerbated the silence, dressing it in a harsh yellow in case you should miss it.

'Shall I make some tea while you get things together?' Kevin said. He didn't wait for a reply but went into the kitchen.

I found a bag in a cupboard and packed Dad's pyjamas, some underwear and slippers, his comb, a flannel, his toothbrush and toothpaste. I'd rarely touched some of these items since I'd last lived with him in my early teens when it had been my job to do the washing, organise the bathroom and check that he didn't answer the door in only a pyjama top.

There were two Mars bars on his dressing table. I added them to the bag. In the living room, that day's *Daily Mirror* was on his chair so I put that in too, and a pencil for the crossword, the habit Doreen had cultivated in him. He hadn't looked crossword-capable in the ambulance but I had to believe.

In the kitchen, Kevin was spooning tea leaves into the pot.

I reached into the cupboard where the money tin was and shook it. Nothing.

'What was in there?' he said.

'Dad's money.'

He said, 'We have a tin like that.'

'I wanted some loose change in case he needs it. I'm assuming his wallet is with him but he may have nothing left.'

Together, from Kev's wallet and my purse, we scrambled together some 10p, 20p and 50p pieces. I found one of my old pay packet envelopes and put the coins in that.

'I'll pay you back,' I said.

'What's yours is mine,' he said, 'as they say in the wedding vows.'

He poured the tea and added a teaspoon of sugar from the bowl.

'I don't take sugar,' I said.

'You do today.'

'Let's drink up. I don't want to be long.'

We slurped at the hot tea, standing in the kitchen, and ripped open a packet of digestives as neither of us had eaten since lunch.

'I feel like I *am* married to you,' I said, 'being here like this.'

'Suits me. Thanks for letting me come.'

'I don't remember a choice.'

We arrived at the critical care ward's reception desk at nine o'clock. Lights were low and a nurse was at the desk, filling in paperwork. I told her Dad's name. She looked over her shoulder as though she thought she was being observed and whispered, 'Visiting's over, but – half a minute.'

Kevin took hold of my hand. I pulled it away at first but he held on. We followed the nurse into the ward. There were seven or eight beds each side, patients lying in them straight and quiet as though they'd been tidied up, blankets pulled tight across their bodies. Grey boxes stood to attention beside some of the beds, their dials and switches keeping watch.

Dad's head was large with thick bandages, his face bruising up. He filled the bed lengthways and widthways.

I leaned towards him. Kevin stood at the end of the bed.

'Dad,' I said.

His eyes fluttered open but I wasn't sure he could see me. He might have been responding to my voice only. 'Pet.' He sounded scratchy, the way he did in the mornings.

'You had a fall,' I said.

He didn't reply.

'You daftie.'

He grunted in reply.

'I've brought your pyjamas and toothbrush.'

'Why?'

'You had a fall. You're in hospital.'

He closed his eyes again. 'I need a fag.'

'I've got your Mars bars.' I opened the drawer in a small locker beside his bed and tucked them in there with the cash. I put the rest of his things in the cupboard below.

He didn't answer.

'Things are bad,' I said to Kevin.

'He'll want them when he's feeling better,' he said.

A nurse arrived and said, 'I need to check your father's obs.'

'Where are his obs?'

'Observations. Basic tests.'

'I don't think he knows where he is.'

She said, 'That's why we do the obs.'

We waited outside the curtain, listening to the nurse say, 'Measuring your blood pressure now, Mr Chadwick.' 'Checking your heart rate now.' 'Just taking some bloods.'

When she emerged, she kept the curtains shut. 'We ought to leave him in peace now.'

It sounded funereal.

'Can I see him before his operation tomorrow?' I said.

'You can go down to theatre with him, all being well. Be here by eight, though.' She looked down at Dad's notes to check she had our phone number.

I said to Kev, 'I need to tell the bakery I won't be in.'

'I'll phone them first thing. You'll have enough to think about.'

'I didn't even remember it was Saturday tomorrow.'

Outside the hospital, Kevin said, as we neared a phone box, 'Do the Walls know?'

'I'll do that when I get back to the flat.'

'Promise?'

'I promise.'

'You could stay with us for the night. Mum asked. You can have the sofa.'

'I'd like to be near the hospital,' I said.

He walked with me to Landor Close. 'Phone me tomorrow.' He kissed the top of my forehead but I put my hand around the back of his neck and kissed him on the lips.

*

At the top of the concrete stairs, which were harder to climb tonight, I found Colin, puffing hard on a cigarette. 'Someone said your old dad went proper arse over tit.'

'How very caring of them.'

'Is he all right?'

'Not really,' I said, and added, for effect, 'He has a subdural haematoma,' tossing the words away as though I said them every day.

'Bloody hell. What's a—'

But I'd put my key in the door by then.

I sat on my bed and cried for all kinds of reasons, glad to be alone with the tears apart from Weston and Super-Mary who seemed to understand, looking down at me from the chest of drawers. Then I washed my face and telephoned the Walls. Nick answered and I told him what had happened.

'Your poor dad,' he said.

'I think he'll be okay.'

'And what about you?'

'I think I'll be okay.'

'Does Heather know?' he asked.

'I'll have to phone her on Monday.'

'Amanda says Heather rang here this afternoon for something or other. Neither of us was home.'

I knew what that was about. But it all seemed like something irrelevant, for another day.

'Come and stay with us,' he said, 'until he's through the worst.'

'I can't do that because ...' I would have to say it. 'You're in my room so that Bridget can sleep properly.'

He couldn't deny this. 'We can work something out.'

'I'm fine here.'

'Hold on a minute.' I thought he'd put his hand over the receiver because I could only hear muffled conversation but then he said, 'All sorted, Jackie. We'll put our Z bed in Amanda's room. She came up with the idea.'

'She did?'

'There's room in there. Or there will be, when she's tidied up, which she's doing now. It's only temporary.'

'How much was the bribe?'

'Honestly, she volunteered.'

I said, 'It might be more than one night.'

'She knows. Shall I come and collect you now?'

'No, don't come out. I'll sleep here tonight and come tomorrow.'

There was a pause and I heard Bridget's voice.

He said, 'Apparently, I'm jolly well fetching you now. Pack a bag.'

'I thought I'd heard wrong,' I said to Amanda later. We were in her room, keeping our voices low. She sat on the edge of her bed, still dressed. I was kneeling on the floor, folding clothes into my bag. I'd changed into my nightie in the bathroom. 'Why would you agree to this?' I said.

'Because I need someone to talk to.'

'That's honest. Nothing to do with offering me sympathy while my dad's critically ill.'

'And that, of course. But, while you're here.'

She took off her blouse. She was wearing a tight vest that looked two sizes too small. She breathed out heavily. 'It's more for the boobs. My tummy's not much different although I let out my belt a notch. I've been washing this vest in the bathroom and drying it with my hairdryer so Mum doesn't smell a rat.'

I said, 'You have to tell them.'

'I can't.'

'Do it while I'm here. That might make it easier.'

'I'm not telling them.'

'I will, then.'

'You promised.'

'You've put me in an awkward position.'

'Mine is more awkward,' she said. 'Hey, look at these

307

marks.' She pulled the vest down to show me fine lines at the tops of her breasts.

I stood to look more closely. 'What's caused those?'

'I don't know. They started a month ago. They look like scratches.'

'It's where your skin is stretching, I think.'

'It might be in the pregnancy book.' She reached for her college bag. 'I keep it hidden in here.' She handed it to me.

'I'll look up stretch in the index,' I said.

'Oh, an index. I'd forgotten about those.'

I found the relevant page. 'It says they're like tiny tears in your skin tissue as it gets pulled tighter.'

'Ugh. Are they permanent?'

I looked again. 'They'll fade.'

'In a hundred years' time,' she said, the way Eeyore would say it.

I closed the book.

'Anyway, I've felt something moving,' she said.

'Let's hope it's the baby.'

'It feels like having a butterfly in there.'

'I don't know anything about babies. Maybe it's indigestion, what you're feeling.'

'Maybe it's terror,' she said, perceptively. 'Turn round while I put my nightie on.'

I focused hard on a Sex Pistols poster on her wardrobe: not the only sacrifice I'd ever made for Amanda.

She was climbing into bed. 'Do you mind if we turn the light out?'

'I have to read or write before I go to sleep,' I said, turning round. 'I've got my torch ready.'

She yawned and turned off her bedside lamp.

I climbed into the sleeping bag that Nick had given me, tucked my mum's ring and Kevin's poem under my pillow, lay on my stomach and opened *Oliver Twist*. I had to concentrate hard on the words, going back over sentences. I kept thinking of Dad, his legs splayed out in the road.

Amanda's face appeared over the side of the bed. 'What are you reading?'

'Charles Dickens. I could read you some?'

'Ugh,' she said, possibly filing Dickens away with stretch marks. She lay down and I could hear her breath slowing. But she said, lazily, 'If you can't sleep because of thinking about your dad, wake me up and I'll talk to you.'

'Okay. Thanks.'

'I might as well get used to broken nights,' she said.

SATURDAY 29 MARCH

When my alarm rang in the morning, Amanda groaned and turned over, settling back under her blankets and putting a pillow over her head. Neither of us had slept well. I'd woken in darkness to hear her shifting about, pulling her bedclothes this way and that, and at one point, when I'd given up on sleep, I'd shone my torch on *Oliver Twist* and she'd said, 'You're blinding me.'

Perhaps I wouldn't stay long, whatever happened.

Downstairs, Nick and Bridget were in dressing gowns on the sofa with cups of tea. Nick asked me, 'Are you getting the bus to the hospital?' and Bridget said, 'No, you're driving her there, darling. Go and put some clothes on.'

So, Nick went to put some clothes on.

Bridget also told him that he must accompany me into the hospital. Turning into the car park later, he said, 'I'll come in with you if you want me to. Or perhaps I should come back later when he's had the operation.'

I tried to imagine the scene, walking onto the critical care ward with Nick, Dad only just come round. I'd heard that general anaesthetics could affect people in strange ways, causing them to behave irrationally. I decided Dad needed no more help with that.

'I'm sure I'll be okay,' I said. 'I can phone if I need you.'

He stopped the car, leaving the engine running. 'Do you have coins?'

'Actually, I gave most of them to Dad.'

He emptied his pockets and insisted I take what he had.

'Thanks. I'd better go. It's nearly eight.'

'Maybe it's best I don't come in after the op,' he said. 'Not everyone reacts well to general anaesthetics.'

A different nurse was supervising the critical care ward, an officious older woman who looked as though she thought the desk was a ship she piloted. 'Yes?' she said, as though she meant no.

'I'm here for Dave Chadwick,' I said.

She waited. She was going to make me do all the work.

'I'm his daughter.'

'Right.'

'A nurse told me yesterday I could go with him for his operation.'

She looked scandalised, as though I'd suggested doing the operation myself and had a scalpel in my back pocket. I think she was planning the nurse's public flogging in the hospital foyer.

'I mean, until he's had the anaesthetic.'

'Hm,' she said.

As if on cue, Dad appeared, wheeled out of the ward on a trolley bed pushed by a porter. His eyes were closed but perhaps he was conscious of us. He was covered in a sheet and a blue blanket stamped *Warwick Hospital*. A young nurse walked alongside the trolley.

'Hi, Dad.' I bent to touch his shoulder.

'Are you Jackie?' the nurse said, smiling widely. 'How lucky is your dad. Join the convoy.'

I looked from her to the nurse at the desk, wondering at their differences, but then remembered that within the dinosaur species come both robin and stegosaurus.

In the anaesthetics room, through doors marked SURGERY 2 I saw the same surgeon who had spoken to me the night before. 'He's been fairly stable overnight,' he said, 'but the sooner we get this done, the better.'

'Sooner the better,' Dad repeated, and I said, 'Hi, Dad,' in case he hadn't heard me the first time. He still hadn't opened his eyes and perhaps it hurt to do so, the lights above being so full of glare.

'Count to ten, Mr Chadwick,' the anaesthetist said, giving Dad an injection.

Dad said, 'One, two, three.' It twitched at my heart to see him submissive like that, in the hands of the doctors.

The doctor said to me, 'Come back at two o'clock-ish. He'll be in recovery all morning.'

'Recovery? That's quick.'

'From the anaesthetic, I mean. The rest will take a lot longer.'

'Oh.'

The friendly nurse pointed me to the hospital exit. 'Don't worry about your dad.'

'That would be a first,' I said.

I stood outside the hospital, wondering what to do. I hadn't thought ahead or expected a free morning. It was nine o'clock.

I could sit in the hospital canteen at the front of the hospital. I'd brought Dickens with me. Or ...

I walked up into Warwick and reached the bakery by twenty past nine. The door tinkled as I entered and, as always, the heat of the ovens welcomed me.

'Hey, you're not meant to be here,' Sheila said. 'Your boyfriend phoned us.'

'Ta-da!' I said, flinging out my hands.

She was organising sausage rolls in the warmer, lining them up like soldiers. It was usually my job. 'I'm sorry about your dad,' she said.

'He's having his operation now.'

'Go home, Jackie.'

'Please let me stay. It'll distract me. Or have you got a replacement?'

She wiped her hands with a cloth. 'No one could replace you,' she said, and I grabbed an apron and put it on before I cried sad tears because of worry about Dad and happy ones because Kevin had described himself as my boyfriend.

When I returned at two, Kevin was waiting outside the hospital entrance. I offered him a currant bun. I had two in a paper bag that Sheila had given me. 'I went into work,' I said.

'You're impossible.'

'It helped.'

He kissed my cheek. 'A smiley nurse told me you'd be back about now.'

'You got the smiley one?'

'That was after a fire-breathing dragon told me that as I wasn't a relative she couldn't possibly give me any information.'

We reached the critical care ward. Nurse Stegosaurus was at the desk, unwrapping a sandwich. She pointed. 'He's just got back. But don't you dare disturb my other patients.'

When we'd passed her, I said to Kevin, 'I expected worse. It must have been hungry.'

In the ward, an auxiliary and the smiley nurse were clearing up the remains of plates of stew and dumplings and dishes of fruit crumble.

'Your dad didn't fancy his, not surprisingly,' the nurse said, nodding towards his bed. 'But he'll have something at teatime, I'm sure. We've ordered him a cheese roll.'

Dad was half sitting, half lying in bed, awake. He had his own pyjamas on. His face looked pale. A drip stood beside his bed.

'Welcome back,' I said, moving towards the chair that sat beside his bed. Kevin hovered.

'Grab that one,' the nurse said to him, pointing to a spare chair in the corner.

Kevin picked it up and placed it next to mine. He sat down.

'Who's this?' Dad said.

'Kevin Price, sir,' Kevin said, stretching out his hand, but Dad looked down at the tubes coming out of his own.

'Sorry, sir,' Kevin said.

'My boyfriend, Dad,' I said. 'You've spoken to him on the phone.'

'Only to say you were out when you weren't,' Dad said. So, whatever had pressed on his brain had been taken away. His speech was slurred but for once this was caused by an anaesthetic that didn't come from the off-licence.

'How are you feeling?' I said.

'Top of the world.' He rolled his eyes.

I opened the locker drawer. 'You've got two Mars bars in here for when you're peckish.'

He said, 'Are there any fags in there?'

The rattle of a tea trolley broke into the quiet hum of the ward. A woman in a yellow overall pushed it into the centre. She came to the end of his bed. 'Cup of tea, Mr Chadwick?' She said to me, 'It'll be the first one after his op. Hopefully he'll keep it down.'

'I am here, you know,' Dad said.

'Hopefully you'll keep it down,' she said.

'Is there whisky in it?' he said.

'Dad,' I said. 'You're in hospital, and all you've asked for so far is poisons.'

He accepted a cup of tea, which she placed on a tray in front of him. He slurped it noisily and batted me away when some spilled onto his pyjamas and I leaned over to dab it with my handkerchief. The woman poured one each for me and Kevin. We sat with the saucers balanced on our palms.

'Did you see me fall?' Dad said.

'You went down like an oak tree in a storm,' I said.

'I'd only had a couple.'

'Of gallons?'

'Hm,' he said.

I glanced at Kevin. Some of the details in my sketches were being coloured in for him. I wondered what he was thinking but his face was impassive.

'I came in the ambulance with you,' I said to Dad.

'Was Casanova in the ambulance?' He nodded towards Kevin.

'No, sir,' Kevin said.

When Dad had finished his tea, his eyes began to close and he lay back. 'That's me done for socialising, pet.'

I pulled the sheet and blanket up and smoothed them down on his chest. 'I'll come back this evening.'

'Good.'

'Make sure you behave for the nurses.'

'I'm a saint for the nurses,' he said, his eyes shut, and I knew he was going to be all right.

Outside the hospital, Kevin put his arms around me and said, 'Are you okay?'

'I'm okay,' I said into his chest.

'Are you hungry? You only ate half that bun.'

It took a while to decide. Other feelings were in the way. I had to part them, like curtains, and there I found hunger.

'They do bacon sandwiches in the canteen,' he said. 'We went in there when my auntie was poorly.'

We sat at the end of a long table, at the other end of which were three nurses, eating eggs on toast and discussing the merits of night shifts and day shifts.

We ate our bacon sandwiches then Kevin bought Bakewell slices and a second pot of tea. As he stirred sugar into his, he said, 'I'm sorry I haven't been very understanding.'

I looked at his eyes. They were blue, like Kim's, but slightly darker, almost purply. 'What haven't you understood?'

He took a deep breath. 'There's a lot about your life that you haven't said.'

'It's hard to know what to pick from the selection.'

'I'm sorry if I got things wrong.'

'You don't get things wrong.'

'Accusing you of not trusting me.'

I said, 'I'm really not very good on trust.'

'You've been let down.'

'How do you know?' I said.

'I just know.'

'Good, then I don't have to go into it.'

He put his mug down. 'You know I love you, don't you?'

I blinked. 'Pardon?'

His cheeks flushed. 'Maybe it's not the time to say it, but – I want to marry you one day.'

'One day?'

'Any day you like.'

'I'll be visiting my dad tomorrow, and on Monday I'm revising.'

'We'll get our diaries out,' he said. 'You told your dad I was your boyfriend.'

'You told the bakery you were my boyfriend.' I reached for his hand. 'I still don't want sexual intercourse.'

'Okay.'

'Not right here, anyway, among the egg and chips and the teaspoons.'

'I understand and I'll never speak of it again.'

I hesitated, taking my hand away. 'It doesn't help that a friend of mine is pregnant.'

'Oh.' He paused. 'That makes sense.'

'It's not my only reason. But it's one of them. I don't want to mess up like that. Call me old-fashioned.'

'It's not old-fashioned.'

'Good.'

He sipped his tea. 'Tuesday for the wedding, then.'

'Tuesday.'

He said, 'Do I know this friend?'

I stayed quiet. He'd met Amanda many times over the last few years when he'd called for me at the Walls'. Sometimes, she'd been to gigs at which he played guitar with his older brother, David, something they did much less often now they were both working.

'Not really,' was the best I could do. But I wanted to tell him everything and I knew I would soon.

SUNDAY 30 MARCH

I spent late Sunday afternoon cleaning Dad's flat and settling back in. I'd persuaded the Walls over a roast dinner and apple pie earlier that day that it was the best solution.

'It's walking distance from the hospital,' I'd said, 'and Kevin's around.'

'Darling,' Bridget said to Nick, 'we've been replaced by an apprentice mechanic.' She added, 'Joke!' but we all knew it wasn't.

Amanda said, 'I really didn't mind your sleep-talking.' She had eaten two slices of pie.

'Did I say anything incriminating?'

'I don't know what that means.'

'Did you learn any of my secrets?'

'I don't need your secrets as well as mine.'

'What do you mean, darling?' Bridget said.

'Joke,' Amanda said.

Another near miss, as well as evidence that people use the word 'joke' for all kinds of reasons.

I arrived in the ward at visiting time with some grapes and a book of crossword puzzles for Dad as well as fresh pyjamas.

'That confirms me as an invalid,' he said. 'Grapes.'

I hugged him gingerly and sat in the visitor chair.

I had a question for him that I didn't want to ask but knew I must. I said, 'Dad, would you like me to try to find Doreen?'

He looked in worse condition now than he had the day before even though it was clear that the operation had been successful. His eyes were still bruised and distorted, as though his eyeballs had expanded. Purples and blues coloured his face. His head was still bandaged and I suspected they'd have had to shave a section of his thick hair for the surgery. I imagined it like a field with one section burned to stubble.

He was also suffering the sudden lack of whisky, sweating and with trembling hands. He said the doctors were keeping an eye as he was at risk of a seizure.

He didn't react well to my question. 'Find Doreen, what for?'

'She'd want to know.'

He said, 'She'd be fussing and faffing, buying me new pyjamas when I've got perfectly decent ones.'

'You mean these pyjamas with the cigarette burns and the frayed sleeves?'

'They'll do fine.'

'She still hasn't sent an address?'

'No,' he said. 'And I don't want one either. She's the last thing I need now I'm going back to the nuthouse to get dried out. Hopefully, this time, I'll have something better to show for it.'

'Going back to Hatton?' I said. 'When?'

He looked embarrassed. 'They sent a shrink this morning to give me the third degree about the drinking. I can go straight from here if I want to. In about ten days, they reckon.'

'Do you want to?'

'No.' He flapped his pyjama top. 'It's bloody hot in here.' It wasn't.

'Do you need to?' I said.

'What do you think?'

'You need to.'

'Well, then. I don't need Doreen around to scupper it all.'

'Okay.'

'Anyway,' he said, putting his hand hesitantly on his

bandages. 'They told me I have a bald patch. No one's going to want me now.'

'It'll grow back, Dad.'

'I might need to reseed it,' he said.

Every time he made a joke, I knew he was making his way back.

'I'm relieved about Doreen, actually,' I said. 'I never got used to Stork.'

'Never mind margarine. That woman makes a bed like she's in the army. A pancake couldn't slide in.'

We both laughed out loud but he began coughing, one of his tubes came out, a machine beeped, and Nurse Stegosaurus came galloping from her swamp, shouting, 'Who's been at his wiring?'

MONDAY 31 MARCH

At half past nine on the first day of the Easter school holidays, I'd washed up my cereal bowl and was making a list for a shopping trip later. Bridget had pressed a few pound notes into my hand on Sunday and said, 'Buy fruit and fresh vegetables. We don't want you living on pies and tinned peas,' which was a shame, as I'd intended exactly that.

The phone rang in the hall. It was Heather.

'Can I come and see you?' she said. 'I've just heard about your poor dad. To think I was meant to be popping in on him today, too.'

'Did Bridget phone you?'

'My phone was ringing as I walked into the office.'

'I would have called you myself if it hadn't happened at the weekend,' I said, and then remembered that my dad's girlfriend had moved in, followed by her son, who had made Amanda pregnant, and my dad had started drinking again, and I was head picking like a demon, and messing up my A levels, and I hadn't called Heather with any of that.

'Also, your school nurse contacted me late Friday afternoon,' she said. 'That was quite a long conversation.'

'Sorry.'

'You're not the one who needs to apologise.'

'Did you tell the Walls?'

'You know I had to.'

'Are they angry with me?'

'Pardon? Angry with *you*?'

'I thought they'd be angry.'

'Oh, Jackie,' she said.

I felt guilty. The news about Amanda was still to come. I didn't know how it was going to come. But come it must, as inevitable as the birth itself.

Heather said. 'I'll be with you in half an hour. I'll bring Wagon Wheels.'

Later, she stood in the kitchen, watching me pour boiling water into the teapot. 'I'm the one who should apologise,' she said. 'I made the wrong decision, relying on you feeling able to tell me things.'

'I thought my dad would get into trouble.'

'I can see that.'

I waved the sugar bowl at her and she shook her head.

'This Doreen,' she said. 'She led your dad back into drinking?'

'He followed like a lamb. It wasn't all her fault.' I put the mugs and teapot on a tray and we took it into the living room.

She sat on the sofa. 'But this has affected your schoolwork. You must have been unhappy.'

I didn't know what to say.

She seemed to be thinking back. 'So, when I came to visit your dad in February – well, I suppose I'll talk to him about that.'

'He wasn't deliberately trying to pull the wool over your eyes.'

She glanced at me.

'Okay, he was deliberately trying to pull the wool over your eyes.'

'You're not to blame, Jackie.'

'It feels like it.'

She said, 'It was silly of me to agree to fortnightly meetings so easily. I'm sorry.'

'Not silly—'

'My manager says so and isn't happy with me.' She dipped into her bag and brought out three Wagon Wheels. 'I thought you could take one to your dad.'

'Have you laced it with arsenic?'

'No,' she said, and smiled.

'You won't have to put up with me for much longer.'

'We don't just drop you after your exams, you know. We'll have a meeting. Make sure you're sorted. Until then—'

'Mason Street? Is it ready?'

'In a fortnight or so, and I'm glad you raised that, and not me. We would advise that you don't stay with your dad on his discharge from Hatton.'

'I've already advised myself of that,' I said. 'I'm tempted to send myself an official letter.'

'Wise girl.'

'And Patsy says she's moving back in, too?'

'She can't wait.'

'And Marion and Harry will feel safe in their beds,' I said.

I thought of Patsy and her big hair rollers and that laugh and the way she shouted at customers in the bakery but they loved her all the same. I missed being in a household with girls my age.

I wasn't sure when I would tell Dad of my decision. He'd gone into hospital thinking that his loyal daughter would be waiting for him when he came back.

'Patsy's room has had a thorough redecoration,' Heather said. 'I'm afraid the budget didn't stretch to yours as there was minimal damage.'

'Did Patsy have a say in the redecoration?' I was imagining hot-pink walls and a chandelier, plus a gold cabinet for the Barbies.

'We didn't risk asking,' she said.

I tore open one of the Wagon Wheels. 'I liked my room as it was, anyway.'

*

That afternoon, I visited the Walls. I knew I must, even though as I put my key in the door, my stomach seemed to disagree.

Nick was at the dining table, a pile of exercise books in front of him and a red pen ready. He said, 'I want to finish all this, then enjoy the holiday.'

I hung my coat up and pointed to the pile of books. 'That shouldn't take too long.'

'There are four piles like this,' he said. 'But you're here now. Terrible essays about the Civil War can wait.' He put the pen down.

'How's your dad?' Bridget said. She was in an armchair, knitting. She found this more difficult now, and projects grew slowly. She'd told me she was knitting a blanket for the baby recently christened.

'Another week at least,' I said, sitting on the sofa, 'and his feet hang over the end of the bed.' I told them about the plans for Hatton.

'And when he's discharged from there?' Bridget said, and I knew she wasn't asking about him, but about me.

'I'll be back at Mason Street,' I said, and she dropped a stitch trying to hide her relief.

Amanda came downstairs.

'Put the kettle on, pet,' Nick said to her.

'I'll do it,' I said, standing up. There was a stillness in the room made up of me knowing more things had to be said and them knowing things were about to be said.

Amanda followed me into the kitchen and pushed the door shut. 'Heather rang them and told them everything,' she whispered.

'I know. Everything except …' I nodded towards her abdomen. 'Which she knows nothing about.'

She put her hand there. 'You're not going to—'

'Of course not.' I put the kettle on the hob.

She let out a long breath.

I said, 'That news might just topple them.'

I could feel the tension coming from her like a force field.

I thought she was afraid that once one secret got out, others would escape, like sheep when a gate opens.

'What are you two plotting?' Nick called.

'Women's stuff you wouldn't want to hear,' Amanda called back, which was both a lie and a truth, and I gave her a thumbs up for the quick thinking.

She went back in and I made a pot of tea for everyone, loading a plate with biscuits.

Bridget poured the tea, holding tight to the teapot handle, her knuckles white. We all tried not to look.

Dunking a digestive, I said, 'I'm here to apologise but I don't even know how to start.'

'We would have helped,' Bridget said, high-jumping straight in. 'You could have come back here any time.'

'Sometimes I thought I would say something but then another thing happened and another thing and it grew too big to handle.'

Amanda stared at me and I realised I could have been describing a pregnancy. 'And Dad was sleeping in her room, anyway,' she said, bluntly.

Nick said, 'That wasn't insurmountable.'

'And your schoolwork,' Bridget said. 'How have you managed?'

'I haven't. But I've been seeing the school nurse.'

'Heather mentioned that.' Her eyes looked wet. She looked at Amanda. 'Did you know all this?'

'Not everything,' Amanda said. 'But she made me swear not to tell you.'

I was annoyed with her, reframing the situation. I felt she deserved a warning. 'It wasn't like that. I didn't want them worrying. I'm sure there are things *you* don't say.'

She went instantly red.

'We *know* there are things you don't tell us, darling,' Nick said to her. 'You're blushing now. What are you hiding?'

Her parents were scrutinising her, surely the opposite of what she'd hoped.

'Nothing,' she said, her arms folded across her chest in case her breasts popped out and yelled, *Look at these beauties!*

'Anyway,' I said. 'My secrets are in the open now and it's a relief.'

'I'm going upstairs,' Amanda said.

THURSDAY 3 APRIL

I'd rung Kevin on Tuesday evening after I'd visited Dad and said, 'Do you want to come round on Thursday and be experimented on?'

For a moment, he didn't reply. Then he said, 'That's a sudden change of heart.'

'I mean *food*.'

'Oh.'

'I bought a cookbook,' I said. 'I needed a project.' The flat had felt motionless and redundant, all the tensions and happenings gone that had seemed to take physical form in corners and behind furniture.

I'd asked for extra bakery shifts over the holidays but Patsy had nabbed most of them, apart from the two Wednesday mornings.

I would learn to cook. It would be a sign that I was ready for independence again.

I'd bought the *Hamlyn All Colour Cook Book* in Leamington on Tuesday morning, one that Bridget used. I'd considering borrowing hers but feared it was attached to her heart by invisible threads and she'd bleed if separated. My culinary skills thus far were at the level of heating up bought pies, stirring beans and making toast. I'd helped Bridget cook hundreds of meals but she'd limited me to mincing meat or chopping apples. In cookery at school, I'd made puff pastry that failed to puff and the teacher had said she hoped I wasn't considering domestic science for O level.

But it couldn't be that hard.

I'd studied the cookbook that evening and chosen a macaroni and tuna layer pie recipe for the main meal. For pudding, I found one for traditional English trifle, except that I'd leave out the sherry. My only recent experience of trifle had been Doreen's and I wanted one that wouldn't set on fire if near a heat source.

After my Wednesday bakery shift, I went shopping and queued at the till. I'd need to make the trifle that evening to set the custard, apparently. 'Someone's living it up,' said the shop assistant at the counter. She said the ingredients aloud as she tapped them in. 'Double cream. Macaroni. Maraschino cherries. Tuna. Ooh, ratafia biscuits!'

'Sounds like a trifle, love,' said a woman behind me in the queue. 'Careful with the custard or you'll have scrambled eggs.'

Another woman said, 'Don't put the trifle under the grill to toast the almonds like my Fred did.'

All three women laughed like a drain. I felt twelve years old and fifty-five at the same time.

'Trifle sponges!' said the assistant. Ting, went the till.

I walked out of the shop with the ladies shouting, 'Good luck, chuck!' as though I'd been nominated for a prize.

I'd put together the trifle that evening after seeing Dad. I made the mistake of telling him about the planned meal and had to reassure him that, no, Kevin and I weren't hosting an orgy.

On Thursday evening, I chatted to Dad via the patients' phone then set the table properly with a red tablecloth Doreen had left behind. I'd forgotten about napkins. I'd bought a candle and lit it but realised I should have bought several.

Kevin rang the doorbell at seven o'clock, wearing a shirt and smart trousers.

I let him in and he kissed me on the cheek. 'Mum sent these,' he said, holding out a box of Milk Tray.

'Thank you.'

He entered the living room. 'Why so dark? Have you got a big spot you don't want me to see?'

I switched the main light back on. The candle looked futile now.

He said, 'You look harassed.'

'Do you want this meal or not?'

'Sorry.'

I pointed to a dining chair. 'Sit here while I fetch it.'

'Do you need help?'

'No, thanks.' I didn't want him in the kitchen, which looked as though some wildebeest had been through on their way to the savanna.

I brought in the macaroni and tuna pie, holding it with a tea towel as we had no oven gloves. But I hadn't put mats on the table. I took the tuna pie back to the kitchen.

'Is that the experiment?' he called. 'All we do is look?'

I came back in, found table mats in a drawer and arranged them. Then I returned for the pie. 'Don't tease me,' I said. 'I don't know what I'm doing and you're not supposed to notice.'

I served him a portion. The pie didn't make it easy, clinging to the dish as though determined to stay. I realised most of the liquid had dried up so what came out was a solid mass which needed carving rather than spooning. It dropped onto Kevin's plate like a sodden sandbag. 'I left it in too long,' I said. 'Dad kept me talking on the phone, complaining about Nurse Stegosaurus, only he calls her the wicked witch of the west.'

'This looks delicious,' Kevin said. He picked up his knife and fork.

'Dig in,' I said. 'Literally.'

'Your dad's missing a treat.'

'My dad's missing beer. He'd take that over a tuna pie, especially one that's died.'

'It's fine.'

'I can hear you crunching.'

'You can*not*!'

'I'm sorry I didn't do vegetables. I forgot about side dishes.'

He said, 'Is your dad getting better?'

'He's wandering around, making a pest of himself, moaning that the meals are too small.'

'There's a lot of him to fill.'

I put my knife and fork down after eating half my portion. 'This is getting more solid by the second.'

The trifle was more successful, although Doreen had taken her whisk with her and I'd had to whip the cream with a fork. I hadn't persisted long enough so we could have drunk it through a straw. Still, Kevin ate two bowls full and then, on the sofa afterwards, snaffled half the box of chocolates he'd brought.

I brought in the *Hamlyn All Colour Cook Book* and put it on the coffee table before sitting beside him. 'Fat lot of use that was.'

'I'd marry you anyway,' he said, 'even if you couldn't cook. But you can.'

'I can't. I should have done a practice run.'

'No, I'm happy to be a guinea pig. Can I kiss you?'

I was looking at the TV listings in our *Radio Times*. 'It's that or watch a documentary about the nature of time. Let's opt for the kissing.'

But when he kissed me, I cried.

'Why are you upset?' he said, drawing me close so that my head lay on his shoulder.

'The cream was meant to be in soft peaks.' I wiped my eyes with my sleeve.

'Soft peaks are overrated,' he said.

'I'm going back to Mason Street before Dad comes back.'

'Have you got a proper kitchen there?'

'No. A two-ring hob. Back to tinned spaghetti.'

He kissed me again. 'You can leave the soft peaks to the Bridgets of this world. And my mum. She likes a soft peak.'

'Will you want soft peaks if we get married?'

'Ah, that's different. We'll need it written into the vows. I promise to love, honour, and make soft peaks.'

I put my head on his chest. 'We should have a cup of coffee with cream now.'

'There's no should,' he said, and played with my hair.

'I don't know what to do with the cookbook. I never want to see it again.'

'My mum doesn't have that one.'

I said, 'She does now.'

SUNDAY 6 APRIL

On Easter Sunday, Bridget cooked lamb, roast potatoes and green beans. She had made the same trifle I'd attempted, but hers looked the same as the one in the book. I didn't mention my failed experiment; she'd have leapt on it and offered a bespoke twelve-week cookery course covering savouries, sweets, snacks and food for special occasions, and perhaps a module in butchery.

I was due later at Kevin's house for tea. His mum Christine had rung to ask me and to thank me for the Hamlyn cookery book.

Nick drove me there and I was slightly early. I knocked and Kevin answered, holding a bag of Hula Hoops. 'They all went for a walk after dinner,' he said. 'They'll be back soon. I'll make a pot of tea.'

I trailed behind him into the kitchen.

He said, 'Have you seen your dad?'

'It won't be long before his dressings can come off.'

'Is he fed up?'

'He's appointed himself official ward spokesman for complaints about the food portions. I think he's enjoying the status. He's told them he had bigger portions in prison.'

'Hey, before they all come back,' he said.

'What?'

'I've got something for you.'

'What is it?'

He took one of the Hula Hoops out of the bag and grabbed

my hand, sliding it on to my ring finger. It wouldn't go past my knuckle.

'Oh,' he said.

'It doesn't matter. I think I get the idea.'

'You can have a real one when I've finished my apprenticeship.'

I popped the Hula Hoop into my mouth.

He said, 'Did you just eat your ring?'

I crunched it and swallowed.

'Happy engagement,' he said.

'Ditto,' I said.

'Shall we tell them all?'

'No, it's between us. Is that okay?'

'That's okay,' he said, and reached for the kettle.

We sat next to each other on the sofa. 'Can I kiss you?' he said.

'You don't have to ask permission every time,' I said. 'I won't make you fill in a form.'

I leaned towards him and he pulled my head towards his. As we kissed, I felt his tongue on mine. He had done this before and I hadn't been sure I enjoyed it but just below my belly button I felt something shift.

He put his hand on my waist and lifted my jumper and then the blouse I had on underneath. I felt his cool hand just below my breast, touching the bottom of my bra.

This, we hadn't done.

'You might have to fill in a form for *that*,' I said, but didn't move away.

His hand cupped my breast and went still.

'You're not going inside my bra.'

'I won't. This feels good, though. Does it feel good to you?'

I kissed him again as an answer. We stayed like that for a few minutes, his hand over my breast which made it tingle, and kissing. Then I could hear Kim's voice outside. He took his hand away and I readjusted my clothes.

'I can hear the kettle,' he said.

'I thought you were going to say you could hear angels,' I said.

'What are you two laughing about?' Kim said as she came in ahead of her mum, dad and older brother David. But I don't think she expected an answer. I could hear how happy she was that I was there. I felt I belonged at the Price household, like a hand in a familiar glove.

'You're a sight for sore eyes, you are,' her mother Christine said. She always made me feel as though I'd had a prayer said over me or that a nun had smiled.

THURSDAY 10 APRIL

In the second week of the holidays, Kevin came to see Dad with me again after tea. We'd eaten together at the flat, this time sausages and baked beans. Kevin had fried the sausages.

'Excuse me. I can't see my dad in the ward,' I said to Nurse Stegosaurus.

'That's because he's busy killing himself in the smoking room,' she said, pointing towards the far end of the ward corridor. She sounded almost hopeful. 'Tell him he's having an enema in half an hour. No one's leaving my ward bunged up.'

I didn't understand but wasn't asking for an explanation and when I looked up 'enema' at the flat later was pleased I hadn't.

We found him puffing away on his own. The one small window was shut and the room was a fug. Dad was in pyjamas but all his bandages had gone. I saw him touch his square of stubble as we arrived, as though self-conscious.

'Oh, Casanova's back,' he said.

'Give it a rest, Dad.'

We sat on a couple of vacant seats. 'How are you, Mr Chadwick?' Kevin said.

'Bloody rough.' He coughed. 'Dicky stomach as well.'

'That money wasn't for fags, Dad,' I said.

Kevin said, 'I'll go and see what chocolate is in the machine.'

335

While he was gone, I said to Dad, 'When are you going to Hatton? The nurse said something.'

'Tomorrow,' he said.

'I'm not allowed to visit you for two weeks. Heather phoned to tell me. I have to leave you time to settle.'

'I'm not a patio,' he said.

'Remember I'm not going to be there when you get back to the flat.'

'So you told me.' He lit another cigarette. I pushed the ashtray towards him.

'You'll be okay, won't you?'

'If you're that worried,' he said, 'you'd stay with me.'

'You know it's not like that. And I'll visit at least once a week.'

'It's not visiting. You make it sound like prison.'

'You know what I mean.'

'You'll soon forget. You'll be applying for jobs after your exams, won't you? You'll have other things to do.'

'You're being awkward.'

But it was true. Exams would be finished by the end of June and I had to make decisions. Mrs Collingworth had urged me to apply for a university place but I wanted to earn my own money and have a place of my own.

'You can always go to university later on,' she'd conceded.

'I will, one day.'

'All your teachers think you should go to university.'

'I know. They've all told me.'

'Sorry. Do you feel press-ganged?'

'It's kind press-ganging, though,' I'd said, and she smiled and suggested I should revise the nature of the press gang thoroughly before my history exams.

'I'll still have time for you, Dad,' I said, now, but then Kevin arrived with three Kit Kats and three Mars bars which he put on the table. Talk between the three of us stuttered along like something running out of battery until Dad began to relax, sitting less awkwardly in his chair. He took a Kit Kat, as did we.

'Thanks, kid,' he said to Kevin.

'What about your poorly tummy?' I said.

'That's hospital food doing that, not chocolate.'

'If you say so, Dad.'

'Anyway, at least the nuthouse has nice grounds,' he said.

I'd been treading carefully in case he didn't want us to talk about Hatton while Kevin was there, but Dad was clearly not fussed. Perhaps it was a hopeful sign that Kevin was accepted. I was alert for optimistic signs like this in case I missed them, like bird spotters miss cuckoos and woodpeckers if they're not fully concentrating.

'Don't keep calling it the nuthouse,' I said.

'That's how it feels.'

'Do you think you'll stay this time, though, until you're properly better?'

'Not much choice,' he said, 'unless I want an early grave.' He screwed up his Kit Kat wrapper and aimed it at a wastepaper bin, then lit another cigarette and ripped open a Mars bar.

'I'm sure there are other ways to achieve an early grave,' I said.

Kevin said to him, 'My mum says she had an uncle who had – who was like you, Mr Chadwick.'

'Did she now?' he said.

'He had to spend six weeks in that hospital – Hatton – but he never drank again. He became a factory manager and won an award.'

'Bully for him,' Dad said, but more mellow, as though he knew Kevin was trying to encourage him.

'He was eighty-three when he died.'

'What killed him, then?' Dad said.

Kevin bit his lip and looked hesitant. He ate a finger of Kit Kat.

'Well?' Dad said.

'He got run over by a truck.'

Dad put his hand over his mouth and I thought it was shock at first but then I realised he was laughing. It was catching. All three of us found it very funny. Dad wiped his eyes.

'I'd forgotten how that story ended until I got to it,' Kevin said.

As we walked back to the ward, Dad shuffling along in slippers, he said to Kevin, 'You don't have to call me Mr Chadwick, lad. Dave will do.' But then he said, 'Unless you mess about with my littlun, in which case you're a dead man.'

'Yes, sir,' Kevin said.

'A slow learner, is he?' Dad said to me but he sounded affectionate, although that may have been because Kevin had given him the remaining Kit Kat and two Mars bars.

Nurse Stegosaurus was waiting for Dad by his bed, holding a long tube with a bag at one end. 'Say goodbye to your dad.'

Dad looked at the tube. 'It's fatal?'

Her face didn't move. 'Your daughter won't see you now for a fortnight.'

She clearly wasn't going to allow us privacy so I gave Dad a quick hug and said, 'Try to be good,' but he tore the wrapper off another Mars bar.

The nurse tutted. 'No wonder you can't *go*,' she said, waving the tube at Dad.

'I can't go because of the rationing and poisonous cabbage,' he said.

He was nibbling the Mars bar round the edges rather than eating it in three bites in his usual manner. I knew he was stalling her deliberately. She stood and watched him, her face set like a stone. She checked her watch.

'I haven't got time for this, Mr Chadwick,' she said. 'I've got Mr Jackson on a bedpan. I'll have to come back to you.'

She bustled to the other end of the ward, still holding the tube and bag. 'Please, no!' I heard a man groan and she replied, 'It's not for you, Mr Jackson. Calm down.'

'Worked a treat,' Dad said. He pulled me close to him

and put his stubbly cheek on mine. 'Two weeks. Don't leave it longer.'

He smelled of hospital soap.

'Bring me some fags when you come.'

'I wish you asked for orange squash like normal people,' I said.

As we left the ward, Kevin said, 'There's someone else who wants to see you.'

'What do you mean?'

'You'll see.'

'You're scaring me.'

'There's no need,' he said. 'It's good news.'

We walked along the hospital corridors. He scanned directions on the wall, and when we saw a sign saying *Dickins Ward*, he said, 'That's the one.'

At the desk, he told a nurse, 'We're here to see Kim Price. I'm her brother.'

She led us to a bed where Kim was sitting up, wearing a hospital gown, her blonde hair in a ponytail. She looked tired.

'Why didn't I know about this?' I said. I sat on her bed. 'You didn't say a word on Sunday.'

'You had your dad to worry about,' she said. 'But I've had the procedure and they reckon it should make a difference, so there's nothing to worry about anyway.'

'But I would have wanted to worry.'

'I have to miss a week of school.'

I said, 'Excellent forward planning!'

FRIDAY 18 APRIL

Mock exam test had followed mock exam test without respite in the week leading up to my return to Mason Street. Although Kim couldn't come into school, I knew she was writing the exams at home. We'd all embarked on what Mrs Collingworth called 'crunch time'. I missed Molly more with Kim away and, rather than sit alone in the dining hall at break or dinner time, I stayed in the library, spreading my textbooks across the expansive wooden tables.

But I felt more prepared this time and it meant I couldn't brood over what was happening to Dad at Hatton. He'd said before his discharge from hospital that the psychiatrist had mentioned electric shock treatment and though Dad had joked about it ('I thought my personality was electric enough.') he'd looked scared.

Again, the flat seemed to know, too. On Monday, a curtain rail had fallen down and the bath had stopped draining water away: both problems Dad could have solved. I felt a weight of responsibility. It reminded me how easy life had been in Mason Street, where issues like that could be reported to Heather, and someone in a council van would turn up to mend them.

On Wednesday, Nick had popped round to deliver the two suitcases I'd used before. I'd told him on the phone about the curtain rail and the blocked drain so he brought tools to sort out the problems. It felt odd, having him in the flat. I wouldn't tell Dad.

I'd also spent time that week spring-cleaning for when Dad came home. Kevin had come round on Thursday evening and helped me clean the tops of the kitchen cupboards and wardrobes. I rewarded him with some kissing and a touch of the other breast so that he'd covered both sides.

On Friday at five o'clock, I heard the beep of Heather's car horn in the car park outside the flats. I was ready, my bags packed.

As I shut the door of the flat, dragging the suitcases, Colin appeared. 'What's happening here, then?' he said, lighting up a Woodbine with an expert strike of a match on the brick wall. 'I heard you hoovering. Don't tell me someone else is moving in. Bound to be bloody triplets.'

'Quins, I heard.'

'What?'

'No one's moving in,' I said. 'My dad will be back.'

'Back from where?'

'Hospital.' I wasn't going to elaborate.

'And where are you going?'

'Somewhere else.'

He took the hint, grunting, 'Right, then,' and went back into his flat.

I heard footsteps. Heather and Patsy were climbing up. 'We thought you might need help,' Heather said.

Patsy was trying to catch her breath. 'Bloody *hell*. It's like *Everest*.'

I managed one case and Heather carried the other while Patsy followed behind. She was in platforms anyway and at risk of death.

'Lie the cases on the back seat beside you,' Heather said, opening the car door for me.

'Her boot is filled with Barbies,' Patsy said.

*

That evening, when we'd unpacked, Patsy invited me into her refurbished room which smelled of fresh paint and recently laid carpet. She'd bought a bottle of Lambrusco – I didn't know how she'd acquired it and I didn't ask - and persuaded me to drink a small glass while she poured the rest into a beer tankard.

Heather had given us each a carrier bag full of groceries so we ate sausage rolls and tomatoes with Branston Pickle, sitting on Patsy's floor, chairs being 'on order'.

'What do you think of the Lambrusco?' she said.

'It's fizzy.'

'Well done, Einstein.'

I said, 'Will you miss Marion and Harry?'

'I'm going to theirs once a week for tea.'

'I do the same with the Walls.'

'Do you get interrogated?'

'Gently,' I said.

'I'll have to plan some answers they'll like.' She topped up her glass and laughed the Patsy laugh.

I opened a packet of Mr Kipling cherry pies and offered one to her.

'I've got a question for ya,' she said. 'About Amanda. Swear to me you'll tell the truth.'

'No.'

'I'll ask you anyway. Is she preggers?'

'What?'

'Is she?'

I peeled the foil from my cherry pie. 'Why are you asking that?' I said, slowly.

'Just curious.'

'Can we talk about something else?'

'I knew it,' she said, but then moved on as though she'd accepted my reticence. 'I can't wait for the summer. I'm going on holiday at the end of August.'

'Where to?'

'Ireland. To stay with that auntie I told you about.'

'The one who helped you?' She had never told me exactly how she'd helped.

'Do you wanna come?' Patsy said.

'Me?'

'I asked her. She says I can bring a friend. She's stumping up for the travel.'

She must have seen my face.

'Don't worry. She's loaded. But she's nice. We have to go on a boat.'

I didn't know what to say.

'Say you'll come. Her dinners are something else. She lives near the sea. Fishermen and everything.'

'It sounds like paradise. Don't I need to ask anyone?'

'Who? You're eighteen.'

'I suppose so. You're not, though.'

'I'll have my birthday there.'

I smiled. 'Okay.'

'That's decided, then,' she said, as though I'd signed on a dotted line.

I didn't mean to eat two cherry pies but the second one got eaten while I tried to absorb the news. I couldn't take it in. I was going on holiday to Ireland, near the sea.

'I suppose, before we go, I'd better tell you something,' she said, mopping up a blob of cherry pie filling from her knee with her finger.

'Go on.'

'You know I said I stayed with her one year.'

'I remember. You told me when I came for my birthday cake.'

'I was there for a reason.' Her voice began to crack.

I waited.

'It's because – it's because I had a baby. A little girl. She was adopted by a couple. They seemed lovely.'

I stared.

'Katy,' she said. 'I called her Katy.' She screwed up the foil her pie had been in. 'I don't know what they called her. The people who took her.'

'Oh, Patsy.'

'She'll be three now,' she said.

'I didn't know.'

'Not many do,' she said. 'Take my advice, though. Let no one into your knickers who doesn't have a Durex, never mind if it's David bleedin' Essex.'

'Thank you,' I said, weakly.

'Anyway,' she said, sighing. 'That's how I know Amanda's preggers. Her skin's glowing like a light bulb and her boobs are like beach balls.'

'Have you said this to Amanda?'

'I don't talk to her.'

I put the two remaining cherry pies in the box for something to do. 'Please, say nothing.'

'Don't tell me the bint is trying to keep it a *secret*.'

'I'm not at liberty to say anything.'

'I'm not at liberty to say anything,' she mimicked. 'We're not in an episode of *Crown Court*!'

'I promised.'

'I'm right, though, aren't I?' she said, and took a triumphant gulp from the tankard.

SATURDAY 26 APRIL

Bridget drove me to Hatton to see Dad on a warm Saturday afternoon, two weeks after he'd been admitted.

'Are you still allowed to drive?' I'd asked, as I climbed into the car.

'You can get the bus, if you like,' she said, and I knew I'd offended her. But, on the way, she said, 'Perhaps not for much longer,' and I looked out of the passenger window rather than focus on how she didn't always get the gearstick first time.

When we reached the hospital car park, she said, 'I'll wait for you. I've brought my knitting.' She'd also brought her curiosity which was like a little dynamo inside her, keeping her going, and I knew I would be questioned in detail on my return.

A nurse took me to a large room with high ceilings and windows that overlooked a lawn and fortunately not the car park, as I wouldn't have put it past Bridget to have binoculars in the glovebox.

Dad was sitting at a table laying out cards for a game of Patience. He stood as I arrived and hugged me. His face looked pale and I wondered if he was ill but then I realised it was the flush of the whisky that had gone. The stubbled patch on his head was growing back softer now.

We sat quietly for a while, less sure of how to begin the conversation again than we'd been after his three years in prison. In the corner of the room sat a black-and-white TV, three or four patients watching. One lady rocked in her chair but it seemed a reasonable response to life.

'What did you say I'd had?' Dad began. 'You're better with words.'

'A subdural haematoma.'

'Subdural haematoma.' He tested it on his tongue. 'That sounds impressive.'

'It's not a competition, Dad.'

'Bleed on the brain doesn't sound half so good.'

'Either way, you could have died.'

Out of the window, I could see two nurses sitting on a bench under a tree, deep in talk.

A young woman came in with a tea trolley on which was a giant teapot and a tin of biscuits. She headed for our table.

'I should have done a full stay here years ago,' Dad said to me, 'rather than discharge myself after a few days.'

The woman began pouring tea, bending to do so, but then stopped, putting her hand on her back. 'Oof,' she said.

'You all right, pet?' my dad said.

She rubbed her back. 'I'm expecting. I don't know what it does to your ligaments but it's doing it to mine.'

'When's your baby due?' I said.

'August time. If I've got my dates right. Ages to go yet.'

'Does everyone get that?'

'Get what?'

'The ligament thing.'

'I don't know, but I do. And don't get me started on the cravings.'

'Tell me about it,' my dad said.

'She doesn't mean whisky, Dad.'

'In my case, celery with salt,' she said. 'I go round the house holding a stick of celery and a pot of salt, dipping it in.'

I thought about Amanda. If she started craving celery, which she normally picked out of Bridget's Waldorf salad, her parents would soon know something was up.

The tea woman said, 'Pregnancy does funny things to your body.'

She left us to serve others.

'You seemed a bit too interested,' Dad said. 'Please don't tell me you've got a bun in the oven.'

Within seconds, I knew my face was pink.

He sat up in his chair. 'Have you got something to tell me?'

'No, of course not.'

'Your lad. Kelvin.' I knew exactly where his mind had gone. I could track its progress in his forehead and eyes.

'It's Kevin.'

'Whoever. I'll kill him.'

He went quiet for a while as though trying to collect the parts of himself together that loved me and the parts that would have found a pregnant daughter difficult news.

He mellowed his tone. 'You know you can tell me. You can tell me anything.'

'Dad, you went white if I mentioned my monthlies. I cannot tell you anything.'

'They come monthly?' he said.

'Very funny.'

'So you're not—'

'No, I'm not!'

'So why are you so embarrassed?'

'You don't believe me, do you?'

'I wouldn't be angry,' he said. 'I'm not exactly in a position to judge people who make mistakes.'

'No, you're not.'

He sipped at his tea. 'You know I'd look after you, pet. And the baby. It would be my privilege. You can come back to the flat any time.'

That broke my resolve not to tell. I said, 'Relax. You're not going to be a grandad. It's not me who's pregnant.'

'So, someone is?'

'You're sworn to secrecy.'

'Okay.'

'Scout's honour.'

'I wasn't in the Scouts.'

'Don't nitpick. It's Amanda.'

'The Wall girl?'

'The Wall girl.'

'Bloody hell,' he said.

It felt like something lifted, saying that aloud for the first time, even though there was nothing Dad could do to help.

'Who's the father?' he said. 'Anyone I know?'

I think it had been a half-joke, but then he frowned and I could sense him thinking back.

'Maybe,' I said, slowly.

'Not – not Doreen's lad?'

I didn't need to nod or say yes.

'The little *sod*,' Dad said. 'What have her parents said? Have they had strokes?'

'She hasn't told them.'

'Surely *you'll* tell them if the girl won't.'

'Stop calling her "the girl",' I said.

'Whatever she's called, they need to know.'

'I can't tell them.' I explained about the night of Bridget's fall.

He said, 'You're too young to have to carry other people's big secrets.'

'Right, Dad.'

There was a pause.

'Except for mine, obviously,' he said.

Bridget was dozing when I reached the car but pretended she hadn't been. 'Tell me all about it,' she said, as she started the engine, so I described the room in some detail, recounted what Dad had told me about a couple of the other patients, and informed her that the woman who'd served our tea was having a baby.

'I love babies,' she said. 'I've nearly finished the blanket for little Rosie and I'll be looking for another project,' and it took all my determination not to say, 'Well, that's timely.'

FRIDAY 2 MAY

On Friday, I ate chicken casserole and mashed potatoes in the school dining room with Kim. 'Your face is so much pinker these days,' I said.

'I was anaemic,' she said.

'What does that mean exactly?' I said.

'You don't have enough iron because of all the bleeding.'

'I think I can spell it but I couldn't define it. Is it A.N.A.E.M.I.C?'

She put her knife and fork together. 'I really don't know how you do that.'

'I'm right, then?'

'I have no idea,' she said.

After lunch, I knocked on Nursey B's door.

'I'm glad you're here,' she said, looking up from her desk.

'Should you be?' I sat in my usual chair. 'You see me because of emotional distress.'

She ignored that, picked up a notebook from the desk and came to sit opposite. 'There's an image in this poem I'm writing. I can't get it right.' She opened the notebook and passed it to me, pointing to the page. 'This bit, here. The second line.'

'Why are you asking me?'

'Just read it out. Does anything sound wrong?'

I read out the line. 'The mind's a wheeling sea, a storm in waiting.'

'Again,' she said.

'The mind's a wheeling sea, a storm in waiting.'

She chewed her lip. 'Something's not right. What do you reckon?'

I looked at the line. How could I say what I was thinking? She'd been published in a literary magazine.

'Say what you're thinking,' she said.

'It's only a small thing.'

'Spit it out. We need to get on to your emotional distress.'

'Well – I mean - could it be wait rather than waiting? A storm in wait. It's free verse, isn't it? You don't need the "ing" for a rhyme or for scansion.'

'You,' she said, taking the notebook, 'are a genius. I knew it needed something. It adds to the sense of threat, doesn't it, that change?'

'It's only my opinion.'

'And that's what I wanted. Your valuable opinion.'

'Okay, then,' I said. 'That'll be a pound.'

She put the notebook on the floor. 'So, how is life back at your bedsit?'

'Not perfect. There's a new girl in the loft room above me who likes Black Sabbath. And my wardrobe door won't shut properly.'

'But, otherwise—'

'Pretty near ideal,' I said. 'I wish I wasn't grown-up.'

'Otherwise you'd stay.'

'I'll have to find something of my own when I leave school and get a job.'

'You can find a flatmate, perhaps. Someone to share with. That's what Mrs Collingworth and I did.'

'How come?'

'Oh, we've known each other for a hundred years. She was doing her teacher training when I was a rookie nurse.'

'I didn't know that.'

'I was talking to her about you,' she said. 'We agreed that when you've finished school, we'd like you to have our phone numbers in case you need a listening ear, or maybe help with choosing where to live.'

'You'd do that?'

'And I'll have your number in case I need help with a poem,' she said.

I sat quietly, taking in what she was saying.

'Anyway, how is your emotional distress?' she said.

'At last!'

'Specifically, how is the head picking?'

'Less and less,' I said. 'I can stop myself now when I get the instinct. I tell myself to write some lines or pick up a book.'

'Or do something practical like some cooking? Do you like cooking?'

'Cooking doesn't like *me*,' I said, and told her about my macaroni pie.

Later that day, I stayed in the library after school to revise some history. The newspapers spread over the library tables all featured headlines about the Iranian Embassy siege in London where terrorists were holding twenty-six people. It was the third day of the siege.

'Strange, isn't it?' the librarian said to me, taking her spectacles off and leaving them to hang on their chain. 'One day we'll know how that ended – please God, they'll be safe – and it'll be in the history books that future Jackies will study.'

I hadn't considered this before, that we were always part of history being made.

I let myself in to the Walls' house at five thirty to find Nick, Bridget and Amanda in the living room, waiting for me. I could smell that tea was cooking but Bridget wasn't in the kitchen supervising in case it misbehaved so something was rotten in the state of Hollybush Close.

Spotless sat with his head on Nick's leg.

'Happy Friday, everyone,' I said, not sure what else to say. I sniffed the air and asked, 'What's cooking?' and meant it on several levels.

'Take a seat, Jackie.' Bridget pointed to an empty chair.

I sat down. 'Am I being interviewed?'

Bridget said, 'Your father phoned us yesterday morning.'

'Dad?' It was an alien concept. 'From Hatton? What's he done?'

No one had offered me tea or lemonade. This alone put me on edge.

'It's nothing *he's* done,' Nick said.

'He had something to tell us,' Bridget said. 'Something you felt you couldn't say.'

I saw both Nick's gaze and Bridget's shift to Amanda's abdomen as though it would come up with a confession of its own.

'Oh,' I said.

I felt two things. One was anger that Dad had betrayed my trust. Two was relief. They were strange companions.

I didn't want to meet Amanda's eyes.

'We couldn't be more grateful to him,' Nick said.

Amanda sighed as though letting out every breath she had. 'You two were going to find out I was pregnant anyway. That's the bit I haven't told you yet.'

'How come?' Nick said.

'Oh, everyone's buzzing with the news. The *Daily Mirror* will be phoning next.'

I waited. When Amanda got witty, significant things were happening.

'Patsy's big mouth at college,' Amanda said. She sounded indignant. 'All I said today was that the perm she'd done looked like tangled wool and she said at least she wasn't having a bastard.'

'Out loud?' Bridget said. 'In front of everyone?'

'What do you think? My tutor took me aside to interrogate

me and then told me that college would be calling you on Monday.'

'I don't know how long Amanda was hoping to keep a baby a secret,' Nick said.

Amanda turned to me. 'Before you say anything, they also know about me taking vodka into college.'

'Which we'd have known about a lot earlier if you hadn't hidden the letter,' Bridget said to her.

'It hardly seems to matter now, darling,' Nick said.

'I wouldn't have said anything about the letter,' I said to Amanda, which seemed hypocritical, bearing in mind that I'd fully intended to tell the Walls about the pregnancy had Bridget not fallen that night.

'You should be proud of your dad,' Nick said. 'He's done this for you so that you don't have to carry the burden.'

'We're indebted to you, too,' Bridget said, 'for supporting Amanda.'

'You're not angry with me, that I kept her secret?' I said, then apologised to Amanda for talking about her in the third person.

'I don't even know what a third person is,' she said.

'We've been angry about a lot of things in the last twenty-four hours,' Nick said.

Amanda said to me, 'You should have been here yesterday.'

'Being angry gets us nowhere,' Bridget said.

'So …' I said.

She said, 'I'll go and check that the carrots haven't boiled themselves to death.'

She struggled to get up from the sofa and I saw Amanda reach out and put a hand to her mother's arm to steady her.

Upstairs in Amanda's room after tea, I said, 'Are you furious with me?'

She sat on her bed. 'No. I was yesterday. But this way, at least I didn't have to tell them myself. I was thinking of running away.'

'Where to?'

She shrugged.

I told her about the tea woman and the discussion about celery. 'That's why I ended up telling Dad. He thought it was me who was pregnant.'

'Ugh, celery,' she said. 'Not likely.'

'What did they say at first, your parents?'

'I'm glad I wasn't home,' she said. 'After your dad rang, Mum rang Dad yesterday lunchtime to get him back from school. Then they phoned Heather for advice as they couldn't think of anyone else to call. All three were waiting for me when I got home.'

'The welcoming committee,' I said.

'They stared at my stomach when I came in so I knew.'

'Do they know who the father is?'

'Your dad told them that, too.'

'I'm sorry.'

'Don't be.'

'So, what's going to happen?'

'I don't know. Dad's been in touch with the builder to get the extension brought forward. That's all I know.'

'Don't think too far ahead. You'll drive yourself mad.'

'It's not as far ahead as I thought. I didn't realise that you count from your last period, not the day you – you know.'

'So it's due ...'

'Probably early September.'

'Right.'

'Mum and Dad say I don't have to go back to college. I can just stay home until the baby is born.'

'Have you seen a doctor yet?'

'Mum's booked me an appointment for Monday morning.'

'I suppose that's to confirm it.'

'I don't think it needs confirming. I can feel it moving right now.'

'So, unless your mum's shepherd's pie was still alive,' I said, 'that's the baby.'

SUNDAY 4 MAY

I went round to Dad's flat on Sunday afternoon and took a box of Matchmakers.

I dared not leave it more than a day as I could tell on the phone that he already felt I'd cast him into outer darkness. He'd been discharged from Hatton on Saturday, had missed the bus home, had to flag down a taxi, and had spluttered over the phone to me on Saturday evening about how much it had all cost. 'And then I got here and it was all quiet,' he'd said. 'Like a morgue.'

'I left you a steak and kidney pie from the butcher's in the fridge. Did you find it?'

'And you've cleaned the flat.'

'Call them your welcome home presents,' I'd said, 'in the absence of caviar and ...' I was about to say champagne.

I would need to take care with my sentences just when I thought those days were done.

'I read your school report,' he'd said. I'd left it on the kitchen counter.

'Is it terrible?'

'Is it terrible that they think you will get three A grades despite some ups and downs? Oh, shocking.'

Now, I stood at the front door ready with my key but decided to ring the bell. The door opened immediately. 'There you are at last,' he said.

'I'm half an hour earlier than I said, Dad.'

A month off the booze had done something to his demeanour, as though someone had given him good news.

'You look well,' I said.

'My hair's growing back, at least.' He touched the patch where they'd shaved him. It would be another couple of months before it looked normal.

I followed him into the kitchen. I wanted to thank him for calling the Walls about Amanda but couldn't think of a route into the conversation. In the end, I said, 'Thank you for calling the Walls about Amanda.'

'Someone had to.'

'I should have done.'

'*She* should have done.'

I said, 'How did Bridget take the news on the phone?'

He took two mugs from the cupboard. 'I thought she wouldn't believe me. People like me don't call people like her with the news that their daughter's in the pudding club.'

'They do now. You're a pioneer, Dad.'

'She asked me whether I thought Stuart would make good father material. Me being the expert, and all.'

'Did she?'

'Of course she bloody didn't.'

We sat in the living room while waiting for the kettle. He lit a cigarette. A couple of job advertisements, cut out from the local paper, lay on the coffee table. I decided not to ask him about them. It was enough that I'd seen and he'd seen that I'd seen.

I said, 'Did you have the electric shock treatment? What was it like?'

'Don't make me relive that, pet. Talk about something else.'

'I'm sorry.' I wanted to hug him but wasn't sure. 'I didn't mean to upset you.'

'You haven't.'

'I really am grateful that you told the Walls. I'd been worrying about it.'

'What's going to happen?'

'They're having an extension so she can live there with the baby.'

'Of course they are,' he said, bitterly. 'Of course, an extension.'

'Don't be like that.'

'Well, some people.'

The kettle began to whistle and I escaped to make the tea.

'There's a letter for you,' he said, when I came back with our mugs. He pointed to an envelope on the dining table. 'It was on the doormat when I came back.'

I set the mugs down and picked up the envelope. It was a typed address, postmarked London.

I slid out the piece of paper and unfolded it. A smaller piece fell out. A postal order for ten pounds.

'Well?' Dad said.

I said, 'Pinch me, Dad.'

'What is it?'

'You know I entered that poetry competition?'

He bit his lip as though trying to know it. 'I can't say I did.'

I thought back, too. He would remember nothing about it. I sent it at Christmas when he was deep and swimming in whisky, like someone who'd waded so far out to sea that they couldn't hear people shouting to them on the shoreline.

He said, 'You haven't gone and bloody won something?'

'I have! I've won ten pounds. And it's being published in a magazine.'

'Fish and chips on you, kid!' Dad said, reliable as the dawn.

I reread the letter just in case I'd got it wrong but I hadn't. I wasn't sure how I would wait until the next day to tell Mrs Collingworth. And Nursey B.

We drank our tea and watched showjumping on TV for an hour. I remembered the box of Matchmakers and opened them. 'We can celebrate with these.'

He took one. 'I've got something to tell you,' he said, biting into it. 'Don't lose your rag.'

'Go on. What have you done?'

'It's about Doreen.'

'Doreen?' My stomach clenched.

'We're just taking it easy. She's not moving in.'

'I *hope* not. She's back in Warwick?'

'I said, don't lose your rag.'

'Where's she living?'

'A bedsit near the racecourse. She was working in Bejam's in Birmingham and got herself transferred to the Leamington branch.'

'I wish I hadn't brought you these now.' I pulled the Matchmakers box towards me.

'Don't be like that, pet.'

'But what if—'

'She's off the drink,' he said. 'She had a blackout. It scared her. She's been teetotal a month now.'

'A month isn't long.'

'I've just done a month,' he said. 'You don't believe in me, either?'

'Of course I do. Don't see her just because you're lonely.'

'What do you expect me to do?' he said. He pulled the chocolates back towards himself.

'What about Colin across the way? Ask him in for a cup of tea.'

'Colin? I'd want to top myself after ten minutes with him.'

There was a silence.

I said, 'Next, you'll tell me Stuart's moved into the flat downstairs and you're playing Rummy together of an afternoon.'

'No, he's still in Birmingham, back with his dad.'

'What if he comes here?'

'I'll wring his bloody neck and I made sure Doreen's told him that.'

I sipped my tea. It was cold now. Possible sentences lined themselves up but none of them seemed worth saying.

It was Dad's life, not mine. What could I do? There were reasons to worry and reasons for relief, a mix of emotions that seemed to come with being alive.

Dad said, 'Doreen told me this morning that Stuart phoned the Wall girl yesterday.'

'What?'

'It sounds as though his dad has knocked some sense into him.'

'What did he say?'

'That's all Doreen knew.'

I said, 'Can I use the phone?'

'Will you stop asking stupid questions? You could *live* here if you wanted to.'

I went into the hall and rang the Wall house. Amanda answered.

I said, 'My dad says Stuart has been in touch.'

'Yesterday,' she said. I could hear Bridget in the background, clanking pans.

'Is it okay to talk?'

'No point in whispering now,' she said, forlornly.

'Do your parents know he rang?'

'Yes.'

'What did he say?'

'He was sorry and was there anything he could do.'

'Like, marry you? Bring up his child?'

'I don't want to marry him.'

'Did he ask?'

'No, he didn't.'

'Do Nick and Bridget want you to marry him?'

'Yes but no.'

'And is there? Anything he can do?'

'He says he's got a job in a garage. He'll send some money to help with baby things.'

'Like what?'

'I don't know. Toys. A potty? When do babies need a potty?'

I heard Bridget say, 'Goodness, it's not even born yet!'

I said, 'Do you think he'll keep his promise?'

'How do I know? He scarpered, didn't he? Anyway, I can't say he promised.'

'I'm glad you're telling your mum and dad things. I've had enough of secrets.'

'I won't ask you to keep any more,' she said.

I said, 'Until you have triplets and hide two of them under the bed.'

I stayed with Dad for another hour. We watched Barbara Woodhouse training dogs. I told him about my holiday in Ireland and he said he'd give me pocket money which I thought was sweet but optimistic.

'I'll have a job by then,' he said.

'I hope so.'

'I might have won a million on the pools.'

'I hope so.'

We also saw the six o'clock news. The Iranian Embassy siege was now in its fifth day.

'Those poor hostages,' I said.

'Can't see that ending well,' Dad said, lighting a cigarette. He'd admitted that he was smoking more since getting sober.

'I don't know, Dad. I'm sure someone's planning a rescue. They must be.'

'Can't think how.'

'They'll find a way.'

When the news was over, I said, 'I'd better go. I've got a practice history essay due in tomorrow.'

'Leave the Matchmakers,' he said. 'Doreen likes those.'

'Be careful, won't you, Dad.'

'Don't you worry yourself.'

He waited while I put my jacket on in the hall. I opened

the front door and reached up to him for a quick hug. He held on, saying, 'You can use your key, you know, when you come next week.'

Subtle, Dad!

'I'd rather ring the bell,' I said, letting go of him.

'Whatever you like, pet,' he said, but not ungraciously.

He watched as I made my way down the steps. I looked up to wave before reaching the lower floor when I could no longer see him.

But I did hear Colin open his front door and his raspy voice saying to Dad, 'Back from the dead, then.'

ACKNOWLEDGEMENTS

I intended to begin with something pretentious such as 'The official definition of acknowledgement is ...' But the *Oxford English Dictionary* says there are *eight* meanings listed, so stuff that for a game of soldiers.

I'll start instead with thanks to everyone – bloggers, endorsers, reviewers, readers – who read *Cuckoo in the Nest*, this book's predecessor, and let me know one way or another how much you loved its protagonist, Jackie Chadwick. Your feedback gave power to my writing elbow for another story about Jackie and kept me going on days when the best I could write was 'They have a Sunday lunch' or 'She gets cross'.

Huge thanks, too, to those who helped during the drafting phase for *Home Bird*: poet-friend Craig Lambert for reading Jackie's poems; writer-friend Deborah Jenkins for reading the synopsis and draft manuscript; and writing-buddy and Zoom-friend Lisa Carey for tactful feedback on scenes I'd clearly rattled out in the twenty minutes before our calls.

Thank you to supportive writing networks including the Women Writers Network on ex-Twitter, the Association of Christian Writers, the Room 204 crew at Writing West Midlands and the Warwickshire contingent of the Society of Authors. Along with my faithful friendship group The Incomperellas and the friends at church who show interest in my writing and seem to really mean it, you are all delightful sources of encouragement and comradeship.

I have loved working with Legend Press on my 'Jackie'

books. Big fat thanks go to the whole team for taking on this second one and for all the keen industriousness behind the scenes. As someone famous should have said, it takes a writer to give birth to a manuscript, but a village to raise a book.

Particular appreciation goes to Cari Rosen, my editor, who I truly believe loves Jackie Chadwick as much as I do and who has championed Jackie and my writing so generously.

Thanks too to Ross Dickinson for a copy edit that was such a boost and especially for loving the poems in *Home Bird*. Not many mention them and my self-belief was sagging.

Ditte Loekkegaard, cover designer: I love the way *Home Bird* echoes the cover of *Cuckoo in the Nest* but has its own vibe. I'm looking forward to showing it off everywhere.

I have some young supporters to thank as well as everyone else in my blood family and foster family. Hats off to Eli (12) and Phoebe (10) for asking Grandma regularly about how the writing's going and precisely how many books have been sold.

To Sarah, daughter and unofficial PR and marketing assistant: if I could afford you and wasn't worried about being continually upstaged, I'd make it official.

To Paul, my husband of forty-two years: it's really true that buying other people's novels is research.